I0772354

BRIAN L. REECE

Stealing Stealth

A Gabrielle Hyde Thriller

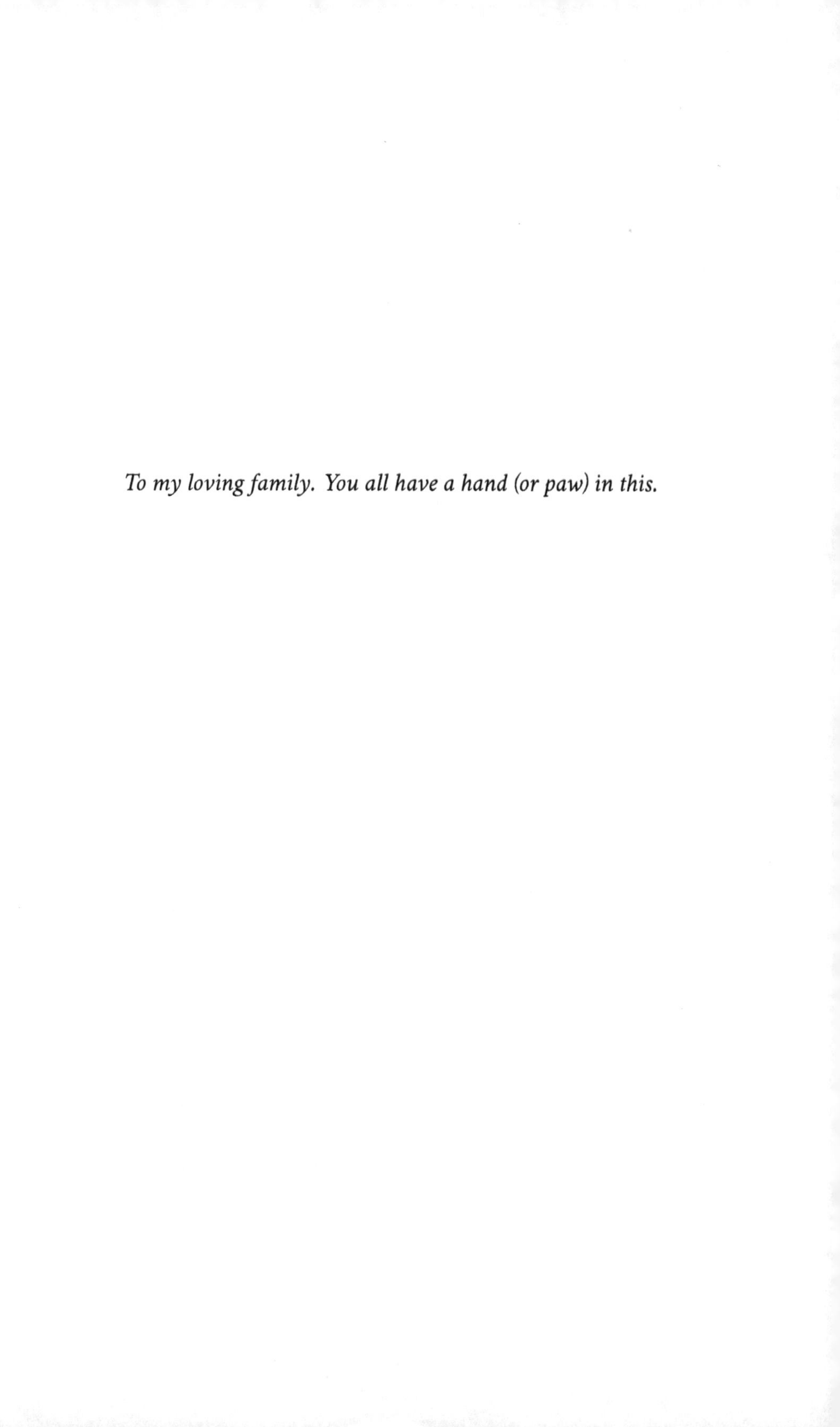

To my loving family. You all have a hand (or paw) in this.

Acknowledgments

I would like to thank all the amazing people who have supported my writing journey. Thank you to my wife, Alyson. You pushed me to go outside of my comfort zone to start this amazing journey. I appreciate everything you did to support my long nights and endless editing circles. Thank you to my kids (and their many animals) for encouraging me, helping when possible, and for limiting how much the pigs and bear typed.

To Mrs. Edwards, Ms. Rice, and Mr. Perryman — thank you for giving me time and space to tell stories in high school. It is something I still cherish. You sparked this journey.

Special thanks to those I served with and to those who shared their stories. Those experiences live on in these pages. This story originated from a debate during dinner in Afghanistan, and everything grew from there. To the wonderful Jay Preston and Megan Hensley, who helped bring the words from the page to life for the audiobook. It's always a pleasure to work with you! Check them out at www.theboothofus.com.

Thanks to the thriller writing community for their guidance and to early readers whose feedback shaped this story.

Finally, thanks to my Mom and Dad, who have been constant supporters, readers, editors, and so much more.

Chapter 1

TORONTO, CANADA

August, 1975

00:15

Emerging from darkness, Gabrielle Hyde savored the silence, anticipating tonight's deception. Stealing for profit alone would never suffice. Too pedestrian. Theft was more than an occupation.

This lesson was fundamental. To thrive, one must elevate their endeavors to artistic mastery. Only the exceptional should endure; natural selection at work. If nothing else, this night represented a personal victory in an ongoing war against a cruel world.

Still air in the ventilation shaft carried a musty scent of old paper that made Hyde's nose itch as she scrutinized the room. Dull burgundy curtains hung limp from neglect, framing windows that offered glimpses of the city's half-finished skyline. Lights from beyond cast muddy shadows across the worn carpet.

Faded commendations and yellowed newsprint adorned wood-paneled walls, bearing witness to achievements now obscure. The office breathed history, but not the kind anyone valued. An antiquated desk calendar remained fixed on 1965, reflecting ten years of disuse, like everything else in this outpost.

This presentation was an almost too-perfect veneer.

The room held more than relics. Hidden beyond the dated pictures and decor lay a meticulously disguised vault. The safe contained many precious things, but Gabrielle only received payment for the classified documents.

Unknown to her customer, those secrets weren't her primary goal.

Her shadowed form unscrewed the air vent cover and lowered it on a slender cable. Exiting the narrow opening in a fluid motion, her shoulders rolled. Years of experience allowed the master burglar to slip through confines that would stop one less devoted.

Descending with feline grace, Hyde's weight barely tested the sturdy oak desk. Her inky silhouette launched forward, body arcing fluidly through the air. Muscles tensed beneath the dark fabric as her long fingers reached out, grasping the exposed pipe running along the wall.

Balancing precariously, Hyde retrieved a tiny screwdriver from a hidden vest compartment and popped open a rusting metal box housing the room's security.

As the wires twisted together with a satisfying sizzle, the dated security system's lights flickered off.

Hyde clicked a compact two-way radio, whispering, "System's down. On timeline."

Producing a small strip of tape from the same pocket, she rubbed it across the edge of the junction box, leaving behind two partial fingerprint remnants. She had obtained it from one of Vasquez's unwitting FBI agents.

"That should keep Bruno running in circles," Hyde mused, dropping to the floor, now free to maneuver.

Gabrielle's gaze swept over the framed clippings of victories against organized crime, a map with fading pushpins, and an untouched '40s typewriter. Her gloved finger straightened the photo of agents at an awards ceremony.

The faint creak of the floorboards beneath Hyde's feet vanished beneath the muffled thrum of street traffic a few stories below. The smell of exhaust mingled with mustiness, while a distant orchestra elicited a twinge of excitement. If they only knew.

Rumors swirled amongst law enforcement agencies that Hyde possessed supernatural abilities, a notion as preposterous as it was useful. Interpol was the worst; they built profiles, analyzed evidence, consulted experts, and never once considered that their phantom might wear heels. Their sexism was her greatest disguise; one she didn't even have to work for.

Yet, it rankled a part of her soul to let their narrow-mindedness persist. Her yearning to shatter their chauvinist illusions warred with the supreme tactical advantage such assumptions provided. Pragmatism won. It always did with her.

None of these automatons could fathom Gabrielle's real aim, for it was a deep departure from her usual quarry. It wasn't about money or data. This was far more important. But such value carried enormous risk.

Sure of the path, Hyde refocused.

In the corner, the massive vault sat unassumingly behind an angled, dusty painting. Her slim gloves traced the painting's weathered frame. Careless hands had left the outer edges conspicuously clean.

The vault's design, studied and analyzed, was almost amateur. A vintage Sargent and Greenleaf, the lock was likely state-of-the-art in its day. Pity surfaced for the government that hid its secrets here. Those seeking absolute protection should expect failure.

With skill, Hyde manipulated the antiquated mechanism. The tumblers aligned with faint clicks, sounding like the ticking of a grandfather clock. The lock clinked open. There was no turning back the moment that latch swiveled.

It was the only way forward. Yet, she froze.

Hyde looked down at her hand. It quivered and then stilled. Was it nerves? This was a big moment, one that initiated a series of consequences even she could not predict.

She lifted her hand, rotating it slowly. Staring at the numbers, their presence soothed her in the most unusual of ways. Like Virgil in Dante's Inferno, Gabrielle was ready to cross the threshold and transcend mere excellence.

The door swung open with a whisper, revealing a barely visible tripwire hook in the top corner of the safe. Hyde noted its calculated placement. This confirmed the intel on her new government shadow.

She smiled. Finally, another who sought to impose order. But this young agent still had a lot to learn.

The two-way radio beeped.

"We have movement. Target's approaching. Sixty seconds."

The setup was perfect. "Copy," she replied.

Her icy eyes found the silver case instantly. That part was simple. A thrill coursed through Gabrielle at the prospect of this new challenge. Yet that joy was pure veneer, a deceptive veil for a lifelong pursuit of liberation.

Those who wielded power controlled everything, never sharing willingly. As with all things, she would have to force the issue.

Outside the imposing single-pane windows, the CN Tower's construction lights distantly blinked as agents flooded the building's entryway. They rushed headlong into the waiting jaws of her trap. Among them was the man she wanted so desperately to meet.

Satisfied, Hyde turned and crafted the scene, creating scuffed tracks from the vault, disturbing papers on random desks along the way with deliberate, almost theatrical flourishes.

"That will do nicely." A smile formed as she anticipated the impending confusion.

The stomping footsteps ascending the stairwell grew louder. The thief sprang up with acrobatic grace, sliding into the narrow vent and replacing the cover just as FBI and Interpol agents heaved against the locked door.

They were too late.

Their arrival was merely prelude to the long and twisted road ahead. It was time to put another shovelful of dirt on the grave of her hideous past.

Chapter 2

A quarter mile away from the safe, a nondescript surveillance van idled on the street. Inside the cramped, ripe interior sat CIA Case Officer John Olson, his lean frame bent forward in concentration. Intense blue eyes scanned the flickering monitors while his slicked brown hair reflected the glow of surveillance equipment.

His finger tapped on his knee until it halted abruptly. He adjusted his straight tie, grimacing as he checked his watch for the third time.

Hyde was the Holy Grail of international espionage. Brilliant. Elusive. Always just beyond grasp. "Unrivaled" was the word his superiors whispered in hushed tones. He craved the chance to make them eat those words.

Honed by two years of obsessive study, his gut told him this was it.

This conviction tested his usual patience. No sign of Hyde. John's hope faded as the hour grew late.

At only twenty-nine, Olson was already years ahead of his peers. His numerous high-profile captures should have been enough to silence his father's disappointment in his career choice. But that shadow lingered, driving him to prove himself.

Sometimes he pushed too hard. Convincing the higher-ups that Hyde's next target was Toronto had become a battle of wills.

John's meticulous evidence and theories clashed with the agency's penchant for murky international affairs. His superiors' focus on career advancement and everything Russian left them blind to all other threats.

If it wasn't about the Soviets, the seventh floor didn't care. That is, until they looked bad.

John's insistence, accompanied by an embarrassing miss in England, finally forced them to listen. But it came at a price: FBI involvement and dire consequences were he mistaken. He'd made more than one enemy through rash actions in the field.

It didn't matter that they panned out. His success only made the cautious bureaucrats more nervous. Despite his methodical approach over the past eighteen months, they wouldn't hesitate to take their administrative revenge when the shoe finally dropped. He couldn't let that happen.

Hyde would show.

In the world of industrial espionage, some dismissed the thief as a ghost story. Olson begged to differ. Hyde's profile differed dramatically from the normal Interpol criminal.

His boldest theory was something he now kept to himself. Bruno had laughed in his face. He didn't dare risk sharing it with the seventh floor after that.

The hard plastic seat dug into John's back, sticky from the humid Toronto weather. His gaze darted between humming monitors and his Second Cup mug, the van's interior thick with tepid coffee, cigarette smoke, and dozing Interpol agents. A reel-to-reel Nagra SN recorder whirred as static crackled over the radio.

The surveillance setup was impressive considering the short notice, but still limited. The grainy black and white monitors offered only fixed angles, and there was no thermal imaging. John had requested the new Minox night vision scope, but requisition delays denied him that luxury.

Only one person shared his intense interest in Hyde: FBI Special Agent Bruno Vasquez. To outsiders, it bordered on fanaticism. Where John was trim and polished in his narrow-lapelled suit, Bruno was a rumpled bear of a man.

With a world-weary face and a heavy five o'clock shadow, Vasquez dozed, drooling on his color-coded dossier of handwritten notes. Even in sleep, his thick fingers clutched a red pen. His meticulous system of annotations stood in stark contrast to his off-the-rack polyester suit, hopelessly wrinkled, and a stained tie that perpetually hung askew.

John's eyelids drooped. He jerked awake as a blinking indicator caught his eye. Hyde had tripped the hidden wire.

John sprang to his feet, hitting his head on the van roof. The sleeping agents stirred at the sudden sound. Agent Vasquez lurched, paperwork creasing his cheek.

"Hyde's here." Olson pointed at the video feed.

Vasquez snatched the radio from John's hand, a string of colorful curses tumbling from his lips. "You were right. I've got it."

Now alert, Vasquez shouted orders as the team poured out. Olson's attention flicked between the monitor and the action unfolding around him. He dropped his mug, spilling coffee across Bruno's typed notes.

At least he won't need them, John thought as he eyed the soaked pages. He jumped out of the van and joined the unit.

The squad rushed toward the target building, their shoes splashing through puddles left by an earlier thunderstorm. Olson's heart hammered as all his hard work culminated in this moment. Agent Vasquez took the lead, whisking through the lobby doors, roaring orders to the men.

"Remember, this is an FBI op. CIA is just observing," Bruno said.

Olson's jaw clenched as he swallowed the retort forming on his tongue. Without him, Vasquez would be chasing shadows in Brazil.

"Yes, sir."

As the agents thundered up the stairs, Olson's senses sharpened. The scuff of tactical boots. Weapons tapped against the railing. Heavy breathing of men who needed more physical training. A nagging doubt surfaced. This was too easy.

An adversary like Hyde demanded respect. John had urged nuance, a chess player's approach.

Bruno, ever the blunt instrument, insisted on a frontal attack, believing in overwhelming force. Their clashing styles epitomized the rift between

CIA ambiguity and FBI absolutes. Despite John's initial reservations, the FBI's plan was working. They had Hyde cornered.

There was no other method of escape. It's what made this trap so enticing.

The breaching unit positioned themselves outside the door. Olson pressed against the wall, weapon drawn. His breathing steadied into the controlled rhythm of his training. The familiar cadence calmed his thoughts.

The ram struck. BOOM. Sound exploded through the hallway. Wood splintered. His grip tightened.

Second impact. CRACK. The door frame buckled.

Third strike. The door exploded inward with a sound like rolling thunder.

In a sweeping surge, the combined forces of FBI and Interpol agents poured through the shattered doorway, fanning out in tactical formation.

Olson followed, hyperaware of every detail.

"Check every corner!" Vasquez barked.

Bruno's chest expanded with labored breath. His pupils constricted as he scanned the scene, nostrils flaring.

He found what he was looking for. A confident smile crossed the FBI agent's craggy features.

"We caught Hyde off guard! He made a mistake." Vasquez pointed to the footprints and displaced furniture. "Take notes, CIA boy. Not many would notice these marks. The trail's faint, but it's there."

He whipped a loose circle in the air with his hand. "You men, follow me!"

As the team moved, John's voice cut through the urgency. "Agent Vasquez, wait! This is wrong."

Everyone stopped and looked at him.

"Hyde doesn't leave trails. Sh… He wants you to go that way," John continued, ignoring their disapproving stares.

"Olson, we don't have time for this. We missed Hyde in Argentina because the agents there were too slow. That won't be me."

He paused. "You have a better wild-ass theory? Let me have it, but make it fast."

Where Bruno saw an obvious trail, John's analytical nature assembled a different puzzle. He scanned the space in quadrants, the way he had taught himself to process crime scenes quickly.

The broken furniture caught his attention. A desk chair lay on its side, but the impact pattern was wrong. No scuff marks. It took force to topple a chair. Someone had placed it there.

Then there were the scattered papers. Too organized for panic. Too deliberate for an accident. The walls told their own story. Undisturbed except at the security system, where distinct fingerprint smudges marked the keypad. Clean and distinct. Not the frantic actions of someone under pressure.

On the surface, the room screamed disaster. But to John, every detail whispered to his subconscious. The chaos was too... purposeful.

Vasquez stole a look at his watch, impatience radiating.

"I don't have one. At least, not yet."

Bruno's tone was surprisingly understanding. "Don't sweat it. You secure the scene. Call if you find Hyde. Everybody else, on me!"

The agents raced out the door in a jumble of footsteps that soon faded. Left alone, John tuned into his surroundings.

"Focus," he whispered.

Aged metal pipes ticked in the walls. An underlying scent of mildew filled his nose. Somewhere far off, a streetcar's distinctive bell rang. Silence. Fresh air hit him from above.

The answer was here. In every case, Hyde escaped without a trace. How?

Olson moved toward the closed vault and traced the footsteps. Twenty-eight inches between prints. The stride was too short for someone in a hurry. The impression was also heavy on the heel instead of the toe, where it belonged. He noted the thin ball-width.

Maybe Bruno was right. Perhaps he ran. The evidence said otherwise.

Except, Hyde never panicked.

His gaze fell upon an old oak desk far from the original trail. As John approached it, he spotted a barely distinguishable footprint imprinted on a piece of paper.

He snatched the sheet and scrutinized it, the corner of his mouth lifting in a half-smile. Why stand here? It offered no obvious tactical advantage.

He refocused on floating particles.

At first, his eyes followed the debris downward, only to retreat to the ceiling. An askew ventilation hood was clean compared to the rest of the room.

Point of entry. Point of escape.

Bruno was chasing a ghost. Again. Olson raised the radio to contact Agent Vasquez, then hesitated. What if he was mistaken? He should verify first, then call. Interpol would come running once he had something concrete.

Everybody wins. Vasquez had shot down enough of his insights for one day.

"Alright, then. Follow the clues."

Olson climbed onto the desk, the wood creaking. He wrapped his fingertips around the edge of the vent cover and kicked off. For a moment, John dangled precariously before hauling himself up into the air shaft. He had a slim figure, but the metal box proved suffocating.

Enveloped by the darkness, John inched forward on his elbows. The duct pressed against his chest, its rough seams catching on his suit. Decades of grime coated his palms, gritty between his fingers. His appreciation of Hyde's agility grew with every uncomfortable shimmy.

The tunnel angled upward, ending at a barrier. John's hands found aluminum grating, cool to the touch and slick with condensation. Cool air whispered through the slats from the other side.

Muscles straining, he braced his palms against the grating, the metal grid pressing into his flesh. He shoved. It gave way with a clatter, and Olson tumbled onto the roof in an undignified heap.

Crisp air stung his face, a welcome relief from the stifling vent. The brisk wind carried distant foghorns from the harbor, helping clear his head. The glittering cityscape stretched around him, lights twinkling.

He spotted a trail of footprints leading to the building's edge. The tracks ended abruptly at a knee-high concrete parapet.

The imprint on the exterior barrier matched the shoe print from the desk. Olson gripped the rough concrete and peered over. Ten feet of empty air stretched to the nearest rooftop. This chasm might as well have been a canyon. Below, the alley plummeted straight down, a hundred feet of nothing ending in unforgiving asphalt.

Wind whipped, tugging at his soiled jacket. The gusts were strong up here. Unpredictable. A leap was ill-advised.

John's thumb hovered over the transmitter.

Call Vasquez. That was the agreement. That was protocol.

But protocol hadn't caught Hyde in London. Or in Buenos Aires. Or in the seven other cities where he'd vanished like smoke.

"Think it through."

If he called now and was right, the FBI would sweep in, claim the victory. Bruno had made that clear in the lobby. Olson would become a footnote in someone else's triumph.

If he was wrong, his credibility was gone. The CIA would bury him in some basement office or third-world outpost.

Everything balanced on a knife's edge.

The radio felt suddenly foreign in his hand, like something belonging to another version of himself.

He knew he should call for backup. But that made him like everyone else—a forgettable nobody. Agent #47 in the credits, just like his superiors wanted. Good enough would never make him special.

"What would Hyde do?"

The timid approach had yielded nothing in over a year. He would take the risk. Catching Hyde would require thinking like him. The thought both thrilled and disturbed him.

Every second of hesitation widened the gap between him and his prey. Between the agent he was and the man he needed to become.

Olson's eyes locked onto the edge as he pocketed the bulky radio. He stepped back three paces, gauging his approach. The wind caught his tie, snapping it sideways. There was no return once he crossed this line.

Hyde had jumped. So would he.

Chapter 3

"This is a bad idea." John closed his eyes, taking three quick breaths. Olson sprinted across the rooftop, each step propelling him faster. The gritty surface gripped his soles, releasing with soft, tacky sounds. His toes found the concrete edge, launching himself. Legs churning, John was suddenly weightless over the ten-foot abyss.

A blast of air whipped against his face. Memories of the CIA's grueling obstacle course surfaced through the rush. Even then, he couldn't escape the insatiable need to prove himself.

The ground flew up. He windmilled his arms, shoulder joints straining as he fought to maintain the proper position for a Parachute Landing Fall. The wind stung his eyes, but he kept them open, focusing on the impact spot.

Knees bent and toes pointed, every muscle coiled in anticipation. He turned sideways at the last second, letting his body absorb the brutal force of the landing. In one fluid motion, honed by countless hours of practice, he rolled forward in a three-point stance, his pistol drawn and ready.

The horizon swayed, and John doubled over. Stale coffee rose in his throat, almost splattering all over the rooftop. He swallowed it back down, wiping his mouth with the back of his hand. John shook his head and regained his bearings.

In the distance, Lake Ontario's misty shoreline blurred the city lights, casting a hazy glow over Toronto's burgeoning skyline. Scanning the ground, John spotted a trail leading to a neighboring building. The gap was only five feet, much closer than the first. In the shadows, a figure lurked at the edge of the rooftop.

Hyde.

Olson stalked his prey, careful not to trigger another round of high-rise acrobatics. He tapped the bulky radio transceiver clipped to his belt, ensuring it was still operational after the jump.

A haunting orchestral score drifted through the night air, the muted swells of violins and cellos adding an eerie undercurrent. John hoped the music would mask the faint crunch of gravel beneath his footsteps as he inched forward.

Keeping to the deep shadows, he advanced, each agonizing step chosen with patience. The surface scraped against his hard leather soles. Each time the sound escaped, he winced.

Olson hopped to the adjacent building as Debussy's Clair de Lune drifted from the gathering below. A blue, white, and red flag snapped against its steel pole, unmistakable even in the dim light. His step faltered.

The ornate limestone façade surrounding him was the French Consulate. This space was sovereign territory. Worse, he no longer had jurisdiction.

Diplomatic technicalities wouldn't save Hyde. Twenty feet away, John rounded a stairwell, weapon drawn, and faced his quarry in the moonlight.

Backlit, Hyde exuded aristocratic poise with her tall, slender frame. Her brunette hair kissed the nape of her neck, and her ageless face was a chameleon of nationality. No doubt her beauty had secured more than one escape, a perfect disguise concealing her true nature.

His breath caught as overwhelming relief surged through his body. He was right. Hyde was a woman.

Every expert had dismissed his profile assessment. But then there were the patterns. Eyewitnesses. Inconsistent physical descriptions. Each agency had built its profile on bias and then labeled him the fool.

The vindication should have made him ecstatic. It didn't. Being right complicated everything.

Hyde wore a stunning silk ball gown, the fabric shimmering. An elegant tuxedo jacket draped over her shoulders. She stood like a statue, her manicured hand cradling a sleek briefcase.

A small, worn, blue forget-me-not pin adorned her lapel; a delicate flower of colored pearl and silver. John's eyes lingered on the tiny brooch, a surge of curiosity coursing through him.

She peered through petite opera glasses. The nonchalance of her actions, set against the backdrop of orchestral music, was disarming.

Against his better judgment, John followed her eyeline, sneaking a peek over the edge. Whatever she watched had to be important enough to delay her escape. Obviously through the Consulate party below.

He spotted a familiar face leading a group of fifteen Interpol agents as they converged on an oversized wooden door. Their boots thumped in unison against the brick street as they stacked up.

Agent Vasquez took point, signaling four men with a battering ram to move in. They heaved the heavy metal forward with grunts of exertion, crashing through in an explosion of shattered wood. Bruno rushed past them, gun drawn.

Flashlight beams illuminated the empty space.

As Bruno swept the vacant corners, the truth dawned on his face. He cursed, ripping the radio from his belt and hurling it. Even from this distance, Olson could see this failure cut deep. Vasquez's shoulders heaved as he exited the building.

A smile spread across Hyde's features. That face. How many fell prey to it?

His weapon rose. "Don't move. You're under arrest!"

"You don't follow orders well. How refreshing."

A look of pure delight caused her eyes to sparkle. It gave John chills. No one should appear this happy to be caught.

"Game's over, Hyde. There's nowhere left for you to run."

Hyde's eyes never left the skyline as she spoke, as if his weapon posed no threat.

"Please, it's Gabrielle." Her voice carried the warmth of someone who'd weaponized charm. "You've been my tenacious shadow for quite some time now. The least we can do is preserve pleasantries, Officer Olson."

How did she know? He'd only recently accessed Hyde's most classified file, which was clearly inaccurate.

"Nice trick," Olson said, tightening his grip. "I'm not easily impressed."

"Such a melancholy city, much like you, John. I make a habit of knowing what's important. Such as your impressive 97% capture rate." She tsked. "Law enforcement. Always building better cages, but never evolving."

His fingers twitched. "My rate's now perfect."

"Perfection. Such a sad endeavor. Our minds are just another cage. Something I believe your father exemplified. God rest his soul."

"Enough!" Olson snapped. "Lie down on the ground, hands behind your head!"

A smirk curled Hyde's mouth as she toyed with the flag cable. "You have no authority here. Even Interpol needs permission."

Her words were a dare. "I'll work jurisdiction with Interpol."

She sat on the ledge, briefcase in hand. "Let this be your first lesson: the best heist is the one no one knows ever happened."

"I don't care. It's over."

"Is it? Or is this the beginning of something you refuse to see?"

She stood. "You follow the rules like a religion, while your superiors ignore them daily."

Gabrielle covered her watch with a long sleeve. Hyde was unconcerned with time, letting him see her complete lack of urgency.

"I've watched you solve puzzles they couldn't fathom." Hyde advanced, her gaze measuring him. "They'll decide you're dangerous once the stakes become real. Toss you away like garbage."

She opened her arms in a welcoming embrace. "You should be some-where you are valued."

He took a step back, eyes darting from the rooftop to the surveillance van below. Hyde could have vanished. The sudden change in MO, the grandstanding.

It was as if she wanted…

The realization hit like a gut punch. He'd walked straight into this. No, he'd dove in headfirst.

She'd planted the evidence that led him to Toronto. Lured him away from the prying eyes of the Agency. Right onto her private stage. This wasn't a robbery or an escape.

Hyde was recruiting him.

As he watched her casual demeanor, doubt gripped him. She was the one in charge. How deeply had he underestimated her?

John, like most case officers, felt the impact of Agency backstabbing and bureaucracy. Hyde clearly thought he'd turn. What could she possibly offer that over-rode national security?

The answer was simple: nothing.

His posture stiffened. "Kick it over."

Hyde studied him, bumping the case with her foot. "I wouldn't open that if I were you," she warned.

He eyed the sleek briefcase. The Canadian Security Intelligence Service was vague about its contents, only stressing its importance to national defense. Typical.

"Is that a threat?"

"Friendly advice," she said. "You know, John, I admire you. Brave, cunning, disobeying orders, breaking diplomatic treaties… Someone who sees the bigger picture. You've been studying me, so naturally, I've been analyzing you. To my surprise, I found you're a man I can respect."

"Respect? You have a strange way of showing it."

"You should be honored." Hyde shrugged. "Arranging this meeting was more difficult than I expected. All the subtle clues. Just enough to make it feel earned on your part."

"The only people you'll meet tonight are Interpol agents. But then again, they're looking for a man."

"Aren't we all."

He ignored her quip, unclipping his radio and adjusting the squelch knob before speaking into the chunky handheld. "It's Olson. Hyde's in custody on the roof at the French Consulate. Request immediate backup."

Static crackled through the speaker. "Are you out of your mind?" came Vasquez's furious voice. "You're on foreign soil!"

"Is that Agent Vasquez?" Gabrielle cut in. "I bet he isn't even dressed appropriately for the consulate party."

"Quiet!" Olson snapped.

The order was simple. The choice was not. Obey and lose Hyde, or defy and get his prize.

John's grip clenched the radio. "Just get here as quick as you can."

Olson lowered the volume completely. He didn't need the distraction of Vasquez's anger.

"Do you think capturing me will change anything?" Gabrielle asked. "There's a grander scheme, and you're too smart for trivial matters. The world's changing. Let me help you before the CIA casts you aside."

"Save it," Olson said, kneeling. "You're not talking yourself out of this. They're on their way now."

"John…"

He released the first latch.

"Don't do it."

"I don't believe you," he said.

Hyde sighed with what seemed like genuine disappointment. "Remember, you wanted it this way. Some people must take the hard road."

Olson traced the briefcase's exterior and snapped open the last clasp. A hiss pierced the quiet as gas erupted from the case.

John tried to hold his breath and leaped away. Too late. Fire burned in his throat as his airway slammed shut. He fought his body's reflexes, but the vise around his trachea tightened.

"Too bad," Gabrielle said as Olson's face contorted. His gun slipped, clattering to the ground.

She kicked the pistol aside, picked up the briefcase, and straightened her jacket. Producing a trim carabiner from beneath her coat, she connected it to a nearly invisible cable attached to the flagpole.

The line was taut, angling downward toward an office tower one hundred feet across the street. A small black helicopter waited in the shadows, its blades beginning to turn. The positioning was perfect. Only someone with the proper equipment could follow.

The Consulate party was just another deception. She never planned it as her escape route. The thin wire hid perfectly, night shadows providing cover. He should have known.

"After you made that first leap, I had so hoped you'd take another. This isn't personal. Capability is the highest form of moral authority. But when the time comes, you'll always have a choice with me."

Hyde held up a small syringe as she hopped onto the ledge, flicking it aside. "That hypodermic contains epinephrine. It'll save your life if you don't delay."

Without waiting, Hyde launched herself off the roof, briefcase clutched tight. She hurtled through the air like a sleek arrow, her ballgown billowing as gravity carried her faster and faster over the glittering city.

As Hyde's form grew smaller, John's gaze fell upon the syringe. The world closed in as he pushed himself to his knees. Darkness encroached as his chest burned. With one foot and then the other, he rose.

Staggering, John bypassed the needle, his lungs searing. Through teary eyes, he watched Hyde glide toward the office rooftop. The helicopter blades were now at full speed, ready for liftoff and shooting debris outward.

Desperation fueled him, trembling fingers aching for the syringe. Even as his vision dimmed, defiance flared. He wouldn't let Hyde win. John pulled a backup pistol from his leg holster. He aimed, hands shaking.

Hyde slid faster, twisting back for one last look. She seemed surprised to see him slumped against the wall, gun in hand.

Another spasm. Hyde's figure blurred and split. Willing his vision to focus, John squeezed the trigger.

A single shot rang out.

The bullet struck true. Hyde jerked and spun, her grip on the briefcase faltering. The case tumbled through the night air, spinning end over end before crashing through the windshield of a car parked on the street below. Gabrielle careened toward the waiting helicopter, mere yards away.

Two figures emerged on the rooftop, shouting in French as the helicopter's rotors whirred. The first was a man with a compact, muscular build and short, dark hair. The other was a slim woman, her long red mane whipping in the helicopter's downwash.

They caught Hyde at the zip line's end, heaving her into the aircraft cargo bay. Gabrielle suddenly sat upright, gripping her side as dark blood poured between her fingers. Olson searched her face, but found no hint of pain. For a fleeting moment, he saw only remorse.

John's finger tightened on the trigger again, but his body convulsed. The gun slipped from his grasp, clinking over the edge. Panic consumed him as the walls closed in. He collapsed and crawled toward the medication.

He cursed, stretching toward the syringe. His fingers brushed it, but it only slipped away further. Oblivion closed in, but he lunged with his last strength and grasped the needle. He plunged it into his thigh, depressing the plunger.

A burning sensation spread as he slipped into unconsciousness.

Flashes of light and muffled sounds melded together. John's body felt leaden. Hyde laughed at his failure. He fell into a pool of water, unable to surface.

A faraway voice yelled his name.

"Olson!" Vasquez slapped his cheek.

John propped himself up on one elbow. "Vasquez," he rasped. He oriented himself as the nearby orchestra hit a soaring crescendo.

"He escaped. Again! This is your mess! You and the damned CIA let him get away!"

Olson tried to respond, but only gravelly noises came out.

Interpol Agent Pierre Dubois rushed to Olson's side. "Agent Vasquez, please," he urged, his French-Canadian accent crisp and professional as he administered first aid. "He needs medical attention."

Vasquez scoffed.

Pierre grabbed his radio. "I need an ambulance and emergency kit to my position, now."

John appreciated the agent's excellent care, but it wasn't what he needed. He cleared his throat and attempted to stand.

Dubois placed a restrictive hand on his chest. "Don't move. Help is coming."

"I'm okay," Olson croaked.

John shoved the man's arm away and staggered to his feet as Bruno sidled up beside him. An icy wind knifed through Olson's clothes, raising goosebumps along his skin. He felt Vasquez's fierce stare, but refused to meet it. Instead, he searched for the helicopter, its form already swallowed by the night.

"I told you to call, you arrogant glory hound," Vasquez growled, flecks of spittle flying. "You think you're the only one who cares about catching Hyde? I've been chasing him since your first day at The Farm. You don't know how much it's cost me."

"The briefcase… it…" John said hoarsely.

A vein pulsed at Vasquez's temple. "My team grabbed it from that Toyota before the locals showed up. Lot of good it did us. The goal was Hyde, and you let him slip through your fingers."

Olson winced. His spotless record was now gone forever. And his superiors, they would take full advantage of this fiasco. Bruno didn't need to rub it in.

"Her." John said with difficulty. "Hyde is a woman. Like I told you. And she was hunting us, if that matters to you."

For the first time since he met the FBI Agent, Olson noted genuine surprise on Bruno's face. His loose jowls twitched, eyes widening as he processed the information.

"How was I supposed to know?" he muttered. His gaze drifted, unfocused. "Damn it." Shaking it off, Vasquez's expression hardened. "Doesn't matter. You still screwed the pooch, kid."

"I'm not making excuses."

"Good." The FBI agent scrutinized him. "Cause I'm the least of your problems. Your boss already had my ass to let you join this op. He'll get my report. I'll be fair, but honest. Buckle up, Bonzo."

Vasquez lumbered away. The Agency didn't tolerate failure, especially not when it was on display. His once-promising future was now as uncertain as the bleak Canadian night sky.

And there would be fallout. He'd violated international law, compromised his own operation, and potentially sparked a diplomatic incident with France. The State Department would have a conniption fit. And the Agency?

They'd either bury him in paperwork or ship him off to some outpost. Exactly as she predicted.

John brushed past the waiting medical team as he departed. He had work to do. Even if his superiors exacted their vengeance, Gabrielle Hyde remained free.

Olson swore he would be the one to bring her justice. Not because it was his job. It was his obligation.

Chapter 4

MOGADISHU, SOMALIA

September, 1977

Two Years Later

07:38

Monsoon dawn swept over Mogadishu's markets, its muted light filtering through golden clouds and damp air. The scents of cardamom and cinnamon mingled with loamy earth as vendors emerged from shadows, filling the streets with excited chatter.

Collar raised, CIA Case Officer John Olson wound through the maze of stalls, pale eyes scanning for danger. Two years of operating in African markets had honed his instincts against ever-present threats. Eyes followed his every move.

John halted at a stall, feigning interest in a polished plate. Turning the platter over in his hands, he tilted the metal surface to view what was behind him. Sure enough, a figure was tailing him. Whether it was one of Xaabsade's men or a rival agent, their presence underscored the value of the package he carried.

His shadow, a grizzled man of fifty, closed the distance. John's pulse accelerated. He slipped between two stalls, quickening his pace as he transitioned to the backstreets that wove through the ancient city.

The figure was persistent, matching his every turn. John's sense of direction was now instinctive. He turned one corner after another before tucking into a small niche to wait. The man passed his location, looking around before continuing.

John hustled, backtracking. After three more turns, he checked his six. No sign of a tail. He was clean.

He felt the promising intelligence packet hidden under his jacket, a glimmer of hope after months of dead ends. After a final check that he was clear, he cut through a dirt parking lot, scattering protesting soccer players.

Time was short.

Olson ducked into an abandoned store with faded signage and dust-caked windows. Inside, an elderly gentleman hunched, gnawing methodically on a root. It was the only thing he ever did.

John caught the man's attention and nodded. The local's dilated eyes observed him with indifference. The old man paused mid-chew, and leaning back, pressed an unseen button under his stool.

He resumed gnawing. John moved briskly through a dim hallway to a solid steel entryway. He pushed it open, stepping into the dull green CIA work center. The air-conditioned chill hit him, a relief to the humid heat trailing behind. The reinforced door snapped shut with a metallic thud.

An odor of burnt coffee, cigarette smoke, and cheap cologne clung to every surface. To him, it smelled like apathy.

He looked up at the oversized clock hanging nearby. Not yet eight o'clock. Good.

John's adrenaline faded as he took in the office. Typewriters clacked in chorus, punctuated by the occasional ding of a carriage return. Hazy smoke hung in lazy tendrils, illuminated by harsh fluorescent lights.

He stripped off his jacket, the intelligence packet pressing against his chest. Case workers hunched over their desks, oblivious. He ignored them.

It took fifteen minutes for the tech to complete the translation, with John hovering over him the entire time. Once it was complete, John snatched it up and moved to his station, itching to review what Xaabsade had sold him.

John leaned back in his chair, allowing himself a moment to unravel the single page. The local dealer usually let intel go easily. But it had taken a bit of prying this time. Three times the normal price.

Then there was that first-class tail in the marketplace.

The usual drone of the office waned as he considered his next move. Footsteps approached, quick and eager. Only one person moved like that.

Nate Balik, a slender African American in his early twenties, approached with youthful eagerness. His styled hair faded from his skin to neatly packed curls, and he favored a pair of old gold aviator glasses that complemented his confident smile.

Watching Nate's eager face, John saw himself three years ago. He was hungry, convinced the next case would make his career. The kid had twice the obstacles John ever faced, and twice the fire.

He brought Nate on as his apprentice, hoping to mold the enthusiastic recruit into a skilled operative. Balik tried hard, but it had been a long road.

"Contact came through, right?" Nate slid in next to John, barely containing his excitement. "Knew he would."

John held up a hand. "Lower your voice, Balik." He passed the sheet. "If this is accurate, we'll need top-level clearance. Soviet industrialists buying intel should be more than enough."

Nate scanned the page, eyes widening. "I knew it!" His voice dropped to a harsh whisper. "This is the real deal. I told you so."

"Yes, you did." John snatched it back. "We have to handle this carefully. I'll talk to Upton." He eyed their supervisor's door. "If he gives us support, you'll get your credit."

"Forget credit, I wanna get in on the action!"

John clapped his shoulder, recognizing the eagerness he once possessed. "Remember what we discussed? Patience. Now, go fetch some coffee and stay cool."

John watched the man bound off. Nate winked at an indifferent secretary, then donned the gold sunglasses as he poured a mug of hot sludge.

The corners of John's mouth twitched. The kid had guts. If this intel panned out, he'd make sure Nate got another shot in the field. He was still overeager, and that could get you killed. But the station needed some fresh blood.

Time to face Upton.

The moment Rupert Upton surfaced in Olson's mind, his features contorted into a grimace. It bundled two years of infuriating obstruction into a single, silent look. His boss was a broken man, the epitome of a busted system.

A sign reading 'Logistics Manager' hung lopsided, the words themselves a weak attempt to inflate Upton's position. Olson knocked. As the door creaked open on rusted hinges, he spotted the usual disorder on Upton's desk. A rotary fan turned uselessly in the corner, its blades clipping the bent frame.

As he stepped inside, John's peripheral vision caught motion. Nate was milling around, failing to appear casual. Olson mouthed a stern "go away" before closing the door.

Upton's perpetual frown deepened. "What is it, Olson?"

John cleared his throat. "Sir. We've got bona fide intelligence. 'Eyes Only' is being moved to a new player. Possible dead-drop. Asset says the buyer is a Soviet hitter."

Upton's salt-and-pepper eyebrows drew together. "We've been down this road. Most of your 'intel' is rubbish. I'm not wasting resources on it."

"Sir, this is actionable, and the asset is clean."

Upton rubbed his eyes and leaned back, the chair creaking. "Have a seat, Olson."

"I'd rather stand."

"It wasn't a request." Upton jabbed a chubby finger at the chair. "Sit down."

John perched on the rickety seat across from Upton's desk.

"You know why you're in Somalia." Upton's fingers drummed the desk. "Insubordination. Treaty violations. The D.I. Chief personally…"

"I was there," John said, cutting him off.

"Well," Rupert sighed, "now you're stuck here with me."

John knew he should keep his mouth shut, but the words escaped. "If it pans out, you'd get all the credit, sir. If it fails, blame me."

Upton removed his glasses, letting out a long sigh. For a fleeting moment, his eyes showed some fire as he sat up straighter. John wanted to believe there was more to the man. Perhaps, once, he was better than this.

Rupert's gaze drifted to a faded photograph on the wall that was hidden behind stacks of paperwork. It showed a younger, sharper version of himself receiving a commendation from Eisenhower.

The look vanished as Rupert's shoulders deflated. His eyes settled into their usual dull indifference.

"You're an excellent case officer, John. The best I've got here in hell." He slid his glasses back on. "Don't blow your chance to escape on bad intel."

"This is different."

Upton let out a humorless chuckle. "Agency brass has been all over my ass. Carter's supposed to meet Kosygin for nuclear talks," he said. "You know what happens if something goes sideways before then? Treaty dies and the Cold War gets hot."

John waited for the inevitable caveat.

Upton leaned forward. "And I get blamed."

"But what if I just…"

"Christ. No!" Upton looked at the calendar. "Give it a few weeks."

"We can't wait," John pleaded. "I need authorization now."

"You need to remember who's in charge."

John clenched his fists under the desk. Every wasted second was another chance for this opportunity to slip away. "The meet is today."

"Not my problem. You're dismissed."

John rose from his chair. His hand hovered over the handle as he stood at the door, hesitating. He turned.

"You should reconsider. We're better than this place."

Upton shot up from his desk. "Look Olson, I'm sick of this shit from you and everyone else telling me what to do. You think I want to sit around with a thumb up my ass?"

"No, sir."

"God damned right. But I've got strict orders to stand down and stay off the streets right now. So, why don't you go get a three-hour coffee or hire some hookers and call it research like Ford? Either way, get the hell out of my office and don't come back till I call you."

A chilling realization hit John as he stared at his supervisor.

Upton wasn't here because of something he did, but what he failed to do. The man was afraid. He was unwilling to take action when it mattered. The prospect of ending up like him was a nightmare. A bureaucrat who valued comfort over duty.

The report crumpled in John's grip as he returned to his desk. He stared at Upton's closed door. John could picture himself with the same defeated posture Rupert wore so easily.

"Well?"

John spun. Nate stood there, vibrating with expectation. Olson glared at his reflection in the sunglasses.

Nate removed his glasses and knelt beside him. "What'd Upton say? He surprised? He was, right?"

John saw his former passion reflected in Nate's bright eyes. Upton's oppressive bureaucracy had extinguished that fire in him. Olson dragged a hand over his face. Upton left him no choice.

"Nate…"

"This is solid gold, boss! When do we move? I'm finally gonna get my shot."

John appreciated the kid's enthusiasm, even as he made a note to work on Balik's professional composure. The news was going to devastate him.

"No," Olson said. "You're not."

Nate froze, his eyes searching for answers.

"Upton wants us to sit tight. With the upcoming summit, he doesn't want to risk stirring anything up."

"For real? No way!" Nate slapped the desk. "We can't sit on this. It's solid, I'm tellin' you."

"Upton was adamant. It's out of our hands."

Nate plopped down in the chair next to him. "Can I at least read the memo?"

"Be my guest."

Nate scanned the page, his face contorting with frustration. "Who translated this? It's terrible."

"Patrick."

"Of course." Nate scoffed. "Well, he got it all wrong. You see here? First off, this isn't a name, that's the word for badger or skunk." He scanned the page again, pointing. "And here, *'miiska-birta,'* Pat translated it as 'industrial,' but that's street slang. It means 'Iron Table.' That's what locals call the secret police. Specifically, the German Secret Police."

John turned on him. "You're saying the Stasi are in town and buying?"

Nate's grin grew. "Yeah, they're buying a badger. Whatever that means."

John jumped up. "Holy crap."

"Does this mean we're back on?"

John looked at Upton's door. "I was explicitly ordered to stand down. I can't go back and ask again."

"My pops used to tell me, when the man gets in your way, find another path." Nate leaned in. "We can do that. C'mon, boss, this is our opportunity. You and me!"

Clocks and typewriters resumed their clicking as John hesitated. Nate's eagerness reminded him of a different time. Balik didn't yet know that good intentions can backfire.

"You don't know what it's like, do you? Having to prove yourself every damn day? This is my shot." Nate leaned in. "Don't be a slave to the man."

John eyed Upton's closed door. The kid was right, and that terrified him.

Two years in this hellhole, and for what? One mistake in Toronto, and they'd buried him alive. But this was real. The Stasi were buying something days before a summit. Not a coincidence. They were positioning for something big. The treaty was the perfect cover for a high-profile operation.

And Upton wanted to sit on it.

John had a responsibility to act. He couldn't follow orders if it represented letting a greater atrocity go unchecked. The moment had come to stop worrying about the past.

He glanced at the clock. Normally, the seconds dragged, but now they were flying by. It was time to take Officer Balik on a consequential mission. It might be their last. At least it would be for a good reason.

"Grab a surveillance kit and meet me at the van in ten." John kept his voice hushed. Nate's face lit up, but Olson silenced him with a look. "We need to move fast."

"Yes, sir!"

He snapped off a crisp mock salute. Then, with a burst of energy, darted away to gather gear. John watched Nate charge down the hallway.

Officer Balik was likely unaware of the risks, blinded by passion. Experience had taught John the cost of unchecked ambition. The toll could be extreme if one were not careful.

But this was a chance they both needed to take. Risk was part of the job. John tucked the intelligence report into his jacket pocket.

Another roll of the dice on an unsanctioned op. If anything went sideways, he and Nate were on their own.

Chapter 5

John tugged at the collar of his djellaba as he stood beside the surveillance van, half a kilometer from the drop site. Despite the loose-fitting robes that concealed his tactical gear, he knew his height and fair complexion would mark him as an outsider. He would need the crowd to blend. Eventually, he would find a hide hole and disappear.

Inside the vehicle, Nate fiddled with a camera strap, his creased forehead reminding John of his own early days in the field. Nate wasn't ready to run point; plus the operation called for a spotter.

"Your job's logistical support and observation. Remain out of sight; maintain a discreet distance. The Soviets are paranoid."

"But I could…"

"We're not debating. Today's not the day." John's tone softened. "Stay in the van. Don't engage."

Nate nodded, his hand tapping on the camera bag.

"We're here to ID the buyer. Don't get overzealous like in Aden."

"C'mon, boss. Aden was ages ago. I've learned since then," Nate replied.

"I'm certain you have. Just listen. Okay?"

"Yeah, yeah. Sit tight. Be vigilant. Avoid trouble. Watch and learn," Nate sighed. "You say that every time."

"Must be important, then." John checked his wristwatch. "Now let's get to work. I'll sweep the area, make sure we're clear. Give me an hour, then move into position. Stay sharp."

Nate flashed a thumbs up and closed the door.

Olson walked away, merging into the dense market crowd. A familiar jolt of adrenaline spiked as he pressed into the churning mass of people.

Vendors hawked their wares, their cries assaulting from every angle. The air hung thick with the pungent aromas of roasting spices and cured meats. Children laughed and shrieked as they wove through the crowd.

Amidst the bustling scene, John spotted two men whose alert postures and sweeping gazes marked them as potential spotters. The pair patrolled the entire corner before exiting together, heading down a nearby alley.

Definitely spotters. With their departure, John circled back to the far side of the square. He situated himself behind a row of vendor stalls, leaning against the wall in deep shadow.

"Position," he whispered into his comms unit. "Couple of owls, but they're gone."

"John?" Nate's voice cut through the static.

"Eagle?" Olson responded, searching the market.

There was a lingering silence. "Oh, right. Not yet," Nate said. "Uh, boss? Quick question."

John's hand clenched the spyglass under his robe. Learn the damn code words. They'd address proper radio discipline in debrief. Tight comms were the difference between staying invisible and becoming a target. "Make it quick."

"Did Upton mention me?"

"What?"

"You know. Did he say anything like… 'That Nate Balik, he's the cream of the crop?'"

"Upton doesn't hand out compliments. He barely tolerates my antics, let alone yours."

Nate was silent for a long moment. "Oh."

John knew all too well the need for validation. "But we're on this op, thanks to you. Remember that. And Nate?"

"I know. Sit tight, observe. The usual BS."

John sighed. "I was going to say, good job."

Nate needed to learn that stakeouts were not therapy sessions.

A glint of metal caught Olson's eye. A convoy of cars was making its way towards the marketplace. If this was their target, then the buyers were arriving earlier than expected.

"Eagle," John said into his mic.

"Copy that, boss."

Black sedans with tinted windows eased into the square. "I have two vehicles approaching," John said. "This should be it."

He leaned forward cautiously as the convoy came to a stop. "Confirm visual ID on the buyer," he reminded Nate. "Do not engage."

The cars sat idling as the minutes ticked by. Finally, the driver's door of the lead sedan swung open and a figure emerged. John's eyes narrowed as he took in the man's appearance. Tall, around six feet, with an athletic build.

"No visual," Nate reported. "Our guy here is just the babysitter."

The man glanced at his watch. Two more bodyguards emerged from the second vehicle. The first, a hulking figure with a shaved head, scoured the area for threats. His companion, leaner and more agile, moved with predatory grace. On the surface, they bore all the typical earmarks of standard Soviet agents: nondescript suits and stern expressions.

The subtlety was the biggest clue. Nate's assessment was spot on.

This caliber of manpower was overkill for a routine intelligence drop. All three men were Stasi.

John's hand brushed his sidearm. "You were right, Nate. This is a first-tier operation. Be ready."

"Stay cool, stay cool," Nate said over the open channel.

The first bodyguard glanced around before producing a radio. He spoke rapidly in Russian.

"Did you get that?"

"*Da, tovarisch.*" Nate's pronunciation was flawless. "The chicken has entered the coop."

Olson searched, soon spotting a figure emerging from a side street carrying a satchel. He was a slim Arab, with a keffiyeh obscuring his face. The heat and stiffness of his movements made him stand out.

"Ten O'clock. Local agent entering the square." John's eyes focused. "Can you ID him?"

John heard the camera clicking. "One of Kafi's guys," Nate said. "I thought he left town."

"So did I. Our bagman is waiting for something."

He needed a better look inside the car. Olson slipped a hand into his robes, withdrawing a small spyglass. He was careful to keep his movements subtle. Lifting it to his eye, he leaned back into the shadow.

The windows were too dark for a visual within the sedan. As the Soviet agents opened the door to confer with the primary, they blocked the view.

"Nate, did you get eyes?"

"Not from this angle," Nate said. "Permission to move?"

"Negative! Stay where you are. Just observe."

"Copy."

Leaving the cars, the Russian trio spread out, once again sweeping the bustling square in calculated movements. One of them altered course, heading straight for the alcove where Olson watched.

"Standby. I may have been made," John whispered.

The man stepped closer and closer. John cocked the hammer of his pistol. Then, just as suddenly, the bodyguard turned, rejoining the others as they circled back to the vehicles. False alarm.

A moment later, an agent opened the sedan door briefly. John caught a fleeting glimpse of the occupant's imposing silhouette before it swung shut again.

"Visual ID, boss. The guy's big, six-two, maybe six-three. Late 50s, salt-and-pepper hair, scar over his left eye, and missing part of an ear."

"That doesn't sound like anyone active in the area," John whispered in return.

"I swear I've seen his file before. Came across it during my language training."

Olson paused. "Name?"

"He was definitely Stasi…" Nate snapped his fingers. "Got it! *Prizrak Berlina*… the Ghost of Berlin."

"Morozov?"

Nate replied, "Yup, that's him. Morozov! Creepy lookin' dude."

Goosebumps popped up on John's arm. Sasha Morozov was a name whispered with fear and respect in the hushed corners of Langley and Moscow alike.

"CIA reports say he died two years ago," John said. "Are you sure?"

"I'm not certain," Nate admitted. "But if it is… guy's looking pretty fly for a corpse."

"Confirm identity."

"I'll get it, boss."

He hoped Balik was wrong. In intelligence circles, Morozov was known as the Ghost of Berlin, but this moniker was derived from his original Russian nickname. Chort. The demon. A defector had once revealed Morozov's history, only to mysteriously die days later under heavy guard.

"Hurry, Nate. It's important."

The rear car's door opened. John eased forward, the moment's gravity pulling him from the shadows. The crowd parted, revealing the hidden figure's imposing stature. Broad shoulders stretched the seams of a dark suit. Cold blue eyes scanned with predatory precision. A scar cut through his left eyebrow, pointing to a mangled ear. There was no doubt.

Sasha Morozov.

"Christ," Olson muttered.

Whispered stories of Morozov's depraved acts turned even Moscow's elite pale. The man was supposed to be dead. This public resurrection after years of supposed death would only amplify his mythic reputation.

Why had he chosen to show himself now? The Soviet's presence confirmed this was no ordinary intelligence drop. In the world of spies: there was great, then elite, and then there was Morozov.

"Nate." John's tone dropped. "You were correct."

The line went silent. When Nate responded, his voice trembled with excitement. "Holy crap, I knew it! I mean… this is bad, right?"

Olson watched Morozov direct his men with quiet authority.

"The bagman! He's on the move," Nate exclaimed.

John cursed himself for not watching the target. Morozov's presence demanded his focus, and now they were behind the curve.

"Where?" he pressed, searching for the man.

"Far edge of the market. He just dropped a small satchel under a vendor's cart next to the archway. Disappeared into the crowd."

John spotted the abandoned parcel sitting in the open. He wiped sweat from his eyes. What was in that satchel? Nuclear secrets? A new weapon? In every scenario, the answer spelled danger.

Morozov's presence, coupled with the secretive dead drop, was a volatile combination. This was no longer a surveillance operation; they were now in the middle of an international crisis.

"Mission change." John stashed his gear and unclipped his holster. "I'm going to secure that package. This is now an active intercept. You're overwatch."

"Boss…" Nate's voice trailed off. "What about the hostiles?"

"No choice."

With that, John slipped from his hiding place, moving swiftly through the dense crowds. The masses provided good concealment, but he had no idea how many eyes Morozov had pre-positioned around the market.

"Combatants approaching from the north," Nate warned.

John found interest in a cart as the two spotters from before walked past. The vendor, an elderly man with milky cataracts, gestured enthusiastically at his array of intricate copper teapots. John waved him off, continuing on his path.

He let out a short exhale. "Thanks."

"You got it, boss. Russians are on the move."

Olson realized his position had put him at a disadvantage. Taking a deep breath to steady his nerves, he mapped the quickest route. The satchel rested under a cart near the archway.

"I'm going for it." John plunged headfirst into the masses.

"Wait! You're exposed."

John's focus shifted from the bag to the Soviet agents as they pressed through the marketplace. Morozov hung back, using his babysitters as a shield. The Soviet's caution was John's only window. John had to move fast.

"Our priority is the drop. The Soviets cannot get their hands on it. Nate, this is your chance to make a real difference. We stop them, by any means necessary."

A beat of silence hung on the radio. "I got you, boss. Whatever it takes."

He felt a swell of pride for his protégé rising to the occasion. "Good man," he said. "You're my eyes. Keep me clean so I can move fast."

"I'll clear the path."

The words emboldened John. The quartet of men was steadily advancing towards the drop site, but they were not moving with purpose. They had chosen caution over speed.

John's muscles coiled as he pushed through the crowd as quickly as possible. Anything faster would be suicide, but he couldn't hesitate either. The moment he made his move, a firefight would ensue.

The mass of people restricted his movement to an agonizing slowness. Sweat beaded on John's brow as he weaved through the bodies, his eyes focused on the satchel.

Seeing an opening, John lunged forward and collided with a merchant leading a camel laden with goods. He twisted past, but his elbow clipped a bag of loosely packed gourds, sending spices crashing to the ground. Vibrant red and yellow dust exploded into the air.

The beast's owner, an older man with sun-leathered skin and a henna-dyed beard, whirled around. His face, etched with hard lines, contorted with rage. "You clumsy fool!" he shouted in Somali, the words exploding from beneath his elaborately wrapped turban. He thrust a finger at the ruined wares, bangles jangling. "A lifetime of trade, destroyed by your clumsiness!"

"*Waan ka xumahay*," John said in apology. He held money up for the man, offering it as compensation for the damage. "*Aan ku bixiyo khasaaraha*," he added with a conciliatory bow.

Nothing appeased the tradesman. His voice rose with each accusation. Out of the corner of his eye, John saw the Russians halt, their attention now focused squarely on him.

The danger of his position was escalating. Pinned down by the irate merchant, with Morozov's men watching his every move, he was a sitting duck. If they recognized him as American, it would all be over.

Desperately, he looked around, seeking an escape route. But the wall of bodies offered no clear path as he tightened the scarf covering his face.

He chanced a look. One of the Russians stared straight at him, the agent's hand drifting toward a pistol tucked under his jacket.

Olson reached for his weapon, realizing a shootout was imminent. Yet another operation slipped into chaos. Tensed for conflict, John's thumb pulled back the pistol's hammer. He visualized his first two shots.

Pull on three. One…

The unexpected sound of Nate's voice registered in his ear. "I got your back, boss," he said in short, rapid breaths.

John barely had time to process before a commotion erupted.

"You cheated me!" Nate's accusation rang out.

John's head snapped to the noise, his eyes widening as he spotted Nate gesturing wildly beside an overturned fruit cart. Oranges and mangoes rolled across the square, drawing everyone's attention, including Morozov's men.

Nate's broken Somali filled the air as he waggled his finger at the bewildered merchant. His youthful features twisted in an exaggerated outburst. The seller's initial bewilderment gave way to a sly grin, recognizing the dance of negotiation. He matched Nate's melodramatic gestures with his own theatrical display of indignation.

Seizing the moment, John slapped the wad of money into the camel owner's hand and disappeared into the crowd.

As Nate continued his dramatic tirade, drawing chuckles and head shakes, John closed the distance. The Russians were engrossed in the spectacle, giving him a few slim seconds. Now he had to make them count.

John gauged the crowd's flow. In one fluid motion, he sidestepped into an opening, pivoted through a narrow gap, and grabbed the bag. He spun and hunkered in the shadow of an empty cart. Nate's distraction still held the attention of the crowd and Morozov's men.

He tucked the satchel under his robes. "Package secured," he whispered. "Extract now."

But even as the words left his mouth, a prickle of unease made John pause. He had an inexplicable sense that he was being watched, a spy's instinctual warning.

John raised his head, following the dread to its source. Morozov was staring directly at him, a glint of cold recognition in his frigid eyes. The man bared his crooked teeth as he pointed a single knobby finger.

Sasha Morozov just marked him for death.

Chapter 6

Sasha Morozov stood ten paces away, his stony eyes revealing nothing. John turned to stone under the Soviet's Gorgon stare. The harsh sun carved the spymaster's weathered features into a mask of unforgiving menace.

As recognition dawned, a predatory smile twisted Sasha's disfigured face, rendering him even more terrifying. Every fiber of John's being urged retreat. The Soviet's voice sliced through the air in harsh syllables.

One of the bulky Russians yanked a pistol from under his coat.

Adrenaline snapped the world back into focus. John leapt to his feet and darted into the dense crowd.

"Nate, get out of here!" he shouted.

Threading his way through stalls and startled shoppers, John ignored their panicked shouts. Gritty mortar scuffed beneath his soles, kicking up waves of fine sand that stuck to his sweat-drenched skin.

A vendor bounded into his path. Without slowing, Olson spun to his left and around the man, the local's gnarled fingers scraping against his tunic but never finding a grip.

A second series of sharp orders in Russian pierced the air.

Bullets whizzed past, tearing through canvas stalls and forcing shoppers to dive for cover. A stray round clipped a hanging pot, shards erupting outward as the market scrambled for safety.

John ducked and weaved through the panicked crowd, barely escaping the deadly hailstorm. The satchel thumped against his side. Even with bullets zipping past, John knew one thing: the Soviets wouldn't get that package.

Gritting his teeth, he veered down an alleyway of hard-packed dirt. The Russians were closing in, shouting commands in their native tongue. He needed distance. Their tactics would involve fanning out to cut off any escape, diminishing their numbers. But he was still trapped.

Mogadishu's narrow streets, flanked by weathered coral stone buildings with arched doorways, formed a sun-drenched labyrinth. One that seemed to close in around him.

He vaulted low walls, his breath coming in sharp bursts. He pushed forward, his boots kicking up choking dust as he zigzagged through the cityscape.

Thinking he was clear, John glanced back just as two Russians rounded the corner. Their shouts filled the narrow passageways. Olson pressed himself into a shadowed recess as one of Morozov's men charged past, cursing.

The sounds of pursuit faded. After a solid twenty count, John slipped from his hiding spot and walked calmly in the other direction. He hadn't gone fifty yards before noticing a few nearby locals taking too much interest.

Confirming his suspicions, a shout describing him rang out as he turned the bend. They were using local teams, casting a net. It was smart. He had to keep moving. Their numbers were now overwhelming.

John scurried down yet another narrow pathway, his feet stomping on muted pavestones. He needed an escape plan. Rounding the corner, he narrowly avoided startled locals, apologies tumbling out. He pressed on, once more swallowed by serpentine streets.

The old city was a maze of contradictions, its winding alleys and crowded markets a double-edged sword. Every turn presented a new opportunity for cover, but each step forward also carried fresh risk. These Soviet hunters were a far cry from the bureaucratic adversaries he faced at the CIA.

John couldn't outrun them forever, not in this maze of dead ends. He needed a new plan. His gaze drifted up to the flat roofs and jutting pipes that crisscrossed the buildings above.

It was risky. But also his best chance.

Surveying the roofline, he caught sight of a promising ledge. Without hesitation, Olson lunged for the sheer wall of the building. His fingers scrambled for handholds on the rough stone, ignoring the sting. He hauled himself up, muscles straining. The Russian agent's menacing yells grew louder every second.

He grabbed a horizontal outcrop of wires just as a bullet whizzed past his ear. Surging, Olson flipped himself onto the rooftop as more bullets impacted the area where he had been a second before.

The surface of the traditional Somali-style roof, covered in sun-baked clay, radiated intolerable heat. In the distance, the Indian Ocean glimmered. A curse came from below as the pursuers realized he was now out of reach.

Olson sprinted across the rooftop, his feet trying to maintain a grip against the hot tiles. The rough, uneven texture scraped against his soles. Sweat-slicked hands grazed the scorching ceramic as he fought to keep his balance.

He launched himself over a gap, arms windmilling as he sailed towards the next building and landed hard. John's legs skidded on the angled surface, loose grit biting into his palms as he scrambled to regain control.

Panting, John looked up. One of the Soviets blocked his path, a cruel sneer twisting his features.

"Where do you think you're going?"

Olson weighed his limited options. He couldn't afford to stop, reinforcements were imminent. But the Russian stood between him and the best escape route. John had come too far to let this obstacle stand in his way.

With a half-smile that cloaked his coursing adrenaline, Olson darted away, creating separation. He needed the spy's trifecta: distance, cover, concealment.

Fighting was a last resort.

A single bullet tore through the sleeve of Olson's shirt, nicking his skin as it blasted the fabric in front of him. That was too close. Olson prepared himself for a second shot.

Click-click-click. He knew that sound. The agent was out of bullets.

Time to go on the offensive. John pulled his weapon and swung around to aim, but was surprised to find the Soviet leaping straight at him with reckless abandon.

Olson sidestepped at the last moment, using the Soviet's momentum against him. His attacker stumbled, off-balance. John seized the opportunity, landing a sharp jab on the man's torso.

The agent wheezed but recovered faster than John anticipated. He lunged again, this time successfully tackling Olson. Breath burst from his lungs in a ragged gasp as the impact drove them both onto the steeply sloped rooftop.

The tiles scorched his body as they careened down the unforgiving surface, grit tearing at his clothes. Grappling with his attacker, Olson's pistol skittered away.

Their limbs tangled as they slid faster and faster toward the precipice of the roof. The edge was approaching, and he needed to get free.

John rammed his elbow into the man's ribs, trying to break the iron grip on his torso. The Soviet grunted but held tight, his fingers digging in with bruising force. He was too powerful. John was at a disadvantage in this fight.

As the roof's end rushed up, Olson twisted violently, wrenching himself around to face the man. His dark eyes burned with fanatical fire. John knew this agent would sacrifice himself without thought.

With a roar, Olson drove his forehead into the bridge of the brute's nose. Cartilage crunched wetly, and the Russian howled, his grip loosening just enough for John to kick free. The man's hands scrambled for support but found only empty air.

John's hand shot out, grabbing a rusted pipe jutting up. His fingers closed around it as his feet slipped over the edge. The vent groaned but held.

The agent wasn't so lucky. A scream rose from his throat, abruptly silenced by a sickening crack from the street below.

Hanging perilously, John clung to his lifeline with white-knuckled determination. A crowd gathered below. Searching for a way out, he spotted an open window a few feet below.

The jump was dangerous, but it was his only shot. More operatives would be on the rooftop by now.

Kicking off with a grunt of effort, he propelled himself towards the opening. The world clouded as he plummeted, wind whistling past his ears. He crashed through the shutters, his body instinctively curling into a tight ball. He hit the floor hard, momentum carrying him into a combat roll. The impact reverberated through his frame as he slammed into the far wall, leaving a small dent.

John pushed himself up, his eyes darting around. Save for a rickety chair and a bare table, the room stood empty. He had mere seconds to regroup before his pursuers caught up. Distant, angry voices suggested his hunters still hadn't realized he had abandoned the rooftop.

For now, their search would focus on the high ground, buying him precious time. He was momentarily safe, but he needed to distance himself from the chase team.

It was important to get back to the streets where he could blend in. Scanning the modest room, John noticed a vibrantly colored scarf hanging over a rickety chair. He inverted his djellaba, exposing a new color. Then, with a swift movement, wrapped the multicolored cloth around his head and neck.

He dropped a few tarnished coins on the bare table as payment. He eyed the crease in the wall.

"Sorry for the mess," he whispered, adding more money.

He peeked out the door, ensuring the hallway was clear. John then slipped down an old concrete staircase. At the bottom, he emerged onto Mogadishu's streets, keeping to the shadows.

Up ahead, a small crowd gathered around the crumpled dead body. Blood seeped out, staining the sand black. Arguments broke out as onlookers debated whether his fall had been an accident.

John's eyes stayed on the growing commotion as he moved at a measured pace, blending into the pedestrian traffic. Too overt an escape would draw attention. He had to fade away.

Passing the still-warm corpse, John chanced a glance back over his shoulder through the scarf's loose folds. There, outlined against the bright sky, were the unmistakable silhouettes of Morozov's men.

Olson knew it was only a matter of time before the agents picked up his trail again. He needed to retrieve his gear and report back to the station before the entire sector locked down.

He scanned the rooftops and alleyways, searching for any sign of pursuit. Nothing. The market's familiar sounds and scents returned as he backtracked, retracing the path of his earlier flight.

Olson soon found his original over-watch position near the square. It was untouched. His fingers brushed over the fabric of his go-bag, retrieving his discarded surveillance spyglass. He raised it, adjusting the focus and sweeping across the scene, looking for danger.

His blood froze.

In a shadowed alcove near the edge of the square stood Morozov. The Soviet spymaster was not alone.

He had Nate.

Morozov's weathered hand was wrapped around Balik's throat, the grip firm but not crushing. A show of control. He zoomed in closer, noting every detail. Sunlight glinted off the barrel of the pistol he pressed against Nate's temple.

John frowned. Something wasn't right. Morozov's posture was too relaxed; his movements too deliberate. There was an unsettling restraint in the spymaster's actions.

His eyes swept the area as if expecting someone.

That was the game. It was a trap.

Blood flowed from a gash on Nate's forehead, staining his face and shirt. Morozov's voice rose in a mocking taunt that John couldn't quite make out.

Even from this distance, the fear in his partner's eyes was obvious. The Ghost was toying with his prey, relishing his power. Every fiber of John's being screamed at him to act.

But what could he do?

Olson's gut churned, a sickening mix of guilt and anxiety. He shouldn't have let the kid get involved. Nate was his partner, his responsibility. Now Balik was paying the price for John's mistakes.

His hand moved to the bag's hidden compartment for his backup weapon. The sleek pistol felt reassuringly heavy. He checked the magazine and chambered a round.

John considered his options. From this position, there was no clear shot. A diversion? Morozov would kill Nate and then turn his attention. They'd both be dead.

The CIA field book was unequivocal on this scenario. Officer Olson was duty-bound to walk away, to let procedure take precedence over his personal desires. Nate knew the risks.

John weighed obligation against loyalty. The rational part of him screamed to follow protocol, to prioritize the mission and the intelligence he'd gathered. It was what they trained him to do.

No intel was worth his partner's life. He would save Nate or die trying.

He raised his comm unit. "Inbound. Thirty seconds out."

Olson pushed through the mass of people, shoving them aside. Pistol brandished, he left it on full display. John didn't care about keeping a low profile.

A crisp voice came across the radio, the words in clipped English. "You have something of mine. Hand it over, and your friend lives."

Men ducked and yelled as John barreled forward, the commotion of his passage drawing attention. Morozov's eyes widened as they found Olson.

He expected to find the staunch confidence of a seasoned Soviet operative. Instead, he glimpsed something else: a flicker of unease.

Morozov had dedicated all his supporting personnel to the chase. The spymaster was alone and vulnerable. And it was clear John had no intention of bending to his threats.

Police sirens wailed, their piercing cry growing louder, promising an impending arrival. Authorities would only make the situation worse.

Faces swirled as Olson propelled himself forward. They yelled and jostled as he tried to fling them aside. He pointed his weapon, finger coiled on the trigger. A throng of people blocked his line.

"Morozov!" John shouted.

For a split second, the crowd parted. Morozov took a step back from Nate, searching for his forces. There was a kind of weary resignation, as if he had played out this scene before.

As quickly as it appeared, the look was gone. The old man tilted his head just before a surging group blocked John's view.

Two sharp cracks split the air.

BANG! BANG!

People scattered, their panic igniting chaos in the already skittish market. Olson swam forward, pushing others aside.

John whispered a brief prayer as he cleared the last set of men. The sight stopped him cold.

Nate lay on the ground, his body slumped. The once-drab wall was now painted a vivid crimson.

Blood poured from two bullet wounds in Nate's gut. His eyes were open but glazed. Bloody bubbles gathered on his lips with each ragged breath. Morozov had left the CIA operative alive just long enough to allow John to watch him die.

"No, no, no!" John dropped to his knees, hands frantically applying pressure to his stomach. "Hold on, Nate. You hear me?"

"You're gonna be okay." The lie tasted bitter.

Balik's hand fumbled for Olson's, their entwined grip slick with blood. His mouth moved, but only a wet gurgle emerged. He managed a faint smile, a mockery of his usual pearly grin.

"I'm sorry." Tears stung John's face. "We did it. You did it."

Nate's eyes cleared, locking onto Olson with fierce intensity. He tried to speak, but nothing came out except bloody drool.

John bit his lip, emotions surging. "I promise to get him."

The fire in Nate's eyes faded until nothing was left. He stopped breathing. Olson felt the grip slacken.

John knelt in the bloody dirt, suffocating under his failure. This time, another had paid the cost. He was supposed to protect Nate.

Sand clung to the fabric of his trousers. The fresh scent of spent gunpowder stung his nostrils. He looked down at his trembling fingers. Guilt and grief welled up.

John's breath sputtered, a ragged sob catching in his throat. He slammed his fist into the dirt, the force sending jolts of pain through his knuckles.

Beneath it, a hard anger took root. Morozov had taken Nate.

The Ghost may have cheated death once. But come hell or high water, John would ensure Morozov's next brush with the reaper was final.

The sirens grew steady, their wail no longer distant. Olson knew he had to leave, but the thought of abandoning Nate tore at him. The local police were pushing through the crowd with great effort, their shouts intensifying.

John took one last look. With trembling fingers, he closed Nate's eyelids.

Rising to his feet, he patted the package, still secure in the satchel at his side. The weight seemed to increase tenfold. He wiped away a stubborn tear, leaving a swath of fresh blood across his cheek.

With a deep breath, Olson retreated into the masses, allowing the disorder to swallow him.

A group of uniformed men arrived on the scene, pushing back the onlookers. John recognized a lieutenant from the Somali Police Force who took charge. The police officer paused over the gruesome body lying in a pool of blood.

The man swiveled around, scanning the crowd, searching for the perpetrator. He found only a wall of inscrutable faces.

"Find out what happened, now!" he shouted.

The police combed the area, their eyes seeking clues. All they discovered was a few bloody footprints. They disappeared to the west, leaving behind only sand and stone.

Chapter 7

CIA FIELD OFFICE, MOGADISHU

13:16

Officer Olson burst through the steel entrance, his clothes blood-stained and eyes feral. The door slammed against the wall with a crash, the intrusion shattering the office's artificial tranquility.

The clacking of typewriter keys tapered off as everyone looked toward the commotion, leaving only the hum of fluorescent lights and an uneasy silence. This bureaucratic machine failed Nate when it mattered most. Olson scowled at their pale faces.

John swept through the room, radiating menace. Seasoned officers recoiled, terror flashing in their eyes at the sight of his bloody shirt and crimson-streaked face.

He clutched an aged satchel in one hand; its contents holding secrets that the Soviets wanted badly. Protecting this intelligence had come at a terrible cost.

Workers stumbled back as John strode through the cluttered workspace. He seethed at the stunned bureaucrats who'd traded morality for comfort. A woman half-rose, mouth open, then sank down into silence as he passed.

Running a hand over his face, Olson winced at the gritty texture of blood and sweat. John's gaze gravitated to the far wall, where a conspicuous workspace sat abandoned.

John approached Nate's empty desk, each step amplifying the finality.

His fingers traced the rough, scarred surface and stacked reports.

An engraved nameplate lay overturned, knocked askew in Nate's frantic exit. John reached across the cluttered space, fixing the plate. "BALIK" was printed in crooked letters. Another detail Upton couldn't be bothered with.

The simple act of touching Nate's things was like a twisting knife in his side.

Fresh grief threatened to overwhelm him. Nate should be there, that infuriating grin plastered across his face. The empty chair was a painful truth. His partner wasn't coming home. If only John had been a second faster, a bit sharper.

Nate's gold-rimmed aviators caught the light, the lenses glinting accusingly. Without thinking, he picked up the sunglasses and tucked them into his jacket pocket.

Olson took a deep, steadying breath, embracing the loss. But he couldn't afford to be consumed by it. There would be time later.

Right now, there was something he had to do.

Olson's gaze locked onto the closed door at the back of the room. Upton's office. The veins in his neck bulged, the memory of their last meeting still fresh. How many times had they butted heads? Upton had always been more concerned with maintaining the status quo.

He barged in, startling Upton.

"Have you lost your damn mind?" Rupert sputtered, rising from his desk.

He sucked in air to launch into a tirade, but it died in a frightened exhale. Seeing Olson's state, his features drained of color. For a fleeting moment, genuine concern flashed in Upton's eyes.

John closed the distance until he was inches from Rupert. His clenched jaw rippled, barely containing the fury. Sweat stung his cuts, plowing through dried blood.

If Upton thought protocol would provide safe harbor, he was gravely mistaken. He was facing a man with nothing left to lose.

Olson slammed a folder onto the desk, technical schematics spilling out.

The manager's gaze darted from John's face to the papers. The bold red letters were unmistakable: TOP SECRET. But even more distressing was the stamp below - POTUS EYES ONLY.

Rupert's mouth opened and closed. "How?"

"I held up my end, Upton. If you'd done the same, Nate would be alive."

"Wuh… wait… Balik's dead?" Rupert wheezed. "That's on you, Olson. I assigned him to you."

John's fist slammed the desk, sending a stack of folders cascading. "Shut up! Own it for once, Upton! Nate gave his life for these. The least you can do is read them."

His finger smashed against the paper, leaving a bloody print. The supervisor looked down at the scattered papers, his eyes narrowing as he retrieved the page. Lowering his glasses, he squinted.

"What the hell?"

"Something you've forgotten. Sacrifice." John growled. He leaned in. "Now, look at it."

Hands shaking, Upton sank into his chair. The paper fluttered as he examined it, turning it over once again.

"Technical schematics? Is that a skunk?"

Upton's eyes flicked to the shredder, his instinct for self-preservation overriding duty. Even now, his career mattered more than national defense.

"Focus," John snapped. "The Ghost of Berlin was there!"

Upton's face paled further. "Impossible. He's dead."

John dropped the camera onto the desk. "Wrong again! He killed Nate, and I need to understand why. What is this!?"

"I-I don't know!" he stuttered. "I've never seen anything resembling this."

John watched as the station chief studied the diamond-shaped diagram, bewilderment deepening across his face. Rupert turned the page upside down.

"What in God's name? Some damn abstract art piece. Triangles and facets everywhere. Almost alien."

John leaned forward. "It's not art, and it's not abstract. Open your mind."

"It's like… a blueprint. But for what?"

John snatched the page from Upton's hand and slid it back into the worn satchel, pulling the strap taut across his chest. He couldn't trust anyone else to keep it safe.

"It's a weapon for a war we're not ready to fight."

Chapter 8

LANGLEY, VIRGINIA - CIA HEADQUARTERS

3 Days Later

08:32

John's polished shoes clicked on the marble floors of CIA headquarters, the crisp scent of pine cleaner stinging his nostrils. It was a stark contrast to Mogadishu's searing heat and spice-laden air. With each step, Nate's absence pressed on him.

It felt like a month since the encounter with Morozov.

As usual, Upton had tried to hide the situation. But the cryptic diagram had triggered top-brass involvement. Within hours, operatives swarmed their corner of the world, tearing everything apart.

The outsiders vanished as swiftly as they had appeared, leaving only devastation. The silence lasted less than a day before the seventh-floor summons arrived. Twenty-four hours of travel on three separate C-130s followed.

Rupert resembled a man led to the gallows, his suit sagging with resignation. "Twenty years. Not once called to see the Director; I like it that way." His gaze dropped. "I miss Somalia."

"It's the Deputy Director," Olson corrected.

"Same thing."

John glanced to his left, where flags flanked a larger-than-life bronze statue of William Donovan. Across the entrance hall stood a somber wall honoring case officers who paid the ultimate price. A team of men was adding a small black star.

Balik's star. That should have been his.

His stomach growled. How many days since he last ate? The trip from Mogadishu had fused into a haze of debriefings and time zone changes.

They ascended a staircase, navigating hallways and elevators until they reached a seventh-floor office. A young secretary perched at her desk looked up as they entered. Her fingers flew over the typewriter keys like machine-gun fire, punctuated by the flick of ash from her cigarette.

"Wait there," she instructed.

They settled into vinyl chairs. John gazed at the heavy wooden door and checked his watch. Waiting was the worst part.

Upton's knee bounced, his breath catching with each tick.

John weighed the likelihood of Rupert's heart giving out. Olson rejected any responsibility, deciding the man's life choices should be blamed for any fatal results.

The secretary barely looked up. Her typewriter clacked in a rapid cadence, each stroke punching into carbon-copied paper. Later it would be filed away, buried in the CIA's archives of deniable operations.

The phone trilled, shattering the quiet. She snatched it, her cigarette shifting as she spoke in hushed tones.

"Deputy Director Avery will see you now."

Upton offered for Olson to enter first. It was not an act of chivalry.

John thought he would have more time before they fired him. He braced himself for another bureaucratic dressing-down.

Upon entering, John's assumptions melted. The room was stunning. Antique firearms and edged weapons adorned one wall. Leather-bound first editions lined the opposite shelves. It validated Avery's appreciation of both strategy and history. This Deputy Director was no ordinary bureaucrat.

Lucas Avery sat behind a massive mahogany desk, its surface covered with classified folders arranged in precise, overlapping rows. He was on the phone, his voice low but authoritative. As John and Upton approached, he held up a single finger, signaling them to wait.

Keen eyes peered out from beneath a prominent brow, framed by neatly groomed, graying hair. A life of secrets was carved into the lines of his face. His classic suit, well-tailored but not ostentatious, spoke more to duty than fashion.

Lucas famously operated in the shadows long before rising to his current position. Everyone knew of his time in the OSS. However, the exact nature of what he did remained a mystery.

"That's an order," Avery snapped, setting the receiver down with a rough click.

With surprising agility, Lucas rose and bridged the gap. His hand, weathered and nicked from years of service, stretched out. Before John could react, Upton lunged forward, his sweaty palm seizing the Deputy's hand.

A grimace flickered across the Deputy Director's features before he wrested his arm from Upton's clammy grip. He extended his hand to John, the handshake matching the man's sturdy presence.

"Officer Olson. So glad you could make it."

Upton stepped forward, his words rushing out. "Sir, Nate Balik was an excellent case officer—cream of the crop. One of the best." He swallowed hard. "Taught him myself. Damn shame."

Avery fixed him with a shrewd stare. "Good to hear."

Rupert wilted, his eyes darting to the exit. His hips and right shoe shifted in the same direction.

"Chief Upton, that'll be all."

The color drained from the bureaucrat's face as he inclined his head in acquiescence, scurrying from the room. Olson had always anticipated being on an island, but he never expected his station chief to abandon him so quickly.

Avery's lips curved into a sardonic smirk. "Is that guy real?"

Olson hesitated, weighing his response. "He's fairly… consistent."

"Diplomatic." Avery's eyes shimmered with approval as he loosened his tie. "But not blindly loyal. Good."

"Have a seat," he gestured to the spot opposite his desk. "You kicked up one hell of a hornet's nest in Africa."

John sank into the leather chair. "It wasn't intended," he said. "But I'd do it again."

He prepared for a reprimand. Instead, Avery let out a hearty laugh.

"That's what case officers are supposed to do. At least, that's what we used to do."

John was speechless. Protocol demanded a head for an operation gone wrong. Lucas's approving gaze threw him off balance. The reaction, unexpected as it was, hinted at a different approach to fieldwork. One more pragmatic in nature.

Lucas leaned against the desk, his gaze unfocused. John sensed that the man was wrestling with a decision. He looked at the hand-written note, nodded to himself, then crumpled it up. Avery dropped the paper into a burn bag as he ambled toward a built-in shelf adorned with crystal decanters.

"I'm considering a brandy. Want one?"

This had to be the strangest firing of a CIA operative on record. "You have whiskey?"

"Ah, a man who understands the history of the region," Avery said, retrieving two cut-glass tumblers. He poured two generous fingers into each before handing one to John.

They each took a savoring sip, enjoying the rich flavors.

Olson set the glass down, senses on high alert, waiting. Something more was coming. He could feel it.

Avery swirled his drink. "You know, John, I was there when we built this place from the ground up." He tapped his finger on the desk. "Wild Bill himself taught me that sometimes, to serve your country, you have to operate with certainty in unstable conditions."

He paused, a smile forming. "We were patriots and outlaws both. Had to be, in those days."

"We've lost our edge, Officer Olson. Become too… civilized." Avery's lips curled in distaste. "We play by gentleman's rules in a back-alley knife fight."

That world of pure action was now a bygone era. John would have thrived in that time. Men could do what was needed, and success was their only measure.

"The CIA was born from the ashes of World War II. The OSS and 'Wild Bill' Donovan. We had a different spirit then." He took another leisurely draw from his glass. "Do you know why you're here, Officer Olson?"

"Until about twenty seconds ago, I thought I was being fired." John chanced a second dangerous sip of whiskey.

Avery barked a laugh, slapping the table. "Of course! John, the agency is crawling with people so goddamn scared of their own shadows that no one's willing to do the hard things anymore."

"But not you," he pointed a finger, his expression growing serious. "Be honest with me. Mogadishu was unsanctioned, right?"

John felt guilt at the reminder, but he straightened his spine and met Avery's inquisitive look. He wouldn't cower, not to a man who seemed to get it.

"I take full responsibility."

Avery scrutinized Olson, then turned his attention back to his drink. "You know what keeps me up at night, John?"

"No idea, sir."

"The Soviets are developing technology we won't see coming," Lucas answered, his voice carrying a hint of bitterness. "I know they are. And if the bastards can't build it, they'll steal it." He paused before taking a deep gulp of his whiskey.

He regarded John with a half-smile. "You stopped my nightmare from becoming a reality." The grin faded. "But an officer is dead, and I have at least five diplomatic complaints that won't disappear easily."

Avery lifted a thick folder from his desk and let it drop back with a thud. "And this isn't the first time, is it?"

"No, sir."

"All my division chiefs say I should fire you."

John tensed, waiting for the ax to fall. But Avery's tone had a hint of… admiration? Everything about this was wrong. The pieces weren't adding up. If the CIA wanted him gone, why the drink? Why the history lesson?

John rose, standing tall as he faced the Deputy Director. It was time to end this charade. "If you were going to do that, it would already be done. Why am I here, sir?"

"Brass tacks. Good. Two reasons." Avery smiled. "First, you have a guardian angel. Apparently, somebody believes your brand of fieldwork is useful."

"Who, sir?"

"You know better than to ask. Even within these walls, there are factions," Avery replied.

John grimaced. Of course. This was how the game was played. "And the second reason?"

"I need someone for a green door assignment. One that requires… creative tradecraft. Perfect for someone with a checkered past."

John's lips pressed tight. Those ops always skirted the edge of legality, morality, and sometimes both.

"How inventive are we talking, sir?"

"High-risk, high-reward. The kind that gives most sane people nightmares. Our enemies are evolving. We need to do the same. Desperate times demand desperate measures."

"I don't get it, sir."

"Excuse me?" Avery replied.

"One minute the agency is telling me to do one thing, now you're telling me to do another. Which is it?"

"Neither, both." Lucas's eyes narrowed. "This mission. Hmm. It's not just off the books. It's between the lines of the words. Danger will come at you from everywhere, across the ocean and down the hall. Question everyone and everything." He straightened the small American flag on his desk. "That's the game. You'll detest it. I guarantee that. Because I already do. Nothing about this is conventional." He gestured accusingly. "But that's why it may work. You're perfect for this assignment. You just don't know it yet."

"And if I walk?"

"Then we fire you. Maybe throw in some extra charges for my own amusement." His stare bored into John. "After all, somebody has to be the public face of this cluster. I'd prefer it to be that sniveling leper you arrived with."

This was a dangerous gamble. John recalled the Senate's Church Committee investigation into CIA assassination plots and illegal domestic operations. Ford had come down heavy on the department for that kind of thing. And now, the Agency was asking him to operate in those same murky waters.

He could find balance. Just because others broke the rules didn't mean he had to as well. Clandestine didn't imply corrupt.

Avery controlled all the leverage. Refuse, and his career could vanish in an instant. Then there was the ominous guarantee that he would 'hate' this new mission. It likely meant delving even deeper into moral gray areas, the kind of compromise that had already cost his friend his life.

If he had refused the last op, would his young partner still be alive?

That didn't matter. He had to stop Morozov. He owed Nate that.

John drained the remaining whiskey in one gulp and slammed the empty glass down. "Sounds like you've got me cornered, sir."

Olson rose, squaring his shoulders. He would accept Avery's challenge and crush it. He had to believe there was a way to navigate these murky waters without drowning in them. It couldn't be worse than anything he had encountered before.

"When do we begin?"

Avery's smile was all teeth. "We already have."

Chapter 9

14:37

Sleek headphones dulled the engine's roar as John scanned the Virginia landscape below. The helicopter's black body sliced through the air, its blades whisking overhead, leaving white contrails. The lush, rolling hills clashed with his memories of Somalia's barren wastelands.

"Any clues as to where we're going?"

Avery's cheeks rippled in the wind. "Laws restrain us, John. Especially with Soviet agents operating everywhere."

The Deputy Director was dodging his questions. Everything about this secretive helicopter ride and the mission's murky details set him on edge.

"After Vietnam and Watergate, the administration is gun-shy," Avery continued.

John crossed his arms. "Ford's reforms were harsh."

"Harsh?" Avery scoffed. "He gutted our operations. And now Carter's human rights crusade has us in a straitjacket while the Soviets run unchecked on American soil."

"If it's within our borders, isn't that the FBI's jurisdiction?"

"Christ, Olson. The Bureau couldn't find a Soviet in the Kremlin. This requires a delicate touch. Especially in the homeland."

"Domestic ops require presidential approval."

"Technically," Avery said.

"But?"

Avery leaned in. "Communism is spreading like a disease, from Angola to Ethiopia. And Carter's too focused on extending the SALT Treaties to see it."

John saw the Soviet influence shift, even in Africa. But this operation seemed a little more dramatic than usual for the Agency. There was a reason for everything the CIA did.

"A black bag op with plausible deniability built in."

"Call it what you want." Avery waved his hand dismissively. "Officially, you're still running dark in Somalia. And given your colorful history…"

"I've bent the rules before. If this blows up, you can pin it on me," John finished for him. "An out that protects everyone else, including you."

"You catch on quick. But don't worry. You and your partner will be our secret weapon to protect this program."

John realized getting fired would've been a mercy compared to this tangled web. Sometimes you're the sacrificial pawn.

"What program? What partner?"

Avery pointed out the window. A sprawling compound materialized below, invisible except from the air. Barbed-wire and heavily armed guards made it look like a military installation.

"We're here."

John's fingers dug into the seat as the aircraft jolted to a halt. The rotor wash kicked up a swirl of dust as they disembarked, the helicopter's rhythmic thump-thump fading. Avery strode toward the entrance with purpose. John trailed behind, scanning his surroundings as the helicopter blades came to a stop.

What seemed imposing before now felt oppressive, its featureless walls stretching in every direction. The compound towered before them, barbed-wire fences and steel barriers casting ominous shadows. John felt the same anxiety he'd experienced as a child watching explorers open King Kong's gates.

Armed men, their faces impassive beneath caps, pushed back the doors on soundless hinges. High-caliber rifles rested against their shoulders as one guard led Avery towards a reinforced doorway carved into the hillside.

As they approached the entrance, Lucas produced a metal key, inserted it into the lock, and then entered without hesitation.

The guards eyed Olson. He followed as the door and sunlight slammed shut, a bead of sweat trickling down his temple. His eyes strained to adjust to the harsh lighting, the warmth of the outside world replaced by a chill.

They descended the concrete tunnel. John's instincts screamed danger, and Avery's silence confirmed it. He glanced at the ceiling, trying to gauge how far underground they were.

"Fifty feet and descending," Avery muttered, glancing at his watch.

They passed checkpoint after checkpoint with unsmiling guards scrutinizing their credentials. Finally, they reached a desolate hallway with a single door.

Avery rotated an object in his hand, the cold metal reflecting the seriousness of the moment. He pivoted to John, his expression unreadable. "You've seen too much to turn back now," he growled.

John couldn't take the suspense anymore. "Look, sir. Cut the act. This is clearly a black site."

"Few know of this place's existence."

John remained quiet, waiting the man out.

With another glance at his watch, Lucas broke the silence. "Remember what I told you about patriots and outlaws?"

"The OSS. Always be ready for a knife fight."

"Sometimes you gotta fight dirty. Fight fire with flamethrowers. KGB style," Avery explained. "But you can't become the enemy. To succeed, you need both sides of the coin, patriot and outlaw."

John took a moment. He was the patriot. And whoever was beyond that reinforced steel barrier, well... they were the outlaw.

"Level with me, sir. Who's behind there? A Soviet defector?"

"Nice thought, but wrong."

"Then who? Another agent? A criminal informant?"

Avery clasped John's shoulder, his grip firm. "I've shielded you as much as I can, son. From here on out, you're on your own."

"That's not an answer."

Avery's eyes met his, a warning buried within. "Sometimes, it's better not to know until you have to." He tapped his coat pocket. "I can't emphasize this enough: trust no one."

He pulled a crisp manila envelope from his jacket. "This is your leverage. Say nothing about the mission or the operation."

Avery pressed a key into Olson's palm. His grip tightened, a subtle gesture that belied the gravity of the situation. But just as quickly, Avery's features smoothed back into an impenetrable mask.

John's fingers gripped the key, the sharp edges pressing into his skin as if to warn him. He looked up for more, but the Deputy Director was already walking away.

"But I don't know anything about the operation."

"Perfect. I almost believe you." Avery's voice floated down the hallway as he receded into the darkness.

"Who's behind the door?"

His unanswered question echoed in the empty corridor.

"Your helicopter transport departs for a formal in-brief in half an hour," Avery's disembodied voice drifted back from the depths. "Both of you be on it or find yourself a room."

A door slammed shut. Silence engulfed him.

Now isolated, uncertainty joined the eerie quiet. Avery made it clear: the only way out was through. The Deputy Director had gone to great lengths not to reveal the existence of a partner until they were on the helicopter.

Black sites weren't for holding Nobel laureates. They were reserved for the worst of the worst. His new "partner" wasn't just a criminal; they were someone dangerous enough to warrant this level of security. And now, he was expected to work with them.

He looked down at the items in his hand, and then at the threshold. Whoever waited beyond, he would face them. He steadied himself and inserted the key, turning it with a slow, deliberate motion.

The heavy door groaned as the lock disengaged, shattering the silence. John heaved it open, revealing an antechamber. He stepped into it.

The first portal closed behind him with an ominous thud, plunging him into darkness save for a small spotlight on a second door's handle. A faint electronic buzz drew him forward.

Was he making another mistake? What lay beyond? He couldn't articulate it, but somehow he knew that whoever lived in this awful place would change the course of his life.

John turned the handle and pushed it open. Despite the day's twists, nothing had prepared him for this.

Olson stood rooted to the spot, feeling as if he'd crossed a threshold into a parallel world. The stark, clinical reality of the black site vanished, replaced by a rich glow.

The room beyond was an inviting, comfortable space that would be welcome in any home. This cage was beyond gilded.

There was a cozy reading nook nestled in one corner, where a plush chair rested next to stacked books on a side table. Paintings adorned the once drab walls, but what caught his attention was a half-finished Matisse recreation resting on an easel.

The room's floral scent, like fresh rain and blooming jasmine flowers, was in discord with the subterranean compound.

His eyes finally landed on a figure seated comfortably in an armchair, their back turned to him. A slender arm extended from the chair, casually tapping ash from a lit cigarette.

John took half a step forward.

Impossible.

The CIA couldn't be this desperate.

The seated figure shifted, head tilting as if sensing his presence. A familiar voice, smooth as silk, cut through the silence.

"Hello, John."

Chapter 10

The heavy door sealed with a muffled clank. Olson blinked, willing his senses to deceive him. Smoke coiled above the high-backed chair as a tanned, bejeweled hand emerged, tapping ash into a crystal ashtray.

The figure rose.

Gabrielle Hyde.

John's face hardened, masking his turmoil. Contempt burned in his gut, warring with an unwelcome curiosity. She defied all he knew about criminals, and that unsettled him more than he cared to admit.

It was easy to fall into her gravitational pull. Instead, John focused on his anger. His hands clenched into fists. This woman had cost him everything two years earlier. He had imagined finding her a thousand times, but never like this.

Hyde tilted her head, as if she had been waiting for him all along. "I was glad to hear you survived our last encounter."

John scoffed, bitterness lacing his words. "This is a mistake."

Hyde's smile faded. "That's all you have to say?" Her tone brimmed with mock hurt. "No *'bonjour, mon ami,'* no 'hello?' Not even a *'See tahay?'*"

John froze at her flawless Somali. How did she know? What did the CIA want with her? He was the last person they should have sent.

"Save it."

Unfazed by his hostility, Hyde glided across the room, her fingernails trailing over the surface of a walnut table. "Then allow me to fill this dreadful silence."

Hyde's nostrils flared. "You've had quite the journey," she said, her eyes narrowing. "Avery still favors that Jet Ranger, doesn't he?"

John blinked. Her smile widened. "Aviation fuel clings to you like cheap cologne."

"Cut the parlor games, Hyde."

"Parlor?" Hyde's eyebrows shot up.

She moved closer, her voice dropping. "Fine, let's make this interesting, shall we?" Her stare lingered on John's hands. "Curious," Gabrielle murmured, reaching for his wrist.

John recoiled, but not before she glimpsed the raw cuts on his knuckles.

"Those scrapes… not from an American brawl." Her voice dropped. "Your tan lines are muddled. Doxycycline? Known to accelerate sun exposure and ward off malaria for those living in Africa. The CIA's Mogadishu station must be busy."

John kept his features impassive as her eyes met his. But his silence spoke for him.

"What were you doing in a fight in Somalia, and why would that bring you to me?"

Her gaze moved up to his face, homing in on the bridge of his nose. "That discoloration on your medial canthus… A recent traumatic event, *non? Cela indique un événement traumatique, n'est-ce pas?*"

John remained motionless.

"That fresh bruise is still healing." Her eyes lingered on the fading spot on his cheek from the fight with the Soviet agent. "Quite a dangerous profession you chose. Enemy or colleague?"

A muscle trembled in John's jaw. He cursed, hating how easily she got under his skin. Her insights were too personal. For the first time, he wondered if Hyde was out of his league.

She stalked around John, her eyes dissecting him like a living document. "You winced when I said colleague," she noted. "Not in anger, but from something else." Her voice softened. "Ah, of course. Tragedy."

Olson fought to stay neutral, but his cheek twitched. Hyde pointed her finger, reading his reaction. She leaned in close.

"Tell me, John. Where is your faithful Sancho Panza now?"

Hyde knew. He trembled, not with fear, but with the force of his repressed emotions surging to the surface. Grief and guilt threatened to shatter his control.

Visions of choking to death on top of the Toronto skyscraper filled John's head, replaced by the bubbles of blood escaping Nate's lips. He saw Morozov's cruel look. His failures crashed down as the world turned red.

It was all her fault.

A volcanic surge of repressed anger propelled John forward. He lunged, slamming Gabrielle against the wall with bone-jarring force. His left hand wrapped around the delicate column of her throat, fingers digging into flesh. His right hand clamped down on her wrist, ramming it against the rough concrete above her head.

"You know nothing," he hissed through gritted teeth, his face inches from hers. "Go to hell."

Hyde didn't flinch. Her eyes, devoid of fear, bore into his with an unsettling intensity. John's grip tightened. He felt her pulse beneath his fingers.

"Is that your wish?"

His grasp loosened. Why wasn't she fighting back? Olson searched her face, finding a haunting sadness. A depth of emotion he'd never contemplated.

"Too late," Hyde rasped, her gaze flicking to her trapped arm. "Already been there."

John's eyes followed. The sleeve of her blouse had fallen, revealing…

His breath caught.

A small, crude tattoo covered the inside of her wrist. It was a series of numbers. He had seen these before in pictures from Holocaust survivors.

He released her arm as if it burned, staggering back. Empathy welled within him, unwanted and undeniable. He pushed it down, clinging to his anger.

"Is that supposed to make me feel sorry for you?"

Hyde rubbed her wrist. "Pity is the last thing I want."

John turned away, running his hands through his hair. Why did Hyde affect him so? His neatly categorized world was dissolving. The truth was hard to accept, but impossible to ignore.

He didn't hate Hyde; he hated himself.

The realization drained the fight from John's body. His shoulders sagged as the ebbing adrenaline left him. "This changes nothing," he said.

Hyde smoothed her disheveled clothes and obscured the tattoo behind elegant jewelry. "I pushed you… too far. There is no greater beast we face than the one from within."

She motioned to the package tucked under John's arm. "I assume that is for me?"

John hesitated, eyeing the fireplace. He could toss the contents into the coals. But Avery's warning replayed: this was his mission, regardless of his feelings.

He thrust the envelope toward Hyde. She took it gracefully, regarding him with an inscrutable expression before pacing the room, flipping the document between her delicate fingers. The package remained unopened as she came to rest. Her calm gaze lingered on the dancing flames.

Hyde was making an actual decision in front of him. This was new. She didn't seem to rush or act on impulse. Instead, she appeared to weigh her options.

John's view of her softened, but then he grimaced. That is what she wanted him to feel.

"Should I burn it, as you desire?" Hyde asked.

"Yes," John admitted. "That was my initial instinct."

Hyde turned to face him, a curious look in her eyes. "I am also reluctant," she confessed. "It's clear what's inside." Her fingers traced the edge of the large envelope, breaking the seal.

John watched as she examined the contents, a faint sigh escaping. "Amnesty? How cliché." She produced a loupe, scrutinizing the document. "Authentic paper, genuine signature," she muttered. "Interesting. Should I accept?"

"No," he replied instantly. He then added, "It's likely a trap. Even if it's not, the CIA could renege on their promise at any time. They don't make deals like this… not without a catch."

"Anything else?" Hyde asked.

"I'm not a good partner. My ops never go as planned."

"Honest to a fault."

Hyde nodded as she reached for a silk scarf, the deep turmeric fabric rippled as she looped it around her neck. "You've talked me into it," she said.

John raised his hand in exasperation. "Which? Accepting or walking away?"

Hyde's lips quirked into an enigmatic smile. "Both."

"I told you, it's a trap," Olson repeated.

Gabrielle gathered select items, stuffing them into her handbag. She seemed unaffected by his protestations.

John hesitated, torn between justice and the CIA's ruthless pragmatism. "The CIA doesn't pardon targets. There's always a catch; you can be sure of that."

"A trap indeed," she replied, a playful glint in her eye. She leaned in. "But for whom?"

"Gabrielle…" John's voice softened.

Hyde stopped in her tracks, turning her full attention to the CIA Officer. John could see a small but subtle change. It was the first time she viewed him as a person, rather than a puzzle to be solved.

"The government doesn't play games."

For half a second, John thought he saw uncertainty. But if it was doubt, it was gone even faster, replaced by Hyde's usual confidence.

Amusement sparkled in her face. "That's why they're so bad at it."

"You should reconsider."

"Your eyes tell a different story," Hyde laughed. "Now, where are we going?" She studied him as she finished her collections.

John considered the answer. He didn't know. Where would the CIA send a thief of her notoriety partnered with a blacklisted operative? Nowhere made sense.

"The Pentagon? Langley?" Gabrielle mused, pausing in her tracks. Her eyes narrowed as if considering. Suddenly, her face lit up with excitement.

"No…" she gasped. "I've always wanted to see it in person."

"But I said nothing…"

Gabrielle grasped the handle. It buzzed, the locks disengaging. She pulled the massive door open. "Sure you did, partner," she said. "What is a circle, but not a circle?" She pivoted. "Now, come along."

Without waiting, she slipped out the door. John lunged, catching the edge before it slammed shut. He stared at the round brass doorknob in his hand.

Hyde's riddle played in his head: "What's a circle, but not a circle?"

The answer was an oval. But that wasn't a location.

John's pupils dilated. Could it be? The audacity of it was breathtaking. He recalled the stamp on the stolen documents: POTUS EYES ONLY. How had Hyde pieced it together?

He then heard a low, distant rumble that grew in intensity. Even from the depths of the room, the thunderous roar of rotor blades was unmistakable.

It wouldn't be any ordinary aircraft. The sheer size could only belong to a Sikorsky VH-3A. Those made up the presidential fleet.

Adrenaline surged, John's muscles coiling with sudden energy as he burst forward. The cool air of the corridor rushed past his face as he sprinted to catch up to her. Their eyes met for a moment, a silent understanding passing between them. Whatever lay ahead, they were in this together.

The thunderous roar of spinning rotors was deafening.

"You realize," Olson shouted, "there's no going back. They think we're both expendable."

Hyde's lips curled into a smile. "No, my dear. We're about to become the most dangerous people in Washington."

The helicopter grew even louder. Marine One was departing for the White House.

Chapter 11

OVAL OFFICE - WHITE HOUSE

21:10

The hum of air conditioning was the only sound in the Oval Office as Secret Service Agents ushered Olson and Hyde inside. Night had fallen, darkness pressing against the windows and highlighting a meticulous model ship behind the President's desk.

The room's grandeur weighed on Olson as lamps cast amber light across rich yellow carpeting and gleamed on the resolute desk. The subtle aroma of expensive wood polish permeated the room. Discarded pens and notes lay scattered near a silent white phone. Most knew it as the "Red Phone," despite its color.

Generations of leaders had occupied this space. Their legacies were etched into every surface. John felt out-of-place. Whatever situation brought them here, it was big.

Political meetings often built expectation for action followed by endless inactivity. He thought of Somalia. The President would almost certainly know what happened there, especially with a CIA officer's death involved.

He tried not to think of Nate, but the memory ambushed him. Nate's gold aviators reflecting the Mogadishu sun, that eager grin as he'd adjusted his earpiece. Missions could go so wrong, so fast. He learned that in Toronto.

Olson looked at Hyde. She was his partner now, God help him. Hopefully, somebody would arrive soon. John turned to the Secret Service Agent standing watch. "Do you know when we could expect someone?"

The agent's weariness etched his eyes, hinting at long duty hours. He had the patience of a veteran. "They'll be here shortly, sir."

Olson sank onto a couch. The striped fabric felt unnaturally still beneath him. John noticed a newspaper folded on a side table, its headline blaring about the ongoing energy crisis. Carter's presidency was barely a year old, and already the global oil shortage had people reeling. Soviet expansion wasn't helping.

John watched as Hyde explored the room, her gaze moving from painting to painting. She paused before a bust, her reflection distorted in the bronze features. "Franklin," she murmured. "Never president, yet we still connect him to its power."

"Admiring or casing?" John asked.

"Can't I enjoy a little history without sending up flares?"

"Not when it's you doing the appreciating," Olson retorted.

Hyde circled the President's desk, her attention fully captured. The agent stepped forward. "Miss Hyde, please keep your distance."

She lifted her hands. "Don't worry, dear agent. I'm just admiring."

On one side sat a worn Bible. Hyde's focus, however, moved to a set of folders strewn across the polished surface. Leaning in close, her fingers hovered mere millimeters above the rich mahogany, never quite touching. She squatted, eyeing a labeled binder bearing a star.

Though playful on the surface, her actions carried a sense of purpose. John recognized that laser-focused intensity. She was hunting. A glance at the Secret Service Agent confirmed John wasn't the only one who'd noticed.

The guard shifted his weight. His hand inched closer to his earpiece, fingers flexing, as if fighting the urge to call for backup.

"Enough games, Hyde. You're like a five-year-old in a candy shop. Sit down."

The admonishment satisfied the agent, who eased his stance. Hyde gave a subtle nod of acknowledgment. "Noted, Officer," she said, taking a seat next to John.

He scowled. "You push too far."

Hyde shrugged. "Worth it. Trust me."

John let out an exasperated laugh. He thought of the gas canister that had almost killed him. "Trust you? That's rich. You lie to everyone."

"I've never lied to you, John. People see what they want, not what's there. I hoped you would understand."

Olson squirmed in his seat, glancing away from Hyde's piercing look. As much as he hated to admit it, she was right. For all her deceptions, she'd never outright lied to him.

He ran a hand over his face. "I'm sorry. I just don't think like you."

A genuine smile replaced the frown, Hyde's eyes brightening. "Give it time. My ways might grow on you."

"Not likely."

The large Oval Office door slid open, and Olson rose to his feet. A man in his early forties swept into the room with an air of effortless authority. His presence commanded attention, filling the space with an almost tangible energy. His tailor-cut suit, a masterpiece of charcoal Merino wool, hugged his frame. A proficient smile played on his lips, warm yet calculating.

He approached them with effortless grace, his eyes flicking to Hyde before locking onto Olson. He extended his hand, the grip slightly too firm, held a beat too long. It was the handshake of a man who measured others by how much pressure they could withstand.

"Officer Olson, what a pleasure," Durbin said, the title rolling off his tongue with polished ease. "William Durbin, President Carter's Deputy Chief of Staff for National Security Affairs and the architect of this clandestine gathering."

He leaned in, a conspiratorial glint in his eye. "And between us, I also lend my expertise to… certain communist affairs. Though that's strictly off the books, of course. I'm sure you understand."

A familiar taste of resentment rose in Olson's throat. Here was another bureaucrat ready to meddle in covert operations. He'd vanish at the first sign of trouble. John caught Hyde's eye, dismayed that he found her more trustworthy than the politicians.

He recalled Avery's words about hating this assignment. So far, he was correct.

Durbin turned his attention to Gabrielle, his eyes gleaming. "And you must be Miss Hyde. The stories of your grace and beauty don't do you justice."

Hyde extended her hand, meeting his gaze with a cool smile. "Mr. Durbin," she said, leaning in close, "you sure know how to flatter." Her tone shifted subtly as she added, "You wouldn't be *the* William Durbin from Oxford, would you?"

A flash of calculation crossed Durbin's face, there and gone like a chess player recognizing an unexpected opening move. "I attended Oxford for my graduate studies. Are you an alum?"

Hyde laughed, placing a hand on her chest. "I'm afraid that institution and I had differing opinions on educational priorities," she said, her tone both respectful and self-deprecating. "But I appreciated your paper on the Calculus of Conflict. Your theories on the Nash equilibrium and noncooperative game theory in communist expansion were brilliant. The analogy to the Englund Gambit in Cold War policies was particularly bold."

Durbin's fingers twitched almost imperceptibly. "Curious, Ms. Hyde. I never reached an agreeable conclusion with my chair. That paper was never published."

"You'd be surprised what one can learn with the right connections. I find controversy infinitely more intriguing than consensus, don't you? After all, the most interesting solutions arise when orthodox strategies fail."

"Controversy can indeed be… illuminating," he replied carefully, studying her with renewed interest. "Though I've found that those who reveal their approach too early often lose their advantage."

Hyde glanced at the entrance. "By chance, will we be meeting with the President?"

Durbin let out a soft sigh, followed by an indulgent chuckle. He remained calm and composed, his posture subtly shifting to mirror Hyde's stance. "The President is still in Georgia. I'm afraid you are stuck with me."

"Well, I understand completely. It's always a delight to meet the true power behind the throne." Then, she added with a sly smile, "Don't you dare deny it."

"An astute observation. Though I prefer to think of myself as more of a loyal advisor than a player."

Hyde kept her attention focused on the man, but John recognized the calculating glint in her eyes. It was a look he'd come to know the hard way. Hyde was seeking advantages.

And Durbin was giving it right back. They were sizing each other up in coded conversation. John couldn't tell if it was for Alpha status or something more meaningful.

Durbin looked away first. "I just make sure this office runs efficiently, staying focused on the long-term goals of the country."

"That is obvious. And having you confirm that, I have a very important question. Just between friends."

Durbin leaned in. "How can I help?"

"Well," Hyde began, "I was wondering…" she let the last word hang, but before she could angle further, a sharp knock interrupted. The door swung open.

A second Secret Service Agent entered and announced, "FBI is here."

Olson winced. The FBI's involvement was troublesome. They almost never worked well with other agencies. John's hand moved to straighten his tie, but he forced it back into his pocket.

The conflict between their organizations went beyond mere sibling rivalry. It was a bitter war fought with budgets and political favors. A presidential directed CIA op in FBI territory wasn't just going to ruffle feathers. It could light a powder keg that made Watergate look like a schoolyard spat.

"Show him in, please," Durbin told the agent.

The door opened with agonizing slowness. Olson held his breath, noting Hyde's sudden stillness. As a familiar silhouette filled the doorway, Olson's suspicions were confirmed.

Of course it would be him.

Bruno Vasquez entered. John felt a shift in the atmosphere, an undercurrent of antagonism that was all too recognizable. He also caught the subtle scent of the agent's aftershave as it mingled with the room's polished wood aroma. Olson's muscles constricted, his posture straightening to military rigidity.

He exhaled through his nose, carefully arranging his features into a neutral mask. The aftermath of Toronto still burned in his thoughts. Vasquez's field report had painted a very skewed portrait of events, omitting John's effort and coordination. It failed to account for FBI oversight and ignored the warnings John had delivered. The report placed the blame squarely on the CIA.

The CIA reassigned Olson to Africa within a week. The injustice of it all still stung. He had put his life on the line, only to be discarded as a convenient scapegoat by his own superiors. With Vasquez and Hyde in the same room, John wondered if history was about to repeat itself.

Vasquez's eyes narrowed. "I should have known," he said. "Heard what you did down in Somalia. Classic CIA, classic Olson."

"Thanks, I think," John replied, keeping his own feelings on a tight leash.

The only consolation here was that Vasquez hated Hyde more than the CIA. Olson watched with intrigue as tension swept over Vasquez's weathered face. "What is she doing here? This woman should be in handcuffs!"

"*Buenas tardes*, Agent Vasquez," Hyde greeted.

He whirled on Olson. "Corporate espionage. Art theft. Forgery. None of that keeps her behind bars?"

Hyde's smile never wavered. "The view was ghastly."

Then, with a pointed look at Bruno's leg, she added with feigned innocence, "How fares the knee? I trust it's mended adequately."

John knew it must be a remnant from some confrontation after his exile. He realized with grim clarity that Agent Vasquez's presence was meant to sow discord. It was a classic move in the inter-agency chess game.

On cue, Vasquez's face hardened. "Mr. Durbin, I'm not supportive of this course of action."

John hesitated, then stepped forward. "I agree with Agent Vasquez. Involvement of incarcerated civilians in operations seems highly unusual."

The unforeseen endorsement took Vasquez by surprise, making his stern expression soften. He glanced at John with a hint of newfound respect.

Genuine disappointment crossed Hyde's features. "Gentlemen," she said, "you may find my contributions more valuable than expected."

Vasquez pivoted, but Durbin raised a hand, cutting off the protest. "Look, I get it. You're not comfortable," he said. "Despite your concerns, I negotiated this directly with the leadership of the CIA and FBI. It's happening, period."

John expected to see the politician annoyed at the strife, but it seemed as if he were enjoying the verbal skirmish. A slight flush had risen to his cheeks, and his breathing had quickened just enough to be noticeable.

Hyde offered a gracious nod. "Thank you."

"But this is…" Bruno started, unwilling to give up.

"I appreciate your concern, Agent Vasquez," Durbin interjected, his voice laced with a layer of politeness that did little to mask the finality. "However, Miss Hyde's unique expertise and connections make her an indispensable asset for this operation."

Vasquez grimaced, swallowing his protest. John stayed silent, recognizing the futility of arguing. At the CIA, the mission always took precedence.

"I'm glad that's settled," Durbin said. He signaled to the Secret Service Agent at the door, snapping once. "Seal the doors, please."

John knew it was time to get to work. "So, what is this mission? And given the President's absence, why meet in the Oval Office instead of a staff room?"

Durbin's reaction suggested he'd been waiting for this question. His spine straightened, shoulders squaring. It was as if he were preparing to step onto a stage.

"Top marks, Officer." He motioned toward the couches. "This office is the only suitable venue in the world. Even I had to pull a few strings."

He walked to the couch facing a portable screen, patting the cushions. "Have a seat," he said. Durbin's voice dropped to a near whisper, forcing everyone to lean in.

"Let me explain how the world as we know it comes to an end."

Chapter 12

John walked in a daze across the carpet with the presidential seal. As he took a seat on the couch, he found it impossible to shake Durbin's statement.

The end of the world as we know it.

The gravity of the situation far exceeded John's expectations. It transformed this operation into a high-stakes game with catastrophic consequences.

A Secret Service Agent entered with a bulky red carton, handing it to Durbin. After signing the chain of custody, he placed the box on the coffee table. As the Secret Service agent left, all eyes locked onto the politician.

With the flick of a switch, Durbin plunged the Oval Office into semi-darkness. The projector sputtered to life, its mechanical whir cutting through the stillness. A pale, ghostly glow emanated.

Durbin broke the seal, the scent of old paper and ink filling the air. His manicured hands retrieved the cylinder of Top-Secret slides. The metallic click as he loaded the machine filled the hushed room.

The carousel rattled as TOP SECRET and PRESIDENTIAL CON-TROLLED INFORMATION stamps blinked onto the screen. John sensed Hyde stir beside him.

"I usually have to steal this kind of information," she commented.

"Be quiet," Vasquez and John snapped, their voices overlapping.

They exchanged a glance. Then they turned back to the display. John's irritation warred with reluctant admiration. Hyde's audacity was, maddeningly, her most effective weapon.

The slides advanced. The Soviet emblem, a hammer and sickle against bright red, flashed onto the screen.

"For decades," Durbin said as he moved to a slide showing a U-2 spy plane, "the US government and CIA worked together on ways to penetrate Soviet airspace. For this, they used Lockheed's Top Secret Skunk Works division to develop innovative and cutting-edge aircraft."

Click. A Soviet missile silo appeared. "To count their missiles." Another click revealed a Russian Air Base. "Map their moves." He paused. "The Cold War, gentlemen, is a game of chess."

"We developed airplanes too high and too fast for counter defenses." William's voice trailed off.

"Despite knowing our flight paths, the Soviets couldn't touch us. Or so we thought." He flipped to a picture of a pilot in a spacesuit. "That hubris came at a steep price."

"Our worst fears were realized on May 1, 1960. A newly developed SA-2 missile shot down Gary Powers over Sverdlovsk. The Soviets captured, sentenced, and imprisoned him until his exchange for Colonel Rudolph Abel two years later."

After a pause, he added, "The political fallout was devastating. That Soviet propaganda victory still haunts us to this day."

At the mention of Powers, Olson frowned. That incident was a significant blow to the CIA and a massive embarrassment on the world stage.

Out of the corner of his eye, John noticed Hyde sitting up a little straighter, her gaze fixed intently on the screen. Even Vasquez seemed to have forgotten his animosity.

Olson turned his focus back to the Deputy Chief of Staff as he explained the need to avoid further prisoner exchange scenarios. President Carter would not get into a situation where he had to negotiate over hostages.

"Our grip on the intelligence battlefield slipped away, leaving us blind behind the Soviet Union's iron curtain." Durbin's gaze swept across his audience. "But gentlemen," he said, "we've found a way to regain our advantage."

His fingers toyed with his gold cufflinks, an air of satisfaction in his stance. "A fresh approach. Short. Precise. Uncompromising."

He paused for effect, then with a practiced flick of his wrist, advanced the slide. A complex wire diagram appeared on the screen. John's breath caught.

Durbin's voice assumed a solemn tone, his features gleaming with a fanatical intensity. "That's why we developed this: the Stealth Fighter. Code-named Have Blue. A weapon so revolutionary, it will tip the balance of global power."

Olson knew this image. It was the unmistakable design from Mogadishu.

With another click, the wireframe dissolved, giving way to a fully realized image of the finished aircraft. The airplane was a nightmarish obsidian demon. Its angles jutted out aggressively, a deliberate affront to aerodynamics. It was more like a triangular shard of midnight than conventional aircraft.

Bruno turned from the screen. "That thing can fly? What's up with the angles?"

"Yes, it can fly." Durbin's reply carried a note of impatience. "And the facets provide the geometry necessary to disperse radar signals." Brushing lint from his sleeve, he continued. "Everything in life is cold, hard math. This advancement," he emphasized, "is perfection."

Hyde's usual nonchalance evaporated as she leaned forward, her attention captured by the aircraft. Her eyes opened slightly. It wasn't awe like Bruno's. Rather, it was a professional appraisal.

"That thing is real?" John asked.

Durbin's nod was solemn. "Very real, and very dangerous." His fingers tapped on the table. "Two years ago, the engineers at Skunk Works made a game-changing discovery. This full-scale aircraft is completely invisible."

"Invisible? Impossible," Olson replied.

"Yet, undeniable," Hyde countered. "Improbable. Not impossible."

John glared at her. Hyde met his gaze, her certainty unflinching. "Sorry, being quiet," she responded, with no hint of apology.

Durbin cleared his throat. The projector clicked and hummed as more images flashed: a meeting with former President Ford; concept drawings; blueprints.

"Project Have Blue." Durbin's voice took on a reverential quality. "The President immediately recognized its potential beyond aircraft. It includes ships and vehicles. An entire arsenal impervious to detection."

His face exuded an intensity that seemed to exceed patriotic pride. "The perfect first-strike weapon."

Vasquez's eyes narrowed with skepticism. "In '73, we screwed the pooch at Yom Kippur because we trusted tech over human intel." He spoke with the tone of someone who'd lived and learned from history. "Now, we're about to put our trust in another piece of technology. This stealth thing? How do we deal with the blind spots?"

John sat back. Bruno was right. Technology had limits that bureaucrats often overlooked in their excitement. He'd seen it firsthand. Plans and reality rarely met in battle.

Durbin's expression flickered between annoyance and forced patience. "Every advancement has its skeptics, Agent Vasquez." His voice carried the edge of someone accustomed to having the last word. "The automobile, the airplane, the atomic bomb—all faced the same doubts you're expressing." He straightened his tie. "We'll find the right balance. But first," he pointed at the screen, "we ensure we are the only ones with this capability."

"Of course," Vasquez agreed, though John could tell he was just being diplomatic.

Durbin flipped to another slide: a photograph of an industrial complex surrounded by high fences and guard towers. "We locked this program down tighter than the Manhattan Project. Not a soul outside the inner circle knew what we were building."

Olson recognized the significance of the comparison. The atomic bomb's development was the most heavily protected secret of World War II. It single-handedly ended the war, and started another.

Durbin's expression darkened. "With all revolutionary ideas, this one has attracted unwanted attention from competitors," he said. "Every program has its weak points. Last week, our biggest nightmare came to life."

Click.

The room fell silent. The screen displayed Sasha Morozov. It was Nate's last photograph.

John's body went rigid. A cold sweat broke across his forehead as the Soviet operative's icy sneer seemed to bore into his soul. He couldn't tear his eyes away. Two gunshots echoed in his memory.

Durbin sighed. "This man is Colonel Sasha Morozov. A high-ranking enforcer within the KGB's First Chief Directorate."

"He's more than that," Olson snapped as he gripped the edge of his seat to steady himself. He clenched his fists, nails biting into his palms. "Morozov's a killer."

"I know too well what sort of beast this is," Bruno murmured. His face was filled with understanding as he gave Olson a brief look of reassurance.

Durbin pointed to John in appreciation. "Three days ago, Officer Olson and his late partner prevented this man from obtaining Stealth research documents. Sasha Morozov is one of the world's most renowned spies." Durbin coughed once. "Our analysts believed Morozov was dead. Intelligence suggested internal Soviet factions had eliminated him in a car bombing, along with his son, daughter-in-law, and granddaughter."

"He's one of the most dangerous men on earth," William added, unable to keep the edge from his voice. "Now he's after our biggest technological advantage. This single incident was enough to spook the President." He paused.

"President Carter has granted me extraordinary powers to address this threat." Durbin pointed at Hyde and Olson. "I can use any means necessary to prevent the Soviets from obtaining this technology and avert nuclear war."

Durbin straightened, extending to his full height. "This includes employing uniquely skilled individuals, such as yourselves, and exploring untraditional methods. The stakes are too high."

A heavy silence fell over the room.

Vasquez's gaze darted to Hyde. "I don't get it," he said. "This seems like an overreaction. Why take the risk on her?"

Durbin's features hardened. "You think I'm exaggerating the threat?" His posture stiffened. He set the remote down and placed both palms flat on the table. "You're concerned about the danger a single criminal poses to your sensibilities. While I balance the fate of the world."

Bruno was at a loss for words. Durbin's eyes flew open as he reached for the controller. "This is the consequence of underestimation."

Click.

John flinched as the room erupted in the blinding glare of a nuclear explosion, the brightness searing his vision. Power and destruction filled the screen.

"Tsar Bomba," Durbin said. "Largest nuclear bomb ever. The Soviets detonated this monster in the Novaya Zemlya archipelago in 1961. Fifty megatons of earth-ending firepower. It was just one-tenth of their original plan and 1,600 times more devastating than Hiroshima."

John fixated on the image: a monstrous, apocalyptic cloud billowing upward, dwarfing the landscape beneath it. The black-and-white photograph cast writhing shadows across their faces. He could almost feel the earth-shattering roar of humanity's never-ending dance with self-destruction.

"Jesus." The word escaped Bruno in a hoarse curse. His hand trembled as he ran it over his mouth, as if trying to wipe away the horror.

"Once they get their hands on stealth technology," Durbin's voice rose. "Our analysts predict the Soviets won't hesitate. The moment they secure it, they'll unleash their newfound capability on American soil."

Each word was like a death sentence.

"Forget notice," Durbin continued, his words echoing ominously, "forget response. We simply cease to exist."

Vasquez's haggard cough grounded everyone. "If I can," he began. "I'm not taking away from what Olson did in Africa. Far from it. Hell of a job."

The compliment caught him off-guard. Maybe Vasquez wasn't such a jackass after all.

"However, I gotta ask one more time: if this operation was as secret as you say, how did this Soviet spy know about it? Better yet, how did we allow the CIA to almost hand it over through ineptitude?"

John felt a swell of anger rise within him. He pushed it back down, knowing it wouldn't help.

"My understanding was that we were dealing with a locked-down operation. How did it get out and end up in Africa?" Bruno tacked on.

Irritation crossed Durbin's face before he masked it with indifference. "Our protocols are flawless." There was a hint of defensiveness in his tone.

It failed to inspire confidence. John scrutinized the man as he smoothed the pleats of his jacket, searching for any tell that might reveal more.

"Only the team at Skunk Works and a select few in the CIA have access."

Vasquez shook his head. "Sorry to sound ignorant, sir. But that didn't answer my question."

Hyde leaned in, a mischievous glimmer sparkling in her eye. "My dearest Bruno," she said, "you ever notice how certainty has a way of evaporating when specifics come into play?"

"What?"

Hyde's eyes shifted from the bewildered Vasquez to the man in the expensive suit. Something in her look helped all the pieces fall into place for John. The secrecy, the off-books operation, Gabrielle's presence.

John snapped his fingers and pointed at Durbin. "You have no idea how the information leaked," he said. The second part hit him just as fast. "There's a mole."

The room froze. Hyde's face showed admiration. Vasquez's entire demeanor changed, his chin jutting forward. His eyes, previously wide with shock, now narrowed with dangerous focus.

All attention shifted to Durbin. He fidgeted, his cultivated composure cracking as he glared back at John.

It wasn't unwarranted. The Soviet Union was an existential threat, and Olson just accused the President's team of botching security on the most closely guarded secret in American history.

John could hear the rapid, shallow breathing of those around him, the soft rustle of fabric as bodies tensed. Only one thing was worse than absolute quiet.

William Durbin didn't deny it.

Chapter 13

This breach was a disaster for the administration's political future. The ticking of an ornate clock on the mantle disquieted John as he met Durbin's gaze. It was impossible to navigate through this operation without getting caught in partisan strands.

He ran through the list of typical suspects, from disgruntled employees to double agents. Each represented a potential threat not just to national security, but to global stability.

The politician pivoted, his tapered fingers pressed the wall switch, flooding the room in light. "Our internal investigation is underway, but time's a luxury we can't afford. We must sacrifice prudence in service of decisiveness."

Bruno fixed him with a penetrating stare. "What do you mean by that?"

Durbin raised his hands in a deliberate act of appeasement and cleared his throat. John detected the faintest hint of self-satisfaction.

"Our enemies, Agent Vasquez, know our vulnerability and are using it to their advantage. They invested heavily in radar and missile advancement, and now they want to pair that with Stealth Technology."

John's face drained of color. If the USSR gained both advanced defenses and stealth technology, it could emerge as the world's sole superpower.

Durbin pointed toward the Capitol building. "Now, those bastards are holding SALT II over the President's head."

John squinted. "SALT Two?"

Hyde grumbled. "Do they not sell newspapers in Somalia? SALT stands for Strategic Arms Limitation Talks."

"Hey, he's not the only one," Vasquez said. "Stop the incredulous looks and explain what you're yapping about."

Gabrielle sighed. "In 72, Nixon and the Soviet Union signed the first SALT Treaty. It limits long-range nukes, and each country agrees to stay out of the other's business." She turned to Durbin. "Sufficient?"

"Colloquial, but accurate. As for relevance... The original agreement ends soon. The Soviets and President Carter will expand and extend it with SALT II next week. This treaty is the backbone of our nuclear strategy."

He balled his hand into a fist and rapped it on the table. "Balance, men. I told the President; now I tell you. Everything here is about balance."

John felt the hair on his neck rise. Nuclear agreements were fragile. A new first-strike capability could undermine the entire situation.

Vasquez leaned back in his chair. "Seems a bit dramatic. Who cares about a treaty they'll ignore?"

"The President cares. I care," Durbin countered. "The President is walking a tightrope here. The hawks in Congress are pressuring him about being soft on communism." He adjusted his sleeve. "We must appear on the right side of history."

"Plus, nuclear war is dramatic enough for me. This breach has forced our hand. If the Soviets expose our program, we'd lose credibility on the world stage," Durbin said. "We're opting for... unconventional solutions."

John looked at Hyde. Radical meant desperate.

"Nontraditional is the CIA," Durbin declared. "Therefore, Officer Olson and Ms. Hyde have been paired. They will investigate and identify our leak, using a combination of their shared skill sets."

Working with Gabrielle was a double-edged sword. "How long do we have?" John asked.

"Until the summit," William responded without hesitation.

Seven days. A year's work compressed into a week, with a criminal as his partner. It was absurd, and Durbin knew it.

"That's impossible."

Hyde scoffed, "Oh, John. Impossible? Never. Improbable? Certainly."

The phone on the President's desk erupted in a shrill ring. Each tinny chime seemed to tighten Durbin's jaw. By the sixth, a vein pulsed at his temple. He strode over, snatched the receiver, and slammed it down.

"Now, where were we?" he said. "Ah, yes. The treaty. If the Soviet Union suspects we've tipped the scales, they'll balk. If they obtain our data, they'll see no need for negotiation. Either way, we lose."

Vasquez slapped John on the back. "Well, well. Looks like you've got yourself in a pickle. But hey, that's what you CIA boys live for, right? Good luck threading that needle."

Durbin wagged his finger. "Not entirely. We have a contingency plan, but it relies on securing the site and capturing the mole. If either of those conditions are not met, the President has no choice but to shut down the entire Stealth Project to protect his vision." His voice was cool. "Not every advantage is a blessing."

He took a dramatic step forward. "Carter will do anything to secure it from Soviet hands. Even if that means barring the door."

"You're asking for a miracle."

"Yes, Officer Olson," he said. "That's precisely what I'm asking for."

Durbin straightened his shoulders, his posture radiating control. "Infiltrate Skunk Works. Find the leak. Trace any compromised intel." The scent of his expensive cologne wafted over John. "Report directly to me. I can't afford any further compromises in the system."

"What assets do I have at my disposal?"

Durbin placed a hand on his shoulder, the grip firmer than necessary. "I mentioned discretion, correct?" He waited, then added, "Only those in this room."

"In seven days?" John repeated.

"The signing is on the evening of the seventh day," Durbin replied.

A shiver of unease crept up John's spine. Failure wasn't just an option; it was certain. "And if we don't meet your timeline?"

"Well, Officer Olson, you'll be dishonorably discharged and charged regarding the fallout from your actions in Somalia, while Ms. Hyde will go into FBI custody."

Agent Vasquez perked up. "About damn time." He rubbed his hands together. "Your CIA protection is gone."

"Always so negative." Hyde turned. "And what, my dearest Mr. Durbin, shall happen if we are to succeed?"

Durbin froze, as if he hadn't considered the possibility. "If you are successful," his voice carried an undercurrent of doubt, "Officer Olson will have demonstrated an invaluable service to national security and may well save the Stealth Project from compromise. An assignment and position of choice shall follow."

He shifted his attention to Hyde. "As for you… let's say your cooperation would be taken into consideration as we honor our amnesty deal."

Vasquez's scowl deepened.

"I'll need full access to personnel files, security clearances, and a dedicated liaison on site," Olson said.

Durbin nodded. "Necessities will be provided."

John cast a sidelong glance at Hyde, whose silence was uncharacteristic. "Why are you not all over this?"

A long moment passed. "I'm afraid this is distasteful." Her usual whimsy was gone. "I'd like to know what happened to my personal assets," she said. "The ones the government took."

Satisfaction stretched across Vasquez's face. "Oh, the FBI seized and liquidated that already," he said with triumph. "We put that ten mil to good use."

John suppressed a gasp. Ten million dollars?

"Well," Hyde mused, "I've always believed in the law of conservation. Nothing is ever truly lost. I'm sure a new opportunity shall arise."

John knew it was a trick. She dangled the bait of financial restitution, but he knew better. For Hyde, money was secondary. She couldn't appear too eager for the mission.

"Amnesty will have to be enough," Durbin stated. "Do we have an agreement?"

"Yes." Her lips curved up. "After all, I find espionage is the best form of therapy."

The casual way she approached life-or-death stakes struck John. It was the same maddening confidence he'd witnessed in Toronto. Hyde swept forward and enveloped Durbin in a firm two-handed grasp.

Durbin maintained his stance. "The Almighty crafted the world in a week. You have the same time limit."

"How apt," she replied.

"This will be a CIA-led operation. Officer Olson is the chief operative on the ground."

Vasquez started to interject, but Durbin cut him off. "But to maintain an appearance of lawfulness, the FBI has joint operational authority." A flicker of satisfaction crossed the agent's face. "Special Agent Vasquez, you and your team will escort Ms. Hyde to California."

Bruno gave a wicked grin. "You'll be under the eye of the FBI. Every. Single. Moment."

Hyde's glare turned dangerous. "Hard pass."

Vasquez charged forward. His rapid breathing, hot and fierce, stirred a stray lock of her hair.

"Enough!" John stepped in. "We're all on the same side here."

Hyde regarded her nails with feigned indifference. He knew it was a mask to hide her distaste for the situation.

"I agree to your terms," John said. Vasquez's smile broadened, sensing victory. But John continued, "But if we are going to maintain a cover, I can't have their agents on top of us. We'll need to work without interference."

Bruno's grin faltered.

"Fine," Durbin conceded. "Ms. Hyde is under the care of the FBI. Once you arrive in California and go undercover at the Skunk Works facility, the FBI'll transition to an observational role." He added, "Gentlemen, I understand your agencies have had their... differences. But this operation transcends usual jurisdictional squabbles. You'll work together. Is that clear?"

"Sir, the Bureau doesn't mesh well with Langley's cowboys," Vasquez responded.

"Decision's made."

"An FBI escort. How blasé," Hyde remarked.

Vasquez's nostrils flared. "You try anything," he warned. "I have a room reserved for you at a facility we just built in Cuba."

Hyde's shoulders squared, chin lifting a fraction. "You never caught me. And you never shall." She met Bruno's glare with a cold amusement.

Durbin coughed. "I need you both on this. CIA's foreign intelligence expertise, FBI's domestic counterintelligence network. I'll run interference, but keep me in the loop. Are we clear?"

Gabrielle broke eye contact with Vasquez. She nodded in Durbin's direction without uttering another word. Bruno retreated, his eyes still locked on Hyde.

John acknowledged for all of them. "Yes."

The politician collected his papers. "I'm glad we can all agree. Now, if you don't mind, I have other areas that demand my attention."

Vasquez pulled out a set of cuffs. "Let the escorting begin."

"Is that really necessary?" Hyde asked, eyeing the handcuffs with disdain. "You haven't even bought me dinner."

Gabrielle sighed, extending her wrists forward with a grace that made the act seem voluntary. Her fingers twitched almost imperceptibly as the metal closed shut.

"Move it, Hyde," Bruno said.

"To be or not to be? Isn't that the eternal question, Agent Vasquez?" she quipped, as if they were actors on a stage and she were communicating with an unseen audience.

Vasquez rolled his eyes.

"Tomorrow, and tomorrow, and tomorrow," she added as Vasquez led her away. "Creeps in this petty pace from day to day, to the last syllable of recorded time."

Her eyes locked with Olson. "Let's hope our little adventure doesn't turn out to be a tragedy. I shall see you there, John."

They disappeared through the doorway. There was something magnetic about someone who refused to be contained by systems. But his thoughts lingered on.

Why was she suddenly quoting Shakespeare? She was absolutely certain with every word she said. The words were far from random. A test, no doubt.

John turned and found himself alone with Durbin.

"What was all that about?"

"Just Hyde being Hyde," John responded.

William nodded, his expression betraying no outward emotion. "John, those two are going to test you. But I have faith you can handle this. This mission is a rare opportunity, one to make a significant difference. You're the right man for the job. Honest and capable."

John wasn't expecting the compliment. "Thank you, sir."

"Don't let Hyde take you somewhere you don't want to be. I know you've got this. If you ever require support, you only need to ask. Okay?"

Not even Avery had supported him with any real assurances. John realized Durbin wasn't the enemy here. "Yes, sir. Once again, thank you. If it's good with you, I've been awake for over twenty-four hours."

Durbin gave him a reassuring pat on the shoulder, sending him on his way. The day had been long; sleep would be welcome, but likely elusive.

As he walked, John replayed Hyde's actions throughout the meeting. She'd been calculating, yes, but there had been moments when she'd revealed genuine interest in the mission. Not just in the opportunity for freedom, but in the challenge itself.

He soon emerged into the night, the cool air washing against his exhausted frame. Strategically placed floodlights bathed the manicured White House lawn in a warm glow.

This mission was filled with agendas. President Carter. Hyde. Vasquez. Durbin. Avery. The FBI. The CIA. Even the Soviets.

Each player would deceive. And now, time itself was an enemy.

He'd face them all for just one clean shot at Morozov.

Chapter 14

SUNNYSIDE HOTEL, VIRGINIA

7 Days Remaining

07:30

John strode down the hotel hallway, clutching a steaming cup of coffee in each hand, the rich scent of roasted beans wafting ahead of him.

The beige walls, faded and peeling at the corners, absorbed the weak light from sconces, mirroring Olson's somber mood. Two FBI agents flanked Hyde's room door, their postures revealing long duty hours and too much caffeine.

"Good morning, gentlemen," Olson greeted. "I'm here to escort Hyde to the airport."

The agents' eyes narrowed as they exchanged a glance. He caught a flash of animosity in their expressions. "Been a quiet night."

John's eyes darted to the door. With Hyde, quiet usually preceded disaster. "Sure you're guarding the right room?" he asked, offering them coffee. The two declined with curt shakes of their heads.

Neither agent seemed concerned. One produced a key and unlocked the room. Olson eased through with his shoulder, the hinges creaking as he entered.

The lingering aroma of Hyde's perfume mingled with the staleness of recycled air. His nostrils flared, recognizing the jasmine scent. Drawn curtains blocked out the rising sun. He yanked the drapes aside, letting warm light flood the room.

An unmade bed dominated the space, its sheets twisted into a bunch. "No rest for the weary, Hyde," Olson snapped.

Silence.

"Gabrielle?" he called louder this time.

He slammed the coffee cups down on a table with a sharp clack, droplets of dark liquid splashing out. John swept the sheets aside, revealing an arrangement of pillows.

She was gone. Vanished, right under the noses of two highly trained FBI agents. It was bold. And reckless. It was classic Hyde.

Olson tore through the room. Closet doors flew open. Dropping to his knees, he peered under the bed. Empty. He spotted something on the wall. A closer look revealed a faint vertical streak in the wallpaper. The ceiling vent cover screwheads showed tiny fresh scratches.

This was twice, and somehow the second round hurt just as much. Toronto had ruined his reputation, and this would end his career. It couldn't possibly happen again, especially under constant supervision. Yet here he stood, staring at an empty bed.

Olson barked a sharp warning to the agents outside. They sprang into action, bursting in with hands on their holsters. They moved like twin storms. The first agent, seeing the vacant room, snapped to his radio. "Secure the perimeter," he ordered.

His partner vaulted towards the bathroom and flung open the door, exposing nothing but an unoccupied shower. Their execution of protocol was impressive, but it yielded no results. Their prisoner was gone.

"Damn it, Hyde," John muttered. This was a game to her, and he knew she always left clues. He thought about the previous evening. "Tomorrow, and tomorrow, and tomorrow…" What did she mean by that?

Heavy footsteps in the hallway interrupted his thoughts. Vasquez burst in, gun drawn, eyes scanning. Escaped prisoners always brought out the worst in everyone. He circled, scrutinizing every corner.

The room soon filled as FBI personnel swarmed in, their urgency and frustration mirroring Vasquez's. Tension crackled, sharp clicks of camera shutters capturing the scene.

Bruno's cheek muscles rippled as he ground his teeth, eyeing both agents from guard duty.

"Shift change was at 0300. She was there," the senior agent reported.

"And nothing else?" Vasquez leaned in.

The agent thought and shook his head. "No."

"You have something to add?" Bruno asked as he caught the second agent eyeing the table.

"We left some food for her. She complained about being hungry," the agent said. "But we never abandoned our post. I swear."

Vasquez spun to face a technician, a man with glasses slipping down his nose. He yanked the napkin covering an untouched meal, revealing a fork with a missing tine.

Vasquez's eyes narrowed. "Did she say anything at all?"

The first agent shrugged. "Nothing. She kept calling me Duncan, which was weird. I thought maybe she was hinting at donuts or something," he said, shuffling in his spot. "Seriously, boss. It was quiet and within protocol."

Bruno spun, glaring at Olson. "Where did she go?"

"I don't know. She was gone when I got here."

The FBI agent's frustration radiated. "I knew this would happen." He jabbed a finger at Olson. "I warned you!"

Vasquez turned and glowered at the agents. John's hand hovered just above his shoulder before resting there. The FBI agent shrugged it off, but the brief contact seemed to diffuse some of the tension between them.

"We'll find her," John responded. "I can help."

"Look, Olson, I know you didn't cause this," Vasquez said, rubbing the back of his neck. "But I'm the one on the hook here. Getting her to California was my responsibility."

"I get it," John told him.

Bruno shook his head. "Nobody keeps me from doing my job. Not you. Not her."

"Understood."

"We just need a place to start," Vasquez declared.

A young FBI agent excused his way through the huddle. "Sir, a woman, could be Hyde, asked for a bus at Matthew's," he said with excitement.

Vasquez's calm evaporated and his neck veins bulged. "Get a go-team assembled," he commanded. "I want 'em ready in twenty minutes."

The agents scrambled to obey, moving fluidly to gather their gear. Vasquez checked his watch repeatedly, his impatience growing.

A second agent burst through the doorway a moment later. "Boss," he gasped. "Got a positive ID. Hyde took a cab to the international airport."

Vasquez spat a curse. The crimson flush drained from his face, leaving behind a mask of stony resolve. "Hyde is a master of misdirection. Don't fall for it."

His gaze swept across the men. "Okay," he snapped. "Morris, get a team to Dulles!" He pointed to an agent who was already halfway out the door. "And prep a squad to raid the train station."

The man froze at the unorthodox order. "Sir?"

"It's the only place she didn't leave a clue," Vasquez said, tapping his temple. "I know how she thinks."

John sat on the edge of the bed as the other agents darted about. This escape was unlike Hyde. She'd never pin that sort of thing on two green FBI agents. She'd do that right in front of Bruno, just to make a point.

It frustrated him. Hyde played with people, moving them like pieces. She was brilliant, calculating, and self-serving. But it was also her weakness. Whatever her goal, it served Gabrielle first and foremost. Olson's gaze drifted to the window. Outside, the world bustled. People flowed along the sidewalks like lines of ants, filled with intent.

His eyes caught a billboard. Normally, he ignored such ads, but this one grabbed his attention. "Escape is only moments away," the tagline proclaimed. A young blonde girl clutching a stuffed purple giraffe pointed at a sleek airplane soaring across a clear sky. The ad was typical. The airport's name was not.

John stared in awe. Hyde's Shakespearean monologue suddenly transformed from cryptic quotation to deliberate breadcrumb. They weren't a flourish, but rather, instructions. The name on the billboard confirmed everything.

He needed to warn Bruno.

"Agent Vasquez," Olson interjected. "If I could just have a couple of your men…"

Vasquez cut him off. "I told you," he warned. "I'll find her. Stay out of the way."

"But, you don't…"

Red flared in Bruno's face. "Back off. This is mine." John stepped aside. "Move out," Vasquez yelled, circling his finger in the air.

Olson accepted the dismissal with a curt nod, forcing himself to remain professional. The FBI was technically in charge until they reached California.

John weighed chasing down Bruno to explain his thoughts, but hesitated. If he were wrong, it would only reinforce the idea that he was under Hyde's influence. And if he was right, Vasquez wouldn't handle it well. Either way, he lost.

"This feels familiar," he sighed.

The bustling chaos faded down the hallway. Olson focused on the clue; he couldn't waste time arguing. Assuming he was correct, every second counted. He could stay in place and wait for Vasquez to return empty-handed. Or he could follow his instincts.

It wasn't even a choice.

Olson soon strode through the hotel lobby. His measured steps contrasted with the panicked frenzy of FBI agents swirling around him. The crisp fall air hit his face as he stepped outside, a welcome reprieve from the stuffy hotel room.

John hailed a passing cab with ease, and he slid into the rear seat. He directed the driver, and a bob of the man's head was all the acknowledgment he received.

To the operator, Olson was just another fare.

Buildings melded into a jumble of brick and glass as the car wove through traffic. Olson leaned back against the worn upholstery, the standard scent of artificial pine filling the interior.

"Tomorrow, and tomorrow, and tomorrow," he mumbled.

Macbeth spoke these lines as he prepared for a war he knew he would lose, and Duncan was the king he betrayed. Hyde calling the agent 'Duncan' wasn't a coincidence. Merely another hint.

He had to know whether he was right. Olson hoped this would work out better than their last encounter. As the cab stopped, John noticed his own contemplative expression in the mirror.

"Here we are," the driver announced. "Macbeth Regional Airport."

Chapter 15

MATTHEW'S BUS STATION

09:05

The station's air hummed with the throb of engines and defunct speakers as the aroma of diesel fuel overwhelmed the space. Weary travelers paraded through the aisles, clinging to their bags. Tinny announcements crackled overhead, barely discernible above the discord of shuffling feet.

Amidst them, a squadron in crisp suits surged through the crowd, parting it like a sea. The team leader's jaw clenched beneath his clean-shaven cheeks. His badge caught the dim light as he plunged into the bus.

The seats, sticky with age, creaked under his weight as he ducked between them. The agent swept every corner with a small, powerful flashlight, its beam revealing only dust.

Emerging from the last bus, he pressed his palms against his eyes. "Boss, bus station's a dead end," the team leader growled into the radio. "Just empty seats and pissed-off drivers."

At the nearby train station, Vasquez led a swift, coordinated sweep through the faded carriages. The odor of upholstery and steel filled their nostrils as they marched in sync through the narrow aisles. Whispered conversations and the rustle of newspapers melded into a background murmur.

This had to be where Hyde was hiding. Bruno knew it.

It was hard for Vasquez to admit, but Gabrielle was smart. Undoubtedly the smartest adversary he had ever faced. There was something personal about her actions. Each time she slipped away, it felt like she was taking a piece of his soul.

The high-wire escape in Toronto had shattered his standing in the agency. Despite his direct supervisor's attempt to shift blame to the CIA, the ax had fallen hard on Vasquez and his team. Two grueling years of hell followed.

Bad assignments, junior personnel, and a decreased budget. He had muscled through every bit of it. He'd slowly rebuilt his world and was finally back where he'd stood before. His squad was at last reinstated.

The director had been silent about the nature of the mission. Just that it had the highest level of support, and he had been requested by name. It seemed like a golden opportunity.

Then John Olson and Gabrielle Hyde reappeared. If Bruno had known those two characters were involved… well, retirement would have been an excellent alternative.

That was a lie. He couldn't retire, not with that failure on his record. He needed this win. Not for himself, but for all the people who depended on him. Rookies, vets like Morris, and all the agents in the middle. Families. Kids.

Hyde's escape put everything at risk. This kind of screw-up wouldn't just end his career; it would affect everyone on his team. And with the White House involved, he'd be powerless to protect them from the fallout.

Vasquez's hand, with its slight tremble betraying his intense investment, reached for the radio. He needed to know how the searches at other locations were panning out.

"Morris, I need an update. Any sign of Hyde at the airport?"

"Just arrived on scene at Dulles, boss," he replied. "Stand by for updates."

Vasquez lowered the radio and swept the train station one more time. His reflection in a nearby window surprised him. The man in the glass looked desperate.

* * *

Miles away at Dulles International Airport, Agent Bart Morris's convoy of four-door Dodge Monaco sedans screeched to a halt outside the departure terminal. Their government-issue tires left rubber marks on the pristine concrete as their cars idled.

Morris burst from the lead car, the roar of jet engines and announcements replacing the quiet of the hotel just a few miles away.

Automobiles honked as the FBI vehicles blocked the congested lanes, causing traffic to pile up. Somewhere in this mob of travelers might be the fugitive, and Bruno was counting on him to find her.

Agent Morris, dark hair neatly combed back and his face a mask of stern determination, led the charge into the terminal. His crisp white shirt and black tie, visible beneath a gray suit jacket, projected an air of professional authority.

Bart's military background as an Intelligence Officer with the 101st Airborne in Vietnam served him well in this moment. The Tet Offensive of '68 had honed his skills in decisive action under pressure. It also motivated him to look for a new way to serve.

His transition to the FBI after returning from Vietnam had been a natural fit. His background made him an asset in the Bureau's counterintelligence division. However, the nation was not as kind to veterans, and he found reintegration difficult.

Agent Vasquez had been Morris's lifeline, patiently mentoring him and helping translate his military skills to FBI fieldwork. Where most saw only a soldier, he had recognized potential. That faith had changed everything.

After the Toronto fiasco, Bart was certain Bruno would be ousted. Instead, Morris had watched as Vasquez absorbed the blame, refusing to sacrifice others even as his career crumbled. It was a lesson in leadership that no academy training could provide.

When Vasquez asked him to help on this mission with Hyde, there was no hesitation. He owed the man a debt he could never repay.

"Spread out!" he ordered, directing his team with sharp gestures. "Eyes on every gate and exit!"

The agents dispersed as Morris approached the nearest airline counter, credentials already extended. A woman in a red coat appeared in his peripheral vision.

Same height and build as Hyde. His hand instinctively moved toward his holster. "Ma'am!" he called out, changing direction.

The target turned, revealing a youthful face beneath a stylish haircut. Not Hyde. Morris offered an apology and returned to his mission.

"FBI," he announced to the ticket agent. "I need the passenger manifests for all flights departing within the next three hours."

The agent's smile faltered as she rummaged through thick binders of carbon-copy tickets and flight logs. Morris drummed his fingers as he scanned the crowd. His eyes, honed by spotting VC movement in dense jungles, swept from face to face for his target.

"Here you are, sir," she said, hefting the heavy books.

Bart flipped through the pages, his finger running down columns of handwritten names. Nothing jumped out, but Hyde was known for using aliases. He pushed Gabrielle's black-and-white photo forward for the woman to examine.

His radio crackled to life. "Sighting at Gate 37."

"On my way," Morris responded, already moving. "No one boards until I clear it."

"Nevermind. False alarm," the voice said just as quickly.

"Vasquez is crazy. We're wasting our time," an agent grumbled.

Morris whirled on the man. "Take a backup to international departures and don't come back until you've checked every flight. Move!"

Twenty minutes later, Morris's last hope vanished as the airport personnel sealed the Los Angeles flight's door. He lifted his radio, pinching the bridge of his nose. He scanned the crowd one more time, but there was nothing here.

Time to report his failure.

"Airport's a bust. We've combed every inch. Hyde's like a ghost; she could be standing five feet away and we'd never know."

Bruno's voice was quick to respond. "Check the car-rental desks. She's not slipping past us this time."

Bart acknowledged, "Roger that, boss."

He signaled to the nearest FBI agent without breaking stride. They split off toward the ground transportation, with two others following suit.

At the airport rental car section, the powerful odor of fresh disinfectant lingered. Morris watched his agents converse with clerks, their voices urgent as they scrutinized records. It was methodical work. Tedious, but necessary.

As minutes ticked by, Morris's hope dwindled.

A clerk, her face pinched with exhaustion, hefted another ledger. As she spread it out, the unique scent of methanol and isopropanol radiated from the mimeograph paper. The agents leaned in, their fingers leaving smudged trails in the carbon-copy ink as they scanned the entries.

Morris recognized the futility. But the job had to be done. One by one, they checked names, yielding no results.

He wasn't giving up, but he had to let Bruno know this was a dead end. The man may not appreciate the outcome, but it was better than blowing sunshine up his skirt. At least, that was the way Vasquez put it to him as a probationary agent.

Morris made the call. "Nothing yet, boss. We'll keep working, but I don't think she's here," he said into the radio.

"Roger. Stay at it."

Another stack of papers thumped onto the desk. Bart fished in his coat pocket for some aspirin he kept in reserve. His headache was only starting.

* * *

Back at Matthew's Bus Station, Vasquez's footsteps scraped against cracked tiles as the station clock ticked past ten. The radio buzzed in his ear with negative reports from other field agents, each transmission delivering another blow.

They were chasing phantoms.

Vasquez rubbed his temples. Hyde understood the fundamental truth of espionage: perception was reality. Creating diversions, distorting truth, making them split resources. It was the same playbook the KGB and CIA used against the FBI daily, only better.

The intense déjà vu was suffocating. How many times had he been here? Hyde always pushed him to make bad choices.

"Sir?" The young agent asked. "Do you want us to expand the search grid?"

Vasquez surveyed the station. Hyde had a four-hour head start. But she was resourceful. Smart enough to vanish wherever she wished.

"Do it."

He couldn't shake off a gnawing suspicion that they were playing right into her hands. As much as he hated to admit it, she'd always been several steps ahead.

How could he break through Hyde's deception?

Bruno grimaced, his thoughts reluctantly turning to John. The CIA officer's instincts had proven unnervingly sharp. He seemed to understand Hyde. Olson's maverick attitude grated against Vasquez's personal style, but it yielded results he couldn't ignore.

A memory from the hotel room surfaced. Olson requested manpower to follow a hunch. In the heat of the moment, Vasquez had shut him down.

That gnawed at him. What if…?

Bruno's approach worked for almost every criminal. Systematic sweeps, multiple teams, overwhelming force. The FBI way. Olson operated differently. Intuitive hunches, psychological insights, creative leaps. The CIA way.

For years, Vasquez had dismissed John's methods as undisciplined. It wasn't true. Bruno just didn't understand them.

It was time he accepted Hyde wasn't a typical criminal. She consistently went in the other direction, evading even his cleverest traps. She addressed the world exactly like the CIA. Maybe that was the reason John grated on him. He was a bit like her. And that gave the spook a unique insight.

Bruno cleared his throat and depressed the transmitter. "Can any unit confirm the whereabouts of Officer John Olson, our CIA liaison?"

Vasquez stood in silence for almost two minutes.

"Boss, he grabbed a cab to Macbeth Regional," the voice on the radio crackled. "Think he knows something?"

Macbeth.

The word hit Vasquez hard. Hyde's stupid quotes in the Oval Office were from Macbeth.

She'd dangled the truth before his eyes, counting on his overconfidence to blind him. She'd weaponized his dismissive nature into a perfect getaway. And in his arrogance, he'd done just what she wanted.

Vasquez's grip tightened around the radio, his knuckles protruding against the skin. A sound, part roar, part wounded animal, tore from his throat as he hurled the device against the ground. It exploded on impact, plastic shards skittering across the floor like shrapnel, the circuit board sizzling before falling silent.

Vasquez stood frozen, staring at the shattered remnants. It was more than broken components and wires. It was his career. He squinted, taking a shaky breath. He couldn't let the team down again.

His empty hand extended, palm up. It was a silent command that was obeyed as another radio materialized.

"All units, converge on Macbeth Regional. Now!" Vasquez commanded.

Triggered, his men sprang into action. The station erupted with the sound of a stampede as agents bolted towards their cars. Within seconds, engines roared to life. Tires screeched, kicking up fine plumes of white smoke, propelling the vehicles forward.

Every second mattered.

The passenger door of the black Dodge sedan flew open. Vasquez lunged inside, the leather seat protesting. The car's suspension dipped, absorbing the impact. His hand slapped the dash as he fixed the driver with an intense stare.

"We need to be there five minutes ago. Move!"

As the car lurched forward, he prayed they weren't already too late.

If they failed now, he might never get another chance.

Chapter 16

MACBETH REGIONAL AIRPORT

09:25

Fifty-five minutes until takeoff.

Gabrielle assessed three potential threats before she'd taken ten steps into Macbeth Airport. The security guard with the ill-fitting uniform. A businessman whose attention lingered too long. The maintenance worker inspecting his radio. She drifted past the clacking departure boards, her outward nonchalance masking hypervigilance as the rhythm of flipping tiles punctuated each seemingly disinterested glance.

The smell of smoke hung in the air as waiting men flicked ashes. A glossy magazine sporting the latest New York fashions dangled from her grasp.

The crisp clicks of her heels on the polished tile underscored her collected demeanor, each step sticking to the thick floor wax. To the world, she was just another traveler.

Clothes and money were always within her reach, easily acquired when needed. Gabrielle's gaze shifted to the enormous clock above the terminal gate, each second ticking by without remorse. Olson was smart. She had faith that he would decipher her message.

Every few steps, her gaze darted over her shoulder. It was a casual movement, like a traveler searching for a lost companion. But alas, there was nothing. John was not here. Patience, she told herself.

Gabrielle idly folded and unfolded her ticket, a prop to bypass watchful guards whose gazes never lingered long enough to detect the underlying threat. Many women resented societal norms that favored men, but she found these norms provided blind spots for exploitation.

Men stole fleeting glances, captivated yet dismissive. Hyde's elegance rendered her both conspicuous and forgettable in the same breath. At least, to most.

A single security guard, frustratingly impervious to her usual anonymity, abandoned his post and tailed her. He closed the gap with long steps, falling into a matching pace on her trail. His pale hair and lean frame seemed out of place, as his focus zeroed in.

The man reminded her of her father. Back when he was young. Before the gathering of tribes. Before the camp. She pushed the unwanted thoughts aside.

Her pulse quickened, tension creeping into her shoulders. Was he with one of the interested parties? She maintained her leisurely pace, ranking the top four escape routes. The man closed the gap with every second. Gabrielle felt a moment of concern.

She spotted an older gentleman only a few paces ahead. No professional wanted to tangle with an elderly civilian relying on an escort. Maintaining her speed, Gabrielle linked her arm through that of the stranger.

"Mind escorting me to my gate?" she asked.

"Of course, young lady," he replied. "Quite a bustling place today, isn't it?"

The man grasped her arm, continuing forward in tandem. Hyde observed the guard shake his head in disgust and return to his post, apparently dissuaded by her companion.

With quick thanks, she broke away from her companion, heading directly for the Los Angeles gate. Floral perfume wafted from Gabrielle as she approached the young woman perched at the door. The attendant's gaze flickered over Gabrielle's tailored suit, the fabric exuding authority.

Gabrielle handed over her ticket. "Busy day?"

"Very," the lady replied. "Please proceed." She glanced down.

Hyde stopped abruptly. The line behind her jolted, then fell still as she waited for the gate agent to look up. Gabrielle's eyes took in the woman's angst, noticing the telltale smudges of makeup concealing a recent domestic dispute.

Neither woman spoke.

Her instincts screamed at her to avert her gaze, to disregard the pain, to follow what she had learned long ago in that place of death. Empathy was weakness. Survival demanded indifference.

Yet, for an instant, the undeniable marks of trauma stirred an inconvenient emotion. Memories of Hyde's childhood flooded back, when she was a frightened girl with no control. This woman's poorly disguised suffering cut through every layer of her carefully constructed defense.

Gabrielle's fingers tightened around her ticket, unconsciously crushing the paper. She forced her hand to relax. The mission clock ticked mentally. Many lives were riding on the next week.

No time for detours. Yet she could not ignore the suffering. With the young woman's anguished face and name committed to memory, Gabrielle made a mental vow. When this was over, she'd return. Some battles were impossible to overlook, no matter how trivial.

Ascending the steep jet stairway, Hyde's fingers latched onto the handrail. Soon she would unlock the most elusive treasure: freedom. Reaching the top of the stairs, she paused at the threshold and cast a glance behind her.

"Shame," Gabrielle murmured. Olson's absence would hurt her chances.

A rare tendril of fear snaked into her consciousness. It wasn't too late to flee. She'd done it before. Hyde shut down the intrusive thought. Desperation was a relic of her past.

She strode into the plane, ignoring the jet fuel and smoke that permeated the narrow aisle. The other passengers still found travel a novelty, but it held no interest for her. As she neared her assigned luxury seat, the banter of two loitering men fell silent.

"Excuse me, miss," one said, stepping aside. "Didn't mean to block you."

"No problem at all," Gabrielle replied.

Her focus locked on the man in the second row. The precise angle of his shoulders, the controlled stillness of his hands. She recognized them instantly. Then she caught the gleam of a concealed weapon beneath his jacket.

Her pulse quickened with anticipation.

She stepped closer, and their eyes met. Hers calculating, his unyielding. A life spent in service had carved those lines around his eyes, hardened that jaw. A kindred spirit, despite everything that divided them.

Hyde's earlier disappointment evaporated. Her lips curled into a slow smile. The most dangerous games required the most capable players.

"I see you still have your touch," Hyde said.

The barrel of John's pistol was aimed at her heart. "Have a seat, Gabrielle."

In that moment, she knew all her efforts were worth it. Olson was exactly the man she needed for her plan to work.

Chapter 17

John wasn't surprised when he caught sight of Hyde. With her, everything was a performance. He shifted forward, knowing that while others gawked at her overt showmanship, the real danger lay in what she didn't show.

He kept his service weapon concealed, but ready. He wanted to savor the moment Hyde realized he had finally gotten the upper hand. But she refused to give him that satisfaction.

Hyde's composure was unshakable. "I see you still have your touch," she said.

"Have a seat, Gabrielle." John indicated the vacant spot beside him.

She complied, sinking into the upholstery. The cabin's recycled air carried a breeze across their faces, blowing back a loose strand of Gabrielle's hair.

"Top marks, Officer Olson."

Even for a seasoned spy, her machinations were overwhelming. "Macbeth Airport, Hamlet, seat 2B. Is this all just a game to you?"

Hyde shrugged. "I don't play games. This was an audition." She paused. "You passed, by the way. Consider yourself lucky. I rarely give second chances." She gestured at his jacket. "Now put that vulgar thing away. It's embarrassing."

"I'm not your monkey," he said.

John wondered if he was trying to convince himself. Every interaction with Hyde was a stubborn reminder that she thrived in this environment, and he merely survived.

His hand tightened on the pistol. An engine stirred to life under them. As Hyde and Olson's silent standoff stretched, a beautiful stewardess approached their seat, her tray and draped napkin pulling his attention.

"Sir, you need to put your things away, like the woman suggested," the attendant said, her thick British accent unmistakable.

Olson dismissed her at first, but then noticed the pistol under the napkin. It was pointed directly at him. A spark of recognition flared.

Jessica Fortner's image had haunted his memory since Toronto. The wind-tossed copper hair and predatory grace were unmistakable. He now recognized her in this stewardess disguise.

The CIA dossiers didn't capture her essence: hazel eyes holding both secrets and threats. The pistol appeared an extension of her will. Controlled and assured, Jessica embodied lethal elegance.

"Don't make me ask again, sir."

John wasn't about to be pressured by a single gunman, especially on a crowded plane. A passenger from the row in front of him turned around, peering over the seatback.

Olson spotted a petite handgun aimed at him through the seat cushions. One look was all it took for him to recognize the second player from Toronto. Matheo Castille.

Damn. They outnumbered him.

John had underestimated Hyde once more. Her allies' presence served as a reminder that she had rigged the game before he'd even begun to play.

Matheo's refined French accent carried a calm authority. "I would listen to her, monsieur."

Matheo reclined as if he were in a Parisian cafe. His dark, impenetrable eyes mirrored the cold sheen of his weapon. His nonchalance projected a silent promise of violence.

Three hostiles, two visible weapons, and at least thirty civilians in immediate proximity. The exit door was twenty feet aft, but he couldn't reach it. The forward galley offered cover, but no escape. Any crossfire would be catastrophic.

Olson lowered his weapon. The calculus was simple. Confrontation was a risk he could not take. And one Hyde had clearly counted on.

"Security at this airport is terrible," he muttered.

Gabrielle gestured to her two accomplices. "I trust you remember Jessica and Matheo? They'll be joining us in LA."

The odds now favored Hyde. John knew she'd seize every opportunity to manipulate him. But his mission directive remained in place: deliver Hyde to Los Angeles and find the mole. At least they were on a flight to California.

"Is everything all right here?" a man asked.

John looked to the airline captain standing before their row in his crisp pilot's uniform. This situation was on the brink, as Hyde's crew showed no interest in hiding their weapons. Only inches from Jessica's pistol, the pilot could turn this into a full-blown panic.

John calculated his options: assert control, de-escalate, or prepare for a firefight. He flashed his credentials. "Nothing to worry about here, Captain."

The pilot remained impassive. That was unusual. Normally, a civilian had some reaction to his badge. This man just smiled.

Olson scrutinized the pilot. The starched white shirt was pressed to perfection, epaulets with their glinting insignia rested on his broad shoulders. But sun-bleached hair spilled from beneath the cap. The man's relaxed demeanor and appearance didn't match his position.

The pilot dipped his head in respect. "I'm sure it is, Officer Olson."

John did a double take. The captain couldn't have seen his name from the brief flash of the badge. He needed to end this. "Captain, I need you to contact the authorities."

The man laughed and then turned to Hyde. "Ready for takeoff, Gabrielle?"

"Indeed, Mr. Simmons." Hyde's voice carried a combination of charm and authority. "We may proceed. I'm afraid the FBI won't be far behind. Thank you."

Gabrielle had only hours. Yet, her preparation outstripped extensive military operations, both impressing and terrifying him.

"Another member of your crew, I presume?" John studied the man as he approached the front cabin.

"One doesn't board a commercial flight without a pilot. I have high standards." She closed her eyes, leaning back.

Frustration coiled in John's gut like a tightening spring. Hyde's manipulation was infuriatingly apparent. As Simmons disappeared into the cockpit, a thought suddenly hit him.

"Is he an actual pilot?"

Hyde stifled a smile, but did not respond.

This would never be the orthodox mission John wanted. From the moment they arrived at the Oval Office, Gabrielle had been pulling the strings, manufacturing and manipulating.

Avery warned him. He should have listened.

Rules and rigor were always going to be an afterthought to Hyde and her crew. For the next seven days, every decision had to be calculated. He had to be ready for anything.

As the aircraft moved forward, a surge of power forced John back into his seat. His gaze drifted to the window. He blinked, certain his eyes were playing tricks.

There, racing down the tarmac, was Vasquez next to the plane with his gun drawn.

Chapter 18

Olson watched Bruno's silhouette shrink against the tarmac, his lowered weapon signaling defeat. A smirk tugged at John's lips. The clink of ice drew his attention.

"Vasquez?" Gabrielle asked.

John nodded, his eyes snapping back. "He's dedicated. But I didn't think he'd go as far as chasing an airplane down the runway."

Hyde leaned close to peer out the window, then settled back. "Admit it. Outsmarting the FBI feels good, doesn't it?"

Her triumphant look irked Olson. However, ever since the Toronto incident, he had harbored resentment towards the Bureau. Seeing Vasquez's frustration was a minor personal victory. The moment of satisfaction was fleeting. The FBI, and Vasquez in particular, wouldn't forget this humiliation.

"What exactly are you doing?"

She took a savoring sip of her cocktail. "Flying first class. Certainly more comfortable than what the FBI would have arranged, don't you think?"

The jetliner's engines roared, sending vibrations through the cabin. Overhead compartments rattled. The lights dimmed, casting long shadows.

"None of this makes sense," John said. "You could have escaped, but you didn't. You warned me, in your own weird way, on where to be. Why not just escape?"

"I had to be sure."

"Of what?" John asked.

"I had to confirm that Toronto was no fluke. That you are, indeed, up to the task." Hyde locked eyes with him. "To be part of my team."

"A member of your... You've got to be kidding. You still think you're recruiting me?"

Hyde's hands spread wide. "We're here, aren't we? Together on a mission for national security and world peace. What could be better?"

"Wait. You're going to take the assignment?"

"John, darling, I was never off," Hyde said with a smile. "Unlike some lowlifes, I keep my word. It's how I've built my reputation. And this task..." Her eyes were distant for a moment. "It could provide a semblance of peace, a lifelong pursuit of freedom that's always dangled just beyond my reach."

She sipped her drink, leaving a lipstick imprint. "The question is, are you still on board?"

John's eyes drifted to Hyde's wrist, where delicate jewelry barely concealed the jagged outline of numbers.

"How could I ever trust you?"

"This isn't about me," she replied. "It's about understanding why you're here. Can you put aside your bias and be open to a new world?"

Hyde's fingers traced the rim of her glass with deliberate precision. She appeared at ease, yet there was something unnaturally perfect about her relaxation, as if every moment was a choreographed performance.

"You and I are more alike than you'll ever admit. We both want retribution. For you, it's..." she paused, "Morozov."

Even though John expected it, the name still sent a tremor through him. For a fleeting moment, he saw Nate's gold aviators. He forced his features to remain impassive, but Hyde's brief pause told him his reaction was noticed.

"Trust is earned, John. I believe in your desire for both duty and revenge. I also respect your character. And if I place my faith in you, surely you could extend the same courtesy to me."

"That's not a luxury I can afford."

"Yet, here you are," Hyde countered, "taking risks on my behalf. Sounds suspiciously like trust to me."

"It's not that simple."

Hyde reclined with feline grace. "Plus," she added, "this is going to be fun."

That was not the way he would describe life and death stakes. Gabrielle seemed to find amusement in the game of espionage as if it were something other than a chess match with human lives.

Her fingers absently drifted to the small forget-me-not pin on her lapel, adjusting its position. The gesture was revealing.

Olson sank into the seat, his body tensing involuntarily as he felt every shudder. The jet's engines transitioned from a dull roar to a high-pitched whine as they reached full thrust. Outside, the Washington Monument transformed from a towering structure to a miniature model. The aircraft banked sharply toward the Potomac.

A vibration hummed through the floor as the landing gear retracted with a muffled thunk. He wondered about the pilot flying the jet. Surely Hyde had recruited him from some military aerobatics school.

Olson eyed Hyde, contemplating the bitter irony of the CIA allying with crooks to catch worse criminals. What he craved wasn't revenge, but redemption.

Fun, Gabrielle called it. But for him, this was far from a game.

As if reading his thoughts, Hyde placed a hand on his arm. "Consider this," she said. "We're about to infiltrate one of the world's most secure facilities. Our goal? Find a mole and avert a global nuclear crisis. No official support, and everyone probably working against us."

"It's beautifully improbable. I love it." Hyde paused, lifting her glass. "But when we pull this off, we'll be legends."

"Legendary criminals is more likely."

Hyde's smile turned sharp. "Justice and idealism rarely walk hand in hand."

The truth of her words stung. Status didn't appeal to him. Closure did. Ending Morozov did. Working with Gabrielle was not his first choice, but it was his only option. If he was going to pull off the impossible, Hyde was the perfect partner.

"Some legends die," he countered.

"Death is inevitable, John. It's what we do before that defines us. When you no longer care, that is when you truly die."

She was correct, as usual. Rupert Upton was a prime example of a man who died inside long before his actual death. John feared that fate more than anything.

His attention moved to the window again. Their takeoff had been suspiciously smooth. No slow taxis, no last-minute delays by the tower. Under standard protocol, Bruno would be on the phone to air traffic control within minutes.

John studied the airport's diminishing outline. The tower should have demanded an emergency recall. Yet the aircraft continued its steady climb, unimpeded.

"Why isn't Vasquez recalling the plane?"

Hyde took another sip. "Maybe he's recognized the futility of it." Her pupils dilated. "Or perhaps… there are forces at work beyond his control."

Her response only compounded Olson's discomfort, stirring a growing unease. Her casual references belied the true depth of her execution. Secure systems had been compromised. Contingencies had been anticipated and thwarted.

And what had she done to Bruno?

Chapter 19

20 Minutes Earlier

"Hyde's on the ten-twenty to LA!" Morris called out, struggling to keep up.

Vasquez barreled through the bustling terminal, his suit jacket billowing behind him. Overhead announcements blurred into white noise as his elbows jabbed through the startled travelers, clearing a path. One hand rested on the worn leather of his holster, a relic from his rookie days.

He flashed his badge at the confused security guards lounging on stools. The demand for easy travel that made airports such vulnerable targets was working against him.

He sidestepped a bewildered ticketing agent and sent paper scattering.

"Sir, you can't go in!" The woman sputtered. "Boarding's closed!"

Vasquez ignored her. He burst through the door, FBI agents trailing in his wake. A sleek Boeing 727 loomed before him, its distinctive T-tail silhouette unmistakable against the tarmac's shimmering heat waves. Its massive engines rumbled to life as it inched forward.

With gun in one hand and badge in the other, Vasquez sprinted alongside the taxiing airplane. His legs churned, matching the rhythm of the plane's acceleration. A jet blast roared, rattling his bones and whipping his tie. The smell of aviation fuel filled his nostrils as his shouts vanished into the deafening noise.

He pressed on. Any second now, he thought, the plane would halt.

The sun-kissed pilot locked eyes with Vasquez, a flicker of recognition passing between them. Bruno tried to place where he'd seen him before. Brushing it aside, he slowed his pace.

Through the cockpit window, the captain gave a crisp, exaggerated salute. In the same fluid movement, his other hand pushed the throttle forward. The engines roared, propelling the plane ahead.

The blatant disregard of authority was all wrong. The pilot should be stopping, not going faster.

The epiphany struck Vasquez like a sledgehammer. Hyde orchestrated this entire scene, turning the airport into a mockery of safety. Then, to top it all off, she and her crew hijacked a jet without anyone noticing.

It couldn't be worse.

Then things got worse. Through the window, he spotted Olson.

Betrayal and fury propelled him into a frenzied sprint beside the accelerating plane. He couldn't let Olson get away with this.

He had to stop that airplane, no matter the cost.

Arresting Hyde topped his list, sure. But snagging Olson? He'd blow the lid off whatever game the CIA was playing. That would be the cherry on top. The White House be damned. That surfer pilot would be right there with them.

Vasquez couldn't afford another failure, not after Toronto nearly ended his career and left him a laughingstock.

He ran alongside the airplane. Legs pumping. Lungs burning. The jet's acceleration was relentless, widening the gap between man and machine with each passing second.

It was futile. His feet slowed until he skidded to a halt.

Ragged breaths heaved his chest while sweat streamed down his flushed face. Nothing remained in the plane's wake but his gasping and the faint howl of fading engines. On the tarmac, scuff marks scarred where his shoes had dragged.

Out-of-breath FBI agents surrounded him. Some looked his way for orders, others bent over, heaving, hands on their knees. The frantic energy of the chase drained, leaving only the hollow ache of disappointment.

Vasquez watched the plane turn, engines spooling. A nearby building displayed the letters "Macbeth" on its side. The word burned like acid. How had he missed it?

Years of chasing Hyde didn't make it easier. Every close call and failure culminated in this moment. He spat out salty saliva and wiped his mouth with the back of his hand.

Pursuing the airliner on foot was a waste of time. But facing his superiors with another setback would mean more than just a reprimand; it could be the end of his career.

Resisting the urge to puke, he scanned the area, searching for a way to salvage the situation. He locked onto the control tower on the opposite side of the field, its glass windows reflecting the harsh daylight.

He couldn't physically stop the plane, but he could ground it.

"On me, now!" he barked, whirling around.

With renewed determination, Vasquez sprinted back toward the terminal, his team groaning and scrambling to catch up.

The open tarmac gave way to the crowded lobby. Bruno stormed through the masses, shoving past confused bystanders. He zeroed in on the gate agent who had tried to stop him earlier.

As he approached, he caught a glimpse of her fumbling with a magazine about Elvis's death. She covered it with scattered oversized green printed pages.

The airline representative met his approach with an apologetic tilt of her head. It was just one more day in hell for her.

Her eyes popped to Vasquez's holster. "Sir, I..."

"Save it."

She swallowed hard. "I told you boarding was complete. There's nothing..."

Vasquez's hand shot forward, slamming his badge onto the podium with such force that the metal shield left a dent in the polished surface. The sharp crack silenced the busy terminal, a toddler's wail cutting off mid-sob.

"FBI." Bruno growled. "There's a dangerous fugitive on that flight. I need your cooperation. Now."

The agent's face drained of color. "How can I help?"

"Get the tower on the horn, now."

The woman winced. "Oh my, sir," she said. "Telephone communication went down an hour ago. We can still take off, thank God. Called a tech, but..." She shrugged. "Still waiting."

Vasquez's right eyelid spasmed, and he forced it still with a finger pressed to his temple. He scanned the room with a predator's focus, spotting a black radio mounted on the far wall. He pointed at it, already marching forward.

"I'll use the radio."

"That's down as well. Strangest thing," she said.

The sabotage was perfect. Enough destruction to hamper operations, but not enough to shut them down. Nothing broken that couldn't be easily restored. Clean, efficient, and leaving minimal evidence. If he didn't hate Hyde with all his being, he might admire her.

As he returned to the desk, the agent's plastic smile and false portrait of calm grated on Bruno. "Is there anything else I can do to assist?" she asked.

"No." Vasquez's curt reply ended the conversation.

He picked up his badge, dragging the metal across the countertop. Around him, the FBI agents watched in tense silence, waiting for orders.

Vasquez stalked to the broad windows. He pressed his palms against the sleek glass, gazing out at the runway. The airplane carrying Hyde and Olson dwindled to a speck, swallowed by clouds that obscured the horizon.

His head dropped as he watched them vanish.

Two years of thankless stakeouts and cold case files to redeem himself, and in seconds, it all just evaporated. Toronto all over again. No, this was worse.

This time he'd seen the pattern, recognized that Hyde required a different approach. He'd even unraveled Olson's methods. But that understanding was too late, and now both were beyond his reach. How many more chances would he get before the Bureau decided he wasn't worth the trouble?

Helplessness surged. No radio, no phone, and no way to intercede. It was as if the universe conspired against him. No. It was Hyde. It was always her.

He thought of Morris. The junior agents who'd just transferred to his unit, careers full of promise. The veterans who'd stuck with him despite everything. All of them would pay for his failure.

They weren't the only ones. He'd endured years of training and countless nights spent away from his family. He refused to let it all go to waste now. Vasquez collected himself, pushing down the pity.

Regaining his full height, Bruno turned back to his team.

Morris stowed his weapon. "What if we send a team to the tower? Maybe they can recall the plane."

"No." Bruno's voice was calm. "Wouldn't do any good."

"Orders, sir?"

"Regroup. Debrief in thirty."

The other agents dispersed, their slumped shoulders and dragging feet mirroring the defeat Vasquez felt inside. He watched them go, then turned around to the window. His reflection stared back.

His hands curled into fists at his sides. Every setback, every near miss, had only sharpened his resolve. He'd chase Hyde to the ends of the earth.

"Morris," he called. The second-in-command turned, renewed hope on his face. "Find me the fastest flight to Los Angeles. And call the LA field office. I want a team ready to go when we land."

Chapter 20

LOS ANGELES WAREHOUSE DISTRICT

7 Days Remaining

15:30

The derelict concrete warehouse reeked of neglect. Amber light filtered through towering windows, illuminating dust in the afternoon air. The smell of industrial chemicals lingered, mingling with a musty odor. The fourth floor stretched beyond the revealing sunlight, long shadows creeping up to rows of tarp-covered equipment.

The CIA provided a small field office near the Skunk Works facility for Olson and Hyde's operation. John intended to use it as their hub, but Hyde persuaded him that her alternative would better accommodate her crew and shield their activities from oversight.

Despite his reservations, John found himself here. "Off the radar," he muttered, "and spacious."

It was a place John would love if Hyde hadn't suggested it. The CIA wouldn't fund this workspace, and the FBI wouldn't approve it either. As much as he hated to agree, the rows of mysterious crates and pallets promised they'd have plenty of resources. If the Agency didn't want these kinds of surprises, they never should have involved a criminal.

The distant rumble of city traffic leaked through the walls. John observed Hyde's team from a safe distance. A plume of smoke rose from Jessica's lips.

A burst of laughter erupted as Douglas Simmons leaned against a cluttered table, his voice rich with a dramatic flourish. He recounted past exploits as he tinkered with a small device. The pilot's uniform was gone, replaced now by a mottled bohemian shirt.

Jessica flicked ash as she detailed her role as a carnival dancer during a job in Brazil. Matheo commented on the still-missing headdress, a gaudy vehicle for smuggling gems. She laughed, countering with Matheo's misplacement of diamonds in Switzerland.

"Ah, yes, Switzerland," Hyde said. "I would fancy that diamonds are, in fact, not forever." The group released a shared laugh.

Olson watched the squad interact. They were more than thieves. A family bound by unspoken connections. He envied their unity, even as he questioned the morality that tied them together.

As an outsider, the crew's tight-knit dynamic would be a problem. To maintain control of the operation, he needed to separate Hyde from the team. But as he observed them, he realized that such a task would be nearly impossible.

Catching Olson watching, Simmons crossed the space with a slight swagger, then wrapped his arm around John.

"Join the gang." A clap on his shoulder punctuated the invitation. "You're one of us, now."

"I wouldn't go that far."

Jessica crushed her cigarette with her heel. "Quite the troop for you, I imagine?" She slithered closer, her movements fluid. "Got stories for the ages. Probably best not to share too much with a copper, though."

John leaned back from her advance. "Yeah, I get it."

"We all have our secrets," she breathed, leaning close enough for him to catch a subtle flowery perfume. "I'll tell you some of mine, if you tell me some of yours."

John grasped Jessica's shoulders firmly and eased her back a step. "Thank you; but as you say, not my cup of tea."

She took the cue, though a predatory smile still lingered.

John asked Hyde, "What does your gallery of rogues bring to this operation? If they're going to be here, I might as well know what we have."

"I owe you an introduction. A proper one this time."

John straightened. "Some talents are obvious; others are not. The CIA has their own roles and titles, ones I doubt you use. So, I might need a translation or explanation for your insider terms."

Hyde laughed. "We have our own language." She motioned to Douglas.

"Pilot." John nodded. "Easy enough."

Hyde held up a finger. "Nobody here has a single job. I chose everyone for their variety of talents." She motioned to the man. "Now, take Mr. Simmons."

As he strolled over, John noticed a small belt lined with handmade tools, the leather worn smooth. The faint smell of machine oil and solvent wafted from his untucked shirt.

"The outside man," Hyde explained, "is our first line of defense. He's the eyes and ears that keep watch for threats approaching from our periphery."

He flashed a wry smile. "Law enforcement, tail-happy agents, you name it. I've got a face they seem to trust. Don't know why, it's just like I'm one of them." He chuckled. "It's cosmic irony, man. I throw on my serious look, and suddenly everyone's tripping over themselves. Makes 'em stick out like a sore thumb every single time. It's beautiful."

A skeptical crease formed on John's forehead. It made sense. Spies needed someone to monitor external threats. But the casualness with which Simmons spoke about manipulation was already raising red flags.

"Douglas is also a multi-platform pilot, forger, electrician, and if I may say so," Hyde added, "a fantastic astrologist."

"That's… an eclectic mix of talents." John paused. "Astrology, seriously?"

"Gotta know if those stars are in alignment before a big job," Simmons said with zeal.

Hyde then motioned to Jessica. "Jessica Fortner, our roper. I'm assuming you remember that one from field ops?"

"I'm familiar."

Jessica sauntered toward John. Her nails trailed along the workbench's edge, every movement calculated to draw attention. "I also do communications and occasional demolition." Her British accent rolled. "I'm skilled at getting into places no man could."

Jessica tilted her head, examining him. "Oh, I do fancy you, John. Easy on the eyes, and deliciously… damaged. It's quite the intoxicating combination, darling."

Her fingers reached out, tracing a line down his chest. John stiffened. "We talked about this."

A soft laugh cut him off. "I get close. Draw them in and find their desires." Her hand moved over his torso. "… command their attention and then…" She produced his gun with a flourish.

John snatched back his weapon reflexively. "I'm going to need you to keep whatever this is… in check."

Jessica's siren face softened. "You're more of a challenge than I expected, Officer Olson."

John re-secured his pistol inside his jacket and locked eyes with Gabrielle. The message of maintaining boundaries was clear. His gaze shifted to Matheo Castille. His broad shoulders and stoic demeanor led to an easy conclusion.

Previous experience taught John to expect certain archetypes in field operations. The man before him seemed more than suitable for fieldwork. He was skilled at both throwing and taking punches.

"I take it you're the muscle?"

The Frenchman's eyebrow quirked up.

It was Hyde who responded, "Matheo's a man of many talents. While he can handle himself in a fight, that's not his primary role."

They caught John's look of skepticism. Hyde continued, "He's our fixer. Matheo often works near the inside man, providing backup and coordinating resources as the con unfolds."

"He's your fixer?"

"The con's most versatile part," Hyde replied. "Matheo has a combination of skills that range from grifting to hitting when necessary."

Matheo crossed his arms, his fingers drumming against his bicep. His deep voice carried an edge of pride. "I also speak five languages and am a premier tailor."

"Tailor?"

Matheo's lips twisted into a frown. "*Quoi?* You have something to say, *Muef!*" he snapped.

Jessica laughed from behind. "Don't take it personally, love. He's French; he hates everyone equally."

Hyde smirked. "There are three important things to remember: The Mark is the intended victim; The Grifter is the practitioner of the confidence scheme; and The Shill is an accomplice with no apparent knowledge of the scam."

John had seen similar dynamics within intelligence agencies. Same play, different cast. "Got it."

"For a long con to work," Hyde said, "it requires a team of grifters who can execute a variety of roles. Some specialize in one area, while others adapt as needed." Her voice took on urgency. "Typically, our jobs take months to set up." She glanced around. "Here, we don't have that luxury."

Olson felt his grip on the situation loosening. Without consulting him, Hyde had broadened the scope of their operation to include her crew. He couldn't let them join. John realized he couldn't risk alienating them either.

He stepped forward. "Look, I understand. You've all got… special talents. But this is still a CIA op. For now, I need everyone to back off until I give you the green light to join."

There was no reaction. John continued, "When that changes, I will ensure you are brought in to help."

Hyde cleared her throat. "All right, you heard Officer Olson. Time is against us. We need this operation tight and flawless. You each have things to do."

With a short clap of her hands, the team dispersed into action.

John waited until they were clear and pulled Gabrielle aside. "They have to stay out of this mission until I decide they are needed. This is non-negotiable."

Hyde set a hand on her hip. "My people aren't just skilled. They're loyal to a fault. I'll keep them leashed, but make no mistake," her gaze razor-sharp, "when this house of cards inevitably tumbles, you'll be glad they're waiting in the wings."

Protecting her team was fair, but it left an open variable. "I'll be the judge of that," he responded.

"I know this differs from anything you've been part of before, but it should all feel familiar too. They can help."

John refused to surrender operational control. "I understand that, but it's still not my way. This isn't one of your cons, Gabrielle."

She drew him further away with a gentle tug on his arm. "We need to discuss this. You say you're not part of this world," she began, "but you're wrong."

Glancing at his watch, John realized time was slipping away. "Perhaps I am, but this is my mission to run. My role is to enforce the law; not fix what you break. And despite what's happened so far, that will not change. I'm in charge here."

"You think what we do is any different from the CIA?" Hyde challenged. "The feds destroy things. You scheme, you plan, you lie. Do you have the authority? Yes. But it's still all manipulation."

"We protect national security. That's the job."

Her laugh dripped with irony. "And how do you accomplish that? You manipulate, extract, deceive. The CIA leverages assets. Terms like legal and illegal are just stamps put on it by the government. You and I are the same."

"The difference is incentives."

"Do you know what we really do?" Hyde's voice dropped.

Olson folded his arms. "You fool people and steal their stuff."

Hyde arched an eyebrow. "It's about filling perception gaps with polluted information. We're the spies of the industrial world."

"Heuristics."

Hyde's eyes widened. "We guide people's thoughts, making them believe what they already want to be true."

John glared. "Sorry, you deceive and relieve. Close enough?"

She executed a curtsy. "As usual, you cut through the pretense."

Olson offered no reply; instead, he turned back to observe Matheo, who was sewing something that required careful attention. But regardless of how similar their tactics might seem, he couldn't come to terms with their end goals.

Hyde moved beside Olson. "You think you stand on the moral high ground," she said. "But when has the CIA kept your hands clean? Did it ever save anyone you truly cared about?"

John's gaze flicked to her wrist. Nate's face flashed in his mind. He heard the ragged sound of his partner's last breaths.

"My hands may not be clean," John admitted, "but I've never lost sight of why I do this."

Hyde nodded with respect. "Nor have I. Perhaps our goals remain the same. We simply bring different tools to the table."

"There are rules. I have to follow them. And so do you."

"Was it regulations that led you to that rooftop in Toronto?" Hyde pressed. "Or helped you recover that intelligence in Somalia?"

He didn't need reminding of the choices that drove sleepless nights. "Orders aren't always clear," he conceded. "I did what I had to do."

She poked him in the chest. "That's precisely my point."

"This is different. Avery made that quite clear."

"And what if this job is not what you expect?" Hyde asked. "There are layers here you might not be willing to consider."

"I'm not sure what you're implying." John's tone hardened. "Our orders were explicit."

"That's the problem." Intensity radiated from Hyde. "Think about it. A leak of this magnitude, in a facility this secure? It's not just about one person with loose lips. You may not like what you find, because this is bigger than you want to acknowledge."

John pointed at Hyde. "That's a dangerous accusation." His voice dropped. "Because if that were true, it could break the entire process." He thought for a second. "Or is that your goal?"

Hyde nodded as if she had expected this. "You can see through the veil of the world, John. It's much rarer than you understand. That's why we'll be great together. Sometimes, the system is the problem."

His eyes snapped back to hers, searching for mockery or deceit, but finding only sincerity. The notion that he shared common ground with Hyde's life of espionage was unsettling. John knew this was her game.

Gabrielle intended to convince him of a grand conspiracy. She wanted him to question his own leadership. All the easier to lead him astray. Hyde's offer wasn't without temptation. It would be so easy to let loose and play the rebel.

His hand brushed against his jacket pocket, feeling the outline of Nate's gold sunglasses. "I'll keep your concerns in mind. But off-the-book decisions have cost me too much. When I doubt the system, it costs lives," he said.

"And probably saved countless more."

"I know what you're doing. The Agency has its own fancy terms, and one of those is called Co-opting. It won't work on me, not here, not today. We're doing this my way." John met her gaze. "We'll conduct a methodical leak search before more lives are lost because of rash actions. If there's a bad actor, I'll find them."

"We only have seven days, less actually."

"I'm well aware of the timeline," John said.

"I have a thought. It's a little unorthodox, but under the time constraints..." Hyde began.

"No!" John's response was swift, severing her words. "I'm running this op, not you. We go slow, we research, then we find our man."

He couldn't allow Hyde to take over. Her ideas would only lead him further into murky, dangerous waters. Hyde lifted her hands in a rare display of surrender, appearing spectral in the afternoon light.

"Understood. We do it your way... for now. It's settled." She smiled.

John nodded, recognizing the temporary ceasefire for what it was. Hyde's too-easy compliance shot a prickle of caution up his spine. In his business, a smooth retreat often hid the setup for a bigger play.

"Let's hope it stays that way," he said. "No more delays. We need to get moving."

Olson's eyes drifted back to the ever-advancing clock on his wrist. If he didn't act now, there wouldn't be time to establish operations at Skunk Works or start the interview process until tomorrow. Delay was not a luxury their mission could afford.

John grabbed a set of keys from the table. "I'll get the car. Meet me downstairs in ten minutes. We're going to Skunk Works."

John paused, as if expecting a challenge from Hyde. When none came, he departed through the steel door without looking back. The steel metal clanged shut. In its wake, a charged silence settled over the room.

All eyes shifted to Hyde.

* * *

Gabrielle could sense her team's unease.

She leaned against a concrete pillar, its surface catching her blouse. Her gaze lingered on the door. The day's complexities had worn her down, but there was no time for fatigue. Especially with John proving to be both complication and catalyst.

"The clock is ticking," she said.

Jessica and Simmons remained static, waiting.

Gabrielle straightened. "The Soviets will not stand by idly. Nor will our government friends. As usual, timing is essential. You have your assignments."

"Matheo." She pivoted toward his workstation.

Glancing up from his equipment, Castille let fly a French expletive. His face winced in a scowl, stained fingers wrestling with the coarse fabric of an olive drab suit.

"*C'est atroce!*" he grumbled. "This material! Like trying to sew cardboard!"

She peered over his shoulder. "Any success?"

His fingers paused. "Two minutes."

As he returned to work, Simmons approached with Jessica on his flank.

"Douglas, I can see you're worried about Olson," Gabrielle said before he could speak.

Simmons cleared his throat, hands fidgeting. "His aura… it's way off. Just sayin'."

Jessica put a hand on Simmons' shoulder. "He seems more than merely on edge; his trauma could boil over at any moment. I'm not so sure about this approach." She nodded toward the door. "He may put up a brave front, but I recognize cracks. That bloke's teetering on explosion." She took a second, then added, "You taught me to take smart risks."

Gabrielle was happy to see Jessica taking her lessons to heart. "I appreciate your assessment," Hyde said. "We all carry our burdens into the fray, but the key is one's ability to lay them aside when it's required."

Olson was disrupting their cohesion. Her team needed to see the potential she saw in him. What fascinated her most was how Olson's moral code had bent but never broken. Unlike others who justified their actions with platitudes, John carried his lines with him.

"A CIA asset is both a burden and our greatest advantage. And that man has way more grit and defiance than that government spit and polish exterior would suggest," Gabrielle told them. "He'll endure because beneath it all, he's a caged tiger looking for a fight."

"And if Olson suspects what we're doing?" Matheo asked.

"That's inevitable. We proceed as planned."

Simmons relaxed. "As you say, boss. You always love the long odds."

He and Jessica returned to their preparations, their motions more deliberate. Only time could prove Hyde's instincts correct. Until then, she would find the subtle harmony between compassion and exploitation.

Gabrielle wandered to Matheo's workbench and examined the finished suit. "Remember," she said, "it's not about creating beauty. Today is about believability."

Castille gave an almost imperceptible nod. He resumed his task with renewed focus. "*Oui.*"

"The pieces are moving," she announced. "Let's ensure we're ready when they fall."

Gabrielle turned toward the window, hiding a frown. She considered the intricate dance facing them, absently rubbing the inside of her left wrist. This wasn't just another simple con. It was a chance to settle all the scores at once.

Yet the future remained maddeningly murky. Only one thing was certain: Olson was the key. John would ensure their success or failure.

Either way, it excited her.

Chapter 21

SKUNK WORKS DESIGN FACILITY

7 Days Remaining

16:15

The rental car swallowed up miles of asphalt as John's thoughts drifted back to the warehouse. Hyde's crew and their unsanctioned actions were a continued concern. The tense standoff with Gabrielle had left him hyper-aware of every shift in her posture.

John eased off the accelerator as they approached the first security checkpoint. The car's engine settled into a steady hum. A bored guard waved them through after a glance at their cover credentials. As the shack receded, the imposing silhouette of Skunk Works loomed ahead.

John's gaze shifted to appraise Gabrielle's new attire, a drab olive suit. It was a clear departure from her usual sophistication, hugging her contours with a precision that betrayed its custom nature.

"Don't pout."

"I'm not," Hyde shot back.

He suppressed a smile. "As long as we investigate normally, the FBI can't touch us."

Gabrielle turned. "And the rats run in the predetermined direction."

"Not everything is a conspiracy."

Hyde shook her head. "Still dwelling on this morning?"

Olson kept his eyes on the road. "Just wondering when you'll pull that same stunt again."

"I never attempt the same maneuver twice," she said with nonchalance. "So you're safe in that regard."

"For now," John grumbled as he eased the car into a spot.

He and Hyde emerged into the shimmering afternoon, working their way to a series of oversized buildings. With each step toward the main hangar, the structure seemed to grow. The enormity of it surpassed his expectations.

Inside, the air hummed with machinery, carrying scents of metal and solvents. Overhead, massive cranes hung from reinforced tracks, ready to move bulky components. The concrete floor bore the scars of decades of use and chemical stains.

Hidden shapes lurked beneath tarps, each surrounded by gear and equipment. Shadows hung over the few skeletal aircraft, each promising technological breakthroughs. He also knew without a doubt that some of these secret concepts had originated through espionage.

Hyde's eyes gleamed.

"We stick to the plan. You promised," Olson reminded her.

"Promises are chains," she replied. "You know," she started in a low voice, "I could probably have the plans for these beauties within a couple of hours."

"We're not here to have fun. We need to find our contact."

"You'll never charm a lady with that kind of attitude," Hyde said with a smirk.

Olson surged ahead, not wanting to give her the satisfaction of a response. He had neither the time nor the inclination for such distractions. Gabrielle's widening eyes were the only sign of imminent danger. He'd been so focused on her that he forgot to watch where he was walking.

As he rounded the corner, Olson collided with an engineer. Her files, a collection of intricate sketches and annotated calculations, erupted into a storm of papers as they both staggered backward. The sheets flew across the concrete floor like leaves caught in a gust.

John's body tensed as he tried to assess the situation. His right hand darted to his hip, grasping at the empty air where his holster should have been.

When the papers settled, he realized it was nothing more than an accident. An apology died on his lips as he became surprisingly entranced by the young woman.

Something about her composed demeanor, the way she moved, piqued his curiosity. Every aspect hinted at an analytical mind. Strands of warm, chestnut hair framed a soft face. She exuded a natural confidence that didn't demand attention. A stained, functional lab coat covered her slender frame.

"I'm sorry," John started, his voice trailing off. "Miss…"

"Andrea." She continued, flicking debris from the sheets without looking up.

John stooped to help, but Andrea swept it from his reach. "It's not like we're already two months behind schedule," she snapped. "This! This doesn't help."

Olson held out a hand in peace. "I'm sorry. We weren't…"

She locked eyes with him, recognition narrowing her gaze. With quick precision, she scooped up the remaining documents and hugged them to her chest. "Do you even have clearance to handle these designs?"

"Yes. I do. I'm John." He resisted the urge to reach for his CIA credentials. "We would like to speak with Dr. Miles. Quietly, if possible."

He noticed Andrea's lips purse, looking at both of them. "You're the security consultants?"

Hyde cleared her throat, clasping her hands behind her back. "Don't ask me. He's in charge."

Gabrielle's uncharacteristic restraint triggered his concern. What did she know? "Yes, we are," John said.

"Then follow me. I'll take you," Andrea said, pivoting and striding toward a reinforced entrance nestled in the far corner.

John and Gabrielle exchanged a glance before following in her wake. Andrea led them past corridors flanked by glass panels, offering glimpses into rooms where engineers hunched over tables laden with blueprints. Periodically, someone would look up from their work, curiosity on their face at the sight of strangers.

Reaching a large door, Andrea glanced back. "Are you coming?"

Her badge swept through a card reader, followed by her PIN, unlocking the first security door with a pneumatic hiss. Each successive barrier carried them deeper into the facility's heart. John watched Andrea navigate the labyrinth with ease, her orange badge and random codes granting passage.

Despite her professional demeanor, she exchanged warm greetings with every guard they passed. Each guard brightened at her approach.

"This took a year of my life to earn," she said, tapping the bright orange credential. "Without it, you're practically a tourist here."

John raised a finger. "We'll need two of those."

Andrea laughed. "You'd have better luck asking for the moon."

They reached a featureless metal door with a sophisticated keypad. "This begins the secure section. Two-person protocol at all times, unless you have orange clearance."

She gestured toward a viewing area as they climbed the stairs. Technicians in clean room suits moved with precision around a skeletal frame, their breath fogging their face shields as they applied layers of a strange substance. The air carried the distinct scent of epoxy and the sharp, almost sweet smell of the experimental materials.

"Testing happens there, but the real work is deeper inside. And the storage vault..." Her expression darkened. "That's beyond even my clearance."

As they navigated the maze-like corridors, the ambient hum of machinery faded, replaced by an oppressive silence. Andrea led them to a nondescript room, indistinguishable from the countless others they'd passed.

"We can talk in here," she said.

Once inside, Andrea closed the door behind them with a click. Her demeanor shifted like nightfall swallowing the day. "I know who you are."

The words were bitter. "CIA. It's written all over you." A harsh laugh escaped. "I appreciate the funding, sure. But why in hell are you screwing with us in the last three months of design-build?"

The air crackled after her tirade. John's muscles tensed, bracing for another outburst as Hyde stood alert beside him. Where was Dr. Miles?

John raised his hands slowly. "We're not here to hinder your progress," he said. "I'm sorry, but before we go any further; who are you?"

Hyde stepped forward, the click of her heels a punctuation to the tense silence. "My dear Officer Olson, we must work on your observational skills."

John cursed. Hyde was about to make him look like an idiot.

"May I introduce Dr. Andrea Miles," Hyde began with an air of recitation. "Thirty-One. Only child. First female graduate from Caltech in engineering, doctorate in thermodynamics. Your dissertation was fabulous. Underrated. Worked at Lockheed for five years, lead engineer at Skunk Works thermodynamics division, and a recent cat owner, a gray and white tabby."

Andrea's jaw dropped. "What the hell? How did you?" She pointed accusingly. "Have you been following me?"

"No. Nothing like that. She does that. It's her thing," Olson said.

Hyde cast a sidelong glance at him. "It's called research, John."

"And you're both CIA?" Andrea asked.

"Oh, dear God, no. He's CIA," Hyde corrected with a dramatic roll of her eyes.

"Gabrielle's here because she's one of the best in the world at spotting vulnerabilities. She's… 'consulting,' but her expertise is unmatched."

"I'm a thief that the government's blackmailing, thank you very much."

"Why couldn't you just say consultant?" John grumbled.

"Consultants get paid. But he's right, I am very good."

"Enough!" Andrea's voice cut through. "I get it; you're the government odd couple. What does this have to do with me and our work?"

John gave Hyde a fleeting glare. He needed Dr. Miles to be more receptive to their plight. "The President believes there may be a security problem here at Skunk Works," he said.

Andrea's face contorted, her anger quickly giving way to disbelief. "What kind of issue?" Her eyes darted. "His office knows our protocols are airtight."

"That's what we're here to determine," he said. "We believe someone is leaking classified information."

Andrea swayed. "No, that's impossible. We compartmentalize our work specifically to prevent that." Her fingers tightened around her lab coat.

"Compartmentalization only works if everyone keeps their mouth shut and their data secure; both are rare," Hyde interjected.

Andrea's eyes lingered on Gabrielle, considering the implication.

"Dr. Miles, we need your help," John said.

After a moment, Andrea exhaled. "I'll assist, but I expect full transparency regarding the CIA's intentions."

"I promise to be transparent with you."

Hyde cut in, her voice sharp. "Are you certain it's wise to share such sensitive information with a civilian? We don't know who we can trust yet."

Andrea whipped to Hyde. "So says the thief."

"Oh, John. I do like her," Gabrielle added. "Doesn't mean you should believe her."

Just as Andrea opened her mouth to respond further, John cut her off. "As lead, it's my call to make. Dr. Miles deserves to be in the know. I trust her."

Hyde stepped back, conceding the floor. John understood the maneuver, a ploy to garner Andrea's trust by using his defense as a lever. It was a deft move, but left him wondering if Gabrielle was truly helping.

John continued. "Thank you. Dr. Miles... please. Your project is breached."

She shook it off. "If someone broke into the facility, we'd know."

"A spy successfully stole compartmentalized information and attempted to sell it abroad."

The color drained from Andrea's face as her eyes widened with shock.

"What? How?"

"Three days ago, I intercepted this." John pulled a worn document from his jacket. "It was bound for Soviet spies in Mogadishu."

Andrea shook as she took the paper, its edges crinkling under her trembling fingers. "This is… It's from Have Blue."

John's expression darkened. "Yes. We are read-in on the stealth program. What am I seeing here?"

Her eyes focused. "It's a preliminary exterior schematic. Just the planform geometry. Thank God it doesn't include critical angles or material specifications." She traced the outline. "But this reveals the project's existence. This shape alone could accelerate enemy countermeasure research by years."

Andrea's gaze snapped up. "This isn't just restricted information," she whispered. "This is my life's work. Three years of sixteen-hour days. Holidays. Nights."

"How did you get this?"

"That's classified," John replied. "What matters is that it exists."

She sank into a nearby chair. "This can't be right."

Hyde stepped closer. "I assure you, it's very real. I would pay top dollar for this sort of thing."

John silenced Hyde with a stern look before kneeling beside Andrea. "I know this is hard to accept, Dr. Miles, but we need to face facts. Someone here is selling classified stealth data to our enemies."

Andrea jerked her head in rejection. "No. Our security protocols…"

"have been be circumvented," Hyde interjected.

"Wait… that's my signature," Andrea said.

John placed a steadying hand on her shoulder. "We know you're not involved, Dr. Miles. You've been cleared by CIA HQ."

"Cleared?"

"Yes," John affirmed. "However, your assistance is essential to identify the true operative before they strike again."

Andrea's posture straightened, a spark of determination igniting in her eyes. John recognized that look. It was the same one he'd seen in field operatives who refused to back down from a challenge. In that moment, Olson knew they had a formidable ally.

"What do you want?" she asked.

John rose, thinking as he paced. "We'll need to interrogate anyone who had access. And press them hard until we find the source."

Andrea nodded, her shock morphing into anger. "No one steals from me." She strode to a nearby desk, pulling out a thick logbook. "We keep impeccable records. I can cross-reference everything and everyone."

"We'll need full access," he said, ticking off the thoughts on his fingers. "Personnel files, clearance documents, work schedules, financials. All of it."

Andrea looked up from her task, her earlier skepticism returning. "And how do I know I can trust you? The CIA doesn't exactly have a stellar record around here."

John met her gaze. "Because right now, we're the best chance you have of protecting everything you've worked for," he told her.

"Two rules," Andrea said after a brief silence. Her voice regained some of its earlier edge. "One, don't lie to me. Second, I'm involved in every step until we uncover the truth."

He appreciated her desire to be part of the solution. "Agreed."

Andrea strode up to him. John looked down at her hand as she stretched it out. He shook, knowing it meant everything to her. She released his grasp and returned to her work.

"It's essential that we trace back each step these designs took," he said. "Every person with authorization, all copies… Uncover every stone, no matter what we might find."

"Okay," she agreed. "Follow the science, follow the data. I can do that. We record all movement of sensitive material," she explained while flipping logbook pages back and forth. "I'll compare and match access times with personnel shifts."

"That's good," John replied as he looked for Gabrielle.

Hyde had been monitoring from her vantage point in the corner. She caught his eye and gave an almost imperceptible nod. It was an unspoken agreement that he was moving in the right direction with Andrea.

"We'll also need security footage and clearance records," John said.

He could tell that Andrea had already become absorbed in unraveling the puzzle. She spoke without glancing away from her work. "You'll have whatever you require."

Ten long minutes crawled by. Andrea engrossed herself in the book, her face locked in concentration. John's fingers drummed on the metal desk while his other hand rubbed the back of his neck. There was one more thing.

"We must maintain our cover as security consultants while here," he said. "This is a covert operation."

Andrea glanced up from her notes, irritation crossing her face. "I know all about the CIA's track record with 'undercover operations.'"

John could appreciate how past interference had left deep scars. Yet cooperation was non-negotiable. He didn't have time to mend fences. "I know our history isn't spotless," Olson admitted. "But this is about more than agency pride. To me, it's about national security."

She held his stare for a moment. "Fair enough," she conceded. "I'll arrange for interviews with the staff granted access to the designs."

The offer played right into John's desire for order and structure. He needed a rigid method that could peel back layers of deception.

From the corner of his eye, John caught Hyde's reflection in the glass, her irritation apparent. She shifted restlessly, the suit's fabric rustling. It was a subtle tell that spoke volumes about her discomfort.

Hyde's voice was laden with skepticism. "Interviews? We'll be chasing our tails while Moscow laughs. You'll never get done in time."

Andrea's head snapped up. "What's the concern about the schedule?"

John glared at Hyde. "Nothing. Leadership just wants us to wrap this up quickly," he lied, already breaking the first rule.

While Andrea's protectiveness could be helpful, it could also become a liability if she knew the true stakes. Now wasn't the time for full disclosure. "Remember, no one can know we're CIA," he reminded her. "We'll start interviews as soon as possible."

Andrea approached a phone. "Make sure you get everyone," John instructed as she picked up the receiver. "No exceptions."

Olson turned his focus back to Hyde, who seemed still irritated. He leaned closer, pretending to inspect the equipment next to where Gabrielle sat.

"I need you here with me, focused."

"You have my attention," she replied.

"I better." John straightened and turned to Andrea. "Once you have all the interview times confirmed, let us know."

"Will do," Andrea said, never looking up.

With a flourish of a pen, she stood up, a stack of personnel folders in hand. "Give me an hour, and I'll set up the first interviews."

"Good," John acknowledged. "We'll go through every detail." He hesitated, then added, "As a team."

He caught a fleeting hint of a grin on Andrea's face, but it disappeared quickly.

John turned just in time to see Hyde conceal her own amusement. It gave him a chill. He'd seen that all-knowing look in Toronto. She was planning something.

Gabrielle was just waiting for her moment. He could not let her out of his sight. Not until they had answers. He straightened his tie, a reflexive gesture of self-mastery.

As Andrea stepped away to make another call, Hyde's attention drifted to the table where a facility schematic poked out from a logbook. Her eyes studied the winding paths through the complex. She didn't even attempt to hide her interest.

"Always know your surroundings," she murmured. "First rule of any operation."

The casual way she studied every corner told him everything. Hyde was already casing the building.

Chapter 22

SKUNK WORKS DESIGN FACILITY

5 Days Remaining

23:45

Olson flinched as the dumpster's rancid odor assaulted his senses. It was a nauseating blend of rotting food, wet paper, and chemical residue. The pungent odors were a jarring contrast to the sterile environment inside the Skunk Works facility.

His boots clanged against the rusted metal sides, the hollow sound bouncing off the narrow alleyway walls. A lamppost flickered, its sputtering light casting a yellow glow. John, clad in tight-fitting black camouflage, melted into the darkness. Penlight in hand, he scrutinized everything. Scrawled equations. Jotted notes. Heaps of discarded debris. Grime coated his hands as he rummaged.

An hour lapsed without success, each scrap another disappointment. As exhaustion seeped into his bones, he exited. The edge scraped hard against his side as he hauled himself over. The brisk air hit his face, a welcome relief from the stench. Olson took a moment to collect himself, fatigue weighing on him.

Standing vigil by the alley's rear entrance, Andrea was alert despite the late hour. John noticed the dark circles under her eyes. Her gaze shifted to him as he landed, her lips pausing at his disheveled appearance.

"Most would've given up by now."

"You're still here," John observed. The set of her jaw reminded him it was personal for her. This wasn't a woman who would wait for a man to fix her problems.

"Someone's threatening my life's work. I can't just watch."

Olson brushed past her, the rotten scent trailing in his wake. "Dedication is one of my virtues, Dr. Miles."

John questioned whether this relentless pursuit was devotion or penance. Either way, he stood knee-deep in garbage, grasping at straws.

"That's not dedication; it's obsession. And I thought engineers were bad."

He chuckled. Her words held an undertone of respect. Both of them had worked nonstop for the past two days. He expected her to quit after the first afternoon. Yet here she was.

Olson added, "Obsession is what it takes."

Andrea remained close despite his aroma. "Dumpster diving? That something you do often?"

"More than I'd like to admit. Unfortunately, standard protocol and two solid days of interviews haven't gotten us anywhere."

"Where to next?"

Olson pointed to another nearby alley. "Up. Best place to observe."

They approached an old fire escape, its metal rungs cool and gritty against his hands. John offered Andrea a hand as she began her ascent and was surprised when she accepted it with an appreciative nod.

As they climbed, the sprawling Skunk Works facility revealed itself. Several low-slung buildings, their concrete walls weathered by winds and salt air, stretched out before them. Sodium vapor lamps cast an eerie orange glow over the compound, creating pockets of deep shadow.

John's scrutiny swept over the perimeter. A chain-link fence bristling with barbed wire encircled the complex. Guard stations punctuated the barrier at regular intervals, while a prominent security checkpoint marked the main gate.

As they reached the top of the fire escape, Olson gave it another review.

"This place is huge," he whispered.

"It's like a small town," she murmured. "A city of science and secrecy."

The metal platform creaked as John settled, the cold steel seeping through his clothes. He unhooked his spyglass from his belt and placed it within arm's reach against the railing.

His eyes swept the horizon. Here, a flood of light; there, pockets of darkness. The facility's security lights created a patchwork. He scrutinized every potential vulnerability, imagining how someone could exploit them.

Andrea settled in beside him. Together, they watched in silence as night shift workers filed in and out of the main entrance. The occasional crackle of a radio from a roving guard broke the evening's tranquility.

"I really expected a lead by now." Olson rubbed his tired eyes.

"Just dead ends, one after another." Andrea's shoulders slumped. "When Hyde said she was a thief, I thought you were joking. But seeing her work, I get it. She uncovers in seconds what I've missed for years."

He tracked a guard's movement below. "She spots what others miss. Knockoff shoes revealing affairs, secret fishing boats…"

"The cabaret-dancing secretary," Andrea finished. She leaned forward, pointing toward the main gate. "Activity there."

John followed her gesture.

"Where do you think she is now?" Her breath was visible in the cool night air.

"I don't know."

Keeping tabs on Hyde would require an entire team. Even then, they'd likely fail. She'd worn him down, chipping away at his reservations.

The interviews confirmed her uncanny ability to slice through deception. John couldn't deny her value, though it came at a cost to his sanity. Fortunately, the FBI had kept its word and their distance.

Olson had made a calculated compromise: Hyde would work alongside him during the day, but roam free at night. It was a decision that would have been unthinkable a few days earlier. He'd learned to move with the tide rather than drown opposing it.

"I had to give her room to operate," Olson responded. "I prefer the present company."

"Speak for yourself. I'm not the one wearing Dumpster du jour," she teased.

Dr. Miles deflected with ease, a skill likely honed from years within male-dominated engineering rooms where personal remarks often had ulterior motives.

Movement caught his attention. He reached for his spyglass, Andrea's fingers grazing his. The unexpected touch sent a jolt through him.

"Sorry," she whispered, tucking a strand of hair behind her ear.

"No harm done," he replied.

He took up the telescope again, focusing on a distant shadowy rooftop. It appeared empty. But his intuition said otherwise.

"What is it?"

John adjusted the spyglass. "Nothing."

He couldn't let go of the feeling that someone was there. Meanwhile, Andrea folded her arms, shifting closer to him on the narrow platform.

"You may think I'm just an engineer, but I get what drives people. Most CIA would be terrified of Hyde. She's unconventional." She stared at him. "The way you trust her says a lot about you."

John kept his focus on the telescope, aware of her gaze. "I suppose."

A lull settled between them. The desert chill had set in, raising goosebumps on John's forearms. Then a flicker caught his eye. He stilled, concentrating on the area with the telescope until an indistinct form solidified into a silhouette.

The figure moved with feline grace. It had to be Hyde. She was surveying the same patch of ground. But what was she looking for?

Olson's breath hitched as he lowered the spyglass. He hadn't anticipated Gabrielle mirroring his own tactics. What was her plan?

It didn't make sense for her to be following him. That wasn't her style. She was a planner, always building layers of deception. And it was impossible for her to see him from her vantage point. So what was her angle?

He should report this to Durbin and the White House. But it wouldn't serve a purpose. Hyde was preparing, but she didn't realize he was watching. He finally had the upper hand.

She couldn't know. No one could.

Andrea followed his line of sight, but saw only the night. She turned to him, waiting for him to share his discovery.

John hesitated before placing the spyglass back into his pocket. "It's nothing," he lied. "Just shadows. All clear." He offered no further explanation.

She let it go, resuming their previous topic. "So, you agree then? Hyde might find what we're looking for? I mean, fight fire with fire, right?"

He released a soft sigh. "That's what my boss said." He met her face in the half-light. "She's a force I can't predict or control. Maybe someday I'll figure her out."

Olson rubbed his chin, the stubble grazing his palm. The irony that his future rested on a criminal's whims grated on him. He couldn't do anything about it.

"Time to call it a night," he announced.

He began the descent down the fire escape. Each step met with a hollow clang, the sound ringing through the alley. The metal rails had collected moisture from the evening.

The moment his soles struck the unyielding pavement, a surge of weariness cascaded through him. Andrea soon joined him, her landing punctuated by a soft sigh. He noticed the redness in her eyes and the slight slump of her shoulders.

Andrea stifled a yawn. "More tomorrow?"

John nodded, suddenly reluctant to leave. "Yeah, last day of formal interviews."

"Yay," Andrea said in a monotone voice.

"Okay, well." John glanced at his watch. "See you, Dr. Miles."

"For the fifth time, Andrea," she responded with exasperation. "We've been through dumpster diving together. I think we're past formalities."

"Sorry. Yeah. Good night… Andrea." Her name felt different somehow. John wandered to the car with a stiff, weary gait. He resisted the urge to look at her receding silhouette.

His thoughts drifted back to where he knew Gabrielle still scouted. What had she seen from up there? What pieces was she moving on her personal chessboard?

Tomorrow's final interviews were critical. Time was a luxury they no longer had. It was their last chance to uncover the truth before they hit a wall.

Hyde seemed to be the only one with a plan. Knowing her, it was likely something ingenious and radical. Most certainly unethical.

As he climbed into his car, a realization crystallized: the line between his methods and Hyde's was blurring. He knew he'd get roped into her schemes, willingly or not.

The thought terrified him. Would he choose results over rules? Worse, he wondered if it made him any different from Morozov.

Chapter 23

BURBANK CREDIT UNION

5 Days Remaining

21:03

Simmons leaned against the paneling of the security guard lounge, staring at the seasoned trio before him. Dim lights cast a green hue over the room. The scent of burned coffee mingled with cold air blasting from the ceiling vents. His first night posing as a security guard at the Burbank Credit Union was underway, and it required him to foster camaraderie with the swing shift veterans.

Clad in a standard-issue uniform, Simmons shifted uncomfortably. The coarse polyester, frayed from countless washes, chafed. Tugging at his ill-fitting collar, Simmons scowled at the previous owner's lingering body odor.

Benson, his new boss, topped six foot three with a bulky frame that made the chair groan in protest beneath his mass. From under bushy salt-and-pepper eyebrows, small dark eyes sized up the newcomer. His skepticism of Simmons' long hair matched the severe creases of his worn uniform.

Douglas learned the other two guards' names were Rick and Luis, and they hovered in Benson's orbit. He had to get these guys on his side, quickly.

Simmons pulled a slim bottle of twelve-year-old Scotch from the inner lining of his jacket, brandishing it before the dubious guards. The same trick had worked on the Nicaraguan border patrol. Hopefully, these three were less rambunctious.

"Little something to help the night go by," he said.

With a soft thud, he placed the bottle on the table. All attention shifted to Benson, whose persistent scowl threatened Simmons' fragile hold.

The supervisor considered the offering, his guarded expression lingering. He could see through the ploy, but would he take the bait? After what seemed like an eternity, he gave a noncommittal grunt that allowed him to accept the offer.

"You got taste." Benson's face lit up.

One hurdle down, but the night was still young. Douglas sweetened the pot by withdrawing a handful of cigars from another pocket.

"You can't have one without the other," he added.

Rick whistled as he plucked a smoke from Simmons' hand. His rough fingers treated the cigar with surprising delicacy. "Nice touch," he said, with a hint of a seasoned smoker's rasp.

Luis followed suit. He rose with the slight stiffness of a man used to long hours, joints cracking as he approached. "Gracias."

Benson accepted both. "Let's see if this lives up to its label."

Uncapping the bottle, he poured Scotch into a coffee mug, swirled it, and took a deep drag. The aroma infused the room, and Benson's face softened. The other men joined in.

Simmons slid toward Luis's abandoned post at the bank of monitors while the others laughed. The vinyl creased under his weight as the hum of the displays filled his ears. He scanned each screen: the main floor where moonlight poured through tall windows; the hallways where shadows stretched; and finally, the one marked 'records room.'

In the small rectangle of surveillance footage, Jessica and Matheo moved slowly. Their blacked-out clothing rendered them nearly invisible while they pulled files, methodically building growing piles.

Taking advantage of Rick's deep laughter, Simmons slid his hand beneath the console. His fingers brushed over the wires, identifying each by touch. He located the target cable, grasped it gently, and with a twist of his wrist, felt the snap of the wire. A slight vibration traveled up his arm as the screen went blank.

Benson raised his glass high. "To the new guy."

Simmons lifted his own cup in salute.

"You know," Benson began between puffs, "most greenhorns come in here thinking they're hot stuff. But you…you get what it means to be part of a team."

Simmons inclined his head, acknowledging the compliment. He was in.

"And you brought good Scotch. Not that crap you drink, Luis," Rick chimed in.

"At least his cigars don't taste like rolled-up newspaper," Luis added, pushing his glasses upward with his middle finger directed at Rick.

Rick's booming laugh resonated while Luis's quiet chuckle barely carried over the buzzing monitors. Despite their differences, both men relaxed.

For the next three hours, breaking the rules made Simmons an immediate member of their club. As the night wore on, he settled into their banter, avoiding actual work with amusing stories while keeping them distracted from their duties.

The chime of midnight shattered the levity. Benson stirred, unfurling from his temporary throne. He grunted as he stretched, checking his undersized wristwatch. "Time for the perimeter check," he muttered.

Benson ambled toward the monitors. His gaze swept across the screens until it landed on the blank one. His fat finger lowered to the crude label, confirming the location.

The records room screen was dark.

Benson kneeled beside the console with a sigh. His fingers probed the underside, tracing the wire to its broken end.

"Damn maintenance, bunch of lazy bums."

He pulled a flashlight from his waistband and inspected the cable. Simmons bit his lip. He could splice the feed in under thirty seconds with two alligator clips and three inches of electrical tape.

Benson's unexpected diligence threw a wrench into the plan. "Likely wear and tear," Simmons suggested. "Things fall apart, just ask my ex-wife."

Benson grunted. "Gonna have to check it out."

"I can do it," Simmons offered, already half out of his chair.

"Let Benson do his thing, man. It's his ship," Rick snorted while Luis nodded in silent agreement.

Benson considered the offer. "I got this, newbie."

Simmons paused, noting their reverence. "Sure, but I can't leave the Boss hanging," he persisted, altering his style to match Benson's gruff authority.

Benson considered him for a moment. Luis and Rick leaned forward, their faces brimming with unspoken bets on the outcome.

With a grunt, Benson said, "Come on then. You can shadow me."

Simmons could tell it was a reluctant acquiescence. Veterans of this business rarely turned down backup when facing an unknown variable.

They moved through the building's corridors as Simmons fell into step behind Benson. Close enough to assist, but at a distance that allowed him space. Their quiet footsteps were the only sound besides the occasional creak.

Arriving at the door, Benson pulled a hefty keyring away from his belt, attached by a retractable silver wire. The metal keys jangled as he searched for the right one.

Cold sweat trickled down Simmons' neck. He wasn't sure if Jessica and Matheo had heard them approaching. "Hey, Benson," Simmons said, his voice intentionally loud, "you think this could be dangerous?"

Benson halted his key search, his dark eyes narrowed. "Keep it down," he growled. "No need to wake every rat in the building."

Simmons felt his cheeks flush. He had overplayed it. "Sorry, I'm just… what if there are robbers or something?"

A chuckle rolled out of Benson. "Robbers? In the records room? Pfft." He shook his head as he found the key. "Those idiots would be more interested in the vault if they had two brain cells to rub together. Papers don't fetch much on the street. You gotta lot to learn."

Benson turned the lock with a satisfying click and pushed the door open with his shoulder. The place was empty.

It appeared untouched. Row upon row of gunmetal gray file cabinets sat silent with drawers sealed tight. Cutting through the black, Benson's flashlight swept its beam across the space.

"Guess it was nothing after all," Simmons said, forcing a smile.

Benson directed the light into each corner. "Seems like it," he agreed, giving Simmons a concussive pat on the shoulder.

While the senior guard focused on relocking, Douglas glanced down the hallway. At the end, behind a large ficus, two figures hid in the shadows. He held his hand down in a fist, signaling them to stay put.

"Benson," Simmons said, "mind if I step out for a quick smoke break? All this… excitement's got me antsy."

Benson regarded him, then nodded once while pocketing the keyring. "Do it on the back loading dock," he ordered. "No smoking in the customer areas."

"You bet."

Benson produced a small brass key. "You've got five minutes. Don't dawdle. I'll finish up here." He tossed the key.

Simmons caught it and flashed a reassuring smile. "Tops," he promised.

With one last glance at Benson, who had already resumed his circuit with methodical precision. Simmons turned and headed down the corridor.

Rounding the corner, he jumped at the sight of two people waiting by the rear entrance. His legs trembled with relief, a rush of warmth flooding his chest. He allowed himself one shudder, his breath escaping in a silent whistle.

He used Benson's key to slip outside. The temperature drop raised goosebumps along his arms as exhaust fumes met his nostrils. He leaned against a rough concrete wall as he pulled out a pack of Ducados stashed away for moments like this.

The lighter's flame flickered and caught, casting an orange hue on his face. He exhaled a cloud of smoke, watching it dissipate. He looked down at the cigarette, wishing it was one of his hand-rolled clove ones instead of the Spanish brand that served for quick fixes.

Jessica emerged from the shadows, her keen eyes scanning the dark alley. Matheo followed close behind, his compact frame tense, a thin sheen of sweat on his forehead as he clutched his stack of folders.

Douglas took a final drag from his cigarette before flicking it away, the embers flashing upon contact. "Anything worth finding?"

Jessica shook her head. "Some tax fraud, a few financial discrepancies. Petty stuff. Nothing obvious. But at least we have our volunteers."

Matheo's expression mirrored hers. "Appears Gabrielle was right again."

Simmons nodded. Hyde had an irritating talent for being correct. Breaking into a bank for records rather than money wasn't his idea of a great Thursday night. Still, Hyde insisted these files were crucial for tomorrow's event.

He wished she were here, but she was busy working on "contingencies." Years ago, he'd learned to stop asking. With less than twenty hours until the gala and the party crasher's flight landing at four, the margin for error was shrinking.

Glancing up at the partial moon, he sighed. "Waxing gibbous. Should've known… need to be flexible and open-minded. On to Plan B at the Ball then?"

A distant sound caught his attention. Footsteps on tile. Simmons' instincts told him time was short. "You gotta go."

Jessica and Matheo needed no further prompting. Moving in silence, they melted into the night.

Simmons turned back toward the bank, sensing someone's presence. Benson's hulking form waited in the starkly lit doorway.

"You talking to someone?" Benson's voice was deep and gruff.

Simmons' pulse quickened, but his expression remained neutral. "Just myself," he replied, forcing an uneasy chuckle. "Happens when you spend too much time alone at night."

He braced himself for a bad reaction, fearing the admission might be excessive. Simmons leaned into his meditation routine, exuding a relaxed vibe. However, he was ready to bolt if the large man made a move.

Fighting that giant was a losing proposition.

Benson stared at him for another heartbeat before his features softened. "You're not alone," he said. "We're all a little weird round here."

The guard motioned toward the lounge with a jerk of his head. "Let's finish that Scotch before the morning crew shows."

Simmons' shoulders dropped as he followed his boss back inside. He glanced out the window and saw Jessica's car glide past streetlights and disappear around the corner.

Locking the door behind him, Simmons rejoined the other guards to wrap up his first and last unconventional night at the Burbank Credit Union.

The security detail would soon forget Douglas as an average face passing through their mundane routine. But for Hyde's team, this operation was just a warmup. Tomorrow was when things got crazy.

Simmons stifled a wry smile. He loved this kind of thing.

Chapter 24

SKUNK WORKS DESIGN FACILITY

4 Days Remaining

13:29

Olson sat in the metal chair, its icy surface seeping through his suit. The harsh light cast forbidding shadows across his face, revealing deep lines of fatigue. Andrea tapped her bitten nails nervously on the table.

Hyde lounged at the room's edge, her hawk-like eyes watching as Dr. Lyle Bishop slouched at the desk. He was the latest subject of Olson's relentless questioning.

"Do you have any foreign connections?" John asked, taking notes at every movement.

"Have you ever plotted to commit a crime?"

John fired off questions: "Any overseas financial holdings? Ever been employed by a foreign nation? Have you committed treason?" Each built on the last.

Olson leaned in, shrinking the space between them. "Have you recently traveled outside the United States?"

Bishop's hand trembled as he fidgeted with his wedding ring. Olson caught the movement. Classic deception.

"Only Canada."

"Why Canada?"

"Dr. Miles, what's this about?" Lyle's voice cracked. "I've worked here for fifteen years. I'm a loyal American."

Bishop looked pleadingly at Andrea, his eyes desperate. She started to speak, but averted her gaze.

"Doctor, I'm asking the questions here. What are you hiding?"

His lip quivered.

"Enough of this rubbish, John. Dr. Bishop's wife is ill." Hyde stood unexpectedly. "Terminal cancer, most likely," she added gently.

Gabrielle pointed at the man. "The constant fidgeting with his ring. Quintessential anxiety and guilt. And those bags under his eyes are worse than Olson's." She approached the table for the first time in days. "That discoloration on his left sleeve. Cancer medications often leave this specific greenish hue. Cheaper in Canada. Probably all he can afford on a government paycheck."

Hyde peered at him sadly. "The treatment she needs isn't approved here, is it?"

"The FDA won't approve it for another two years." Bishop wiped away tears. "In Canada, she could start immediately."

John closed his notepad. He had failed to uncover what Hyde had intuited from a fidget and stained shirt. Dr. Bishop was desperate, but not a spy.

"You can go," Olson said.

As Bishop hurried from the room, John turned to Hyde. "How did you know?"

She smoothed the sleeves of her blouse, a gesture John recognized as her way of regaining composure. This wasn't her usual clinically detached observation.

"Terrible disease, cancer. But there is quite an international black market. I've dabbled. I'm sure I could find a better source for his wife." Her voice held a touch of empathy that felt strangely genuine.

Olson scratched the name off his list. "Who's next?"

"He was the last one," Andrea replied.

They'd reached the end, revealing nothing but dead ends and personal lives laid bare. He noticed the disappointment in Andrea's eyes. The chair screeched as John stood. He strode to the window, peering into the darkened hallway.

Hyde pushed off from the wall as she approached. "You're thorough; I'll give you that."

Olson watched their reflections meld together on the glass. "This needs a fresh perspective," he declared. "We need to start over."

"That would be counterproductive," she said dismissively.

John's instincts screamed they were close. Yet the evidence, or lack thereof, contradicted him. He was certain they covered every detail. "We're missing something. What do you recommend?"

Hyde cast a glance at her watch, a sleek antique piece. "You should walk the space, consider alternative concepts. Meanwhile, I shall explore my track," she announced.

"You have a lead?"

"No." Gabrielle slid a folder into her bag. "A personal appointment. And I cannot be late."

"With whom?" John pressed.

Hyde folded her arms defensively. "It's private for a reason. Some threads of this investigation are best left obscured. You're better off not knowing everything."

Her typical spark of excitement was conspicuously absent. John had never seen Gabrielle reluctant to pursue a lead. It was disturbing. What could make Hyde uncomfortable?

John returned to the table and stared at the files. It was maddening working with someone who operated this way. Andrea placed a supportive hand on Olson's arm. He caught her eye and regained his composure.

"Why should I let you go?" John asked. "We have nothing. No information. No leads. Absolutely bupkis."

Gabrielle paused with a hand on her hip, her silhouette framed against the hallway's dim light.

"Tell me something I don't already know," he challenged, "and free time is all yours."

Hyde locked eyes with him. "You've been misled. The stolen data did not come from within Skunk Works. It's a ruse."

Olson's jaw dropped. "That's impossible. We were explicitly told…"

"Improbable as it seems, the truth remains the truth," she responded. "I have a source who can confirm this. Someone who may reveal what's happening."

"Who?" John demanded.

"Someone who knows the real story. That's all I'll say for now." She moved toward the door. "You need to trust me."

"I do. But…"

"Then it's settled." She crossed the threshold. "Occam's razor also cuts. Sometimes deeply. Good day."

The room seemed to tilt. Durbin and Avery had insisted it was an inside job. But if Gabrielle was right, who was lying to them? The FBI? But then what was their endgame?

Hyde was almost never wrong on these kinds of issues. Was it possible the stolen data never originated from Skunk Works? That was the simplest answer. But if that was true, then someone was working against them.

As he looked back up, he found nothing but an empty doorway. He hated Hyde's penchant for issuing a proclamation and then disappearing. She should have waited for his approval.

Frustration whirled.

Andrea touched his shoulder. He looked up, meeting her sympathetic smile, feeling the anguish recede. "John," she said, "I know this isn't going how you wanted, but I have something to show you."

With a sigh, he rose from his chair. "Okay. Lead the way."

Andrea took his hand and led him down a route he'd been before. They navigated the twisting halls until they reached a security vestibule. The guard glanced at John and then at Andrea. Without hesitation, he retrieved an orange badge on a Skunk Works lanyard from a drawer.

"Dr. Miles, as you requested," he said with a respectful nod.

Andrea approached Olson with the credentials in hand.

"How did you secure this?" John asked.

"Nevermind that. Now you're all official. And significantly faster than a year." With a sly smile, she draped it over his head and snapped it into place. Her fingers brushed against his neck while adjusting the strap.

"Thank you."

Irrational irritation grew as John looked at the badge. It was too late for such access to help the investigation. Andrea had obviously pulled several high-level strings to secure this for him. He noticed her hands still lingered, fixing his collar longer than necessary.

He took an involuntary step back, reestablishing the professional distance. But there was no hiding the light pink that now colored his cheeks. He needed to remain focused, though he had formed an undeniable attachment to her in just a few short days.

"I want to show you something else," she said. "Just as important."

Curiosity piqued, John followed her through a series of corridors. They ascended a metal staircase, emerging onto a catwalk suspended seventy feet in the air. The platform offered a panoramic view of the sprawling main testing space, the heart of Skunk Works.

Below, the hum of industry buzzed. Engineers hunched over blueprints, their pencils scratching furiously. Technicians weaved through a maze of workbenches. Half-assembled engines resembled metallic sculptures. Fiery sparks danced from the end of an acetylene welding torch.

John took in the living system. Everyone scurried about like ants executing their respective tasks. It was both impressive and daunting.

"Initially, I focused on finding the individual who did this," Andrea began. "But somewhere along the way, I hoped we would fail. It's not personal. Someone stole that data. But I couldn't accept that one of my people did it."

Olson watched silently.

"If a person I trusted did that..." Andrea swallowed hard. "That betrayal. I don't know how I'd handle it." She looked below. "My team would never compromise our mission or each other."

The intensity of her speech struck John. Her eyes shone as she spoke about her colleagues. It wasn't just a job. This place. These scientists. They were her family.

"The personal issues we uncovered during interviews were merely that. Personal. Not one person down there would deliberately hurt this country."

John watched a technician calibrate a piece of equipment. It seemed innocent.

"This is more than just a job; it's a calling," she added. "My calling. It's who we are."

John stood next to her. "I want to believe that. But my job requires that I question everything, regardless of intent. It's a burden that comes with intelligence work." He shrugged. "It all points here."

"Forget the evidence for a second, John. Look deeper." Her eyes narrowed. "What makes you think someone could beat this security? Who could do that?"

"Hyde could," he admitted. "She thrives on the impossible."

Andrea's expression softened as she considered his words. "But we're not talking about her. These are regular scientists, real people. Even the notorious Gabrielle has limits," she countered. "You caught her once, which means you're smart enough to figure this out."

Olson bit his lip. He had not revealed his absence from Hyde's actual capture. It was an omission, not a lie. He was a failure. A fraud. Just ask Nate.

Despite his attempt to push it back, the thought hit him hard. A tear traced down his cheek. With a subtle swipe, he dashed the moisture before it betrayed him.

Andrea moved closer, now touching at the hip. "You okay?"

He mustered a half-smile. "I'm fine."

She rubbed his back with a light touch. "No, you're not. You've been dealing with something since the day we met. I've seen it before." She bumped him with her hip. "Remember, you promised to be open."

He couldn't lie anymore.

John's voice faltered, the words burning his throat like hot sand. As he confided in Andrea about Nate, the knot in his shoulders unwound. The story spilled out, a torrent of suppressed grief and guilt. He shared the ill-fated mission in Africa. He wasn't authorized to share the facts, but he didn't care.

"Nate was barely twenty-five," John said. "Wore these ridiculous gold aviator glasses, even during night ops." His voice cracked. "Morozov put two bullets in his chest."

Andrea remained silent.

John pushed away another tear. "I owe him," he concluded, his breath coming in shallow pulls. "And I've failed him at every turn."

The relief of sharing caught him off guard. John suddenly felt lighter. But it was too much, too fast. He wouldn't blame Andrea for walking away.

Andrea's eyes glistened as she studied him. She reached out, her hand hovering momentarily before settling. "I had no idea. I'm so sorry about your friend."

John searched for pity or judgment in her expression. He found neither. His gaze settled back on the workers below. They stood together, silence falling between them.

"Thank you for trusting me," she said.

The words were a knife. He wanted to tell her the rest. About the danger to her program. He turned, ready to betray his oath.

"We'll just have to figure out another angle," she added, cutting off his confession. "It's what engineers do."

John felt Andrea squeeze his hand, and he marveled at her resilience. Despite the setbacks, she refused to give up. He couldn't destroy her in this moment. Scientists might thrive on solving puzzles with tangible pieces, but spies? Spies dealt with the intangible. Their universe was built on deception.

Spies lie. He had lied to Andrea several times, justifying his actions with moralistic reasoning. Gabrielle was right. He was no different from Hyde.

Once upon a time, he was the CIA boy genius. John thought that facing Hyde had ruined his life. But it wasn't true. Everything that happened resulted from his choices.

It was his fault, not hers.

Ironically, Hyde may be the only person in the world who always told him the truth.

Every instinct screamed against putting faith in her. Unpredictable. Unorthodox. Morally ambiguous. He'd fought so hard to resist, he never considered that maybe Gabrielle was the answer.

"Andrea," John began. "I need to be more open."

She smiled. "That's the spirit."

He took a deep breath. "I'll start... by trusting Hyde."

Chapter 25

OXNARD MUNICIPAL AIRPORT

4 Days Remaining

15:30

The limousine cruised onto Oxnard Municipal Airport's deserted airfield. Matheo's cautious driving was at odds with Gabrielle's preference. The engine's soft hum was too tranquil for the moment.

Seven years ago, the Air Force abandoned this property, surrendering its World War II-era base to the city. They neglected it. Cracks spread across the tarmac, and the yellow lines faded. Now it served as a convenient location for meetings.

She felt a kinship with this desolate stretch, a remnant still bearing the scars of its past. Nature had reclaimed the edges, persistent weeds forcing through. Rebirth was not an overnight endeavor, but a battle of wills.

"He is here," Matheo said.

Her attention snapped to the silhouette of a Super King Air 200. She inhaled sharply, dread coursing through her. A single concern preoccupied her mind: Olson must remain unaware.

"Not a moment too soon." Gabrielle stretched her neck to relieve the strain.

Matheo cut the engine. "I believe in your vision, but this…" Rare worry lines creased his jawline. "This measure is extreme, even for us. I don't like it. Or him. *J'ai un mauvais pressentiment.*"

Hyde watched the approaching plane, knowing that Castille's judgment had never led her astray. Gabrielle's survival had always hinged on her sixth sense. Its current silence vexed her.

"Any issues with the flight plan? Or with evading the FAA's tracking?"

"None," Matheo assured. "Routed through three different countries and changed tail numbers twice. The paint probably isn't even dry." Satisfaction gleamed in his eyes. "Invisible and untraceable."

The invasive growl of propellers carved the air as Hyde stepped from the car. The scent of tar and exhaust filled her nostrils. She stood her ground as the airplane lumbered closer, its engines winding to a stop.

The aircraft door folded down, and two armed men appeared. Their boots clunked as they scanned the area, hands hovering over weapons.

Sasha Morozov emerged. His polished shoes gleamed, but the temperature seemed to drop as he set foot on California soil. His presence radiated danger.

Hyde stood motionless, her dress rippling in the breeze. Behind dark sunglasses, her eyes tracked Morozov. Cataloging details. The bulge of a shoulder holster. Mangled ear. That deep scar bisecting his eyebrow. She steadied her fingers, grateful for the concealment her glasses provided.

These reactions couldn't be trained away, only hidden.

"Welcome," she greeted.

Morozov advanced with swift, imposing steps. His cold eyes locked with hers, and an exiled feeling of helplessness surfaced. She admonished herself. He no longer wielded that same power. She was his equal.

No, she was his superior. He just didn't know it yet.

As he closed the distance, she wondered what would happen if she killed him right now. She had broken his nose once. Today, she could rid the world of this blight.

Not now, she told herself. Not like this. She knew what she had to do.

He extended his arms, his embrace a deathtrap disguised as warmth. To an outsider, they might seem like old friends. Hyde's smile never faltered. She mirrored his gesture, faces brushing in the practiced European manner.

"Gabrielle." His Russian accent hardened. "Years pass. You remain… unchanged."

She exited the greeting with fluid grace. "Good to see you as well, Sasha."

Morozov glanced at the plane. "Thank you for helping me avoid… complications."

"Everything is covered. No one is aware of your presence."

She gestured toward the vehicle, where Matheo waited. Hyde opened the door and offered Morozov first entry.

"Do you have what I need?" he asked.

"Be patient."

"Time is short. Others are interested. I must have it."

"I've never disappointed you, and I won't start today," she replied.

A grin flickered across Morozov's features. The man was hard to read, as are all psychopaths. His seemingly genuine smile could be amusement, or a prelude to lethal action. Without another word, he dipped into the limousine.

Hyde frowned, scanning the taxiway.

Her intuition screamed warnings about the location. Helping the Soviet enter Los Angeles during this current operation was inadvisable. Unfortunately, he left her no choice. The man had the subtlety of a sledgehammer.

A salty afternoon breeze blew from Mandalay State Beach, washing across her face. The air tasted of freedom and possibility. She inhaled deeply, savoring the simplicity others took for granted. She would adore a stroll through the city's historic Victorian-era architecture, but that was a pleasure for another lifetime.

A fleeting flash of light caught her attention, but it vanished into the untended vegetation. She cursed, realizing she should have insisted on a nighttime arrival. Discretion was crucial to her plan.

If it were a rifle scope, then they had already missed their opportunity. She slipped inside the limousine. They needed to leave.

"How long?" Morozov demanded.

Hyde offered a smile. "All in due time, my friend. Impatience is a tool employed by amateurs. This endeavor is still developing."

All the warmth disappeared. "I have no tolerance for delay."

This was unlike Sasha. He had suddenly reappeared. Now, he was acting impetuously. Something, or someone, had him rattled. Morozov cracked a knuckle against his cheekbone. She recognized this long-standing habit, a tell of underlying stress.

He didn't bother to look at her. "Find me results. Or I will make them."

Chapter 26

SKUNK WORKS DESIGN FACILITY

4 Days Remaining

15:40

Secrecy clung to the walls of Skunk Works. As John trailed behind Dr. Miles through the administrative section, the tension in his shoulders tightened. Four days. That's all they had before the President's ultimatum took effect. No one here was aware, but they could sense something was wrong.

Employees hunched over their desks, eyes darting. While Andrea might have been able to ignore the lingering stares, Olson felt them acutely. Word of the interrogations had spread, and more destructive rumors would follow.

They halted at a worn desk, its surface barely visible beneath a chaotic skyline of papers. A simple nameplate reading 'MILES' peeked out from behind a precarious stack.

Andrea's cheeks flushed. "Sorry about the mess."

John suppressed a laugh. "Einstein once said, 'If a cluttered desk is a sign of a cluttered mind, of what, then, is an empty desk a sign?'"

Andrea tucked a strand of hair. "Didn't take you for a man who'd quote Einstein."

He shrugged. "Hyde seems to think I'm not as straightforward as I appear.

Perhaps there's some truth there."

The mention of Gabrielle made John glance at his watch. Time was slipping away, and Hyde's mysterious appointment may be their only lifeline now. They needed a breakthrough, not distractions. Hopefully, she could deliver.

A man approached them with an unhurried gait. Dr. Grant Wheeler exuded seasoned wisdom. Silver threaded through his beard and the ring of hair circling his bald head. Subtle lines etched a face that had spent decades over blueprints. The scent of pipe tobacco clung to his clothes.

"Andrea," Grant said, looking at her station. "You've got to stop stealing my thunder. My desk was the reigning champion of creative disarray until you came along."

"I'm just trying to keep up with you, Grant," she replied. "Not everyone can redefine Bernoulli's principle on a Tuesday morning."

Grant's presence tempered Andrea's usual guarded poise. Camaraderie resonated in their shared laugh, speaking volumes. "And you must be the famous Olson," he said, extending his hand.

"In the flesh. Not sure about famous."

Grant eyed John's orange badge. The doctor let a smile emerge upon reaching a silent conclusion. The man was sharp. Everything about John screamed CIA, but Wheeler ignored it.

"Dr. Wheeler is our resident genius with aerodynamics," Andrea interjected.

"Resident old-timer is more like it," Grant corrected. "How goes the rest of the security review?"

She glanced at the large project board. "Almost done, barring any stumbling blocks. With luck, I'll be back to the heat dispersion problems in the third-stage compressors after Monday. Those J85 engines are still giving me fits."

Guilt twisted in John's chest. They had days to uncover concrete evidence for the President, or their program would be shut down. Grant would be packing boxes instead of solving intricate puzzles.

"Ah, entropy; it just isn't what it used to be." Grant laughed at his own joke. "Speaking of the weekend, are you planning on attending the party tonight? I was about to head out and get ready."

A stiffening of Andrea's posture caught John's attention. She shuffled papers on her desk, feigning a search. "Oh, the gala..." she mumbled. "I'm not sure I'll make it. There's so much to do."

Grant interrupted her with a firm voice. "Andrea, you've been working late for weeks now. You deserve a break. We all do."

She let out a breath, avoiding Grant's gaze. "I know, but these engines won't fix themselves."

Grant's eyes twinkled with grandfatherly compassion. "We all know you're the heart of this project, but even you need a break. You can't solve the world's problems in one day."

John recalled the nights he'd seen Andrea working long after everyone else had left. Her timesheets confirmed it, and Grant's worried words were born of experience. He recognized her drive because it mirrored his own.

Grant clearly wanted something better for her. "Take the night off. Bring your friend, it'll be fun."

She offered a noncommittal hum. There was more than dedication behind Andrea's deflecting behavior. John wondered if the problem was constantly needing to prove herself.

The culprit had to be the party. It served as a dark mirror to Andrea's professional life. In the lab, her brilliance spoke for itself. At parties, whispers most assuredly followed her. Judgments about her nontraditional career and marital status. Mostly from other women.

Grant seemed to sense it too, but chose not to push further. His pat on Andrea's shoulder emphasized their longstanding camaraderie. "I'll see you two bright and early on Monday," Grant said as he made his way toward the exit. "Don't forget to have at least some fun!"

As Dr. Wheeler's footsteps faded down the corridor, Andrea offered a weak smile. "Parties aren't really my scene."

John observed a vulnerability he hadn't witnessed before. While he'd always seen her as the tough, efficient professional partner he desired, something had shifted. Andrea stirred an emotion deep inside him that caused him to want to let go.

"Don't look at me like that," she snapped.

John stiffened. "Like what?"

"Like you're trying to figure me out."

"I'm not," he said, passing a hand through his hair. "I was thinking that I don't know anything about you. Not really. Outside of work, that is." John scuffed his feet. "Forget it. Sorry."

She shifted. "Well, uh, I recently adopted a cat," she stammered.

The response was so endearingly Andrea, that John couldn't help but laugh. It was a genuine reaction that felt foreign to his CIA life. The shared humor eased the lingering awkwardness.

"What about this party tonight?" Olson asked. "What's it for?"

"Oh. Nothing. Just the annual corporate event to thank the employees here for their work."

"Sounds like more than nothing." John rubbed his jaw. "Who attends?"

"Everyone important. Engineers, scientists, administrative staff, managers. Senior executives too." She glanced away. "I've never had a good reason to attend."

Olson caught the unspoken truth. Social gatherings transformed her from "Dr. Miles" to "the woman at work." She knew the event mattered, but parties demanded a performance she had no interest in giving.

John shrugged. "Maybe you should go."

"Me? At the party?"

"Yeah. Why not? You belong there." A bizarre curiosity compelled him to understand her beyond her role as Dr. Miles. "I could go with you."

The spontaneous invitation caught him off guard. He hated parties, the tiny plates, small talk, and most of all, the crowds. He was constantly on edge. Still, he was excited about the idea of going with Andrea.

Her composure faltered. "You would do that?"

John adjusted his tie mechanically. "Sure. I mean, think about all those people. Every division head, engineer with access, and executive—all in one room. This might be our best shot. It's a goldmine for vetting," he rationalized.

The words were out before he could consider their implications. Part of him recognized the tactical merit of attending. However, the real draw was Andrea.

Something else nagged at him. Hyde surely knew about the party. Was that the reason she disappeared this afternoon? Interviews weren't her style, but this event would be her preferred hunting ground. And he'd nearly missed it.

"Okay," Andrea said after a delay. "I suppose it could be useful."

"Great. I'll pick you up at eight."

Realization of their plans seemed to settle on her. "Eight o'clock," she repeated.

As she jotted down her address, John thought about the ticking clock. Time was running out for both of them.

Olson turned and left, carrying his burden of secrets. His only hope for salvation was a party he'd never planned to attend.

Chapter 27

LOS ANGELES WAREHOUSE DISTRICT

4 Days Remaining

17:25

The warehouse base hummed with activity. Matheo's iron sent billows of steam rising from the uniforms he pressed. The hiss punctuated the clinks of Simmons threading CO_2 canisters into copper pipes.

Olson ran his fingers over his black suit. The worn material rustled under his fingertips as he studied his reflection in the warped mirror. The man staring back was both familiar and increasingly foreign.

His wardrobe contained nothing beyond his everyday CIA attire. Andrea wouldn't care.

A pair of arms slid around him from behind, a soft giggle warming his ear. Jessica pressed close, her embrace flirtatious. "Oh, honey, you've got that 'impress the lady' look."

"It's called professionalism, Jess," Olson countered. "Tonight is work, nothing more." He pulled at a sleeve.

Simmons stopped tinkering. "So says the man wearing a red aura."

John shot him a glare, but Douglas had already turned back to the canisters.

Jessica's head tilted. "When's the last time you went on a date?"

"It's been a while." The CIA left no room for intimate connections.

Relationships were distractions. "Attending the Skunk Works' party is fieldwork. Nothing more."

"*Il est un imbécile,*" Matheo scoffed.

Olson frowned. "Why do you say that?"

Gabrielle cleared her throat. Standing in the doorway, her opulent black dress clung to her curves, its elegant train whispering against the floor. The faded blue forget-me-not pin on her strap stood out. The embellishment was an enigma, like Hyde herself.

"Matheo thinks you're full of it, John. Should I disagree?" Hyde asked.

Olson's muscles tightened as he met her gaze. He trusted her candor. "How do I look? Be honest."

Circling, her scrutiny dissected every detail, from his polished leather oxfords to the set of his shoulders. She nodded once before turning to address her team.

"Matheo," she began, snapping twice. "Tonight, he's not CIA. I need him to be one of us. A gem in the rough."

A surprising warmth spread through him. This wasn't condescension. Hyde was including him. He was not deserting the Agency, he reminded himself. For success, he needed to blend in while making a lasting impression.

The team stopped working, all eyes fixed on Olson. He shifted, tugging at his cuffs under their collective gaze.

"What do you want, boss?" Jessica asked.

She waved her hand dismissively over his outfit. "Fix this."

Simmons winced, his face contorting as if he had bitten something sour. Matheo muttered a sharp French curse, his eyes narrowing before cracking his knuckles.

"You know what to do," Gabrielle said, departing for another work table piled with blueprints.

Though the collection of schematics piqued John's curiosity, he was aware of Hyde's team encircling him.

"What does she mean?"

"Don't worry, luv," Jessica purred. "This won't hurt."

Moving as one, the crew descended upon Olson like a pack of wolves.

"Stand still," Jessica ordered, her measuring tape snapping against his shoulders as she called out numbers.

Simmons rifled through a trunk of fabrics. "Too gauche… too pedestrian… ah, perfecto." He held up a midnight-blue material.

"I can dress myself," John protested.

"*Non,*" he replied flatly. "You cannot."

The next two hours passed as John endured their incursion, feeling as though he were a recruit in basic training instead of a seasoned CIA officer. By the time they finished, he grudgingly conceded their expertise.

He barely recognized the stranger in the mirror.

* * *

19:50

The sleek black limousine cut through the evening traffic, its tinted windows reflecting the city's neon glow. During the ride to Dr. Miles' apartment, John struggled to focus on the mission. Lights blurred past as his concentration wandered.

He caught his reflection, polished and refined. He wondered if his father would recognize him.

"Quite the transformation," Hyde observed from her position.

"Just playing the role," John replied, adjusting a cufflink.

"Are you?" she asked. "The officer I met in Toronto would sooner die than collaborate with thieves. Yet, here we are."

"This is different."

"Indeed." A smile crossed her lips. "And Dr. Miles? Is she part of your new view on life?"

"That's not relevant."

"Everything's relevant when the stakes are this high." The car came to a halt. "Time to collect our scientist."

Try as he might, John couldn't stop thinking of Andrea. He didn't know how it could ever really work, but that was a problem for later.

After climbing the stairs, John rapped on her apartment door. The hollow sound reverberated. He smoothed his custom tuxedo, fidgeting with the unfamiliar silkiness.

It was eight on the nose, just as promised.

The door swung open, and John's composure faltered. The glow from Andrea's apartment silhouetted her figure, the jewel-toned gown accentuating curves he'd consciously ignored. Her light brown hair, usually practical and pinned back, cascaded over her shoulders in gleaming curls.

John retreated a step. "Wow. You look… beautiful." Clearing his throat, he added, "I mean, you clean up nice, Dr. Miles."

A rosy flush warmed her cheeks. "Thank you," she said. "I never would've had the guts to buy this. And check you out, Mr. CIA. 007 would be jealous." Her laugh was musical.

John shook his head. "I'd like to take credit, but it was Hyde's team of super criminals. They're apparently also fashion experts. Who knew?"

Andrea laughed, stroking her gown once more. "People won't believe it's me," she murmured with a hint of self-consciousness.

"Yes, they will." He wanted to let her know she looked stunning. "This suits you."

Her eyes met his. "Thank you for sending the dress. You saved the day."

John's forehead creased. "The dress? It wasn't…"

"A problem at all. John insisted," Gabrielle said, cutting him off as she stepped forward. "I took the liberty of having it delivered. I hope you don't mind."

Andrea's smile faltered. "Oh, I see," she said. "It arrived with plenty of time. How you got the size so perfect is a genuine mystery."

"Officer Olson's understanding of fashion is without compare," Gabrielle replied, her tone dripping with sarcasm. "Don't dally now; we can't be late," she urged. "I have designs for this evening, and as always, timing is everything."

"Hyde never misses a trick." John's lips tightened. "She's even invited herself to the party and insists it's crucial to the mission."

"And what exactly does she have planned for this event… attended by all my supervisors?"

"Your guess is as good as mine. She's keeping this one a secret." He popped his fingers out from his head like an explosion. "I know, shocking, right?"

Hyde's crew used the day as cover for their preparations, leaving him in the dark. There were signs. Matheo's steaming. Simmons and his strange canisters. The mysterious boxes.

Andrea sighed, clicking the deadbolt. "Okay then." She tucked her elbow through Olson's arm. "Then, by all means, let's not be late."

Gabrielle moved immediately toward the stairs. John could hear the soft swish of fabric as Andrea's dress brushed against his leg. He felt his weapon sway, happy Matheo stitched in a secret compartment to accommodate his request.

He drew her arm tight. She leaned in, her breath tickling his ear. John fought the temptation to pull her closer.

"Seriously. Scale of one to ten, how worried should I be?"

"Around thirteen," he admitted. "But it'll be memorable. And probably less than legal."

"It's okay. It'll be fine. Nothing to worry about."

Olson contemplated his absurd situation. He was escorting a beautiful doctor to a party filled with the smartest scientists on Earth, where he would let an international thief have an unfiltered run at rooting out a Soviet mole before they could trigger World War III.

What could go wrong? The answer was simple: everything. From the inconvenient to the catastrophic, Gabrielle thrived on creating havoc.

John squeezed Andrea's hand. "Not at all worried."

Chapter 28

EXCELSIOR HOTEL

4 Days Remaining

20:40

The limousine coasted to a stop at the Excelsior Hotel, depositing John, Dr. Miles, and Gabrielle into the gathering crowd. Music and laughter greeted them as they ascended the steps to the grand ballroom.

A jazz quartet's music welcomed John as he entered the elaborate 1920s aviation-themed soiree. Overhead, biplanes and WWII fighter models swayed from wires. Aromas of roasted meats wafted through the air as waitstaff in crisp pilot and stewardess uniforms weaved through the crowd.

"This is incredible," Andrea said, her hand grasping John's.

Hyde leaned in. "Ready to uncover the truth?"

"Yes," Olson replied, "but we need to remain discreet."

"I blend unconventionally," Gabrielle responded.

They needed to find the wolf hiding among their ranks. John swept the sea of faces, a nagging feeling tugging, but he couldn't quite place it.

A man brushed past, causing Olson to double-take. Simmons, dressed as a server, slipped something into a guest's pocket. At two o'clock, he spotted Jessica. Her seasoned sleight of hand flashed gold as she "helped" a woman with her coat.

He spun to confront Gabrielle, but she had vanished.

"Hyde?" John said.

"Wasn't she just here?" Andrea asked, her eyes darting.

John expected her to act, but not without warning. His grip on Andrea's hand dropped as his concern grew. He turned back to the entrance, searching for her.

"What's she doing up there?" Andrea asked.

Olson followed her pointed finger to the stage. Applause rose from the throng of guests. Time seemed to stop as John watched Hyde ascend the platform.

"She can't be that crazy," he whispered. "She'll compromise everything."

Andrea grabbed his arm, holding him back. "It's too late," she said. Her nails dug into his skin.

He watched helplessly as Hyde grabbed a microphone, illuminated by a single spotlight. A glance up revealed Matheo dimming the house lights. It was a pattern. Extravagant theatrical diversions masking a deeper purpose. This was what made Hyde so dangerous.

"Good evening, ladies and gentlemen," she greeted the crowd.

A smattering of claps came in response. She took the meek reaction as a challenge. "Is that the best you've got?" she chided. "I said, good evening, Skunk Works!"

The room erupted with applause, giving her their focus. Now she could steal what they valued most.

"My name's Gabrielle Hyde, and some of you may recognize me from this week." She paused. "What I do is… oh, you almost caught me… it's a secret. But I assure, I'm the best in the world. Just like you."

Laughter bubbled up.

"But tonight," she continued, "I'm going to entertain you while I work. Is anyone interested in having a little fun?"

Cheers answered her.

Andrea patted his hand. "Trust her. It might be our only shot. Remember what you said."

Their discussion on the balcony came rushing back. He would be patient.

His resolve lasted three seconds; a new personal Hyde record.

"Tonight, we will identify dangerous international thieves," she announced. "But I can't do it alone. I'll need your help," Gabrielle instructed. "If I point at you, please come join me on stage."

Her finger darted through the guests, selecting unsuspecting people. A middle-aged man who was pushing 300 pounds. Another with slicked-back hair. A woman in an ornate dress. John looked at each in sequence. These weren't random.

Applause propelled them forward like an invisible hand.

Hyde's arm extended again, this time to the far end of the ballroom. "You."

The man she indicated pointed at someone else, trying to deflect attention.

"Not him. You, sir. Come on up."

The crowd's applause swelled, drowning out the man's protests. Andrea stood on her toes, gaining a clear line of sight on the last volunteer.

Her fingers dug into his arm. "You've got to be kidding."

"Let's give them another round of applause for being such good sports and taking part in our little game," Gabrielle added as they climbed onto the stage.

"What does she mean by game?" Andrea asked.

"I wish I knew," Olson said as Marion Johnston stepped into the spotlight.

CEO of Lockheed, he was not simply any participant in this charade. If Hyde humiliated or implicated Johnston, the whole operation would crumble.

"I... I can't. John, you've got to stop this."

There was nothing to be done. "There's no taming a hurricane," he said.

Andrea grabbed a glass of champagne and took a measured sip. John noticed the liquid jostling as she struggled to stay still. He instinctively steadied her with a gentle touch on her back.

Hyde continued her act. "Tonight, together, we will catch a criminal in our midst." She indicated toward the people. "These four individuals are bandits, thieves, rogues... you just don't know it yet. Some dinosaurs believe you need good detective work and old-fashioned techniques to find a culprit. But that's long and, oh, so boring." She paused. "I'm assuming you prefer a more enjoyable method?"

A round of applause answered her question.

"That was meant for you," Andrea whispered.

"Yeah, I caught it. Sarcasm. A common Hyde trait."

"You have to admit, she's a natural."

John winced. "She's a menace."

Andrea hesitated. "But do you trust her?"

"I trust her to be Gabrielle Hyde. I'm not sure to what end."

With a flourish, Hyde produced four large cards from nowhere. "Greed, Vanity, Opportunity, Desperation," she announced. "These are the motives of criminals. Choose your fate," she commanded, offering the fanned cards to each participant.

"Don't show it to me; don't look at it," Hyde directed them. "The fates will drive your choice and reveal your crimes to everyone in this room."

Each volunteer plucked out their selection. Andrea's eyes remained fixed on Johnston, whose casual expression belied the white-knuckled grip on his card.

"And now," Gabrielle announced with a sly grin, "let's reveal what fate has decided."

Despite himself, Olson admired her audacity. Any illusion of power had vanished. Hyde prowled the stage, eyes sparkling.

"Now Virgil," she said accusatorially, "I detect you can't get enough of some things."

The color drained from his face. "How'd you know my name?"

"Stay with me, Virgil. Couldn't help yourself, could you? Now, did you or did you not steal money from petty cash?"

He shook his head. "No! That's—that's ridiculous."

The denial only fueled the performance. "Why don't you reach into your right pocket and show everyone what you have?" Hyde said.

The fat man's hand trembled as it delved into his pants and pulled out a wad of bills secured by a gold clip. "This isn't mine!"

"Of course not," she soothed with an empathetic tone. "It belongs to the company. Greed has a way of forcing poor decisions."

She produced a cloth bag from thin air and opened it. "Put the evidence in here." Virgil stuffed the money into the sack.

"Now," Hyde said, "your card."

He flipped it over: GREED.

A burst of applause erupted from the crowd, mixed with chatter and gasps of surprise. Hyde moved on to a slender man who swayed on his feet.

"Andy, you know how this works," she said.

He nodded. "Yeah, I got it."

"Andy here finds immense pleasure in his work. Always precise. Always on point. But he also takes pride in his appearance." She leaned in. "You have the time?"

He glanced at his wrist reflexively and froze as he saw the gold Rolex. "Hey…"

"Into the bag," Hyde directed.

Andy fumbled with the clasp before dropping it into the pouch and turning his card: VANITY.

The crowd buzzed; they were hooked on Hyde's performance. She moved to a young woman whose interest had piqued.

"Charlotte." Hyde addressed her with an inviting smile. "Are you ready?"

"Yes," she replied.

"You couldn't help yourself," Gabrielle continued. "It was there. You had to take it while you had the chance. Opportunity often only knocks once." She paused for dramatic effect before leaning in and whispering.

With a mischievous grin, Charlotte reached into her shoulder sash and removed a gold coin with exuberance. "Can I keep it?"

Hyde shook her head. "Only if you want to end up in handcuffs." She laughed. "Which might be too much, even for our distinguished audience tonight."

Charlotte deposited the coin and flipped over her card: OPPORTU-NITY.

Guests were eating up the display. Andrea pulled away momentarily, snatching another flute. She took a deep gulp.

"Easy there, Dr. Miles," John said. "We've got a long night ahead."

Andrea's laugh was brittle. "This is madness. How can you be so calm?"

"I'm not. I just hide it well. Like being nervous on a date, you have to roll with it."

Andrea opened her mouth to respond and then closed it, a faint blush coloring her cheeks.

John diverted his eyes. But instead of looking down, they looked to the shadowy crevices and corners. An aching suspicion of danger hit him. But it passed as quickly as it appeared. He redirected his attention to the stage.

Gabrielle turned toward Johnston, the last remaining participant on stage. The CEO stood stoic. However poised, there was no escaping the spotlight.

Hyde's voice rose above the applause. "Mr. Johnston, as president and CEO of Lockheed, I'm sure this audience is familiar with who you are."

Marion waved to the crowd, and they cheered. It was clear he was well-liked. "I hope so. Thank you, everyone!"

"Please flip your selection," Hyde told him.

Johnston flipped the card, revealing the word 'DESPERATION.' A gasp spread.

Hyde's expression turned solemn. "I'm certain everyone is asking, what would drive the kind and generous Mr. Johnston to be so desperate."

He remained unemotional, but his jaw twitched. "I assure you; all is well, everybody."

"You are wrong, sir." Hyde raised a hand in dramatic fashion. "All is not well. Spies! There are undercover agents everywhere. Maybe in this room right now." People looked around at each other. Hyde continued, "They wish to steal your most treasured material. It's in danger."

Johnston stepped forward, a little angry. "Not true. I don't know where you got your information, Ms. Hyde, but our work is perfectly safe."

Everyone cheered.

Hyde stepped closer to Johnston. "Hold on, sir." Hands seemingly empty, she reached into his inside jacket pocket. "Sorry about this," she said, "but

I need to reveal what you're hiding."

She extracted a piece of paper. She unfolded it, revealing a bright red TOP SECRET. The room fell silent as she opened it further, revealing the wire diagram of the stealth aircraft. She held it up for all to see, the audience stunned.

Andrea's jaw dropped.

The classified document sent a jolt of panic through John. This was more than just a show gone too far. Hyde was dancing on the edge of treason.

"That's not mine. I would never!" Marion stammered.

Gabrielle raised the document for the shocked onlookers to see. "I believe him; what do you folks think? Is Mr. Johnston innocent?"

Scattered applause followed, but it grew. As more looked upon their flustered boss, the volume escalated until it was deafening.

Hyde leaned into the microphone conspiratorially. "Then we have to help the company. We must aid Mr. Johnston." She paused. "You want that? Do you wish to save these criminals?"

The screams were a crescendo of support.

"Then, fellow rogues, we need to destroy the evidence," Hyde continued. "Along with all the other stolen items, before the government shuts you down."

John noticed Andrea shift. Her posture stiffened, and her eyes darted to him. "What did she mean by that?"

He avoided her gaze. "We can discuss it after she's done." Andrea's fingers tightened, but he pretended not to notice.

On stage, Hyde stuffed the incriminating sheet into the bag with Virgil's cash, Andy's Rolex, and Charlotte's coin. "Now, let's make this contraband disappear," she declared, holding it high. "I will crush the gold and paper together. Fusing them until the evidence is gone, like it never existed."

The crowd fell so silent John could hear the rustle as Gabrielle manipulated the bag, pressing it deeper and deeper into her grasp. Hyde's arms trembled with exertion, veins standing out against her skin as the pouch seemed to dissolve.

Her palms were now flat against each other. She lifted them to her face. "Thank you, everyone," Hyde called out. "And remember, secrets are fragile. Tread carefully!"

With a deep blow from her lips, glimmering flakes burst from Hyde's hands. John glimpsed Simmons behind the stage, twisting the handle of a large CO_2 canister. With a hiss and pop, gold confetti erupted from hidden canisters. The metallic strips launched upward and caught the light, creating a dazzling curtain.

Sparkling confetti descended, obscuring his view. As the golden veil cleared, Hyde had vanished from the stage. The crowd erupted in applause, their cheers drowning out John's thoughts.

He felt a mix of relief and unease. Was Gabrielle trying to flush out the spy, or was there some other purpose? With Hyde, anything was possible.

Andrea's grip on his arm tightened. "We need to talk," she hissed. "Now."

Before he could protest, she dragged Olson towards the edge of the ballroom. The noise of the crowd faded. A cool draft from a vent raised goosebumps on his arm as they reached a corner near the entrance.

"They're going to do it, aren't they?' Her voice trembled. "Shut down Skunk Works?"

He hesitated. "Andrea, you're overreacting..."

"Don't patronize me." She covered her face. "How could I be so stupid?"

John wanted to dismiss her concerns, but he struggled to find the words. He could lie again, but she would see through it.

"If this is about what Hyde said on stage, she doesn't know when to stop talking."

Andrea gripped John's hand, her nails biting into his skin like tiny daggers. "She knew. A shutdown is so logical." She turned, pacing. "That wasn't an act. Those were specifics only someone with inside information would have." Her eyes narrowed. "Details you had."

"I can't discuss it."

"Don't play games with me."

"I'm not," he said after a pause. "If I don't locate the leak in the next four days, the President will shut your program down. But I promise we're going to find out who did this."

"That means nothing," Andrea spat. "You lied." Her accusation was harsher than he expected. "You promised you'd be transparent, but that was just another CIA lie, wasn't it? You're all the same!"

Her eyes flashed with anger, then cooled to something worse. It was a look he knew all too well from his late father. Disappointment.

John's loyalty to the CIA now felt like shackles. Guilt crashed over him, drowning him. He had never meant to betray Andrea, but his orders left him no choice.

"I opened up to you, made an exception to my rules. And for what? Another CIA jerk who can't be honest? I should have known better. I did know better."

"I wasn't allowed. I didn't intend…"

Andrea tore her hand from John's grasp.

"Just let me explain," John said.

"No! I need time to process, to figure out what I do next." Bitterness and betrayal intertwined in her voice. "I'll find my own way home."

"Andrea, wait…"

She turned away, eyes filled with tears. Andrea pushed through the crowd without looking back. The scent of her perfume hovered momentarily before dissipating. The distance between them stretched until she burst through the doors and out of view.

The room's swirling joy now felt alien to John. He stood alone, trapped between competing loyalties. Mechanically, he took a champagne flute from a passing tray. The bubbles did nothing for him.

He had chosen this life of secrets, a world where no one was clean. Not the enemy, not the CIA, and not Hyde. The filth of delusion left him miserable.

His gaze drifted aimlessly across the room. The strips of confetti flickered in the ballroom lights, creating a dizzying effect. Through this, something caught his attention.

Shrouded in darkness, a specter of a man lingered on the far side.

The figure, a shadow among shadows, stood motionless. The same predatory stillness he had witnessed in Mogadishu.

This unsettling presence cut through the ambiance. Even the confetti seemed to shy away, as if repelled by the man's cruel aura.

The room faded as John's vision tunneled.

Those unforgettable eyes bored into him. The same calculating gaze that had assessed Nate's worth and found it expendable. In that moment, all his failures crashed down upon him. This was the man of his nightmares.

Sasha Morozov was here.

Chapter 29

The ballroom's splendor, the model aircraft, the golden confetti. None of it mattered. The only thing that mattered was Morozov. Rage surged through John.

The flute slipped from his fingers, exploding on marble in a spray of glass and champagne. Laughter from oblivious guests swallowed the sound.

A shrill scream pierced every corner of John's mind. He felt Nate's slick, bloody grip as if it were happening now.

Unwillingly, he flashed back to Mogadishu. The market's spice-laden air filled his nostrils. Morozov's cruel grin before he killed Nate. Sweat coated John's face, beads rolling down.

The edges of his vision constricted, tunnel-like, focusing only on the liquid at his feet. Around his shoes, spilled champagne morphed into a crimson pool of blood. He saw the life leave Nate's eyes as desert heat burned his skin.

He shook off the memory. Was he hallucinating, or was Morozov truly here?

It couldn't be.

Unless he was here to meet a contact. The mole. Morozov was real.

Sasha dipped his hat and took a sip of his drink, the gesture unrepentant. In that moment, John felt something within him snap. A primal, vengeful force overwhelmed him.

This was his chance to make Morozov pay. Retribution consumed him, overriding every other instinct. John charged through the crowd, shoving people aside. He wove through clusters of tuxedos and evening gowns, his hand finding the weapon inside his jacket.

He seated his palm on the grip, cocking the hammer. His fingers tightened against the textured surface, ready for action.

But as he approached, a fresh puff of confetti clouded his vision. The room swayed like a ship caught in a squall. People crowded around him, obscuring his view. He spun, causing a man to spill his drink. The man grabbed Olson's shoulder, demanding an apology.

"Pardon me. Emergency," he said as he shoved past.

But his target had vanished. Morozov was gone.

John stood frozen as flakes clung to him like tarnished armor. He had failed on every front. Vengeance. Duty to the agency. Andrea's trust. His promise to Nate.

He added the entire nation.

Desperation mounted as John scanned the room. The space where Morozov had stood was now occupied by a laughing couple. He made one last futile sweep, searching for that unmistakable silhouette.

Nothing.

A server passed carrying a tray of empty glasses, pausing to collect more. "Excuse me." Olson grabbed the man's arm. "That man who was just here. Tall, scarred face. Which way did he go?"

The waiter glanced back in confusion. "Sorry, sir. I didn't see anyone like that."

Was Morozov ever there? The question ravaged John's sanity. Had it been a cruel trick of his fractured judgment?

The surge of adrenaline ebbed, leaving him hollow. One failure compounded another. First Andrea, now this.

His mind wandered back to the explosive argument in the dark corner of the room. Her heated words replayed in his thoughts, her tear-filled eyes as vivid in his memory as Morozov's cruel smile.

Spotting the nearest exit, a familiar sensation of detachment washed over him. He needed to leave. John stumbled through the Excelsior's lobby into the cool autumn air. He hailed a cab and collapsed into the back seat.

"Just drive," he muttered. "I don't care where."

The car lurched forward, melding into the chaos of Los Angeles at night. Olson slumped against the worn leather seat. The glittering Excelsior Hotel faded behind them, replaced by a blur of flickering streetlights and shadowy figures.

"Bad night, huh?" The driver's voice floated from the front seat.

John stared blankly at the man. He offered no response.

As the taxi wound through the desolate streets, John's thoughts drifted.

"This good?" the driver asked, receiving only a vacant nod.

Olson paid the fare robotically and stepped out into a night that mirrored his unforgiving mood.

* * *

John's feet dragged across the deserted streets as he approached the warehouse headquarters. A biting salt breeze whipped at his face, momentarily clearing the smog. The glittering opulence of the party was gone. There was only industrial grit.

Reaching the building, he pushed against the metal door, its hinges groaning in protest. The familiar scent of dust and concrete enveloped him as he stepped inside.

He trudged up the four flights of the stairwell, each step clanging metallically. The railing beneath his palm was cold.

He wasn't sure why he had returned. With no home, no friends, and an agency that likely no longer wanted him, the warehouse, despite its mechanical atmosphere, had become a twisted kind of refuge.

Hyde would know he cracked. Jessica would see it and use it to her advantage, too. Reaching the landing, he shook lingering confetti from his hair. Muffled conversation drifted from the room, confirming the team's presence.

John's mind churned with self-doubt. He'd let everyone down. Facing the others seemed impossible when he was already suffocating.

His hand hovered over the doorknob as laughter from inside warped and distorted, blurring reality. John realized he needed help. But his pride stood in the way, preventing him from confiding in the very people who might understand.

With a weary sigh, he turned to leave.

A figure stepped from the recesses.

"John?" It was Jessica's voice, uncharacteristically soft.

Olson pivoted, bracing for sarcasm or another seductive test. Instead, her eyes held what seemed like genuine concern. The siren was gone, replaced by some different version of her.

She was the last person he wanted to see.

"Not tonight, Jess," he said. Too exhausted for pretense, he didn't bother concealing the streaks of dried sweat. "I can't do it. Not now. Please."

She hesitated, her hand halfway extended, as if trapped between two worlds. His broken posture seemed to unlock something within her.

"Yes, now, luv."

She stepped forward and carefully wrapped her arms around him. The power of her gentle embrace caught him off-guard. He wanted to struggle, to pull away, to preserve the last shreds of the tough disguise he was forced to wear.

But the warmth of contact after the night's emotional onslaught proved too much. John's defenses crumbled, and he collapsed.

"It's okay," Jessica whispered. "We've all been there."

He felt her hand steady against his head. It wasn't the practiced touch of a seductress, but the earnest support of someone who understood what it meant to break.

Pent-up emotion and pressure came flowing out in a torrent. He buried his head in her soft shoulder, tears soaking into the fabric as he wept.

Chapter 30

LOS ANGELES WAREHOUSE DISTRICT

4 Days Remaining

23:01

Enveloped by the stairwell's silence, John stood motionless, his face buried in Jessica's shoulder. The night's events swirled in his mind like a toxic fog. Time escaped him.

The fresh wounds of his failures burned raw. Vengeance. Duty. Trust. Promises. Each ideal threatened to drag him under. In the unlikely asylum of Fortner's embrace, John confronted his oldest scar.

His father had been a strict disciplinarian. Service under Patton during the Battle of Metz left him both grievously injured and resolute that no man should ever show emotion. This unyielding code was rigidly enforced in the Olson household.

As a teenager, John found his father's Purple Heart hidden in a sock drawer. When he asked about the medal he had never seen, it resulted in a lashing he never forgot. The lesson was clear: pain was to be endured, never acknowledged. His dad was a good man but deeply unhappy. He couldn't trust anyone, and it affected his relationships. Just like John.

Olson swiped at his eyes with the heel of his palm, emotions swirling. His old man's iron standards clashed with the unexpected relief flooding through him.

He took a centering breath, meeting Jessica's gaze. His mind was still reeling from the evening's events. The phantom Morozov, the argument with Andrea, the suffocating doubt.

"Sorry. Hell of a night."

His red-rimmed eyes revealed a man consumed by demons. He could no longer hide them from Jessica. The rubble of his carefully constructed walls was scattered everywhere.

Jessica patted his cheek. "There's none of that macho, tough-guy hokum round me. We all got secrets. Feel better, luv?"

John wiped his nose with his tuxedo sleeve. "Different. But yeah."

"Good."

Olson didn't want to talk about it. Maybe someday, but not now.

"You're important, John," she told him. "I see that now."

"I broke down. How's that for a CIA field operative?" He pushed strands of hair back into place. "I'm also losing my mind. I swear I saw Morozov tonight." A chill coursed through him. "You know how insane that is? I can't even trust myself."

"Bollocks. You're not crazy." Her voice lacked its normal playful lilt.

"You'd be better off without me. I'm hurting your operations."

Jessica's hand landed on his shoulder. The gesture was uncharacteristically platonic. "I used to think that too," she admitted. "But you've shown you're more than some government stooge. You care, John. I can feel you're ready to break free of those chains."

She eyed their surroundings before adding, "Gabrielle believes in you."

"I'm a liability."

Jessica shook her head. "You're not."

Desperation wormed in. "What makes me worthy?"

"It's complicated."

"Not good enough!" He slammed his fist into the wall. "Hyde has a reason for everything. She could've escaped a hundred times. Everyone here makes sense but me. I need to know why."

His rising voice stopped abruptly, plunging the stairwell into a tense silence. Jessica opened her mouth to speak, then hesitated. Her eyes darted around as she tapped her fingers on her lips.

She leaned in close. "What I'm about to tell you… it can't leave this spot. Ever."

Her words made Olson's skin prickle. He nodded. "I swear."

Her voice dropped. "Hyde had a brother." She paused, letting the secret vanish. "His name was Jan."

"What?"

Her head whipped over her shoulder, eyes scanning the shadows. "He was her hero, her protector. And she lost him… He was taken in the most horrific way imaginable."

The revelation clawed at the edges of his mind. Little things Hyde told him started to make sense.

"Gabrielle couldn't save him, and she loved him deeply. Her brother was kind and virtuous. To a fault." Jessica took a second. "It's why they executed him in front of her."

"Who?"

Jessica bit her lip. "Who else? The Nazis. To break her."

John slumped against the metal railing. Chipped paint embedded in his hand.

"She sees him in you."

"That tattoo's real?"

She nodded. "When Gabby was twelve, Hitler expanded the Holocaust beyond Jews. Her family, Masonic Gypsies, became prisoners in a concentration camp under the Nacht und Nebel decree. It was a bloodbath."

He calculated Hyde's age. Forty-six, maybe forty-five. Much older than she looked.

"Her father, knowing he wouldn't survive, trained his children in Freemason crafts. Ancient knowledge passed along bloodlines. Gabrielle was the only one who made it out alive."

John winced. "Why didn't she say something?"

"Fancy reliving your worst nightmare, do you? Thought not," Jessica said. "That blue forget-me-not pin she always wears. It was her mother's. All that's left of her family. All gone. Murdered in that place."

How often had John seen that pin without a second thought? He recalled Hyde's protective movements whenever anyone came too close to it. No sock drawer could ever hide that trauma. She wore her pain for all to see.

Such horrors would have broken anyone. It should have broken her. "I never believed," he breathed.

"Few do. In helping you, Hyde's atoning." Jessica looked sad. "She's trying to save her brother. Maybe to preserve what's left of herself."

Olson's mind grappled with the story. To have endured that hell. Her cunning, her resilience, her unstoppable drive. These weren't just the traits of a master thief, they were the hard-won spoils of a survivor, tempered in unimaginable suffering.

How many times had he judged her? All her dualities came into focus, like a complex Polaroid.

"I didn't ask to be saved," John said.

"Neither did I." A shadow crossed Jessica's face. "But she did it anyway. Why she still believes in me after what I did is anyone's guess." She cleared both eyes with her thumbs. "She trusts all of us more than you know."

John reflected on his CIA mantra: trust no one. That principle had cost him with Andrea. But if Hyde could trust these people, maybe he could learn to do the same.

"Thank you, Jess."

"We're a team," she replied. "We need to rely on each other."

"I blew that with Andrea. We lost her." He sighed. "Okay, I lost her."

"You didn't lose her," Jessica insisted.

John's eyes widened. Had she missed the fight at the party? Unlikely for someone so perceptive. "What do you mean?"

Jessica gave a knowing smile, the kind that always made him bristle. She pointed towards the entrance. "Look for yourself."

John strode to the door. He cracked it open and stared. Andrea was engaged in an animated discussion with Hyde. They huddled together over a table covered in blueprints.

"Andrea's here," Jessica said, a smile spreading.

John's shoulders slumped. "She doesn't want to see me."

"She'll come around, you know."

As much as he wanted to believe, experience had taught him otherwise. "I'm not so sure about that."

"Just be yourself, John. Maybe throw in a little snog and a bit of the old how's your father…" she said, her tone playful.

"I'm sorry. Are you even speaking English?"

"The Queen's, darling," Jessica replied with a wink.

His laugh was more of a release of tension than genuine amusement. He marveled at Jessica's ability to inject playfulness into the bleakest of moments.

His fingers curled hard around the handle, the scarred metal biting into his palm. He took a shallow breath, preparing himself. He could already imagine the hurt in her eyes. At the last moment, he buckled, letting his hand fall.

Jessica came up behind him. "What's the problem? She's right there, love. I know she wants to see you."

"That's not it." John sighed. "I can't be trusted. I lied to her. We fought. And then… Morozov appeared, but he wasn't really there. That's what happens to people when they lose their minds, right?"

"You're not insane."

"What if I am?"

"Maybe you should consider every possibility," Jessica countered, "before jumping to absolutes."

The words sank in, and a terrible clarity dawned. If he wasn't losing his mind, then Morozov's presence was real. The man's appearance foreshadowed the storm. Hyde broke the rules, and so did the Soviets.

The rule book protected a static, predictable world. Washington was ill-prepared to fight asymmetric warfare. The CIA conditioned him to trust systems, not people. But institutions could never understand human motivation. They were messy and tangled.

Only people could overcome impossible odds.

It was time to adapt. This mission had crossed from intelligence gathering into a fluid field operation.

With Morozov present, the danger was immediate. They needed a plan of action. In this, the team had to be strong and united. Their very survival depended on it.

John glanced at Jessica. "We don't have a moment to lose."

She nodded, a silent gesture of encouragement. Drawing strength, he turned back, squaring his shoulders.

"Go get 'em, tiger." She slapped his backside with a playful swat.

He jumped and moved out of her reach. John's hand hovered over the handle. With a deep breath and a swift, decisive motion, he pushed it open and stepped through.

As he cleared the threshold, the door slammed shut behind him, the bang announcing his presence. Andrea's and Hyde's heads snapped up from the blueprints, their eyes widening in a mix of surprise and curiosity.

John tried to speak, but the words died on his lips. His instincts screamed at him to run, but it was too late. Jessica positioned herself in the doorway, cutting off his retreat.

As the hush stretched, John's gaze lingered on Andrea, his mind racing. Would she forgive him? Something told him she had been waiting for this. What had she and Hyde been discussing?

Desperate, John searched for a way to apologize. His mind drew a blank, rendering him speechless. She deserved more than an apology.

Andrea crossed the room, each step heavy with unresolved emotion. She stopped a mere foot from him, her proximity both thrilling and terrifying. Her eyes flickered with pain, her lips pressed into a thin line.

The air between them crackled, the silence broken only by the soft rustling of blueprints. John's palms grew damp, and he resisted the urge to wipe them on his pants.

Perhaps everything would be okay.

In a blur, Andrea's arm arced forward, her palm impacting John's cheek with a sharp crack.

Chapter 31

The sharp crack of Andrea's palm against John's cheek shattered the silence. His head snapped to the side, the sting spreading across his face. His hope of a simple solution crumbled. Hyde and Jessica's shocked expressions blurred as he regained his balance.

As the ringing subsided, John knew that earning her forgiveness would be worth it. He blinked, fighting the instinct to rub the tender cheek. Memories of their heated argument earlier flooded back.

"I deserved that."

"Don't you ever lie to me again," Andrea snapped.

John swallowed hard. He knew her intensity was a cover for hurt.

She closed her eyes, drawing in a long breath. When she opened them, something had shifted. The wrath gave way to her scientific mind, and her fingers uncurled.

"Do you know what hurt the most?" she asked. "Not the lie itself, but that you didn't think I was strong enough to handle the truth."

He fumbled for the right words. "You're the strongest woman I've ever met."

Her expression softened. The rage dimmed as she pressed her fingertips to her temples. "John, I'm trying to be mad at you here."

"I'm sorry." John hung his head.

"Where was I?" she asked.

"On how I should've trusted you. Told you everything," he answered immediately.

Her lips quirked in a half-smile. "Right," she said, a hint of shame creeping in. "I may have overreacted. It's a bad habit, one I'm trying to break, but sometimes the heat of the moment still gets the better of me."

She took his hand, her fingers brushing against his skin. "I was so mad when I thought they would destroy my work." Andrea's face crumpled. "I wanted to demand someone, anyone, realize what a huge mistake they were making."

She let out a weary exhale. "I realized that sulking wouldn't accomplish anything." The anger drained. "I could stay angry, or focus on doing something productive. So, I came here to find you and Gabrielle." She shrugged. "Plus, I've never been to a secret hideout before."

John looked around. It was not much of a hideout. He turned back to her. "You have every right to be angry."

Andrea's shoulders squared. "No. Emotions don't help. They make things worse. Passionate thoughts produce poor decisions."

John flexed his jaw. "Like assaulting people."

"I thought you were tough."

"Not at all." He looked at the table behind her. "What did you have in mind?"

"Right. Well, collaborative problem-solving yields statistically superior outcomes. Then we optimize the solution matrix." She noticed John's confusion. "Sorry, we figure it out together."

"I'm just not sure which direction to take," he said.

Andrea grimaced. "Exactly the issue we've been discussing."

"What did you decide?"

"No simple resolutions." She seemed lost in her thoughts. "On my team, when we face a tough engineering problem, we often run in circles. The key to a breakthrough is adapting a fresh approach."

Andrea peered at Hyde. "Sometimes, the optimal answer can seem a little... unorthodox. The best ideas always do."

Gabrielle had been unusually quiet, letting Andrea lead. It was smart. Whatever they had discussed prior to John's arrival, they both knew it would play better coming from her.

"Don't worry. I'll listen. I want to be part of the solution."

"Welcome back, John," Hyde said. "I'm glad you've decided to join us. We'll need all hands on deck." She gestured to where blueprints lay scattered across a marred table. "Let's get started, shall we?"

He surveyed the sprawling dark-blue schematics. The pages flipped rhythmically under his thumb, the scent of ammonia hanging. Coffee cups lined the edge, leaving overlapping round stains. As he leaned forward, the table creaked under his weight.

"What am I seeing here?"

"Oh, John," she mused, "you're still thinking like a bureaucrat. Forget those. The papers are prologue. We start somewhere else. It's the people who tell the story."

"What people?" John asked.

Andrea cut in. "Gabrielle, explain the financials." Before Hyde could speak, she added, "Don't forget the behavioral prediction!"

Olson's gaze ricocheted between them. "Would somebody please say something that makes sense?"

"Ask nicely." Hyde said. "To appreciate my methods is to respect the results."

"Gabrielle, I would love to hear more about your plan and the folks who led you there."

With a curtsy, Hyde replied, "Why, John, so nice of you to inquire. Several nights ago, my team acquired the financial records of all Skunk Works employees."

John leaned back. "Acquired?"

"Burbank Credit Union. Just listen to her," Andrea piped in.

Once all eyes were on her, Hyde continued, "We invited individuals with any unusual activity to the stage. My volunteers."

"She used micro-behavior on them!" Andrea injected.

"What on earth are you talking about?" John asked.

"Micromomentary expressions," Gabrielle said, tapping her finger on the table. "The amygdala betrays us all. Our brains trigger involuntary reactions before conscious thought in the neocortex can suppress them. These tells are science, not magic." Her eyes narrowed. "Academia is always the last to arrive. Professionals have relied on these perceptions for centuries."

"The show was an interrogation," John mused.

"Traditional methods fail because subjects know they're being examined. They prepare, hiding their shadow selves." She gestured broadly. "I eliminated that barrier. Two hundred and seventy-three simultaneous interrogations, and not one was aware of the test."

Olson crossed his arms. "I could've questioned those five suspects myself."

"The CIA handbook is for amateurs," Hyde countered. "It's insufficient for our timeline. This operation exposed in seconds what would have taken you days."

"You disclosed a sensitive document to the entire crowd. Wait," he said, raising a finger. "How did you get that?"

"Recreated it from memory." She waved her hand dismissively. "More importantly, I was able to read everyone in that room."

Andrea grinned. "The statistical improbability is remarkable!"

"All those faces, only one truth," Hyde said. "The theater creates that moment of pure, unfiltered reaction. Our rational minds are always a step behind our emotional responses."

"So?" John asked. "Was our mole in the two hundred…"

"And seventy-three," Hyde finished. "No. Everyone there was innocent."

Andrea jumped in. "I knew my people weren't to blame. Isn't that great news?"

"I disagree. We're worse off than before." John massaged his palm with his thumb. "If that's true, then something's wrong."

Hyde's eyes glinted. She was withholding. A quick look at Andrea confirmed it.

"Okay, let me think this through," he said as he paced. "If nobody there reacted to the stolen document, then the thief wasn't in attendance."

"We've already established that. What's next?" Hyde asked, her manner reminiscent of John's university professors.

"We're back at square one. The assignment was to investigate Skunk

Works. If you cleared everyone with access during the party, then… the job is done, except it isn't."

"The absence of an answer is just as telling as a solution itself." Hyde rolled her hand end over end. "Keep going…"

John's eyes narrowed. "The mole isn't at Skunk Works."

"Agreed. And that leads us to an even more crucial problem."

John considered the problem from a fresh perspective. If there was any doubt, why the obsessive focus on the facility? The CIA and the White House were insistent that the California station was the source. That certainty seemed odd.

"They lied."

"Lies are for children and philandering men." Hyde moved closer. "This is manipulation. Elegant and layered. Positioning us to act against our own interests."

Her eyes glittered. "It's rather beautiful. The classic con elevated to art."

"No." John's denial was instinctive.

"What's the cardinal rule of any successful confidence scheme?"

He remembered their conversation. "Make the mark believe they're in control while they are actually being exploited." He gripped the table, knuckles flexing. "Son of a bitch," he hissed. "I'm the mark."

From the corner of the room, Matheo uttered a short, *"Très bien."*

When John looked over, the Frenchman was already back at work, head bent over a stack of papers.

"So, if there's no mole, why send me and you on this wild-goose chase? Who benefits from this phantom search?"

Hyde waited patiently. John would have to find his own answers.

"Someone wants us distracted," he said slowly, "running in circles to hide their real agenda. This entire investigation in nothing more than bureaucratic cover."

"And to what end?"

His skin prickled as the answer crystallized. "Someone," he said, "wants the program shut down."

"Precisely my thought," Hyde said.

"Besides hurting US capabilities, what do the Soviets gain if the program dies?" he asked. "It would cut off their access to source material. Obviously, I'm missing something."

"Dr. Miles, please tell Officer Olson what happens if any Skunk Works initiative is ever shut down," Hyde said.

"At our facility, everything is closely monitored. But there's a catch. If the government terminates a classified project, all related data—every blueprint, every calculation—is packaged and sent to a secure location in Washington, DC." She paused. "And once it arrives there, any top-level executive would have direct access. Without being tracked."

Her gaze moved to the blueprints. "They'd have unfettered control of the world's most transformative military technology. Our early warning systems rely on a frequency range negated by the angles and RAM coating. They could strike anywhere, anytime. No notice."

John felt his synapses firing. It all made sense: the CIA investigation was a ruse from the start. Someone intended for him to fail, then serve as the patsy. And once he did, procedure demanded that Skunk Works ship the data directly to the real culprit.

Olson immediately cataloged the suspects, building a threat assessment matrix. Avery had initiated the operation. But he didn't strike John as a pawn. Maybe another unknown CIA player leveraging his authority?

Durbin presented a cleaner profile. Money was clearly not an issue, and he already had a seat at the table of power. He had access, but the least obvious motive. Ideological incentives could drive him, but as the President's advisor on communist threats, that was incompatible.

Despite the lack of evidence, John's instincts pointed to the FBI. He'd seen the pattern before: rival agencies exploiting jurisdictional conflicts to conceal deeper agendas. The thought of a traitor in their midst made his blood boil.

"Bastards," he grumbled. His hands clenched and unclenched at his sides. "How could I have been so blind?"

"Don't be upset," Hyde told him. "Even I find it… unsettling… to be on this side of the equation." Her smile turned rueful. "They picked the ideal pair. Who better to blame than an industrial thief and her disposable CIA partner? It was a nearly perfect con."

He knew she was right. "Success was never an option for us."

John looked up, realizing Gabrielle was still holding back. There was more to it.

"Wait. You claimed it was 'a *nearly* perfect' con." Hyde had set the line as bait. "What did you mean by that?"

"Every scheme has flaws," she answered. "It's a principle the great ones understand. There's always a thread waiting to be pulled, a string the puppeteer never considered. Something brazen and unexpected that flips them from victor to victim. Their arrogance is our opportunity."

Olson bit his lip. That gleam of cunning invariably led to trouble. Whatever it was, she and Andrea had arrived at it together. No matter what, it would push the boundaries of legality.

"What do you have in mind?"

John expected the dramatic pause. Hyde relished making him wait.

But it was too much for Andrea. She thrust forward in her ballgown, gripping the table's edge, unbridled hair cascading across her face. She smiled devilishly.

"We have to steal it."

Chapter 32

LOS ANGELES WAREHOUSE DISTRICT

3 Days Remaining

09:10

The sun pierced through towering windows, casting angular shadows. The musty scent of old paper and machine oil hung in the air. John, Dr. Miles, and Gabrielle's team bent over a battleground of blueprints.

With only three days left, every moment mattered.

Andrea straightened the schematic. "Skunk Works isn't just some government warehouse. It's an impregnable fortress with four-foot-thick walls. A designed nightmare."

Simmons spread another sheet. "The foundation is layers of cement capped by ten feet of granite with engineered honeycombing." He grabbed a ruler from his pocket and measured the distances.

"*Merde*," Matheo muttered. "*Sous-sol inaccessible.* No digging."

Hyde seized the blueprint, crumpled it up, and threw it to the side. "Forget looking for weaknesses in the design. We go old school." She tapped the table. "Subterfuge, social engineering and imagination will be our tools. People are always the weakest link. But each action must be precisely applied and timed."

John considered this option. Nothing was ever straightforward in fieldwork. "So, how do we do that?"

"We use this building's own defenses against it," Hyde answered. "Every system has a flaw, no matter how well-designed it may be. We must find and exploit it. Its very strength is a weakness."

"That makes no sense. We need to study the interior layout." John turned to Andrea. "Do you think you could draw it from memory?"

Andrea's face pinched tight. "No way. Too many winding paths."

The door burst open, and Jessica strode in, her bright red beret arcing through the air before settling on a chair. She tossed her hair back and strode forward, a set of rolled-up documents tucked under her arm.

Hyde gave her a nod of approval. "Ask, and you shall receive."

Jessica unfurled the diagrams with a flourish, the crisp paper revealing a detailed layout of Skunk Works' interior.

John scowled. "How did you acquire these?"

"I have my methods," she said.

Simmons peered over John's shoulder. "Well, lookie here. Physical defenses are dated," he noted. "Twenty-five-year-old locks. That's a gift, my friends."

Andrea waggled her finger. "Don't underestimate the security. It's military-grade." She pointed at a space. "The outer door is protected by ex-military with .45s and shotguns. Two armed men, two keys turned in sync to gain access." She drew an oversized X. "Beyond that? Two more guards with clear lines of sight and no cover."

That was a death trap. Hyde, however, seemed unfazed. "Move along. We'll cross that bridge later."

Andrea sighed. "Getting past the guards is the simple part. The vault's our real problem." She circled the safe room in red ink.

Simmons clapped a hand on John's shoulder, a confident grin spreading. "We've faced worse." He winked. "Gotta take the world as you find it. This is always a hot mess at first." His eyes gleamed with the thrill of the challenge.

Jessica gestured. "Vault's a proper nightmare."

"Department of Defense contracted the Mosler Safe Company," Andrea said. "Same as at Fort Knox."

Matheo bent over the table, his scarred finger traced the vault's outline. "*Vingt-sept pouces*. Twenty-seven inches," he clarified. "Plastiques?"

Jessica sharply inhaled. "We'd bring the whole place down. And you with it."

"There's one more sticky wicket," Jessica continued. "The vault's time mechanism only allows access during business hours. Electronically sealed."

"What about cutting the power?" John asked.

Matheo glanced up. "Triggers the alarm. Armed response in minutes."

"But theoretically, would killing the power disable the time lock?"

Matheo nodded. "Theoretically, yes." His eyes met John's with newfound respect. "But you're talking a coordinated reaction. Guards. Police. Everything they have. And on the clock."

Simmons tsked. "Even then, it still has that combination lock. Can't skip that part." He let out a low whistle. "Mosler uses gears protected by a cobalt sphere and glass re-locker plate. Drilling's out."

"What?" Andrea asked.

"Cobalt's too dense for standard bits, and those that can handle it shatter the glass. Tumblers unusable. We'll need to get ahold of that combo."

"Only the daytime head of security has it," Andrea said. "And they change it weekly."

Silence enveloped them for a long moment. Hyde tapped her chin. "Once we're in," she said, "what then?"

All eyes shifted to Andrea. "Even if we get inside, we'll find two Cray-1 supercomputers." She pointed at two large rectangles. "These things are enormous. Eight feet tall, twelve feet wide, connected by 2-inch cables. Each weighs 5.5 tons, with 1,662 modules performing up to 160 million calculations per second."

These were the fastest computers in the world. John had seen advanced technology, but nothing like this. Running his finger over the schematics, he followed several large pipes. "What are these?"

"Freon cooling. These machines radiate intense heat and require cryogenic refrigeration." Andrea paused, looking unsure. "We'll have to download the data from both systems and be out of the room before the guards change shift. Reprogramming will take time."

Jessica cleared her throat. "Can you do it?"

Andrea shook her head sheepishly. "I don't know. I've never tried."

Simmons finally broke the tension. "If anything goes wrong, if we trigger any alarm, we're cooked." He held up seven fingers. "Cops respond in seven minutes. Seven. That's all we've got before they're swarming us."

The atmosphere in the room deflated with Simmons' warning. Hyde scanned the pile of blueprints, then scrutinized each team member.

"This will be difficult. Any last-second concerns?"

"I'm worried about the time circuit." Jessica chimed in. "Might require a dedicated resource. But yeah, I'm in."

Simmons gave Hyde an assured nod. "I'll follow your lead, boss-lady."

Matheo cracked his knuckles. *"Oui. J'en suis."*

Andrea raised both her hands. "I made it clear last night. I have no choice, not really. This is my life's work, and I'm going to fight for it."

John looked down at the plans. The sheer magnitude of the obstacles, combined with the burden of his past failures, bore down on him. They were stealing U.S. government secrets.

John's head drooped. "I can't do it," he whispered. "This is not just crazy; it's treason. And I took an oath." Andrea's forgiving smile twisted the knife deeper. "You'll do better without me," he added.

Something in him had fractured between Somalia and last night. He knew how to calculate odds, to recognize when an op was compromised. This had crossed the line.

A small part of him rebelled against the idea of walking away. The brash nature excited him. But then again, a similar scheme led to Nate's death. "I can't be responsible for another person getting hurt… arrested… or killed. I'll go back to Washington and work the angle from that end. You have my word. It's where I can do the most good."

Olson tapped his hands and put them up in resignation. "Best of luck."

Simmons' head dashed between his team and John. "Boss?"

Hyde held up a hand. The corner of her mouth twitched almost imperceptibly. She gave an accepting nod that seemed too composed. With that, John pushed back and walked away, his steps heavy.

He could feel their stares on his back.

Hyde's voice sliced through the silence. "I'm making a new list of responsibilities." Her pen moved at a deliberate speed. Within moments, she handed one to each person. "We have no time to waste," she instructed. "This will continue to shift until the very last moment."

As the team dispersed to their tasks, John drifted towards an unoccupied corner. He felt overly exhausted, trying to remember the last time he had slept through the night.

He reached into his pocket, fingers brushing against the cold plastic of his agency pager and the leather of his badge casing. He pulled both out and set them on a nearby table before plopping down with resignation. His eyes fixed on the cityscape.

The scrape of a box crate on concrete yanked John from drooping eyelids. He blinked, realizing he'd lost track of time. Turning, he saw Andrea settling down next to him.

John's attention drifted back to the team, watching as they worked with a sense of purpose he envied. Matheo hunched over a table, soldering iron in hand, carefully connecting wires on circuit boards. Next to him lay what resembled plastic explosives.

Jessica, now clad in oil-stained coveralls, wielded her welding torch. It hissed and sputtered as she fused a flat plate to a machine. The arc light flared in brilliant, erratic bursts, casting harsh shadows that danced across the walls.

Simmons, meanwhile, tinkered with a large box, a tangle of wires protruding from its hidden heart. He connected two cables, emitting a small beep as a red light switched to green.

John felt the chasm swallowing him whole. Their shared purpose only highlighted his inner turmoil.

"Are you okay?" Andrea finally asked.

"No," he admitted. "Everything I believed, it all feels like a lie. And it's tearing me apart."

She squeezed his arm. "You're a good man, John. Just lost."

"I want to go." His eyes moved back to the window. "My instincts tell me I should stay." He glanced at Gabrielle. "But what Hyde expects me to do… well, it's impossible."

"She would tell you there's no such thing." Andrea scooted closer. "When I told my dad that I planned to attend college, you know what he told me?"

"No idea."

"Impossible. Girls don't do that." A trace of old pain crossed her face. She paused, the silence between them oddly comfortable. "When I wanted to be an engineer, my advisor said the same… impossible. Girls aren't engineers." Her fingers twitched.

"Every step of my career, someone told me it couldn't be done." She sniffed once.

John covered her hand with his, feeling her strength. His life was threat assessments and finding flaws. A mindset of obstacles. But this woman didn't focus on that.

"But I learned," Andrea continued, "nothing is truly impossible."

He completed the thought, "Merely improbable."

Their hands remained joined, neither letting go.

In theory, it all made sense. Part of him yearned to follow her and Hyde into the fires of hell. But Andrea hadn't experienced the same crushing remorse he lived with. Her optimism was based in academia. She didn't understand.

"Don't do this, Andrea," he said with sudden urgency.

"What do you mean?"

"Your path is inspiring, but this is different." His words carried a pragmatic harshness. "In the field, when things go wrong, people die. We're not talking about breaking glass ceilings. This could break you into a million pieces."

He gestured toward the team. "What Hyde is proposing won't just end your career. It could end you. I can't watch that happen." The fear in his eyes betrayed him. "If you're lucky, you'll only wind up in jail. Right before the CIA throws away the key."

Andrea withdrew her hand. "This project, Stealth, validates every struggle I've ever endured," she said. "Someone is trying to take that from me."

"And I'd rather be in jail than stand by and do nothing." Her voice grew louder. "I thought you'd understand."

"I do."

"So what's stopping you?"

"Sasha Morozov."

"The spy who killed your friend?"

"My need for revenge is destroying me." He closed his eyes, trying to shut out the visions. "I see Morozov even when he isn't there. I saw him last night. Jess insists I'm not crazy, but I don't know."

"You're not," Andrea told him. "But if you want real justice, you need to stop this man. Do it for Nate. Just do it your way."

She was right. As usual. He needed to let go of the guilt. "That's the first good plan I've heard in a while."

Andrea smiled. The morning sun cast a warm glow across her, highlighting the faint sheen on her face. John caught her perfume, a delicate blend of floral notes. His gaze dropped briefly to her lips, then back to her eyes. He noticed his own breathing. It matched the subtle rise and fall of her shoulders.

A slight tremor ran through her hand on his.

Andrea's smile softened as she leaned closer. John felt himself drawn forward.

Her eyelids lowered, a silent permission. He ignored the awkward angle of their bodies. They were millimeters apart now. The warmth of her breath swept across his lips.

A pager's loud chatter shattered the moment like breaking glass.

They both jumped. The abrasive buzzing jolted them apart. John searched for the source of the noise. Andrea's posture stiffened as her head swiveled.

Self-consciousness crashed over him. He stood up, brushing the dust from his trousers before offering Andrea his hand. "I think that's mine."

She clasped his palm, rising to her feet.

Hyde's head whipped in irritation. "What in God's name is that infernal racket?"

The plastic box vibrated against the metal table. John strode over to the large black puck. The agency used pagers for urgent and covert communication.

"Sorry. Got it." John's thumb jabbed at the button, silencing the buzz. "It's a work pager." He squinted at the small display. "Coded message."

Andrea moved to his side. "What does it say?"

"Ah, hell." The expletive slipped out. John's fingers tightened around the pager. "It's Deputy Director Avery. He's in LA and wants an update. Immediately."

A hush fell as Olson analyzed the situation. Avery never left Washington without cause. Now, his presence jeopardized their entire operation.

Had their security been compromised?

John swallowed hard. If his boss suspected even half of what was happening here, they were already burned.

Andrea rubbed her neck. "Can you delay him somehow? Buy us time?"

Olson shook his head. "No, the message is clear. He wants to meet now. In person. I have to go. Right now."

As he stepped towards the door, Gabrielle intercepted him. "Surprise is the only thing we have left in our corner," she said, voice intense. "The FBI and CIA will not understand what we're doing."

John knew too well how agencies reacted to unexpected developments. Gabrielle continued, "You can't—and shouldn't—trust anyone."

The warning was clear: the Deputy Director could be dirty. They couldn't afford to tip him off. The stakes were too high; the risks too great. But the CIA never dealt in guarantees, and Avery had been in the game for decades.

"I can't make any promises," John answered. "But I'll do what I can."

Hyde's expression was filled with concern. She released his arm, stepping back to allow him to pass. John gave her an understanding nod.

He couldn't ignore the gnawing suspicion that this meeting would have consequences. There were so many ways this could go wrong, and Hyde made a convincing argument that someone in power was manipulating the situation.

If Avery was the mole, one errant word could jeopardize the entire operation. Or worse, put Andrea in immediate danger. Avery had to stay in the dark.

Was he walking into a trap set by a Soviet agent? He winced.

Everything was based on believing Hyde. He couldn't ignore the danger in putting his faith in a criminal. She was, after all, pushing a plan to steal highly classified data he was sworn to protect.

He pushed open the door and stepped into the stairwell. His mind cycled through what Avery might already know. He was a legendary figure who could read deception like others read newspapers.

This meeting put everyone in immediate peril.

One wrong word, one flinch, is all it would take. Then Andrea's life, Hyde's freedom, and his own career would collapse like a towering house of burning cards.

Chapter 33

EL COYOTE MEXICAN FOOD CAFE

3 Days Remaining

11:15

John slipped into the El Coyote Mexican Food Café, blinking as his eyes adjusted to the dim light. The rich aroma of spices and sizzling meat enveloped him, mingling with the faint scent of stale beer. Multicolored Christmas lights cast a warm, kitschy glow over the seating area.

Navigating through the restaurant, he pushed aside his underlying unease. He noticed the "Sharon Tate Booth" placard at one of the empty tables. A prickle ran across his skin.

The Manson murders haunted the city for years. Did Avery choose this location as a subtle warning? Charles Manson had a reputation for manipulating people to his twisted desires. The CIA viewed Hyde similarly.

Deputy Director Lucas Avery waited in a deep burgundy booth, his steely eyes fixed on John as he approached. Across from Avery sat the familiar face of FBI Special Agent Vasquez.

Olson attempted to hide his surprise as he slid into the seat next to Bruno. Vasquez's presence here was an unexpected complication. The agent's ongoing feud with Hyde threatened to spin this situation out of control.

Avery didn't offer pleasantries. "I expected an update before now. I shouldn't have to chase you down."

John met the man's neutral expression, searching for any hint of ulterior motives. "The investigation is progressing. Nothing concrete, but we're close."

Bruno slammed his fist onto the table. Forks clattered as the salsa bowl tipped, spilling blood-red juice across the white mat.

"I'm done with this bullcrap, Olson." He wiped Pico off his sleeve. "Hyde made a mockery of us in DC." Nearby diners glanced over, but the agent was oblivious.

"I tried to warn you about her plan, but you dismissed me." John paused. "And for your information, I have Gabrielle handled."

"You really believe that?" Bruno scoffed. "She's running circles around you, cowboy. And you're too blind to see it. This is Toronto all over again."

"That was different."

Vasquez rolled his eyes. "Whatever."

"Planning to blame me again?" Olson snapped. "Like your report from last time?"

The FBI agent looked at him, surprise crossing his face. For a moment, the ambient sounds of the cafe faded. "Is that what you think happened?"

"Oh, I'm sure of it." John seethed. "Because of you, my life went to hell. I was exiled based on your report's slander and lies. You made it like I was the one who let Hyde escape. Like I was the only person who screwed up."

Vasquez sighed, shoulders slumping. "I didn't write that report."

"What?" John's eyes widened in surprise.

"Trying to set the record straight was what derailed my career," Bruno responded. "I tried to clear your name, but my superiors had already agreed to let the CIA take the fall. When I protested, they buried me in crap assignments until now."

This couldn't be true. Two long years of hating Vasquez. He'd just assumed. "I'm sorry. I didn't know."

Vasquez dismissed it. "I don't want an apology. We're on the same team. Forget it." He leaned in. "You want to make it up to me? Help me put Hyde behind bars."

Despite the revelation, he still couldn't trust Bruno with the truth. He needed to delay. "You'll get a chance soon. For now, she's under my supervision."

Avery shared a worried look with Vasquez. John's gut twisted.

"What aren't you telling me?"

Lucas interlaced his fingers. "John, I think it's time we had a frank discussion about Ms. Hyde. It's my fault you're in this mess. But I'm afraid her involvement in this matter was a grave mistake."

They were hiding something. Or creating a story to drive a wedge. Obviously fabricated. Deception and lies. The CIA special. He had to protect Gabrielle until they could find the double agent.

"I'm listening."

"John," Avery began, "sometimes things aren't what we'd like them to be."

Olson's eyes darted between them. Were they in this together? That seemed unlikely. Bruno just wanted Hyde. The deputy could be protecting someone. John's hand inched towards his holster, ready to defend himself.

Lucas continued, "We're operating within a web of international politics and hidden agendas that make everything you've seen up to this point look like child's play."

Vasquez cut in. "We've been tracking movements of many people, not just Hyde's. She's involved in this way deeper than we expected."

The table seemed to shrink. Three opposing viewpoints. A triangle of mistrust. He knew he should remain silent, but the accusations were too much.

"I've been working with Hyde. Despite our initial concern, she's been a tremendous help, believe it or not."

"Look, we know how good she is at playing people," Vasquez said, turning towards him. "At playing you."

"Stop the act. Just tell me."

Avery scratched his chin. "Show him."

"I'm... I didn't want it to go down this way."

Vasquez slid a plain manila envelope across the tabletop. John snatched it, the rough texture of cardstock scratching his fingers. Olson hefted the folder once and then upended it, dumping out a stack of blurry black-and-white photographs. The glossy surfaces caught the light as they scattered.

The grainy images were unmistakable. Hyde stood next to a sleek limousine, with Sasha Morozov beside her. A twin-engine airplane was parked on the tarmac behind them. John felt like he was falling. In one, Hyde's lips brushed the Soviet's cheek. In another, she helped him into the limo. His hands trembled, the photos popping against each other.

Hyde was the traitor all along. These photos were proof.

"When were these taken?"

"Two days ago," Avery said. "Here in LA."

John's head snapped up. "What? How is that possible?"

"Somehow, Morozov got into the country," Vasquez explained. "With help from Hyde."

Hyde's manipulations flashed through his thoughts. Her late-night strategy sessions, her moments of vulnerability. It was all a lie. The blood drained from his face.

He berated himself for believing Hyde's lies. She had seemed so genuine, so committed to their cause. How could he have been so blind?

Vasquez noticed. "Listen, John, Hyde's a con artist. Maybe the best in the world. And you're her mark."

Avery locked eyes with Olson. "Did she ask you to doubt us? The CIA? The FBI?" he asked. "To trust her instead?"

Olson's throat went dry. He couldn't deny it. Hyde had subtly undermined his faith in the agencies, encouraging him to rely on her.

It was just her game.

He nodded, unable to meet their eyes. Avery and Vasquez exchanged knowing looks. They both understood what it meant to be played.

Despite all the hard proof, part of Olson wanted to cling to his belief in her, to find some explanation that made sense. But the evidence was damning, and he couldn't ignore the facts.

He tucked one picture into his coat pocket. The photograph seemed to burn against his chest through the fabric.

The cafe's atmosphere thickened as his collar clung to his neck. This would kill Andrea. How could Hyde do that to her? The thought of setting the dedicated engineer up for arrest made his skin crawl. It seemed unthinkable.

He flashed back to the warehouse, to Andrea's hand on his. That moment that almost was. How quickly he'd let himself believe in Gabrielle, abandoning better judgment. He let Hyde weaponize his trauma.

The questions flooded in. Had everything been calculated? If she was colluding with the Russians, then what was the endgame? Somehow, it all connected to their planned operation at Skunk Works.

He looked down at the photographs on the table, at Hyde's smiling face next to the Soviet. He had trusted her.

"If Hyde and Morozov are working together, then we can't tip our hand. I will bring them in, you have my word."

Director Avery placed his weathered hands on the table. "Enough is enough. I'm shutting this whole thing down."

An icy dread settled in. This meant the end of their operation. It also erased any chance of catching Morozov.

"I'll inform Deputy Chief of Staff Durbin to coordinate with President Carter," Avery said. "It's a matter for his National Security Affairs team. They'll shutter the Stealth program and work with the FBI to pick up Hyde and anyone in her company."

The hair on the back of John's neck bristled. His thoughts turned to Andrea. She was innocent in all of this, caught up in Hyde's web of lies. The idea of her being arrested, career and reputation ruined, made him sick.

"I still have three days."

Avery gave a deliberate shake of his head. "Not anymore," he said. "Soviets moved up the summit. Treaty's now scheduled for tomorrow evening in DC at eight. That's five p.m. in LA. There's not enough time."

The change struck John. He calculated time zones, the hours lost, and sorted the operations yet uncompleted. Twenty-nine hours to execute a plan that no one had ever accomplished. And he'd have to beat Hyde at her own game, too.

It was impossible. Time had run out.

"The President was clear." Avery's tone was grave. "If we can't plug this leak by then, he'll terminate the project himself."

"I can get it done," John insisted. Impossible or not, he'd rather go down swinging. "I just need a chance."

Vasquez appraised Olson. His expression was inscrutable before turning to Avery. "Give the kid a shot, Lucas. We've got nothing to lose at this point."

Lucas seemed torn between his duty and his trust in Olson's abilities. "You don't get a second more than tomorrow afternoon at 5," he conceded.

John exhaled. "Thank you for the chance," he said. "I won't let you down. I'll be in touch soon." Then he remembered. "Sorry. I need one more favor."

Avery raised his eyebrows. "Your favors are almost expired."

"I need you to pick up Morozov. Take him off the board. Without Hyde knowing, if possible."

Vasquez gave Avery another leery look. "We tried yesterday," he said. "Morozov killed three of my men before disappearing. He's in the wind."

Anger surged. Losing the FBI agents transformed the spy from a personal vendetta into a shared threat. John sensed a sadness in Vasquez's demeanor. "I'm sorry, Bruno. I know what it's like. Your men deserved better."

"I had you wrong, Olson. And I'm sorry, too." He extended his hand. "I won't let it happen again."

John studied the man, searching for deception. But all he saw was a seasoned agent who had learned the hard way about the costs of bureaucratic machinations.

They shook hands. John knew they could both finally let go of the past. "Me either."

With a quick, affirming nod, Olson stood. He straightened his jacket with a sharp tug, excusing himself. His mind was already planning the next steps.

Only one day to stop Hyde and Morozov, to save the Skunk Works project and prevent a catastrophic leak of classified information.

He'd have to look Gabrielle in the eye without flinching. Pretend everything was normal. The worst part was he'd have to distance himself from Andrea. She couldn't know the truth. It was the only way to protect her.

As John strode towards the exit of El Coyote Mexican Food Café, his eyes lingered on the Sharon Tate booth. Its tragic history resonated with the dark thoughts. The senseless murders of the actress and her friends by the Manson cult had left an indelible mark. Even in the most civilized settings, true evil could lurk.

Rumor had it Steve McQueen, one of Olson's favorite actors, was supposed to be at Tate's party. McQueen had built his career playing heroes who bucked the system, men of action who made their own rules.

John had spent years dismissing such Hollywood fantasies, but now he understood their appeal. When institutions crumbled, a man had to forge his own path in the wilderness. The world was full of victims and villains, and sometimes that line was blurred.

He knew the consequences. He had failed before, letting Hyde slip through his fingers. But now he had the upper hand. Her schemes were vulnerable to a skilled, tenacious man like himself.

The bell tinkled as Olson pushed through the exterior door of the restaurant. Warm, inviting light spilled out, caressing his back. It died upon reaching the cold, harsh world beyond.

Time had become another merciless foe. Previous failures had broken him. But now he had clarity. But he hadn't shattered. He had hardened.

The rule follower was gone. Regulations were shackles. To bring justice and protect his country, he'd have to operate above them.

In the realm of shadows, clear-cut morality was obsolete. Hyde had brought him into her dark world. That was her first mistake.

There was a lot to do, and not much time. John looked at his watch, making a mental list. Hyde would soon learn a hard lesson. Officer John Olson wasn't a victim. He was a hunter.

Chapter 34

LOS ANGELES WAREHOUSE DISTRICT

25 Hours Remaining

15:31

The chill of the concrete stairwell seeped into John's bones. The rough texture scraped against his palms as he gripped the railing.

Years of CIA operations had taught him to guard his emotions, never letting them become a liability. But Gabrielle had tainted that. Life before her was simple. Clear objectives, clear morality.

Now the lines had blurred beyond recognition. He knew what he had to do. The irony wasn't lost on him. Becoming what you hunt is the ultimate hazard.

The FBI surveillance photo burned against his chest. John pushed it deeper into his jacket before shoving open the door.

The warehouse air was thick with the scent of burned plastic. Jessica's cigarette smoke churned in shafts of afternoon light. A rat's nest of clipped wires sprawled across Simmons' and Matheo's tables, their exposed ends glinting. A power drill whirled in the distance.

The room felt alive.

Schematics plastered Jessica's workstation. Nestled in the middle was a homemade transmitter. Urgency crackled like static electricity, everyone moving in a frenzy.

Simmons rushed by, his mouth set tight. His hair stuck out at odd angles, as though something had shocked him. He clutched a tangle of wires and circuit boards to his chest, glancing at John as he passed.

"What's going on?" John called out.

Douglas wiped sweat from his face. "Gabrielle moved up the timeline to tonight," he said. "We're scrambling to get everything ready." He gripped the cables closer. "I've only got three more hours. Every minute counts."

"Why the sudden change?"

"No clue, but we're on a razor's edge here," Simmons said, shifting his equipment. "I've still got to calibrate the signal modulator or this whole op gets a no-go."

As he hurried off, a sinking realization hit him. How did Hyde know about the time change?

It could only mean one thing: the Russians told her. He had to prevent this catastrophe. If Hyde delivered the stealth technology to Morozov, the Soviets would enter tomorrow's treaty negotiations with an insurmountable advantage. Global power would shift overnight. Millions of lives hinged on what happened next.

His eyes swept the bustling room, each face suddenly a conspirator. Jessica and Matheo huddled over blueprints, their voices low. Hyde was nowhere to be seen.

Andrea stood at a table, crushing a white substance into a fine powder. She saw him and pulled off her face mask and nitrile gloves, striding toward him with barely contained energy.

Andrea's smile hit John hard. Unguarded. Trusting. He returned her grin, hating himself.

"You've been gone for hours. I was getting worried. How did everything go with Avery?"

Olson shrugged. "It went well." The less she knew, the safer she'd be.

"John, seriously. What happened?" she pressed, grasping his arm. "Are you okay?" Concern filled her eyes.

"Just the usual. Avery was getting antsy, but I worked it out," he assured her. He tried to appear nonchalant, fighting the impulse to spill everything.

"Trust me, Andrea. Everything's under control."

He glanced around. "Where's Hyde?"

On cue, Gabrielle rounded the corner of a large crate, a checklist in hand. She paused when she saw John, her eyes unreadable. A nearby fan rustled the papers on her clipboard, wafting the faint scent of her perfume.

"How did the meeting go? You were gone for quite a while," she asked.

Andrea crossed her arms. "That's what I said."

John straightened his shoulders, facing their stares. "We're clear. The agencies are in position, but they're chasing shadows and fighting red tape. By the time they realize what's happening, we'll be long gone."

Hyde examined him. He held his ground, keeping his expression neutral, believing his words were true.

Andrea quipped from beside him, "It's almost sad. They won't ever even know."

John locked eyes with Gabrielle. "I've changed my mind. I'm in for tonight's operation. Avery informed me of a timeline change. We're out of time. The Soviets moved the treaty signing to tomorrow night. If we don't move now, it's all over."

Hyde nodded. "I have the same intelligence."

John leaned against a workbench. "That intel's fresh," he said, his tone casual. "Last I checked, it was compartmentalized. Your source must be something special."

Gabrielle waved a dismissive hand. "I'm glad you're in. We were always one person short. Your participation shifts the odds significantly in our favor," she said. "Your operator skills are just what this job needs to succeed."

"Tell me everything."

Hyde's gaze turned cold. "What prompted this sudden shift?"

He expected the question. "I need to do this." Subtly, he brushed his hand across his jacket.

It was calculated.

"What do you have there?"

Blood rushed to John's face. "Nothing," he lied, his voice tightening.

Hyde shook her finger. "Oh, John. Lies are truly not your color." She stepped closer. "That item in your pocket is practically screaming. Not only did the lizard portion of your brain direct you to touch it when I asked, you also subconsciously placed it next to your heart."

John marveled at her perceptiveness. She could detect blatant lies, so half-truths were safer. "It's nothing."

John remained defiant.

"What's gotten into you two?" Andrea pointed. "John, just show her."

He crossed his arms. "No."

Andrea inched closer. "It's okay."

Relenting, John reached into his pocket, his fingers closing around the gold frame of Nate's sunglasses.

As he withdrew them, he ran his thumb along the edge. They had been part of Nate, an extension of his vibrant personality. He embraced the guilt. Hyde and Andrea's faces both softened.

Andrea put a hand on his shoulder. "Are those…?"

"Yeah. I couldn't just leave them behind. Not after…" His voice trailed off.

"I understand now." Hyde cleared her throat. "I'm sorry I pressed you. He'd be proud of what you are about to do."

"You have no idea."

She watched as he stowed them for safekeeping. For a moment, the room's action halted. John released a breath, feeling a rush of self-affirmation. He had placed the sunglasses in that pocket just in case Hyde pushed him.

Though he loathed using Balik's memory as a ruse, it effectively covered his underlying emotion. Step one was complete.

"All right," Gabrielle said, breaking the silence, "you need to get changed, and then study the parameters and assignments sketched on the wall."

John's mind snapped back into operational focus. He had to absorb each detail and his role in the heist. The mission allowed no room for ambiguity.

Andrea's hand shot out, grasping his fingers. "The adrenaline's really kicking in now," she admitted. "I'm glad you'll be there to keep me grounded. I've never stolen anything before." She cocked her head, and her eyes went to the ceiling. "Can you truly steal from yourself? Is that even theft?"

He wanted to tell her to run, to get away.

"Not sure. But I'll be there, right till the end." He smiled at her, then withdrew his hand and headed towards the changing area.

Glancing back, he asked, "How much time do I have?"

Hyde checked her steel Cartier watch. "We go live in three hours. It's a tight window, but it works."

"Perfect."

John paused at the changing room door. He glanced over his shoulder at the bustling team, the hum of activity filling the air. His focus landed on Hyde, deep in conversation with Matheo.

Doubt gnawed at him. Keeping his knowledge of Hyde's treachery a secret felt like a betrayal. The urge to challenge her was almost overwhelming. But he pushed the impulse away. He needed to play this smart.

Inside the room, John caught his reflection in a cracked mirror. He barely recognized the vengeful man staring back. The rules had once been his armor against a cruel world. Now he spun lies within lies.

He pushed aside doubt, worry, pride, and even his feelings for Andrea. Staying focused on the mission was the only way forward. It was the only way he knew to keep her safe. He couldn't afford to let emotions cloud his judgment.

He glanced at his watch. There was no more time for second-guessing.

Morozov waited in the shadows, confident of his invulnerability. That arrogance was now John's best weapon. When he had the leverage he needed, Olson would make his move. Brutal and merciless.

John tore off his tie and unbuttoned his starched shirt. From this moment on, he was calling the shots.

Chapter 35

OUTSIDE THE SKUNK WORKS FACILITY

20 Hours Remaining

21:01

John watched Simmons scale the telephone pole, his lithe silhouette etched against the moonlit sky. The technician's gloved hands clutched the weathered wood, his legs anchoring on the rungs as he ascended. Douglas soon reached the junction box, his fingers coiling wires and clipping connections.

John patted his jacket, confirming his badge was there and ready. Andrea gripped the steering wheel beside him, her hands rotating forward and back. In the rear, Matheo's eyes were fixed on his watch's luminescent dials.

Simmons' van lurked thirty feet behind them on the dimly lit street outside the Skunk Works' western perimeter. A long cord dropped to the ground, the wiring unraveling.

"That's our cue," Hyde said. She slipped out the door and approached the open passenger-side window. "Andrea, give us at twelve minutes before you proceed with Matheo."

John's gaze lingered on Andrea's white-knuckled grip. "Everything will be fine," he said, forcing a smile.

"Easy for you to say," Matheo scoffed. "I hide in this tin can while you stroll right in. No way out if they catch me."

John didn't appreciate the tone. He turned to face the Frenchman, noticing beads of sweat on Matheo's forehead and his labored breathing. He looked scared.

Andrea glanced in the rearview mirror, her eyes alight with idealism. "Don't worry. With my credentials, they'll let me through. No one will look twice at the van. *Vous m'avez, monsieur.*"

Matheo leaned forward and kissed her on the top of her head. "And you have me, *mademoiselle*." His breathing steadied. "*Merci.*"

"I didn't know you could speak French," John said.

Andrea's smile melted John's heart. "Just a little. When this is done, we'll have time to learn these things. Trust Gabrielle. We'll get through this."

"Nothing in the field ever goes according to plan. If I tell you to walk away, you do it. No questions." She started to protest, but he gripped her arm. "I mean it. Your safety is my top priority."

He climbed out and trotted toward Hyde, who was already climbing into their waiting sedan. One last look back.

Andrea gave him a thumbs-up. He returned the gesture and jogged ahead.

As they neared the checkpoint, John felt his nerves kick in. The installation's security had increased dramatically. Adrenaline surged. This was more than pre-mission jitters. Something was off.

The crisp night air crackled with tension as John approached the gate. Guards gripped sleek black assault rifles, the metal absorbing the moonlight. Their eyes, sharp and alert, scanned each vehicle with predatory intensity. The hum of floodlights buzzed from above, casting harsh, angular shadows. Their faces, half-illuminated, presented an aura of menace.

The rhythmic crunching of boots on gravel punctuated the eerie silence, signaling the patrol of additional guards along the perimeter. A bead of sweat trickled down John's temple.

This level of force protection was overkill. The CIA would use more discretion. There was only one explanation: Vasquez.

The man didn't know the meaning of discreet. His zeal was going to derail everything.

At the checkpoint, Hyde's demeanor shifted subtly. She straightened, chin lifting just a hair. She presented her badge with a practiced nonchalance, but John sensed tension beneath her calm exterior.

An older guard gave them both a wary eye before reluctantly waving them through.

Once past the gate, John and Hyde made their way across the property towards the Research hangar. They scuttled across the polished concrete, approaching the first series of offices. Hyde peeled off, heading toward the bathroom.

John entered a cramped security office he knew would be empty at this hour. Rows of monitors lined the walls, their screens casting an eerie, monochromatic glow. He settled into an old, creaking chair with a well-used lab coat draped over the back. A cracked name tag dangled from its pocket, surrounded by chewed blue pens that had leaked and soaked into the white fabric.

He switched between the different camera feeds, searching for the areas he needed to observe. Hyde slipped in behind him. She now wore a sleek black outfit that clung to her frame, melding with the shadows. Only she could find a garment perfect for a heist.

John frowned as he noticed an orange badge clipped to Hyde's black leather belt. His attention returned to the security feeds, finding the one trained at the front entrance. He soon spotted Andrea's van as it turned onto the last stretch before the gate.

He picked up the radio. "Andrea, security's tight. Take another lap."

A crackle of static. "I'm okay. Proceeding as planned."

John switched channels. "Jessica, you're up."

Hyde leaned casually against the wall. "Vasquez must have made a call. His timing is particularly problematic."

John hoped the FBI wouldn't ruin everything. "No kidding. He's sure you're up to something."

"For once, he's not wrong. But he has no idea about our true plan, or our inside woman."

John opened his mouth, but his retort died. Movement on the monitor caught his eye, and time seemed to slow. Two more guards materialized at the front gate.

Andrea's vehicle inched closer to the checkpoint. Each rotation of the wheels felt like a countdown to disaster. He leaned forward, willing her to turn around, but she kept advancing, oblivious to the danger.

The sentries approached the van in unison, their hands resting on their weapons. The men moved with military precision, their synchronized approach like a tactical assault team.

His fingers clenched the radio, causing it to flex. Olson tried to keep his voice calm. "Andrea, abort. Get out, now!"

Static crackled, each second of silence amplifying John's dread. He wanted to yell again, but the guards were so close that his voice might expose her.

Desperation gripped John as he searched for a solution. He swung around to Hyde with a pleading look. "We need a distraction before they search the van. This is your mission. You must have a plan." He gestured to the screen. "We can't leave her out there."

Hyde's expression hardened, a perceptible tightening around her eyes. Her gaze remained fixed on the monitors, but John caught a look of concern. Her fingers drummed on her arm.

"Come on, Andrea. Get out of there!"

The ring of guards still trapped the van. Worst-case scenarios bombarded John's mind. Each second felt like an eternity.

Hyde's unreadable expression offered no solace. She was behaving strangely, and he didn't have the time to decipher it. Vasquez, Hyde, Andrea, the heist. All of it collided in this moment.

If Andrea were to be saved, it had to be now. It had to be him. He scanned the room, finding nothing. On the monitor, Andrea talked with a guard while others circled the van like sharks.

His fingers fumbled with the radio. "Need help? One click for yes, two for no."

Only static answered.

A tall, broad-shouldered guard's hand moved towards his pistol. The gun slid free from the holster, his finger on the trigger. He raised the weapon; the barrel glinting menacingly under the floodlights.

John flashed back to Nate. The pistol, the sharp crack. Blood. His eyes snapped to the screen. Not again. Not Andrea.

The guard shouted a command at Andrea as he reached for the side panel door.

How would she respond? John knew he was too far away to intervene. The entire operation, the fate of the Stealth project, and countless lives hung in the balance. It all came down to the next few seconds.

"What are you going to do, John?" Hyde asked.

* * *

Andrea glanced at her watch. Thirteen minutes since John and Hyde had left for the facility. Plenty of time. She started their approach.

John's behavior over the last couple of hours nagged at her. Something deeper than concern about the heist. She would ask him when they met again.

The radio in her ear crackled to life.

"Andrea, security's tight. Take another lap," Olson told her.

She bristled, tired of others dictating her moves, but the irritation vanished as she spotted the entrance. Bright floodlights forced her eyes to narrow. Reality hit hard, her fingers clenching the steering wheel.

Too late to change plans. Retreat would only raise suspicions. This was their only shot.

She drove on. "I'm okay. Proceeding as planned."

With a controlled exhale, she removed the earpiece and switched off the transmitter. John might be spooked, but she could handle this. No room for fear or hesitation now.

She reminded herself to play the role. She plastered on her practiced, serene smile. One she had perfected through years of navigating the patriarchy.

The hum of the engine vibrated through the seat, matching the nervous tremor in her hands. Andrea's mind instinctively turned to numbers, calculating the ideal speed to approach the gate without raising suspicion.

"Hide," she hissed.

Matheo's eyes widened as he surveyed the van's interior, filled with equipment. His gaze darted around before he tore open two medium-sized cardboard boxes filled with wires and metal plates.

"*Où?*" He stammered. "Where? There is no space!"

"Anywhere," she replied, continuing the van's approach. "I can't go any slower."

In the back, Matheo dumped gear from one of the cardboard boxes. He stacked equipment around the box, creating a hollow.

In the rearview mirror, she caught glimpses of Matheo contorting his body, folding himself into the box with surprising flexibility. She heard rustling and the soft clink of metal as he yanked gear to cover himself. When she risked another glance, the box appeared to be nothing more than a jumble of tools.

Drifting to a stop, several armed guards approached the vehicle. A guard readied his weapon. She tried to hide the tension in her shoulders as she handed her credentials to Charley, a portly, gray-haired gate guard in his sixties with a full beard.

His weathered hands grasped her ID. "Evening, Dr. Miles."

"What's up with the extra security and all the additional guns?" Andrea nodded towards the menacing men.

He glanced at her credentials and handed them back. "Sorry 'bout all this hullabaloo, Doc," Charley said, lowering his voice. "FBI's got their undies in a twist about some insider threat nonsense. You know how it is. Better safe than sorry, right?"

Several of the guards eyed the van with suspicion.

"I see. Well, I appreciate your diligence. Not to be a bother, but I'm running late."

Charley's eyes flicked to his clipboard. "We're doing searches on everyone tonight."

Andrea frowned. "Not a great time, Charley. You know me, and my credentials. We had a test emergency...."

"Sorry, Dr. Miles. Wasn't my idea. Orders are orders."

Andrea added a hint of worry to her tone. "Charley, I'm seriously late. The director will have my ass if I don't get this equipment inside ASAP."

Charley nodded, pointing to the vehicle. "We'll be fast then, but it wasn't a request."

Andrea's hands tensed on the wheel as the guards circled the vehicle. One guard loomed larger than life as he approached the side door, weapon drawn. Another stepped into the van's path. There was no bypassing this checkpoint.

She cataloged their positions and movements, searching for any exploitable weakness. No effect. Her expression remained neutral even as her palms grew damp with sweat.

She was trapped, and they were going to find Matheo within the first five seconds. If this went south, it wouldn't just be the mission that failed; she'd lose everything she'd devoted her life to accomplishing. Time to form a new hypothesis.

The muscular guard slid the door open with a swift, decisive motion. He exposed stacks of gear and a tangle of wires, squinting as he scrutinized the cluttered interior.

Relief washed over her as she let out a silent breath, thanking whatever higher power had guided Matheo. Her solace was short-lived, however, as the man's attention settled on the two cardboard containers.

"What's in these boxes?"

"Test equipment. Sensitive test equipment. Please don't touch it."

As the guard moved forward, Andrea spoke up, adopting a tone of authority. "I said not to touch that! It's delicate and calibrated. Any mishandling could alter the resonance frequency by several hertz. Do you want to delay our testing by weeks?"

The guard paused, his hand hovering before slowly retracting. The big man nodded, as if satisfied by her explanation. His eyes flicked to Charley, waiting for instructions.

Andrea's chest tightened. The box concealed Matheo. Would Charley insist on looking inside?

Memories of her PhD advisor's lectures on quick decision-making flashed through her mind. She weighed her options in a split second: stall the guard and risk suspicion, or let him search and hope Matheo stays hidden? Her gaze flicked to the gas pedal. A third desperate option.

Just as the tension reached a breaking point, Charley tapped his board. "Dr. Miles, I apologize for the inconvenience, but we have to be thorough."

"I understand, Charley. Security is paramount."

He gestured. "Go ahead."

The guard's oversized hand reached for the first box. A sentry still blocked her way forward. The man pulled open the lid and rummaged through the equipment. His eyes moved to the second box.

Andrea's fingers twitched, sweat trickling down her neck. Maybe if she just...

Just as the guard's hand touched the lid, a commotion erupted outside. Their attention shifted up the street.

"Doctor Miles!" a familiar voice shouted out repeatedly.

It sounded like John.

Andrea craned her neck, squinting against the bright floodlights. John was in an oversized lab coat, sprinting down the street. His chest heaved from exertion.

"Doctor Miles!" he yelled through labored breaths.

"You know this guy?" Charley asked.

Olson's hair was wild and his clothes rumpled as if he had started running after taking a nap. The slap of his shoes against the pavement grew louder. The wheezing really sold it. She fought back a smirk.

Andrea recalibrated her approach. She leaned in toward Charley. "He's new," she explained. "Tends to overreact about... everything."

Olson gasped for air, hands on his knees. "Dr. Miles," he managed, "they need you—immediately—in the test bay." He straightened up with effort, eyes filled with feigned panic. "The compressor section fell off the engine…"

Andrea widened her eyes just enough to sell concern. "We good, Charley?"

He glanced at Olson. "You got a stain on your shirt." John looked down, acting surprised. Charley waved her through. "Looks like you have your hands full. Go ahead."

Olson scrambled into the passenger seat. Andrea released a frustrated sigh. She could tell Charley was still watching. "I told you not to start without me! You'll be lucky to keep your job if the engine is damaged."

John hung his head in shame. Charley gestured to the guard, who slid the door closed. The man blocking their path stepped aside as the barrier arm went up.

She jerked the van into gear, moving forward at a smooth crawl. She could see Charley shook his head as another vehicle approached the entryway. The armed men resumed their stance for their next customer.

Andrea let out an exhale. Years of navigating male-dominated spaces and awkward power dynamics had prepared her for tense confrontation, but this was entirely new. She shot Olson an amused look.

"The compressor section fell off the engine?"

He shrugged. "They didn't know either."

A loud crash came from the back. Andrea flinched, pivoting to see the cardboard box explode open. Components and wires scattered across the floor. Matheo emerged from underneath them, cursing in French.

Olson whirled around, his eyes widening at the sight of Matheo covered in the wires. "Where the hell did he come from?"

A sharp laugh escaped Andrea. "I'll tell you all about it later."

Matheo sat up, stretching his arms. He fixed them with a stern look. "You must never speak of this. I deny everything."

Andrea smiled. "*Oui, monsieur.*"

They were already fifteen minutes behind schedule as Andrea pulled into the underground garage. She eased the van into their marked spot, but before the van stopped, Matheo jumped out, grabbing gear and tools.

Andrea followed, her nerves still shot. While Castille focused on the equipment, she studied their surroundings, searching for any sign that their infiltration had been discovered.

"Time for you to shine."

He grunted in response.

Andrea glanced at Olson, seeing the familiar determination on his face. Despite everything, she trusted his abilities.

"Jessica is in position at the station. We don't have long." He put a hand on her shoulder. "You ready?"

Andrea pushed aside the lingering fear. They had risked far too much already. Gate entry was supposed to be the straightforward portion. She gave him a resolute nod.

"We're in." John said into his radio.

There was no turning back. Hyde's plan was in full swing, and so were they.

Chapter 36

As the quartz clock of Jessica's 1975 Mustang inched forward, the tiny numbers ticked away precious moments. The car's leather seats released a faint, nostalgic scent that failed to soothe her. The team was running late.

She needed time to complete her mission. Exploiting the human element was a tricky endeavor, especially on a timeline. Tapping her fingers on the steering wheel, Jessica listened to the hum of the engine, diverting her frustration back to the schematics sprawled across the passenger seat.

She traced the layout with her groomed nails, committing every detail to memory. She mentally marked her top three escape routes, picturing each path through techniques learned from Hyde.

Satisfied she could navigate the station blindfolded, Jessica folded the annotated charts.

She breathed deeply, trying to purge the stress. A haunting memory surged forward, lifeless eyes staring up from the murky water, the soundless scream of drowning. In ops, death was always a risk, but it was preferable to the guilt of failure.

Jessica banished the morbid thoughts. She couldn't dwell on the past.

Hyde's belief had been a lifeline, pulling Jessica back from a desperate edge. Forgiveness was easier said than done when your job was to destroy and disrupt. Hyde had cautioned her: never be a prisoner, especially to yourself. Embrace who you are.

Jessica applied vivid red lipstick. It served both as armor and a weapon. Her hair was perfectly coiffed, not a strand out of place.

From her bag, she retrieved glasses and a Department of Energy badge, pinning it to her sweater strategically. The positioning drew attention to a hint of cleavage. A smirk formed; no man was impervious to such calculated vulnerabilities.

The radio crackled to life. "Jessica, you're up," Olson announced.

She let the nerves melt. Hyde was trusting her to get this done.

Exiting the vehicle, she strode toward the power station. Halfway there, she stopped, spun on her heel, and darted back to grab her purse, tucking it under her arm. Inside were two bricks of plastic explosives connected to a slender remote-trigger.

Matheo's handiwork was artistic perfection. As a token of appreciation, she would procure a bottle of Armagnac from Château de Gensac. He preferred white wine to the rich Tannat grapes of his homeland. There was no accounting for taste.

Squaring her shoulders, she marched toward the power substation, armed with charm. Success hinged on playing her part flawlessly. Within three steps, Jessica Fortner disappeared, becoming Jessica Danielson, an overeager DOE inspector.

Ms. Danielson stepped into the building, her heels clicking against the polished floor. As she approached the reception desk, a trio of security guards surrounded her.

With a disarming smile, Jessica reached into her purse and produced a stack of official-looking documents. Her credentials were a forged masterpiece; she had meticulously crafted each watermark and signature.

"Evening, gentlemen," she said. "I'm from the Department of Energy, here for a pre-inspection."

The guards exchanged skeptical glances. Jessica gestured to the embossed letterhead and state seal on the papers. "I have all the necessary paperwork," she said, the hint of authority unmistakable.

The security team didn't disappoint. Within moments, they ushered her through the checkpoint, their initial suspicion replaced by eagerness to assist. Jessica noted how each man's eyes lingered on her strategically placed badge, their attempts at subtlety laughable.

Roger, the night manager, emerged from his office. His beige cardigan and collared shirt attempted to impress, but they only highlighted his insecurities. Jessica had studied him well. A 48-year-old divorcé. Repeatedly passed over for promotions. And starved for attention.

She felt a twinge of regret. Men like Roger feared obscurity and were easy targets. She pushed the feeling aside and fixed him with a dazzling smile, her hazel eyes sparkling with feigned admiration.

"Mr. Roger Thomason, I presume?" she asked, extending a manicured hand. Roger hesitated, glancing around before returning the handshake. "I've heard so much about your exemplary work here."

Roger's face flushed, his grip lingering. "It's delightful to meet you, Miss...?"

"Danielson," Jessica answered, her fingers brushing against his wrist as she withdrew her hand. "But please call me Jessica. I'm here for the pre-inspection."

Her voice was a melody meant just for him. His posture straightened, removing nonexistent lint from his sleeve in a display of competence.

"I wasn't informed of any pre-inspections."

Jessica placed a soothing hand on his arm. "Oh, you wouldn't be. It's a recent mandate from the Department of Energy. Just to ensure everything is up to the latest standards."

She leaned in, pulling him closer. "Oh, don't worry. From what I've seen so far, you are doing well." All suspicion seemed to melt away.

For the next twenty minutes, Jessica worked her magic. She laughed at his jokes, touched his arm at just the right moments, and listened intently as he vented about the senior administrators. Each word pulled Roger further into her orbit.

As they strolled, she pointed toward a plaque. "I noticed the safety award on the wall. You and your team must be proud."

"Few people recognize how much effort we put in."

Emboldened by her interest, Roger became increasingly eager to show off the control he seldom felt. Seizing the opportunity, Jessica steered them towards the entrance of the off-limits section. She asked how their transfer area operations were compared to the rest of the station.

"We don't really let people into this part of the facility," Roger said, a trace of uncertainty crossing his face. He eyed the "Restricted Access" sign, then returned his gaze to Jessica's encouraging smile. His need for appreciation won out.

"But I keep a close eye on my operations, and we can make an exception," he added, puffing out his chest.

"Really? That would be amazing!"

She took his forearm as he led her into the restricted section, explaining that only someone with her understanding of Department of Energy policies could appreciate it.

Jessica released a calculated gasp. Banks of analog meters and switches filled the walls, their glass faces gleaming under bright lights. The air felt charged, heavy with the scent of warm vacuum tubes and electrical components. In the secluded space, Jessica leaned in closer.

"These light fixtures are fascinating." Awe laced her voice. "What are they?"

Roger's attention followed hers. "State-of-the-art high-pressure sodium lamps," he declared. "I sourced them from General Electric to reduce energy use here. They're much more efficient than the old mercury vapor lamps. I'm always thinking about the future."

As Roger continued his explanation, Jessica shifted her weight, allowing her purse to slip from her shoulder. With a subtle movement of her foot, she nudged it into the tangle of wires beneath a nearby console. Task accomplished, she returned her attention to Roger, her expression one of rapt fascination as he concluded his impromptu lecture.

She glanced at her watch, a choreographed gesture of regret. "I'm afraid I must be going," she said, lips forming a pretty pout. "But I have no doubt you'll excel in the real inspection, Mr. Thomason. Just try to act surprised when they arrive, okay?"

"Are you sure there isn't anything else I can show you?"

Jessica dipped her head, a nuance meant to leave them wanting more. "I'd love to stay, but I mustn't overstep. Maybe I can join the examination team as an observer."

That was all the man needed to hear. He nodded, eyes glazed with adoration, and escorted her back through the echoing corridors. At the front desk, the security team waited eagerly.

"Thank you," she said warmly, waving off multiple offers to walk her to her car. Unnecessary attention was always a bad idea during an exit.

She flashed the guards a final dazzling smile as she left, her hips swaying. None noticed her purse-free stride.

Back in her Mustang, she removed her glasses and the badge. The mission wasn't over. A grin spread across her face as she retrieved a small transmitter with a telescoping antenna from the glove compartment.

She cast a last glance at the power substation, a flicker of pity in her eyes. She extended the antenna and flipped a cover, revealing a glowing red button.

"Sorry, Roger."

Jessica offered a silent prayer as her thumb hovered over the button.

Redemption would have to wait. Her best talent was tragedy.

* * *

The van was still rolling when Matheo jumped out the door. He craved fresh air, even that of a parking garage.

The overwhelming fear churning in the pit of his stomach had to be pressed down.

That damn cardboard box was a suffocating prison. The overzealous guards left him no choice. Only Hyde knew of his childhood-induced fear of claustrophobia. Her failed attempts at hypnotherapy had only confirmed the dread would never leave him.

Andrea gave him a reassuring touch on the arm. No words required. It anchored him, quieting the anxiety. He said nothing; actions were his language.

With a sigh, Matheo prepared himself. Tonight, he would confront his terrors more than once. He questioned, not for the first time, why he subjected himself to this torture. Hyde, as usual, anticipated this concern.

She looked him square in the eye. Tapped his wrist twice, and then said, "We're more than our fears."

Five words. Five important words.

Matheo had a job to do. He unloaded the equipment with deliberation, pressing through the discomfort.

"Time for you to shine," Andrea said as she disappeared into the building with Olson.

Matheo would have only minutes to complete a task that should have taken two days. He knew success hinged on his ability to work quickly and efficiently. The pressure, rather than paralyzing him, sharpened his focus.

He slipped on his flip-front welding goggles and ignited the acetylene torch. The nozzle hissed, spitting yellow fire that twisted into a focused, searing blue. The intense heat pressed against his face, the smell of burning metal hitting his senses as he sliced through the grate. Sparks erupted around him.

Matheo completed the cut, wrenching the floor grate out of position with one gloved hand. He trusted that Hyde and Olson had deactivated the sensors. Lowering the heavy equipment into the hole, his muscles strained as sweat streamed down his face.

He surveyed the garage with worry. At any moment, a guard could stumble upon him or an alarm could trigger, unleashing a full security response. He must hurry.

As he lowered the last piece of equipment, Matheo caught his breath, sweeping the perspiration from his face with the back of his hand. His chest heaved with exertion, but he pressed on. There was no opportunity to rest.

He tore off his goggles and paused, a brief concession to the lurking fear. He glanced at his watch. *Oh mon Dieu.* A quarter of his time was gone, yet so much left to do. Staring into the black, Matheo braced himself.

He zipped up his coveralls, the rough fabric chafing. Gripping the coarse rope, he felt the fibers dig into his gloved hands as he lowered himself into the dark hole. A stale, earthy scent filled the space. Darkness engulfed him like a smothering blanket, the walls closing. His pulse pounded, each ragged breath a battle against the terror.

"You are more than your fear," he repeated.

Matheo's boots thudded against the concrete below, dust swirling in the flashlight's narrow beam. Gritting his teeth, he grabbed the first piece of heavy equipment and started dragging it down the corridor.

Following Hyde's basic map, he moved forward, guided by the beeping of a device he had designed. The slick tunnel walls wept moisture like the throat of a great beast waiting to devour him, the oppressive darkness inching closer with each step. Matheo forced himself to focus on his straining muscles.

As he moved, the beeps from his device grew louder. Adrenaline surged through him as he neared his target, driving him forward despite the fire in his muscles.

Three turns later, he found the reinforced concrete support structure. Exactly where Gabrielle said it would be. His device confirmed it with a steady tone. Setting down the equipment, Matheo wiped away the sweat. The real work was just beginning.

He scurried back for the remaining gear, muscles screaming in protest. Jessica's metal plates fit seamlessly around the beams. Her craftsmanship was clear, even in the dim light. Matheo admired each welding bead.

Jessica was a magnificent woman, despite her unfortunate taste for the wrong things in life. Mostly men and wine. If this machine performed as promised, he might have to swallow his pride and buy her a bottle from Madiran, perhaps from Château de Crouseilles.

No, that was untenable. Jessica preferred bold, tannic flavors. Maybe something cut with a Syrah would be palatable enough for them to enjoy together. But now was not the time.

He removed his drenched gloves and grabbed an air-powered rivet-gun, its weight familiar. The sudden hiss of compressed air pierced the silence as the first rivet fired into place. The gun bucked and roared as he fastened the plates to beams and wall, making Matheo acutely aware of the metric tons of concrete above him.

Despite the adrenaline, his movements stayed precise. Rivet after rivet, sheer willpower kept his focus on the task.

With the plates secured, Matheo connected the two jackhammers, their pneumatic extensions linking into the wall brackets. Though primitive, he knew the device would get the job done. He had built similar contraptions many times, though never one so complex.

He studied the crude machine, pride and disbelief washing over him. It validated not only his technical skill, but Hyde's sheer audacity. Only she would dare ask him to build something so unorthodox.

He cracked his neck and looked down at his hands, coated in grime and grease. A river of sweat poured down Matheo's back, highlighting his growing anxiety. Each breath became a struggle as distracting purpose faded.

Approaching the machinery, he adjusted one final dial. It had to deliver precise pressure. Not too little to be ineffective. Not too much to collapse the building.

There would be no escape from that, only death through his greatest fear. As Hyde always preached - balance, balance, balance. Of course, she wasn't the one who would be buried alive.

Matheo glanced at his radio, every crackle and hiss a dreaded preamble. He had to be ready to act the moment Hyde gave the signal, without hesitation.

He tried to push down the anxiety as he eyed the ceiling. Matheo knew that if he failed, it could endanger them all. He must protect his family, at all costs. That was greater than any fear.

The radio crackled, static hissing. Hyde's voice broke the silence with the command, followed by a countdown. Matheo inhaled sharply, his hand trembling as he flipped the switch. The machine roared to life, the vibrations promising to tear the complex apart. A deafening noise filled his ears, drowning out everything.

The earth trembled beneath his feet as if it would swallow him whole.

Matheo closed his eyes and patiently waited for the worst of fates.

"Je suis plus que ma peur."

Chapter 37

Monitors cast an eerie blue glow across Gabrielle's face, turning her dark eyes into pools of reflected light as she watched the action unfold.

John sprinted down the asphalt towards the front gate. His quick thinking and invented persona were just the right mix.

Watching him convince the guards to release the van filled Hyde with satisfaction. Forcing John's hand had been an agonizing but necessary test. She'd kept her expression neutral, even as he shot her pleading looks.

John's newfound tenacity was impressive but suspicious. His demeanor had shifted after meeting with the CIA, the vague details only heightening Hyde's suspicions.

The only practical solution was a test. An inadvisable gamble for sure. But the situation offered no other elegant alternative.

Forcing his hand had paid off. John showed he would choose action over protocol. But Hyde remained wary; it was far from conclusive.

She watched the van vanish from the screen. They were behind schedule, but recoverable. The plan would still work.

It was the variables that bothered her. The increased security was proof that Agent Vasquez was onto her. The man was not subtle. Much worse, Bruno likely knew about Morozov.

The Soviet's presence was a poison pill. Not only did it put the FBI into play, it also complicated the situation with John. She needed to keep him focused. Volatile players were nasty saboteurs.

Hyde mulled over the complexities and outcomes. The Starling Contingency might have been worth the considerable trouble after all. The faint sound of approaching footsteps snapped her back to the moment.

The control room door burst open. Andrea's flushed cheeks revealed a woman trying to balance adrenaline and anxiety. She held a glass vial containing an off-white powder in a trembling hand.

"Ready?" Hyde said.

"You promise it's safe?"

"Precisely calibrated," Gabrielle assured. "Temporary effects only."

John entered, bearing two steaming cups of coffee. "Ready to go?"

"Yes," Andrea responded. She unscrewed the cap and added powder to each cup.

Hyde glanced at her watch. "We need to keep moving."

Exhilaration surged. This moment was where the line between success and failure was razor-thin. She thrived under pressure, her mind working in overdrive to anticipate every scenario.

John passed one cup to Andrea and kept the other. Hyde noted the concern on both their faces. "Stay composed. As Homer would say, 'Success and the strong force of fate are waiting.' Let's not give it any further reprieve."

With a collective breath, they stepped out. The stale air of the dim hallway enveloped them as they walked. Flickering fluorescent lights buzzed overhead, casting distorted shadows. Hyde's fingertips brushed against the pocked wall, the texture feeding her hyperactive tendencies.

At the first intersection, Dr. Miles assumed point.

Andrea had chosen the route in advance, plotting a circuitous path that avoided manned checkpoints. Hyde admired the woman's careful observation and dedication. Both were invaluable.

As they entered the outer perimeter room to the vault, two guards popped to attention. Hyde noted their stance and demeanor. Despite acknowledging Andrea with respect, they showed an undeniable hint of skepticism. These were professionals.

Jacob, the head guard, was in his early thirties. He had an open, friendly face that belied the seriousness of his position. His thinning light brown hair was cropped short in a conservative style, his lean build hinting at past physical training. Still, he retained an undeniable presence from his years on the Los Angeles Police force.

"Dr. Miles." Jacob's forehead creased. "You shouldn't be down here at this hour."

Andrea responded with a smile. "It's cleared. Our consultants requested a full security assessment. The facility doesn't sleep, neither should our evaluation."

Jacob started to speak, but Andrea continued, "And considering the time, I brought some coffee to help you maintain focus." She took both cups and held them up. "Simultaneous benefits."

Despite the perceptible sheen of sweat on Andrea's face, the guards accepted the drinks. The second guard downed his drink in three gulps. Jacob, however, took a more measured sip and then set his hot coffee on a makeshift desk.

"I appreciate the gesture, Doc." Jacob's voice hardened. "But I can't allow access to the vault after hours. Even for cleared personnel."

Olson stepped forward. "No problem, sir. We respect your position."

A sudden thud cut him off. All eyes snapped to the corner of the room where the second guard had collapsed, his body slumping to the floor, limbs sprawling awkwardly.

The sedative had taken effect faster than expected. They were supposed to clear the room first.

Jacob's focus shifted to his fallen colleague. Without hesitation, he dropped to his knees beside the senseless guard, reaching out a hand in concern.

The guard's compassion impressed Gabrielle. He hadn't leapt to accusations, instead prioritizing his comrade's wellbeing. Jacob's dossier revealed he had left the LAPD after his partner's death. He cared too deeply. It was an honorable quality ill-suited for the streets of LA.

Hyde observed Jacob as he took in the scene. His partner was unconscious on the floor. This happened immediately following three unexpected guests in a secure area after hours. He'd piece it together.

Realization dawned as betrayal and desperation flashed across Jacob's face. Hyde felt a sliver of remorse, but she buried it beneath layers of necessity. There was a tense pause as Jacob stood. His body swayed, the spiked coffee taking effect.

Impaired but not incapacitated.

Then, like a gunfighter from the Old West, Jacob scrambled for his holstered weapon. John lunged forward, closing the distance. His fingers dug into the guard's wrist and twisted. With sudden force, Olson yanked the man's arm upward, forcing the guard to shift his weight against straining tendons.

In a fluid motion, John wrapped his other arm around Jacob's neck. He tightened his chokehold, Jacob's face turning a deep purple as they strained against each other. The guard turned his head into John, gasping for air and kicking wildly. Their bodies skidded across the floor as both fought for position.

Jacob's elbow jabbed into John's ribs, a desperate attempt to break free. Olson winced, his grip faltering momentarily before he readjusted, straining to maintain control.

Jacob thrashed like a cornered animal, legs flailing as he sought leverage to escape John's iron grasp.

Hyde reached into her satchel, her fingers closing around the grip of her Cap-Chur tranquilizer pistol. The skirmish had escalated to a dangerous point. She whipped out the weapon and took aim, her nose scrunching as she zeroed in. The sharp click of the trigger registered in her ears as the dart flew true, striking the guard in the neck with a soft thud.

Jacob's eyes met Hyde's for a fleeting moment, a look of disbelief in them before unconsciousness claimed him. John lowered the man carefully to the floor and then released his hold.

Olson shot Hyde a reproachful stare. "Cutting it close there."

"You managed."

Despite the nonchalant exterior, concern grated at Hyde. Only two darts remained. No margin of error now; every variance was adding up, compounding negative probability.

Andrea's eyes widened as she took in the sight of the drugged guards. A slight tremor ran through her hands, barely noticeable. She glanced toward the inner vault door, then back to Hyde. "They may have heard the struggle. If so, they probably called for backup."

Hyde gave a curt nod. "The only way out is through. You ready, John?"

He turned to the door. "Yes."

There it was again. Eyebrows lowered and drawn together in a vertical line. Eyes narrowed. Lips pressed firmly together, with the corners of the mouth turned down. Jaw jutting out slightly. Dilated nostrils.

Olson was angry. He was angry with her.

Good. He'd need it. She savored the danger for a second and moved on.

Hyde keyed the radio. "Matheo. Jessica. Simmons. It's time."

She paused, absorbing every detail. No one had ever attempted something like this. The risk was worth it.

"Three…" The number hung in the air.

"Two…" The anticipation made her pulse race.

"One…" The word was rhapsody.

The following pause was almost theatrical, a suspended moment where fate held its breath. Then, without warning, it began. At first, it was a low, ominous rumble.

Then it built.

The room erupted in violent tremors, the ground shuddering as the walls groaned in protest. A small picture frame on the wall rattled and shattered, raining shards of glass onto the floor. Jacob's spiked coffee toppled, the dark liquid snaking through the glittering debris.

Gabrielle basked in the ingenuity that had orchestrated this moment. Even as the vibrations grew more violent, threatening to tear the very foundation apart, a part of her reveled in the destruction.

The lights faltered, plunging everything into darkness.

Chapter 38

Perched at the top of a telephone pole overlooking Skunk Works, Douglas Simmons popped open the junction box. The rough wood scraped against his legs as he shifted, wincing at the tangled mess of wires.

"State electrical code? Ever heard of it?" Simmons muttered. Skunk Works clearly played by its own rules. Sort of like Hyde.

There was no choice. All the facility's critical alarm systems ran through hardened underground cables. Their depth and shielded cases rendered them too difficult to reach. Only the phone lines remained accessible.

Simmons unclipped a cord from his utility belt. The custom-made junction could route every telephone line into a single output. He gripped one end, the rest unfurling with a whoosh as it snaked to the earth below. A quick glance down revealed Hyde and Olson moving like shadows beneath the starlit sky. His grip tightened.

It was go-time.

Simmons pulled and reconnected wires. It was delicate work, requiring a steady hand. With each splice, he became an urban alchemist. Instead of lead or gold, he transformed turmoil into a fellowship of harmony. The irony wasn't lost on him. Bringing order to Hyde's chaos seemed to be his role in this world.

Of course, alchemy came with risks. One wrong move would create disaster.

As he worked, Simmons glanced up at the stars, taking a moment to orient himself. The celestial bodies usually provided reassurance, but tonight, they appeared out of sorts.

"Gonna be a long night."

Within moments, he noticed Andrea drive off, disappearing into the darkness before turning toward the blinding front entrance. Simmons admired her courage, stepping out of her comfort zone. It struck him how remarkable all these women were. Hyde, Jessica, and now Andrea. No wonder his personal life was so drab.

He shook off the thought. Time was running out. With care, he color-coded each wire with tape, creating a map of complex circuitry before reconnecting them. Not a single line could be missed. It was slow work, but success hinged on his ability to hijack facility communications.

"Done and dusted." Simmons admired his handiwork. "Paracelsus, eat your heart out."

He chuckled, imagining Hyde's appreciative smirk at the reference. Her knowledge of famous alchemists had first drawn him to her, a shared interest that balanced her penchant for anarchy. As he connected the red wire, Simmons reflected on how Gabrielle subconsciously sought equilibrium.

A modern Taoist balance. Matheo's brashness complemented Jessica's finesse. Hyde's complexity found its yang in Olson's steadfastness. Of course, she wouldn't admit it. Out loud or to herself.

A sudden fizzing sound erupted from the electrical unit. White smoke puffed out, stinging his eyes. Simmons flinched, fighting the urge to cough, the taste of burned plastic lingering in his throat.

"Oh, come on!"

A surge of panic threatened to upset his serenity. He exhaled, forcing himself to find his Samadhi. The Buddhist state of concentration helped clear his self-pity and fear.

With renewed determination, Simmons tore into the wires, yanking them from their connections. As he worked, burned strands left sooty smudges on his fingertips. He was acutely aware that any delay could put the entire team at risk. Above, the disarrayed heavens seemed to mock him.

Sweat trickled down his temples as his singed fingers moved with precision. He grunted, wrenching out a stubborn wire with charred insulation, tossing it aside before plotting a reroute. His fingertips danced over the multicolored strands, each connection a minor victory. A burn on his pinkie throbbed, the price of carelessness. With a final twist and cap, the box looked neater.

Far from pretty, but it would do.

Gritting his teeth, he inserted the red wire. Sparks erupted with a sharp crack, and he recoiled, snatching back the cord with a hiss of pain.

He wiped sweat away with a grimy hand, the stench of ozone and burned plastic filling the air. Simmons glanced at his watch, then at the tangle before him. Something was overloading the network.

With a sudden burst of insight, he traced a tangle of wires back to its source. He found the problem: a mislabeled node acting as a conductor, shorting it out.

"Gotcha," he murmured, stripping the end and splicing it.

Holding his breath, he plugged in the red line.

To his delight, it was stable. No sizzle, no sparks. The wires hummed with a steady flow of electricity.

The tension faded, but there was no time to savor the victory. He was cutting it too close. Sliding down the telephone pole like lightning, the rough wood and steel holds bit into his hands and feet. Landing with a soft thud, the impact jarred his old knee injury, sending a sharp twinge up his leg. He winced, the pain throbbing as he limped to the van.

Equipment cramped the interior, but he quickly linked his custom cord to his homemade communications control box. The device sat silently for a moment, then the red light blinked out.

After half a second, a secondary bulb illuminated, casting a green hue across his triumphant grin. Simmons had successfully hijacked the facility's phone transmissions. But his celebration was short-lived as the crackle of Hyde's voice on the radio called for action.

The countdown was melodramatic, but it was her way.

A thunderous boom shattered the night's silence. His ears rang as he whipped around to see a distant orange glow blooming on the horizon, followed by a thick plume of smoke spiraling skyward.

Jessica's handiwork, no doubt.

The green light on his control box blinked insistently, signaling an incoming call from the facility's security team. "Showtime," he whispered, adjusting his headset's microphone.

He pressed the transmit button. "Switchboard."

On the other end, a worried voice spoke with a blend of fear and intrigue. Just as Hyde had envisioned. Simmons listened intently, his mind already preparing the rehearsed response.

"No worries at all, sir. The seismic system tripped. Power's out. We'll dispatch a team immediately. Hang tight."

As the call ended, Simmons couldn't help but chuckle. Faking an earthquake was a fresh scratch from his bucket list.

The green light blinked, indicating more incoming calls. He composed himself, ready to maintain the illusion. He glanced at the stars once more. Maybe their disorder reflected the mayhem they had unleashed. Maybe he was turning copper into gold after all.

He answered the phone, his calm voice repeating the crafty lie. Every second counted, and the team needed as many as possible.

As Hyde would say, this was just the opening act.

Chapter 39

SKUNK WORKS VAULT SECURITY ROOM

Emergency bulbs snapped on, bathing the security chamber in a crimson glow. As the lights pulsed, sinister shadows slithered along the walls. Once John's eyes adjusted to the dim lighting, he spotted the unconscious guards sprawled on the floor. He knelt beside Jacob, searching his pockets.

The guard had two sticks of gum and the keys. Rising to his feet, Olson held one key out for Hyde. A glint of determination reflected in her eyes. In exchange, she handed him the Cap-Chur pistol. He gripped it, testing the balance.

"Two darts, two guards," Hyde said. "Make them count."

John tucked the tranquilizer gun into his belt. "I don't miss."

They moved in unison, each inserting their key into the dual lock system. The mechanism clicked as they registered.

Andrea pressed her ear against the door. "They've called in the situation. They're waiting for a technical team."

Hyde motioned to Andrea. "Stand back."

As she stepped away, Olson reached into his pocket and retrieved two flash-bang grenades. He held them up to catch Hyde's eye. She gave a curt nod. He pulled the pins, holding the small canisters' activating levers closed.

He raised his right hand, fingers splayed in a silent countdown. Three...

two… one… They turned their keys simultaneously; the lock disengaged with a soft click. The heavy door cracked open, revealing a sliver of the room beyond.

A surprised voice came from inside. "Wow! You got here fast!"

Olson slipped the flash-bangs through the narrow opening. The levers sprang free, metal casings clinking against the floor. He pressed his back against the wall, bracing himself, ears covered.

The flash-bangs erupted with a searing light and a thunderous boom. John's skin prickled from the pressure shockwave as it hit his chest. The smell of burning chemicals was overwhelming. Even though he shielded his ears, the blast left them ringing painfully. Pushing through, he seized the dart gun with his dominant hand.

Olson burst through the door, sliding into the room on his knees. Smoke from the grenades clouded his vision, but the familiar smell of gunpowder sharpened his focus.

Two guards staggered toward the door, their faces contorted in confusion. Hands clapped over their ears, they were trying to regain their bearings. John fired the tranquilizer pistol twice in rapid succession. The darts found their mark with unerring accuracy, striking both in the chest. Despite the slower results, he couldn't risk aiming for the neck and missing.

The men swayed, reaching for their weapons. One managed to unholster his gun and point it before the tranquilizer took effect. His finger slackened, and both men crumpled to the ground.

"Clear!"

Andrea stumbled into the room. Her eyes widened at the sight of the unconscious guard with a gun still in hand. She grasped the doorframe to steady herself as she turned to John. He recognized the look of someone confronting violence for the first time.

"I'm okay. And so is he," John said, hoping to keep her focused.

It seemed to help. Andrea turned her attention to the imposing vault door at the far end. She stepped closer, examining the system mounted above.

"The alarm is off… We got lucky."

John sprinted to the hallway, seized the green Army duffle filled with equipment, and rushed back to the inner security checkpoint where Hyde waited.

At the control panel, Andrea's fingers grazed over switches and buttons. The unsettling red glow illuminated her face as she analyzed the readouts.

"The electronic seal lock is deactivated," she announced. She turned, confusion on her face. "But how did that work without triggering the alarms?"

Olson knelt by the duffel bag, laying out the tools. He looked up, seeing a familiar sight on Hyde's face. It was the look she got when she was about to reveal something clever.

"This facility sits right on top of the Mojave segment of the San Andreas Fault," Gabrielle said. "Under the 1942 California Building Code, seismometers were added to all federal installations, including this one. By 1965, that same code mandated overriding lockdowns during power failures caused by earthquakes."

Her hand pushed the wall. "Matheo's machine provided the proper resonance. Then, Jessica cut the electricity for the entire sector. The system and personnel bought it. They opened the door for us."

"Safety first, as they say."

Olson couldn't help but smirk. Only Gabrielle Hyde would concoct a scheme as bold as faking an earthquake to infiltrate a vault. It was absurd. And brilliant.

Vasquez would undoubtedly lose his mind when he discovered the ruse. First a curse, then his face would turn that telltale shade of reddish-purple.

John inspected the tools. "I've got everything ready, but I don't see how we proceed. Simmons explicitly said drilling was out."

"We aren't drilling. We'll use the code."

Andrea frowned. "Gabrielle, I don't have it. Only the head of security has that combination."

"It's all right, my dear. I've got a better way."

"What way?" John asked.

He had expected a brute-force method. But, as usual, Hyde had been coy with her plans. She removed her gloves and kneeled, letting her delicate fingers slide over the massive steel door with reverence.

"Ever heard of Harry Miller?" She didn't wait for a response. "In 1940, he devised a pioneering scientific method for cracking safes. Still used today."

"Miller was an innovator," she continued. "He was the first to treat it with nuance. Understanding its nature. You must feel the lock's pulse, coaxing it into alignment. The safe," she whispered, leaning close, "wants to be opened."

Hyde's fingers closed around the large dial, her touch gentle. The dial's subtle clicks intensified in the silence, each turn accompanied by the faint rasp of metal on metal.

"You're going to crack it by hand? Hyde, this isn't some backroom safe. It's state-of-the-art. Impossible."

"Such an absolute term, John. You should know better." She spun the dial, letting it come to a slow stop under the friction of her fingertips. "Now, please pay attention. Sometimes, knowledge is more important than skill."

Her concentration went back to the task as she unconsciously bit her lower lip. "In a safe, each piece is a dancer in a grand ballet."

John clenched his jaw, stifling his retort. Arguing with Hyde was futile.

She rotated the knob again. "The combination dial connects to a spindle and drive cam. The drive pin pushes the wheel fly as the cam rotates." Her fingers moved with surgical precision, switching directions. "Turned in the correct order, notches allow the fence to drop into the groove."

Olson watched, transfixed. The indicator clicked. The soft metallic sounds were almost thunderous. Each time she stopped, paused, and sped up in the other direction.

With a dramatic click, Hyde raised her hand away. A series of clunks emanated from within the safe as tumblers fell into place.

"The fence gone, the bolt now slides," she said, rising to her feet. The vault thumped. "And the impossible is now probable."

Grasping the safe's large wheel, Hyde gave it a firm spin. The bolts retracted with a smooth, well-oiled sound, and the massive steel door swung open with a rumbling groan. Cool air rushed out, carrying the overwhelming hum of whirling Cray-1 computers.

Andrea's hands trembled as she gestured at the swinging door. "That's… that's not possible. No one should be able to…." She leaned in. "I have to… How?'"

"I don't normally divulge secrets for free." Gabrielle stared at Andrea, relenting with a clasp of her hands together, as if praying. "I'm sorry, old habits. For you, my dear, I'll share."

"Every safe is manufactured with a pre-programmed combination. People assume it's secure," she explained. "A footnote in DoD Regulation 5200 prevents removing the primary code. Users simply establish a separate combo for day-to-day operations, forgetting the original still exists."

"Bureaucracy can be useful." Hyde winked at him. "Miller's first rule: know the combination in advance. I will spare you the tale of what it took to acquire that scrap of critical intelligence."

Her cunning was beyond compare; Hyde was no mere thief. It only confirmed he could never be complacent. She'd broken into one of America's most secure facilities without tripping alarms, causing major damage, or hurting anyone badly.

The next part would be just as difficult. Maybe more. They needed to retrieve the data and escape.

Illuminated by a haunting red glow, the chamber resembled a scene from a dystopian nightmare. Towering Cray-1 supercomputers, each standing eight feet wide and seven feet high, filled the space. Their imposing structures hummed with latent power as miles of internal wiring trailed like veins through mechanical giants.

The air crackled with electricity, carrying a distinct smell of hot wires and machinery. Steam hissed from the pipes, creating a hazy atmosphere that added to the scene's surreal nature. The temperature dropped, chilling John's skin. Large tanks lining the walls housed fresh and used Freon. Rhythmic clicks and whirs from hidden tape compartments pulsed like a mechanical heartbeat.

For a moment, the scene captivated him. A spectacle few outside Skunk Works would ever witness. It also reminded him they were far from done.

Andrea's urgent voice snapped John from his worries. "We have less than two hours before the guards change shifts."

John glanced at his watch and grimaced.

"The decoy, please," Hyde said, turning to Andrea.

From the duffel bag, Andrea pulled two oversized metal wheels. The spindles resembled movie theater film reels. "Note the red color on the outer wheel," she said as she handed them over to John for inspection. "It's how we distinguish them from the real tapes inside the computer."

Hyde's plan got them into the vault, but it was Andrea who addressed the long-term problem of the missing data following the heist. Stealing the original data from the Skunk Works facility wasn't enough.

She had briefed everyone on the process of a shutdown. "Once the program closes, the government cannot ship these enormous computers. Instead, they'll send the tapes."

If someone stole or destroyed them, the facility programmers would simply produce another copy. But if the administrators felt the tapes were undisturbed, they would ship them without checking. As a director, Andrea could influence that decision. Without engineering expertise, no one could tell the difference.

John suggested empty tapes, but Hyde scoffed. "Blank tapes were just as bad. The Soviet scientists would discover the ruse and return to the source. This leaves the problem in place. The Soviets must think they won."

Andrea had the perfect diabolical alternative. She could hand them a poison pill. "Bad data is worse than no data," she told them. "I have copies containing our most disastrous research. Years wasted chasing a promising idea that turned out to be completely wrong. We can grab them on the way to the vault."

To outsmart the Soviets, they needed to give them what they wanted. A swap would preserve America's technological advantage and hurt the USSR. The best part, according to Andrea, was the mole would deliver it directly to the enemy.

Andrea tapped her head. "Their belief in its authenticity will be their weakness. They'll spend years trying to make sense of it before realizing it's all wrong. By then, they'll have dismissed other ideas that could have helped them advance their research. It's a double whammy."

She even proposed hiding the original tapes among the non-shipped materials. That way, the real data would stay on-site, safe from manipulation. In her mind, this wasn't a heist. It was a rescue mission.

This was a new side of Andrea. Her voice took on a confident edge, and John realized she was reveling in the chance to outsmart their adversaries. And her own security. Even Hyde had given her a tip of the cap. John was proud, but also ashamed of bringing his dark world into her life.

John stood at the brink of the crimson vault, staring. The towering Cray-1 supercomputers emitted a low, constant hum.

No more theory. Time to put her plan into motion.

John looked at Andrea with admiration, motioning to the dummy tapes. "If I didn't tell you before, you're brilliant."

Andrea glowed under his praise. This was her domain. He would help her defend it.

Hyde's sharp clap shattered the spell. "All right, you two, let's get moving. *Tempus fugit,* and such."

John took a deep breath. He needed to lead by example, to prove he was capable of hard choices. His and Andrea's future depended on what happened next. So did the fate of his nation.

Stepping into the computer room, he felt the polished white tile sink beneath his weight with a faint click.

An ear-piercing alarm suddenly wailed.

Chapter 40

The alarm's wail shattered the silent atmosphere. Harsh floodlights snapped on, casting sharp shadows across John's shocked face.

"Floor alarms?" Andrea said, her face turning white. "That wasn't in the schematics!"

"We all missed it," Hyde said. "I have to give it to them. Hidden yet effective."

John froze. This twist derailed their plans, despite being so close. Would they abort and split up? He had always expected the second part, but he needed the physical tapes to deliver on his promise.

Andrea held up the red reel, pointing to the computers. "I need at least ninety minutes to reprogram the system and get the tapes out," she shouted.

Simmons' voice crackled over John's radio. "What's happening in there, boss? Phone lines are blowing up!"

Hyde seized it from John's belt. "Douglas, you need to hold them off for as long as possible. Buy us more time."

There was a brief pause. "I'll do my best, but I can't promise anything. You better hurry."

Andrea's body trembled as she grappled for control. John stepped closer, giving her hand a reassuring squeeze. "Is there anything we can do about the alarms?"

"No, the security system is external. There's nothing. We're done."

Hyde stalked the room, thumb rubbing her chin. "What about the computers? Some way to get to the tapes quickly? It could be anything," she said. "Think! Don't hold back."

Andrea paced in a circle. Her eyes widened. "There's a fail-safe," she blurted.

John leaned in. "What kind of fail-safe?"

"The computers... if they overheat, they'll eject the tapes to prevent damage." She pointed at the machine. "The internal heat sensor, if it activates, triggers an ejection."

She paused, biting her lower lip. "The panels should open automatically."

Hyde's eyes narrowed. "Should?"

"In theory," Andrea replied, hesitating. "The discharge sequence is a secondary system. Never tested." She glanced at John, looking for assurance. "I didn't mention it because an over-temp would harm the computers. They cost over two million dollars each."

Hyde grabbed her by the shoulders. "Can you trigger it?"

Beads of sweat dotted Andrea's forehead. "I can't fake an overheat. Not with the time we have."

"Plan B," Hyde said, grabbing a large wrench from the floor.

Without hesitation, she swung it at the Freon lines that snaked along the walls, connecting the massive computers to the mounted tanks. The first strike resounded like a cannon. Liquid and gas spewed from the ruptured line, hissing and sputtering.

"What the hell are you doing?" John demanded.

Hyde struck the pipes again. "They're Freon-cooled. No coolant," she grunted. Clang! "No cooling!"

She turned to John, pointing with her wrench. "Get in here and help me!"

John jumped into action. Grabbing a second tool from the floor, he struck the lines with all his strength.

Metal shrieked against metal, reverberating. Freon sprayed, coating their skin and clothes in a fine, icy mist. The sickly-sweet smell filled John's nostrils, a nostalgic whiff of car coolant that transported him momentarily to his late uncle's auto repair shop.

As the Freon interacted with the other gases in the vault, it sank to the floor, forming a thick fog that swirled. The Cray-1 computers responded to the sudden loss of cooling liquid with a series of loud, urgent beeps. Internal components clicked, protesting the rising heat.

Andrea picked up the radio as Simmons broadcast again. "Security team incoming. You've got seven minutes tops."

John turned to Andrea. "How long for the override?"

Andrea's eyes darted back and forth as she did the mental math. The temperature in the room climbed rapidly. John felt sweat beading on his forehead.

"It doesn't need to be perfect."

She shrugged. "Seven, maybe eight minutes. At least."

John hissed a curse. It wasn't enough.

A deep, rumbling groan filled the room. John's head snapped to the vault door. To his horror, the massive metal slab was closing, inching its way towards the frame.

Andrea rushed to the doorway, her hands pressing against the smooth surface in a futile attempt to halt its progress. John recognized the futility of her actions.

He locked eyes with Hyde. "They're locking it down remotely! Get out while you can."

John dropped his wrench, the metal clattering to the floor as he rushed to Andrea's side. "Follow me," he said, grabbing her hand and pulling her along.

She refused to move. "We can't abandon her!"

John released his grip. "We're not. But we have to act now!"

He sprang over the unconscious guards, approached the imposing oak desk. 'Help me!' he barked, already bracing his shoulder against the wood.

In a blur of desperation, John and Andrea heaved the solid desk. It scraped and grated on the floor, fighting every inch. With a shove, they wedged it lengthwise into the door. The desk creaked and groaned against the pressure, but the sturdy wood held firm, keeping the pathway open.

"John! Get her out of here," Hyde yelled. "You need to secure the escape path!"

John felt conflicted. He had vowed never to let Hyde out of his sight.

But he also needed to protect Andrea. No matter the choice, something valuable would be lost.

Hyde seemed to sense his inner turmoil. "I've got this. Get her to safety."

A lump formed in his throat. He grasped Andrea's hand, their fingers intertwining. Together they ran, leaving Hyde alone in the vault.

John and Andrea burst through the security room door, their steps in sync with the deafening alarms. The hallway stretched out before them, its blank walls carrying their footsteps. John pulled Andrea, her hand gripped tightly in his.

As they ran, the chaos faded behind them. The immediate danger receded, but a new tension took its place. With each foot down the hallway, Olson moved further from justice. He had to make a choice and needed to make it now.

John skidded to a stop.

Andrea's momentum almost pulled him off balance. "What are you doing?" she asked.

John's chest heaved as he searched for the right words. "I can't abandon Hyde."

"She ordered us to leave, John."

She didn't know the rest of the story. John was drowning in this ocean of secrets. He had an agenda he couldn't trust to anyone. Not even Andrea.

His thoughts drifted back to Hyde's earliest teachings. She had once emphasized that a successful con often relied on a fabricated emergency. It forced the mark to make hasty, ill-advised decisions based on a false sense of urgency.

Was this entire moment orchestrated by Hyde? Surely she hadn't triggered the alarm on purpose.

"The less you know, the safer you are," he said. "I have to stay."

Andrea shook her head. "You stay, I stay."

"Go. I can't..." He swallowed hard. "You need to get Matheo out. Only you can do that."

"No, damn it!"

Those were the words he wanted to scream as well.

Andrea's face was dirty and weary, but her eyes resembled two speckled, hazel moons. The emotion underneath was dark and powerful, like a storm at sea. They begged with an unspoken plea for him to go with her.

Reaching out, he gently cupped her cheek. "I'll find you," he promised. "Trust me."

Andrea leaned in. He pressed his forehead against hers, savoring the moment. The world fell away. No alarms, no aching muscles. Just them.

"I do," she whispered. She squeezed his hand, her fingers intertwining with his.

She turned and ran, slipping through one of the far doors. As Andrea vanished, John wondered if he would ever see her again.

Probably not.

John allowed his heart to break, then sprinted back. Despite the lies, manipulations, and betrayals, he wouldn't abandon Hyde. Everything coming depended on her.

He bounded past the unconscious guards and into the outer chamber. As he approached the wedged desk, John didn't slow down. He launched himself, sliding across the top and landing on his feet inside the computer room. A foot-deep mist swirled around his legs.

From beneath one of the Cray-1 supercomputers, Hyde emerged. Her face was streaked with sweat and grime.

"I told you to leave!"

John met her gaze. "Never leave a woman behind."

Hyde rolled her eyes, but John could have sworn he saw a trace of gratitude in her expression. Respect, perhaps.

She slid him a wrench. "Make yourself useful."

John caught the tool. He gave the cooling pipes three more overhand hits, severing the connection. The supercomputers whirred louder, their internal components straining under the oppressive heat. Fans went into overdrive trying to compensate for lost coolant.

Hyde worked with focused intensity under the first computers. A series of sharp clicks came from within the Cray-1, the sound of multiple latches disengaging.

"First set is out!"

John's blood pressure skyrocketed as he watched her replace the genuine tapes with the decoy. The sirens shrieked, a reminder that the security team was imminent.

Steam hissed from the computers' vents, the metal casings now hot to the touch. John could feel the heat on his skin, his shirt clinging to his back, damp with sweat.

A sudden groan and creak was followed by a loud crack. John whirled around, his mouth dropping as he saw the oak desk cave under the immense pressure.

"Hyde! The door won't hold!"

Hyde emerged, face slick. "First set secured," she said, holding up the tape.

The desk gave way with a sickening crunch, the wood shattering into a thousand pieces. Fragments exploded across the floor, disappearing in the mist. The vault door, no longer impeded, began to close with a deep, resonant rumble.

John sprinted to the opening. "I can't stop it! We gotta go!"

Hyde slid under the second Cray-1. "Seconds away from the second reel."

She wasn't going to make it.

John's eyes landed on an oversized neon-yellow fire extinguisher mounted on the wall. He dashed over, yanking it free. He sprinted to the vault door and shoved the heavy three-foot cylinder into the narrowing gap. The metal groaned and crumpled.

Behind him, John heard a click as the next compartment popped open. He glanced over his shoulder just as Hyde swapped out the second reel of data tapes. Crack. The fire extinguisher's steel skin buckled, the surface twisting grotesquely.

They had seconds, at most.

"Come on! Come on!" John ducked into the security room. "Hyde! We're out of time!"

As Hyde stood, cradling the tapes under her arm, the extinguisher let out a tortured groan, the metal tearing like paper. Fire retardant streamed out, pushing John back.

Hyde lunged forward with a burst of speed, leaping into the narrowing gap. She disappeared into the mist and closing void just as the extinguisher collapsed with a deafening bang, exploding in a blinding white cloud of compressed gas.

The vault door slammed shut with a resounding boom. John staggered back, coughing and sputtering as the dense chemical fog forced him to shield his face.

"Hyde!" he called out. "Where are you?"

No answer.

The disorienting alarms persisted. Squinting through the haze, his pulse raced. Had Hyde made it out?

John swiped at his eyes, attempting to clear away the retardant. He spat, trying to rid the taste of chemicals coating his tongue.

"Gabrielle!"

He took a tentative step forward, shoes crunching on debris.

Dread spread through his body. He had come too far, risked too much. After all he'd endured, this couldn't be the end.

Not when he was so close.

Chapter 41

The caustic fire suppressant cloud thinned, and harsh light knifed through the haze, casting distorted shadows. A silhouette materialized.

Hyde. Tall and ethereal, data tapes clutched under her arm. John closed the distance in two strides.

Her lips curved into a victorious smile. Reaching out, her fingers curled around John's shoulder. "Thank you." Her eyes sparkled. "You know, we may make a thief of you yet."

Leave it to her to find humor at the worst of times. He looked up at the blaring alarm. "Let's get out of here."

Together, they sprinted out the door and into the labyrinthine of corridors. The hallways stretched out before them, an endless maze of twists. Thunderous footsteps announced security teams at every corner, forcing numerous detours.

As they ran, the radio attached to John's belt crackled to life.

"Anyone copy?"

"This is Olson."

"It's Jessica." Static broke up her words due to the thick walls. "I'm back with Simmons… Primary… compromised. I repeat… exit's compromised."

They had planned every detail around that exit, and without it, their chances of escape plummeted. Was this another manufactured crisis, or the real thing?

Hyde seized the radio from John's hand. "Copy that," she said. "Moving to the alternate."

Hyde never mentioned a backup plan or an alternative route. He skidded to a halt, yanking Hyde back with him.

"Keep moving, John," she urged.

"No. We need to hide these somewhere in the building," John said, gesturing to the backpack that now held the precious data tapes. "Secure them. Then, Andrea finishes the plan tomorrow. The last thing we want is being caught with these on us."

Hyde shook her head. "The priority is to clear the facility," she countered. "Andrea can return them later. We must get to the alternate exit immediately."

"You didn't tell me about this."

Hyde shrugged, unfazed. "I didn't have time to brief every detail."

John gritted his teeth, fighting the urge to lash out. Hyde had changed the plan, just like she always did. If anything, it was the only predictable thing she ever did.

"Where are we going?"

Hyde was already moving down the corridor. "West building."

John followed, suppressing a reaction. The West building. This confirmed everything.

They resumed their dash until they reached an access stairwell leading to the roof. Hyde led the way, taking the steps two at once, her feet clanging on the old metal.

They burst through a door and emerged onto the rooftop, the night air a welcome respite after sprinting through the facility. The city sprawled on the horizon, a glittering medley of lights.

Hyde wasted no time. She pulled a carabiner from a hidden harness and jogged to the edge of the building.

John lagged, closing the door firmly behind him. He reached into his pocket and withdrew an old key he'd stolen from the security office. With a deft motion, he locked the metal door's deadbolt and snapped the key off in the lock.

No one follows. No one leaves.

This moment was years overdue.

John turned to watch Hyde look for her escape line. This was the same stunt she pulled in Toronto. Did she think he hadn't learned?

Hyde reached up to clip her carabiner onto the zipline, but her hand grasped at empty air. The line, which should have been taut and ready, hung limp and frayed, its steel end unraveling.

It had been cut. There was no escape.

She spotted a discarded set of bolt cutters, blades glinting in the moonlight. Gabrielle spun to face John, her eyes wide. Confusion and, for once, shock etched her features.

John steadied the gun, leveling the barrel at Hyde's chest.

"Why?" The word escaped Hyde in a whisper.

"You can't change who you are, Hyde. Always looking out for yourself. But this time, I win." John spoke the words he had been waiting years to say. "Gabrielle Hyde, you are under arrest."

A shadow of concern flashed across Hyde's features. It vanished so quickly he almost convinced himself he'd imagined it. Recovering, she adopted an impatient stance. "Stop with the shenanigans, Olson. We're running out of time."

"You're correct, Hyde. Your time's up."

Hyde smirked. "We've been down this road," she said. "We both know how this ends."

He advanced, each step sending pea gravel flying. "This isn't Toronto. I'm not the same man."

Hyde tilted her head, assessing the situation.

"I knew you'd try to play me, Hyde. Three nights ago, I saw you on this roof, supposedly scouting the facility. But it didn't add up."

Hyde's eyebrows raised.

"Then it finally hit me," John continued. "This is a terrible scouting site. The line's wrong, the vantage too low. But it's a perfect escape point."

John gestured to the cable. "After my meeting with Director Avery, I came to this spot and found your escape route. So, I cut it off."

Hyde's eyes darted to the frayed wire ends. She looked surprised, but then her expression turned indifferent again.

"I realized you and Morozov planned this from the beginning. Using fear of a Soviet mole to force an overreaction. Brilliant, really."

At the mention of the spymaster's name, Hyde's left hand jerked, her fingers instinctively tracing the edges of the hidden tattoo. Her face tightened as she forced her hands idle.

"It's not what you think. Sasha is only a means to an end. I can explain everything. Trust me, I'm still on your side."

John was furious. His anger bubbled up, threatening to spill over. Even now, cornered and caught, she couldn't be honest. His gun trembled so much the bullets rattled.

"Enough!" John's voice cracked. "I saw the pictures of you and Morozov. I know the truth."

A rhythmic thump cut through the night air, distant but growing closer. Helicopter blades.

She opened her mouth to speak, but John silenced her with a sharp gesture of his gun. "I'm done, Hyde. Your lies, your manipulations. I'm finished with all of it. Everything with you is an act." He cocked his head. "Do you even have the capacity to tell the truth anymore?"

For a moment, Hyde was silent. Then she let out a slow breath. "If only the world were as black and white as you see it."

"Morozov is evil!" John spat. "How could you align yourself with him? That man killed my partner. In a way, you killed him too. Go to hell."

"There's more to this than you know."

Olson's finger hovered over the trigger. "Then explain it to me. Because from where I'm standing, it looks like you've betrayed everyone. Me, Andrea, this country. You used all of us."

He pulled out the photo of Hyde kissing Morozov on the cheek and threw it at her feet. "This picture paints it pretty clearly."

Hyde opened her mouth to respond, but stopped. Her eyes fell on the picture.

The sound of footsteps thundering up the stairwell cut through the tense silence. His head snapped towards the doorway. The cavalry had arrived. He just needed one more minute for the confession.

Hyde would give him a confession. He just needed more time.

Something crashed into the entryway. Boots trying to kick in the locked door reverberated across the roof like a countdown. The frame shuddered with each forceful blow, muffled shouts growing more impatient.

"FBI! Open up!" A man's voice boomed.

"We need to go before they get through that door. I'll explain everything," Hyde said. Her voice sounded strained.

John's grip tightened. "You've been working with Morozov this entire time. There was no shadow government agent. Just another clever ruse."

"No." Hyde shook her head.

"Don't lie! I was always the mark. Your mark. You're the mole, Hyde," John shouted.

He pointed the gun accusingly. "I don't know how you manipulated this whole thing into existence, but it has Gabrielle Hyde written all over it. Everything… everything… done to gain you access to the stealth data. And you used my pain to get it."

John felt tears forming, but he blinked them away. The betrayal cut deeper than any physical wound. But he refused to show weakness.

Hyde inched forward, hands raised. "It's not that simple, John. Morozov is a tool, a means. But he has certain… leverage. I had to go along. You wouldn't have understood, so I kept it from you. Our pain is more alike than you know."

Hyde's eyes met his, and John thought he saw regret.

No, not regret. It was something deeper. More primal. Fear? But Hyde feared no one. Or did she?

"Try me."

The kicks at the stairwell gave way to the rhythmic crash of a battering ram. Each impact sent tremors through the concrete, threatening to tear the door from its hinges.

"To be free, you must learn to smile in the devil's face. Sometimes, monsters can be useful."

Her words, so casually spoken, left John reeling.

A Bell 206B materialized from the darkness, its rotors slicing through the air with a deafening whomp-whomp. Gusts of gale-force wind whipped across the rooftop, plastering John's clothes to his body.

"You're right. Morozov is the devil," he yelled. "And so are you."

The words tasted bitter, but he knew they were true. Hyde had played him from the start, manipulating him like a marionette. And he had let her do it.

"You're the same, both of you!"

Fury blazed in Hyde's eyes, demolishing her composure in a way John had never witnessed before.

"No! Not the same!" She surged forward, disregarding the gun. "You think you know me? You don't!"

The helicopter circled, its downdraft whipping their hair and clothes. Debris pelted them from every direction.

"That place… that hell," she stammered. "In the camp, my father and the others trained me to be a weapon against the Germans. They thought a child could slip under the radar. But my father… he didn't realize the extent of the Nazis' cruelty."

The downwash swirled her hair chaotically. Hyde's eyes, usually sharp and calculating, now seemed to look through John, focused on some horrific memory. The rooftop, the helicopter, the storming FBI agents. It all faded into the background.

The helicopter took another pass, giving them a moment of reprieve.

Hyde's voice dropped, forcing John to lean in. "I was all alone by the time the Russian soldiers took the camp. That's when I first met him, Commissar Sasha Morozov, an officer of the Workers' and Peasants' Red Army."

He wasn't interested in rationalization.

Hyde's voice faltered, her eyes distant. "I thought I knew evil. I presumed I had seen the depths of human cruelty. But nothing… could have prepared me for what came next." Her hands trembled openly. "They broke me. Shattered in ways I never imagined possible. And I… I put myself back together, piece by jagged piece. I then became the weapon my father envisioned."

Olson's grip on his gun loosened. What had Morozov done to her? But then, the countless times Hyde had deceived him came rushing back. He refused to fall for it again.

"Enough with the lies!"

"You don't know pain, John. You think you do, but you're wrong," Hyde cried. "Morozov took everything from me when I was just a girl. Things even the Nazis wouldn't dare to do." Her fists clenched, nails biting into her palms as she curled inward, making herself smaller. "You can't imagine what that does to a person."

As Hyde's last admission left her lips, she seemed to deflate, eyes shimmering with tears. She looked absolutely fragile. John saw a woman haunted by an endless battle.

Her constant bravado wasn't real. It was the true mask.

He staggered back, his boots scraping against the rough rooftop. Hyde's story was laced with such raw anguish, her pain so genuine, that for a moment, he was tempted to believe her. Tempted to embrace the humanity he saw.

He shook it off. Her tale wouldn't sway him, no matter how horrific or convincing.

"Enough! I'm done with your slick stories. Shame on you for exploiting others' horror as your cover."

"It's not a story. It's my life." Hyde's expression hardened. "I was using Morozov. Trying to find his partner in the government. He kept it well-hidden, even from me."

The door frame buckled under the assault behind them.

Voice raspy, Hyde continued. "I knew from that day in Virginia that you would do anything to get your revenge, just like I once did. I used your pain to lure Morozov closer, and for that, I am sorry."

Olson's trigger finger tightened. "I'm not playing this game."

With a sigh, Hyde lowered the bag containing the data tapes and tossed it at John's feet. She met John's gaze, her expression etched with resignation.

"I never wanted you to shoulder this burden alone."

John looked at the sack before returning his attention to Hyde's face.

Tears streaked down her cheeks, pooling at the corners of her slim lips. He crouched down and ran his fingers along the rim, inspecting the red color on the reel.

"It's the originals," Hyde said.

"You expect me to believe you?"

"I'm a thief, not a liar."

For a moment, he had doubts. But Hyde's betrayals were too extreme. "You weave lies to survive. And I fell for every single one of them. What's worse, so did Andrea."

The helicopter approached again, its blades unleashing a fresh roar. John squinted against the wind, his eyes watering. Hyde lowered herself to her knees, interlacing her fingers behind her neck in surrender.

John looked at her. Bent and broken, waiting on her knees. For a moment, he saw beyond the manipulator to a broken survivor, scarred by unimaginable horrors.

Victim or not, she had still used him. The disclosure of her past didn't absolve her present actions. And now, with the FBI at the door and the helicopter anchored overhead, she was beaten.

"John, the law doesn't always mean truth. You know that's true." Hyde's voice was barely audible. "Trust yourself. Use your heart to decide."

She knew how to twist his emotions. "Be quiet."

Hyde pressed on, undeterred. "Beware, John. You're being deceived. Whoever takes those reels. Oh… and they will demand them… they're Morozov's true partner."

Why was she clinging to this line? Hyde was Morozov's partner.

Or was there a second partner? Hyde might be telling the truth. In that case, someone else, someone he trusted, was working for Morozov. A secret accomplice. Names and faces flashed through his thoughts.

No!

He wouldn't let Hyde play him again. "I'll keep them safe."

With a booming blow, the steel door's bottom hinge exploded. Screws scattered across the gravel as the frame buckled inward. They had seconds left.

Hyde's laugh rasped, her eyes catching the harsh light. "That's naive."

"Be quiet!"

"You're wrong, and you know it," Gabrielle insisted, her voice demanding to be heard. "I didn't do what you say, Officer Olson. They'll never let you keep that data."

Hyde raised her head and stared at him. "They'll shut down the Stealth program, and Morozov wins," she continued. "You stopped nothing and lost everything."

The steel frame buckled with a tortured shriek. The hinges exploded from their mounts in a shower of twisted metal and concrete dust.

Her gaze bore into his. "It's not too late," she whispered.

The door burst open with a crash, fragments pinging like shrapnel. FBI agents stormed through, weapons raised and voices hoarse with shouted commands. They fanned out across the rooftop, their jackets flapping wildly in the wind.

Olson looked at her kneeling before him. A part of him wanted to believe her. He lowered his gun, his shoulders slumping with exhaustion.

"Yes, it is," he whispered back.

The episode left John in a strange, detached state of calm. He watched, almost distant, as FBI agents swarmed the rooftop like a well-drilled unit, their movements seeming to slow in his perception. Countless boots thudded.

John stepped backwards mechanically, decocking his service weapon. Hyde, the center of his world for the last week, was no longer his problem.

She waited, kneeling in surrender, hands laced over her head. John handed his pistol to an agent, who took it into custody as part of protocol. He would get it back later, after the dust had settled.

Two more agents stepped forward, assuming custody of the prisoner. One stripped the radio from her bodice and tossed it aside, the device landing with a clatter.

As the agents snapped cuffs onto her wrists, John watched Hyde's vulnerability vanish, an air of detached control replacing it. Her usual confidence and composure reasserted themselves so quickly, he wondered if he'd imagined her earlier anguish. He longed for just five more minutes to get answers.

Whatever truth that existed, it was now long gone. The walls had returned, and she would never lower them again. That hurt more than anything else.

He retrieved the deceptively simple bag containing the reels. As he slung it over his shoulder, the weight of the data tapes inside seemed to multiply, as if suddenly filled with lead. Olson vowed no one would take it; the research would return to where it belonged.

As the FBI lifted Hyde to her feet, their eyes met a final time. The connection sparked a vortex of conflicting emotions. Relief, regret, anger and loss. He glanced away, unable to confront the complexity.

It was then that John caught sight of a familiar weathered face rushing onto the scene. FBI Special Agent Bruno Vasquez strode confidently across the rooftop, a triumphant grin spreading.

He didn't waste a second before extending his arm to John. "Great work, Officer Olson," he said, shaking John's hand with enthusiasm. "You did it. I never thought you'd do it. But, hot damn… you got her."

"Thanks, Bruno."

John's response felt forced. There was no victory here. Lies and double-crosses had tainted it. He had betrayed Andrea to get the job done. She would never understand, but at least she was safe.

He hoped that one day she could forgive him, but he knew that was unlikely. John saw the parallel between his own actions and Hyde's justifications. Considering everything, he wasn't any better than she was.

Hyde met his gaze. Any hint of vulnerability was gone. Even with cuffs snapped onto her wrists, she exuded an aura of control.

Deputy Director Lucas Avery emerged from the stairwell a moment later, joining Vasquez and John in front of Hyde. His demeanor was more reserved, but no less relieved. Avery extended his hand to John as well, his grip firm and assured.

"I'll be damned, Olson," Avery said, raising his voice over the helicopter's racket. "I had my doubts, but you actually pulled it off. Just like you said you would. Few case officers could execute this kind of operation. Big things are in store for you. Big things."

John inclined his head. Hyde's words were still a nagging itch he couldn't reach.

Avery turned. "Vasquez! Could you please get that damn helicopter out of here? I can hardly hear myself think!"

With a curt half-salute, Vasquez pulled a radio from his belt and stepped away to make the call. Within a few seconds, the helicopter dipped its rotors and vanished into the night.

John caught Hyde eyeing him. "I always knew you were capable of this," she said. Her tone suggested a deeper game at play, one that extended beyond their current circumstances.

Vasquez's face contorted with pride. "Well, well. The great Gabrielle Hyde. Outsmarted by us common feds. How's that ego holding up?"

Her smile didn't falter; if anything, it grew more serene. "It must torment you to know that you still have yet to be the one to capture me. A mere woman."

Vasquez's grin vanished. He lunged forward, his face inches from hers. "I've got a cell reserved just for you. Half a mile from Castro's summer villa. Let's go, move it!"

He gripped her arm tight, jerking her towards the shattered metal door. She offered no resistance, moving with fluid grace despite her restraints. As they approached the exit, Hyde looked back over her shoulder, her eyes finding John.

"Until we meet again, *mon ami*," she said, her voice tinged with a bittersweet note.

Then, with a shove from Vasquez, she was gone. Within moments, Vasquez led her to a waiting SWAT transport, pushing her inside the armored carrier and slamming the door.

As the tactical vehicle carrying Bruno and Gabrielle disappeared into the night, John stood motionless, clutching the bag. The sudden moment ushered in strange thoughts.

Would he ever see Hyde again? Her arrests always seemed transitory, at best.

The bustling agents and twinkling lights blurred into a surreal backdrop. His thoughts turned inward. Had he succeeded, or merely paved the way for a greater ambush? He considered the notion for a long while.

Hyde's words were a haunting refrain he couldn't silence, infecting the empty spaces of his mind. Had he done the right thing? Or had he been played, manipulated by the very institutions he thought he could trust?

Taking a deep breath, John forced himself to push those doubts aside, if only for the moment. The gritty surface shifted beneath his feet as he turned to face Avery, who approached with a more relaxed demeanor now that the mission was complete.

"That was one hell of a covert operation, Olson," he said, clapping John on the back. "I can't believe Hyde manipulated the whole thing from a Black Site. She's even more cunning than we gave her credit for. The FBI's got their hands full now."

John nodded. Hyde's talent for elaborate schemes was legendary, yet her moments of vulnerability felt authentic. He was haunted by that glimpse of raw sincerity. Was it her most masterful performance, or a rare moment of truth? The uncertainty left him questioning everything.

"Yeah," John replied. Nothing about this seemed right.

"No matter. We have our mole. Case closed. You did good work, Olson. The White House already sent its congratulations."

How could Avery be so sure? Everything happened so fast.

Lucas walked towards the mangled door, but then paused, turning back. "I nearly forgot with all the excitement," he said, almost casually. "I'm going to need those reels of data."

As John's hand instinctively went to the bag, his fingers tightened around the strap. The hair on the back of his neck rose, recalling Hyde's warning. The threat had ended. They needed only to walk downstairs and return them.

Surely Deputy Director Avery would understand the danger of leaving the facility with the tapes.

"That's unnecessary, sir. We can put them back into the vault. They'll be secure here."

Avery's forehead creased along worry-lines, his smile fading. "I'm afraid that's not in the cards, Olson," he said. "Skunk Works is being shut down, White House orders. I'll oversee the data's security until the dust settles. Standard protocol in these situations."

"I've never heard of that, sir." John pushed the bag further back on his shoulder. "With all due respect, that doesn't make sense," he said, choosing his words carefully. "Skunk Works is the most secure facility we have. We should use it to our advantage."

Avery's eyes narrowed. "The world's a messy place, Officer Olson. Sometimes, we just have to roll with the punches and follow orders." He extended his hand, palm up, his fingers beckoning. "The reels, please."

John hesitated, his grip on the bag tightening. Every instinct screamed at him to run. Why was Avery so insistent on taking the tapes?

Hyde's warning resurfaced in his mind. Whoever came for the data was working with Morozov. Just like she said.

Avery snapped his fingers twice, the sound sharp and impatient. "I won't ask a second time, John."

John slid the sack from his shoulder and stared at them for a long moment. The danger posed by the critical intelligence within was staggering. And now he was being asked to hand them over without question.

Were orders that defied logic and protocol still legitimate orders?

Reluctantly, he passed the bag to Avery, his fingers brushing against the fabric one last time before letting go. Despite his misgivings, Olson knew he couldn't risk openly defying the Deputy Director of the CIA.

Avery took them, satisfaction crossing his face before he tossed them over his shoulder. "The evidence is in excellent hands now. You did the right thing."

He gestured towards the door, the twisted metal frame gaping like an open wound. "Come on, John. We need to debrief. There's still work to be done."

As they descended the stairs, each step carried John further from certainty. He couldn't shake the feeling that this was far from over. The Deputy Director's explanation made sense on the surface, but Hyde's warning about Morozov's hidden partner lingered.

Could he trust anyone? Nobody remained.

Andrea was safe, but would never forgive him. Hyde's team would vanish like smoke. Even his own agency might become his enemy if he made a move. His only potential ally was in FBI handcuffs and bound for Cuba.

Then there was Morozov. He was still free, patiently waiting for his opportunity.

The tapes had to be destroyed. It was the only path forward. John knew it would get him fired. Maybe make him an outlaw. But this was a red line only he could cross.

Nuclear war hung in the balance. His career, his reputation, even his freedom were nothing compared to that. As John rushed to catch up with Avery, his hand brushed against the railing.

The path ahead was clear. Despite the cost, he would secure and destroy the tapes.

He thought of the Greek god Atlas. He was a man forced to shoulder the weight of the world, a task he could only bear alone.

Chapter 42

Andrea sprinted through the corridors, tears blurring her vision. Each ragged breath scraped her throat raw as her chest tightened. The image of John standing alone left a hole in her heart.

Why did John get to stay while she had to leave?

Part of her wanted to turn back. But the pragmatic part understood she would jeopardize everything.

He had his reasons. The man was the most capable she had ever met. But not everything had to be a solo operation.

Andrea scrubbed her tears away. She'd never been good with emotions.

She navigated the twisting hallways. The blank concrete walls and fluorescent lights created a disorienting maze, but she knew every corner. As she turned a sharp bend, a security guard with his weapon drawn stepped into her path, raising his hand.

She skidded to a halt as the guard's eyes fixed on her orange badge, his lips moving as he read her name.

"Dr. Miles. Did you see anything unusual? Anyone that doesn't belong?"

Andrea swallowed hard, fighting the urge to throw up. John and Gabrielle needed more time. She adopted a look of concern.

"Yes." Her lip quivered as she pointed. "Three men ran toward the central hangar. Am I in danger?"

The guard's eyes widened, spotting her tears. He keyed the radio. "All units, three male suspects heading to the main hangar. Converge and contain!" The guard put a reassuring hand on her shoulder. "Don't worry, ma'am. We'll get them."

Andrea let out a muffled sniffle.

"Get somewhere safe and stay out of sight," he added.

As he disappeared down the corridor, she turned and ran to the parking area, the planned rendezvous for their escape. Of course, that was before the alarms.

As she burst through the garage doors, she spotted Matheo as he was throwing the last of the equipment into the vehicle. He slid the door shut with a decisive thud and turned, grabbing Andrea's arm as he whisked her toward the entrance.

"What about the van?"

"We go on foot," he explained. "They'll be searching vehicles. The gear is a dead giveaway, and we no longer need it."

Andrea followed Matheo to a shadowed corner near the garage entrance. He took a small telescope from his pocket and scanned the front gate.

"Looks clear," he whispered.

In one smooth motion, Matheo ripped off his jumpsuit, revealing slacks and a button-up shirt underneath, perfect for blending in with engineers. He tossed the coveralls into a trashcan and slid on glasses.

"I'll go first," he said.

Andrea grabbed his arm. "Wait. They'll detain us at the gate, clear or not. I might get through, but they'll never let you out without credentials."

Matheo's forehead creased as he considered Andrea's observation. She realized this wasn't an outright frown, just how his face looked when he was engrossed.

"This is your turf. What do you suggest?"

All the normal exits would be guarded. "There's another way," she exclaimed. "A back exit that scientists use to access the overflow parking area. They mostly utilize it for smoke breaks."

"*Montrez la voie.*"

Andrea led Matheo through two narrow alleys and then across the expanse of a sprawling parking lot. Ahead, she spotted the metal turnstiles, concealed within the towering barbed wire fence.

This was their best shot at escape. Hiding inside the facility was no longer an option. Security teams would eventually find them.

A stillness filled the air, broken only by the low, persistent hum of security lights. Swarms of insects circled the bright fixtures, their bodies casting shadows before disappearing with a crisp, electric zap. Andrea hoped to avoid the same fate.

Andrea glanced over her shoulder, then dashed across twenty yards of gravel to the exit. She pushed against the turnstile, the metal harsh against her palms. Its arms groaned, reluctantly giving way.

Matheo followed close behind, his lanky frame wedging between the interlinking bars. A screech of metal. The sound reverberated like nails on a chalkboard.

Two sentries snapped to attention. As Andrea and Matheo approached the second turnstile, the guards sprinted towards them.

"Hey, you! Stop!" the first guard shouted, shining his flashlight.

Andrea shoved Matheo through the last gate, the metal arms spinning. As the red-faced guards reached their unauthorized exit, she swiftly raised her badge.

"Sorry! The gates only work one way. We'll come back around."

The guards, convinced by her apparent ignorance and proper ID, blocked the turnstile to prevent additional exits. Andrea and Matheo moved a few yards further, waiting until the men weren't watching. They ducked between vehicles toward the street.

Once clear, Matheo pulled out his radio, switching the channel. *"Demander un ramassage,"* he whispered. "Extraction point, east auxiliary road."

Moments later, a familiar van rounded the corner, headlights off. Simmons scanned the surroundings as he coasted up beside them. Andrea hopped into the passenger seat while Matheo climbed into the back with Jessica.

As Simmons hit the gas, Andrea braced herself against the center console, glancing in the mirror. More guards patrolled the parking lot, searching for any lingering personnel.

Andrea slumped as her thoughts drifted to John. They had left too much unsaid. Why had she abandoned him?

"What happened in there?" Jessica asked.

"There was a floor sensor," she said. "It triggered the alarm, and they shut the vault door remotely."

"Bollocks!" Jessica slammed her fist against the sidewall. "How'd I miss that?"

Matheo placed a calming hand on Jessica's arm. "Bah, we all missed it. No use pointing fingers now, eh?" he said, his French accent thickening.

The van swerved, forcing everyone to brace themselves.

"How'd you get out of the vault?" Simmons asked, eyes on the road.

Andrea gripped the overhead handle. "We braced the door open with a desk." Simmons twisted the wheel quickly. "Where are we going?"

"Western escape route." He nodded at a hand-drawn map. "Hyde's shifted to Plan B." The van lurched.

"So, they're okay?"

"No need to fret. Hyde's got this sorted." Jessica nodded. "She always has backup plans. Contingencies within contingencies. Rarely shares 'em, mind you. But they'll be just fine. John's in good hands."

Simmons navigated the narrow streets with sharp turns, the facility receding from view. Within five minutes, he pulled off the road into a small clearing.

Glancing at his watch, Simmons noted, "Ten minutes behind schedule."

A sudden movement in the sky drew Andrea's attention. She leaned forward, her pulse quickening as she caught sight of a helicopter circling. Its powerful spotlight sliced through the night and cast its beam across the rooftop.

Dread spread within her as she rolled down the window, night air rushing in. What was happening? Hopefully, John and Gabrielle weren't still trapped inside. Andrea craned her neck, trying to get a better view.

"Matheo, your telescope," Andrea demanded. She snatched the device, twisting in her seat to peer at the rooftop. Agents swarmed like ants.

"Security everywhere. Looks to be FBI," she reported. She gripped Simmons' arm. "John and Gabrielle. Are they okay?"

"*Ne t'inquiète pas.* They're fine," Matheo assured. "Gabrielle? She's the best. And Olson? He's not too shabby either." He paused, looking at the others. "Please don't tell him I said that."

"Thank you, Matheo."

"Pas de problème."

Simmons' attention was locked on the side-view mirror. "Heads up. Bogeys at six o'clock," he announced. "ETA… ninety seconds, tops."

Andrea leaned out, a gust of wind whipping her hair as she spotted three men in dark suits and windbreakers with bright "FBI" lettering jogging their direction. The lead agent never took his eyes off the van.

The team radio crackled. "Um, is someone there?" a voice asked.

Andrea reached for it.

"Wait," Jessica's hand shot out, stopping her. She keyed the radio. "This is a secure law enforcement channel. Who is this?"

"FBI. Who's this?"

Jessica glared at Matheo. Andrea watched something pass between them. She felt like an outsider witnessing the nonverbal communication of a lifelong couple.

Simmons' eyes remained fixed on the side mirror, his knuckles flexing. "We're out of runway, folks."

"Go. Now!" Jessica ordered.

Simmons stomped on the gas pedal, and the van jerked forward as the back end fishtailed. The engine roared as they sped away. The scent of burnt rubber filled the air, mingling with the cool breeze whipping through the open window.

Andrea watched the FBI agents grow smaller in the mirror, chasing after them. Their arms pumped as they tried to keep up, and despite their unholstered pistols, no shots were fired. She made the sign of the cross.

The momentary relief evaporated as she whipped her head back around. "Are we leaving John and Gabrielle behind?"

"Negative. We just couldn't stay. We'll find another way."

Simmons tapped the steering wheel, then slammed his palm on the dash. Glancing over his shoulder, he clenched his teeth. "You realize what this means. Pull the trigger, Jess."

A hint of resignation hung in the air. Jessica looked down and then at Matheo. His almost imperceptible nod pushed her.

"You're right."

Jessica leaned forward, reaching past Andrea into the glove compartment. She rummaged briefly before pulling out a second radio with a green casing. She hesitated, thumb hovering over the button.

"Initiate Operation Surrogate Starling," she commanded. There was a double-click response on the radio, an acknowledgment without words.

Simmons wrenched the steering wheel. The van skidded as the tires shrieked against the asphalt. Andrea's cheeks turned bone-white, nausea churning in her stomach. This was worse than that looping rollercoaster at Magic Mountain.

"I never heard of this Starling thing. What is it, and why do you all look concerned?"

Matheo leaned forward. "Ah, *ma chérie*. Let's just say it's one of Hyde's… how you put it… more unconventional ideas." He smiled. "Best not to ask too many questions, *non*?"

Andrea stuck her head out the window, trying not to puke.

The Skunk Works facility shrank in the distance. Once her home, its silhouette now felt alien. Flashing red and blue lights from FBI vehicles pulsed weakly through the trees like a beacon of hope fading away.

She closed her eyes. The image of John standing alone in that hallway burned.

So many unvoiced feelings and abandoned promises.

She moved to another mystery. What happened on that roof?

As the facility disappeared from view, Andrea felt a piece of herself vanish with it. The night enveloped them, offering no answers.

Tears trickled down her cheeks. She'd lost everything.

Chapter 43

CIA SAFE HOUSE

17 Hours Remaining

23:58

Olson shifted uncomfortably in the sparse room, shadows lurking in the corners. The wooden chair creaked as he leaned forward, its armrests protesting as if ready to collapse. The depressing atmosphere seemed to be standard in CIA safe houses.

He ran a hand through his hair, trying to shake the tension seeping into his bones. Seventeen hours until the nuclear treaty signing between Carter and Alexei Kosygin in DC. Each second felt like a countdown to a doomsday scenario only he could see. Somehow, he needed to destroy those tapes.

Maybe after that was over, perhaps Durbin could persuade the President to reinstate the stealth project. It was a longshot, but the only one John had.

The door creaked open as Deputy Director Lucas Avery strode in, the bag containing the Stealth data slung over his shoulder. He dropped it on the table with a thud, two feet from John.

Avery marched straight to the small refrigerator. He opened the door, revealing a modest mini-bar. The bottles glinted in the interior light, casting a kaleidoscope of colors upon Lucas's weary features.

"You know, John, I find a drink helps take the edge off after a successful operation. Old habits from the war days, I suppose."

He turned to face John with a smile. "Care for one?"

When John remained silent, Avery added, "Another whiskey, perhaps?"

John needed a clear head, but turning down the drink might set off alarm bells. "I'll have whatever you're having."

Avery's smile widened. "Two whiskeys it is, then."

The clink of ice and a slosh followed. John fidgeted as he strained to see what Avery was doing. The Deputy Director's broad frame blocked his view, leaving him to squirm with unknowing.

Avery placed the tumbler of amber liquid in front of John. The rich, smoky scent of the liquor filled his nostrils. Lucas settled into an old burgundy recliner, the leather creaking under his frame.

John's untouched drink sat inches from the bag with the data. He could grab it at any time. But what then?

The Director lit a cigarette with an antique OSS lighter, the flame casting a warm glow over his features. He exhaled slowly, smoke spiraling upward.

"All that trouble for this bit of information. Must be more valuable than we thought." The man's eyes seemed to glaze over. "Makes you wonder."

"Wonder about what?"

Avery waved his hand. "Nah, nothing worth mentioning."

This might be his only chance. "No, really. What do you mean?"

Avery took another puff. Leaning forward, elbows on his knees, he cradled his glass. "Sometimes, the choices we make feel meaningless." He twirled the drink. "But if you could do it over. Pick any life… What would you choose?"

The question caught Olson off guard. He hesitated. Was this some kind of test?

"I don't know," John replied.

Avery's hand drifted to his holstered pistol. It seemed casual, but unmistakable. John stared, wondering if it was an unconscious habit or a threat.

"If I could do it all over, I suppose I'd choose baseball," John said.

"Running bases, cheering crowds. A simple game with clear rules. That clarity feels like a fairy tale now."

Avery squinted. The response seemed to intrigue him. His foot tapped absentmindedly against the bag on the table, the tapes shifting with each impact. It was a gesture so casual, yet loaded.

"Like DiMaggio?" he said after a long silence. "Hell-of-a player. Married Marilyn to boot. Good answer." A dreaminess washed over his face. "Funny how even clear rules can get… complicated."

The refrigerator compressor kicked on, blending with the ticking clock on the wall. All of it needled at John's patience.

Hyde's warning replayed in John's mind. Olson was the only other person who knew Avery had the tapes.

He stared at his untouched whiskey, the ice cubes crackling. Condensation rolled down the side, leaving wet rings. Why had Avery taken so long to pour it? Poison?

He glanced up, catching the Director's curious gaze. John cleared his throat. "What about you? What did you want to be?"

Avery leaned back. "Wanted to be a banker once, like my old man. Then came '29." His voice hardened. "Damn coward didn't have the guts to deal with what followed."

John recognized the veiled reference to suicide. It was a loss similar to his family history. Was Avery trying to establish a connection, or was it just a manipulation tactic?

"First the Depression, then the war…" Avery continued. "Cruel paths opened. But that's life for you. I got swept into something bigger." He fixed John with an unreadable look. "Makes you wonder about our choices, doesn't it?"

John nodded, unsure how to respond. Avery's legendary role in building the CIA reminded him of the personal sacrifices required for their line of work. Perhaps the Agency drew tortured souls like moths to a flame.

Avery slid John's untouched glass closer, the ice cubes settling. "You look like you need this more than I do."

"I'm good for now, thanks."

Avery studied John. With deliberate slowness, he grabbed Olson's drink, and took a deep slug. "Waste not, want not. Obviously you didn't live through the Depression." Avery took another drag and clicked his tongue. "This is good. Totally unfair."

"What's unfair?"

Avery blew smoke from the side of his mouth. "People like Hyde. They thrive in the shadows, flaunting rules as if they don't apply. It's as if they believe they can enjoy the luxuries without ever paying the price."

"I guess that isn't true anymore." Avery laughed. "It's tempting to desire the finer things," he said. "One small compromise, and you could have it all. Almost too easy."

John's unease mounted. The Deputy Director's statements seemed loaded. Was he admitting something? John's hand crept towards his hip, seeking his weapon.

Nothing was there. The FBI confiscated it an hour ago.

Avery shook his head, a flicker of regret in his eyes. "We took the other path, you and I," he said, pointing at John. "I respect you, Olson. Not everyone would've had the stones to turn in their partner." He tipped the glass. "Duty over desire."

A sharp knock at the door jolted both men. Did Avery invite someone else to this meeting? John turned to face the entrance.

Two enormous guards in black suits entered. They looked like linebackers, their massive shoulders filling the doorframe. Their movement screamed military.

"Clear, sir," announced one.

William Durbin strode in, his broad smile infectious, teeth gleaming. His tailored suit hugged his frame, polished shoes reflecting the room's dim light. He flicked his wrist nonchalantly, as if brushing away an invisible speck of dust.

Avery crushed his cigarette into the overflowing ashtray, the embers hissing and smoldering. He finished Olson's last sliver of whiskey in one swift gulp. Lucas straightened his spine, squaring his shoulders in a reflexive display of military bearing. Though his expression remained impassive, John detected a subtle tightening around the man's eyes.

"Op's over," Avery whispered. "In step the politicians. Hope you're ready."

Durbin's gaze swept the room, lingering on the worn furniture and whiskey glasses. As John and Avery rose stiffly from their chairs, he closed the distance between them with long, aggressive strides, his hand extending.

He seized Avery's hand in a vise-like grip, honed by years of political maneuvering. Then he turned to Olson, pumping his hand enthusiastically. Durbin's grasp was ironclad, his fingers tightening a fraction too much in a silent assertion of power.

"Man of the hour!" Durbin exclaimed, his voice honeyed. "I had to come down and thank you in person. The President himself sends his congratulations."

The praise grated on John. Durbin couldn't understand the cost of this moment. It wasn't the politician's fault, but it still burned.

"It was a team effort," John said, glancing at Avery. "FBI and CIA both played crucial roles."

"Are they all this modest?" Durbin asked with a chuckle.

Avery grunted. "To a fault, it seems."

The Deputy Director's gruff tone sounded almost deferential, a subtle shift from the weary arrogance he displayed earlier.

"But I suppose that's what makes men like him so valuable to the CIA. Sees the bigger picture."

John shuddered. The image of Hyde kneeling on the rooftop, her haunting look of resignation and defiance, played on an endless loop in his mind. But it wasn't the expression; it was her warning. Was he missing the bigger picture?

Avery's voice interrupted his thoughts. "Gabrielle Hyde has been apprehended as the mole," he said. "And we've recovered the data. I'll be working with the FBI personally to find Morozov, but the Soviets are hindered for now. The treaty signing should still be on track."

"Everything I could have envisioned, and you two made it a reality."

Durbin clapped Avery firmly on the shoulder. "A true triumph for all involved."

Avery glanced at his watch and sighed. "Gentlemen, as illuminating an evening as this has been, I have reports to file and an early flight to DC."

The Deputy Director stretched his back with a groan. Lucas leaned over and picked up the sack, feeling its weight.

If Avery left the room with those tapes, it was as good as handing them to the Soviets. John couldn't allow it. He had to destroy them.

Durbin and the two bodyguards complicated the problem. Then again, they could be an asset. He just had to express his concerns about the insider threat.

He just had to accuse his boss of being a spy with no proof.

John froze with indecision. The Director stared at the bag for a moment, as if considering. Then, to John's surprise, he extended the satchel.

"Here," Avery said, handing it to John. "You deserve to make sure this is done to the end. Don't let that evidence out of your sight until it's in the federal depository. I wasn't any older when the Jedburghs first trusted me. Just as I now trust you. I'm glad Hyde didn't get to you."

Why would Avery give up the tapes if he were working with Morozov?

Then it hit him: the Deputy wasn't a traitor waiting to shake his junior case officer. He could have slipped away at any time. Avery was testing John's loyalty.

He had passed.

Olson took the bag. The fabric rasped against his fingertips, its unexpected weight settling into his grip. It felt like holding onto the future.

John let the stress melt. Hyde had been making it all up. Just one last desperate attempt to save herself.

"Good luck, Officer Olson. I'll meet you in DC."

Without another word, Avery adjusted his jacket and strode out. The door swung shut with a quiet click, Lucas's footsteps fading down the hall. Despite his earlier doubts, John now saw his boss for what he truly was: a man dedicated to the CIA. Now, that man was trusting Olson.

The room fell silent. John's grip tightened on the bag as he shifted his weight. Now he could destroy them and end this nightmare. But as he looked up, the two guards stood in front of the door, blocking his exit.

John realized he'd been so focused on Avery, he'd forgotten the full meaning of Hyde's prediction. *Someone will come for it.* He'd assumed the first to arrive would be the only threat. The warning said nothing about order.

Avery left empty-handed. But another had shown. Someone unexpected.

His senses sharpened, hyper-aware of every subtle sound and movement. A faint rustle of fabric. The scuff of a shoe across the low carpet.

Then he heard it. The unmistakable click of a cocking pistol.

John's head snapped up, body tensing. He turned.

Gone was the charming politician. In his place stood a cold adversary. Durbin's gun was aimed squarely at John, its barrel reflecting the light with a malevolent gleam. All warmth had vanished; his eyes were as pitiless as death.

John swallowed hard, his throat constricting.

Repressed feelings surged. The rules he'd bent. The people he'd hurt. For what? His faith in the system was about to be repaid with a bullet.

Durbin's head listed to the side, his cold eyes assessing John with a clinical detachment that bordered between amusement and condescension. John felt like a specimen, a helpless insect trapped in the grasp of a cruel child, uncertain whether he would be crushed or tortured.

"Yesterday, I would have shot you in the back," Durbin said, his voice eerily calm as he took a step forward. "Today, I feel like talking."

"We need to discuss your future."

Chapter 44

SKUNK WORKS FACILITY

FBI Special Agent Bruno Vasquez savored the moment as he guided Hyde toward the SWAT tactical vehicle. Agents lined both sides of the street, watching in awe. For Vasquez, it was a career-defining win.

The metallic thud of her restraints against the bench seat was beautiful music. He had finally captured Hyde. The thief of thieves. He wouldn't let her out of his sight.

Bruno turned to the onboard guard. "I'll handle this one myself."

The man paused.

"Let me rephrase. Get out."

The agent exited the vehicle, leaving Vasquez alone with Hyde in the cramped transport. The steel door slammed shut with a resounding clang that reverberated.

Vasquez settled onto the bench opposite his prize, savoring the success. His gaze locked onto Hyde's face, treasuring the moment he'd sacrificed so much to achieve.

"Driver," Vasquez called. "What's your name?"

The lanky man in his early thirties turned, his buzz cut and perpetual frown visible in the rearview mirror. "Clyde, sir."

"Well, Clyde. Get us to Burbank Airport, direct to the tarmac. If anyone gets in the way, run 'em off the road. We don't stop for nothing. Not even red lights. Got it?"

Clyde's eyes widened. "Yes, sir."

The vehicle rumbled to life, its heavy frame shuddering as it pulled away. Vasquez settled into the bench seat, his sight adjusting as the interior light cast shadows across Hyde's face. The massive engine vibrated through the metal walls.

Hyde's wrists were bound, but her shoulders relaxed. Her cool face met Vasquez's scrutiny with an unsettling serenity. The familiar smugness he expected was replaced by an enigmatic calm that unnerved him.

As the vehicle navigated the dark streets, Vasquez caught a glint of color. A small blue forget-me-not pin on Hyde's jumpsuit. The delicate flower seemed out of place. He stared.

His interest was too obvious. Hyde brushed the brooch, and her mask of cool indifference slipped. It revealed… what? Nostalgia? Pain? It was gone too fast.

"Didn't take you for the sentimental type."

"It was my mother's. The only thing I have left of my family. War robs us all." She met his eyes. "You understand that, don't you, Bruno?"

Vasquez stiffened, the unexpected vulnerability throwing him off. He had always seen her as a heartless adversary. That line about war was too close to home. Suspicion replaced the sympathy.

The FBI agent cracked a knuckle, his method of crushing sentiment. He couldn't afford to see Hyde as anything but a criminal. Too many times, he'd watched her slip through the fingers of justice. Not this time.

"Touching."

The silence stretched, broken only by the engine's hum. Hyde turned her attention to the driver. "You know, Clyde, it's been a long night. Why don't you just drop me off downtown? I'm sure Agent Vasquez won't mind."

Vasquez's nostrils flared. "Ignore her."

The driver's gaze flicked to the mirror. "Ignored, sir." Clyde tucked a green handheld radio from the dash into his cargo pocket and tightened his grip on the steering wheel.

Bruno caught a flinch. A subtle movement Hyde meant to hide. She was up to her usual shenanigans.

He couldn't relax for a second until they were airborne. He reached across and checked the handcuffs. One was loose. She could have slipped out. He'd read about this technique used during cuffing, though it was supposed to be exceptionally painful.

"Nice try." He clicked the restraints tight.

Hyde reclined against the wall. Vasquez got a tingle in his nose, an internal warning signal. Something about her composure.

"You're wasting your time, Bruno. Think you've won? They're using you."

Vasquez inhaled sharply, struggling to remain calm. "Save it," he snapped. "Your psychobabble won't work on me."

"Is that what you think? That you're the hero in all this? That by capturing me, the agency will accept a Hispanic as equal? Try being a woman. You'll have to break the rules if you want to win."

Even in captivity, her composure mocked him. He lurched forward, invading her space. "This isn't a game," he growled. "It never was. Not to me."

"Oh, Bruno," she said, using his name with a familiarity that made him fume. "You still don't understand, do you? I'm not the devil you seek. I'm more like you. There's always more to the story."

Vasquez shot to his feet, leering at Hyde. "You're done."

She seemed unfazed. "You know, Bruno, I've been running the numbers. There's a decent chance you might be the mole."

Vasquez recoiled in disbelief. "I have no idea what you're implying. But I'm not interested."

Hyde shrugged, the handcuffs clinking. "I can see it," she replied. "The way you operate, the secrets you keep. It's not a stretch to envision you working for the other side. Even unwittingly."

Vasquez's hand twitched. "Shut your mouth. You don't know a damn thing about me."

"Oh, I can picture it now. You at a press conference, chest puffed out, all eyes on you. Telling everyone how you 'bagged' the bad guys." She leaned forward. "But did you, Bruno? Or were you just a pawn?"

He felt his hands curl into tight fists, his knuckles turning white with the effort of restraining himself. Each word was precision-aimed to get under his skin.

"I said shut up!"

"If you're honest," Hyde continued, "and I doubt you are, when the real culprit is unveiled, you will have your eyes opened. You might even thank me."

Something snapped. This was his moment, but Hyde's incessant needling threatened to ruin it. He wanted nothing more than to silence her, to wipe that smug look off her face.

Vasquez eyed the black hood hanging on the wall next to Hyde. He'd gotten into trouble before for hooding prisoners, but he couldn't stand for her mind games.

This time, it felt necessary. Justified.

She wanted him to break the rules. Well, he could comply.

In one motion, he grabbed the hood from its hook. Her face slackened.

"Now, now, Agent Vasquez," she said, a note of concern creeping in. "Let's not do anything rash."

The FBI agent felt the coarse fabric. "You know what the best part of a bag and tag operation is?" he asked. "The bag."

Hyde's eyes narrowed. There and gone in an instant. Another attempt to control him.

He was in control here.

Bruno yanked the hood over her head, roughly pulling it down. Hyde struggled, her muffled protests barely audible through the heavy material. Vasquez secured the hood tightly, leaving only a delicate wisp of her hair poking out from under the edge.

"If you don't shut up," Vasquez threatened, "I'll knock you out right here and now. I don't care if you are a woman."

He justified the harshness, telling himself it was necessary to maintain command of the situation. It worked. For once, Hyde fell silent. The engine's hum seemed louder now that her taunts had ceased.

As the miles rolled by, Hyde's words replayed in his mind, sowing doubt. He hated how she got to him. He couldn't ignore the notion that she was still running her game.

The vehicle's tires crunched on gravel as it pulled onto an access road leading to the tarmac. Clyde maneuvered easily through the security gates.

"ETA, one minute."

Vasquez kept his eyes trained on the hooded figure, ensuring there were no sudden movements. Even bound and gagged, she had proven how dangerous she could be.

The SWAT vehicle hooked a sharp turn, tires squealing, before lurching to a halt. The awaiting FBI transport plane sat behind them, its sleek form bathed in an unforgiving wash of floodlights.

"We're here," Clyde announced.

Bruno Vasquez leaped from the tactical vehicle, his shoes hitting the taxiway. The night air, thick with jet fuel, filled his nose as he slammed the door shut. He locked the door with a decisive click, ensuring his captive remained secure. Hyde wasn't going anywhere.

Vasquez's gaze settled on the plane. Its sleek matte black form gave it a sinister quality that seemed to swallow the light. He scanned the tarmac for movement.

A man in a fluorescent vest and headphones leaned against the wing, his face hidden by the brim of an aging Lakers cap. As Vasquez strode towards him, the technician glanced up.

"How much longer?" Vasquez demanded over the generator's drone.

The man shrugged. "Five minutes. Just toppin' her off."

"Make it three. We need to be wheels up in twenty, no delays."

The worker continued unhurriedly. "Can't rush safety, boss. We'll have you up and out as soon as we can."

Vasquez stormed off. His eyes darted between the refueling process and the SWAT vehicle as he paced, one hand resting on his holstered weapon. He scanned the shifting shadows, alert for trouble.

A sudden breeze whistled, causing Vasquez to spin around, his hand flying to his pistol. It was just the wind.

Footsteps approached. Bruno pivoted to see the technician, wiping his hands on a rag.

"All done, sir." The man gave a thumbs-up. "Fueled up and ready to go."

"Good. Now get out of here. We're taking off."

As the worker departed, Vasquez strode to the SWAT vehicle. His hand hesitated on the door handle. Hyde was in there; he was sure of it. He was still in control.

He wouldn't let her ruin his victory.

Taking a deep breath, Vasquez yanked open the SWAT truck door. The interior lights flickered on, revealing Hyde's hooded figure sitting motionless on the bench.

"Time to go," he said, gripping her shoulder.

Hyde didn't utter a single word. Her silence was both satisfying and unsettling. She always had the last word.

Vasquez recognized the trick. Her lack of speaking was a strategy. Another attempt to mess with his mind.

The FBI agent pushed her forward, slamming the SWAT vehicle's door shut. He banged twice to signal the driver. He stepped back, frustrated that the refueling process had delayed their departure.

The truck's engine roared to life, and it lurched before coming to an abrupt stop. Gears ground as the driver reset the manual transmission, and then the vehicle sped off into the darkness.

"Cool it, Clyde! Ten miles an hour!"

Shaking his head, Vasquez guided Hyde by the shoulder, urging her towards the waiting plane. Halfway there, Vasquez noticed something odd about her gait. She shuffled with short, stuttering steps, her large boots scraping against the tarmac.

A thrill of satisfaction ran through him. She was finally getting a taste of what it felt like to stumble through the dark.

"Move it." He gave her another push.

At the aircraft, Agent Morris and a pilot waited at the base of the stairs. Morris stepped forward, gripping Hyde's arm and guiding her up the steps.

Vasquez turned to the captain. "I want to be in the air in ten minutes.

No delays. Straight to Cuba."

"Understood, sir," the pilot replied, climbing into the cockpit.

Alone on the tarmac, Vasquez swept the area, searching for movement. The airfield was eerily quiet, save for the gentle whine of the plane's engines. It was too perfect. No guards, no security, no unexpected complications.

Could it be this easy? Vasquez couldn't shake the feeling that he was missing something crucial.

Satisfied that there were no immediate threats, Vasquez allowed himself a moment of relief. In less than six hours, Hyde would be in a maximum-security FBI cell. Her days of eluding justice were over.

Vasquez climbed the stairs. As he reached the top, he paused, savoring the moment. Then, with a decisive motion, he grasped the door handle and pulled it shut. The locking mechanism engaged with a reassuring click.

Vasquez made his way down the narrow aisle, a strange euphoria spreading. Hyde sat rigidly, the hood obscuring her features. Morris stood nearby, hand on his holster.

Settling into his seat, Vasquez watched Morris slide Hyde's seatbelt across her plain black jumpsuit. He examined her one last time for any concealed weapons or tools, but was interrupted as the pilot's voice crackled over the intercom.

"We'll be airborne shortly."

The engines roared to life, a deep rumble that pulsed through the fuselage.

As the plane taxied, Vasquez's eyes locked onto Hyde. Her powerlessness brought an unexpected reaction. The sight was almost sad, robbing him of his enjoyment. The thrill of victory was already fading.

He leaned back, closing his eyes with a grunt. As the wheels left the tarmac and just before he drifted to sleep, FBI Special Agent Vasquez pondered if anyone could ever win in this deeply rigged game of theirs. Nothing ever remained static.

Control was an illusion.

Chapter 45

LOS ANGELES WAREHOUSE DISTRICT

00:10

Andrea stumbled into the control center. The lights flickered on with a hum, casting a harsh glare over the disarray of equipment and scattered papers.

The chaos from the failed operation clung to Jessica and Matheo like a second skin. Grime streaked Simmons's face, his jaw clenched as he slammed a piece of communication gear onto the table. The resounding bang made Andrea flinch.

She'd never seen Simmons lose his cool. He was always so steady. But now, he was like a coiled spring ready to snap. It was unsettling, adding to her anxiety. She wondered if this was how they felt after each mission.

Matheo hunched over his workstation, muttering rapid-fire French curses. His muscular hands grabbed radio components from a pile, soldering them into place. He paused only to wipe sweat from his face, leaving a smear of soot.

The air soon filled with a distinct smell of melting solder. The scent drew Andrea in, evoking countless hours in her lab. But this differed from a research facility. This was real. And dangerous.

They were in trouble, and no one was willing to tell her.

Questions raced through her mind: Why was the FBI on the roof? What happened to John and Gabrielle?

Jessica stalked like a caged animal, her heels crunching on the concrete floor. Her usual mask of cool had slipped, revealing a fierce intensity. She absentmindedly toyed with a lock of her hair, mumbling to herself.

"We should go back," Andrea insisted. It felt wrong to be here, safe, while John and Gabrielle were in danger.

Jessica froze mid-stride. "It's too late. We wait here."

Andrea couldn't shake the feeling that something was terribly wrong. "You saw what happened. The helicopters, the security. What if they were taken?" It had been a miracle that she and Matheo had escaped.

"We follow the plan," Jessica snapped. Seeing Andrea's face, she softened her tone. "Gabrielle always has a plan."

Andrea wanted to trust Gabrielle's ability to outsmart anyone who stood in her way. But fear gripped her, unwilling to let go.

Matheo looked up from his work. "They'll be fine," he said. "Have faith."

"I do," Andrea replied. "But I also saw what happened. The FBI was waiting for us. Someone set a trap."

She glanced around as everyone stopped working. She had their attention now. "Think about it logically. Whoever is behind this… they played us. They have influence at the FBI. And now they have what they wanted. Gabrielle and John…" She took a second. "They're not coming back."

"She's right. They'll be on the offensive." Jessica pointed. "Beta Protocol."

Both men nodded and started moving.

"What's Beta Protocol?" Andrea asked.

Jessica's lips twisted into a frown. "It means we're buggered."

Simmons rifled through documents, his eyes darting across each page before cramming them into a nondescript backpack.

Jessica heaved with a crowbar against the cover of a large crate. The splintering wood groaned as the nails bent. With a resounding crack, the lid gave way, revealing an arsenal of black handguns and rifles nestled within the padded interior.

She stacked the weapons onto a nearby table. "Simmons!" Jessica called out. "I need a hand."

When he didn't move immediately, she added a terse, "Chop, chop!"

Simmons hustled across the room, his muddy boots thudding. Andrea noted a slight limp in his long strides, wondering when he had injured his leg. He joined Jessica at the table.

They fell into a rhythm, inspecting and loading their weapons. The pungent blend of gun oil and cordite violated Andrea's senses. The rhythmic clicks of pistol slides and the thuds of ammunition clips pounded in her ears.

Pitiless dread seeped into Andrea's veins as her focus snapped to Matheo. He pulled several pale, oblong objects out of a duffel bag. Even with her limited knowledge, she recognized plastic explosives. Whatever was happening, it was worse than she had imagined.

"Why does Matheo have explosives?" she blurted.

Jessica and Matheo exchanged a glance. With a grim expression, Matheo muttered, *"Une garantie."*

Of what? Safety? Destruction? She was used to using her imagination to solve problems, but right now, it was her worst enemy.

Matheo attached detonators to the explosives with meticulous care. He occasionally adjusted the placement as if following an unseen blueprint. Each connection, each wire, was a step closer to a violent end.

A heavy silence fell. This wasn't an escape plan. They were preparing for mortal danger. Fortifying against an invasion they seemed to expect but hadn't explained.

Andrea choked back her emotions.

Fear turned into crushing guilt. The vault was her responsibility. She should have predicted the hidden sensor. If she had just been more careful, more vigilant, none of this would be happening. Total failure was unfamiliar territory.

Jessica dropped a bulletproof vest unceremoniously in front of her. "Put this on," Jessica commanded.

Andrea's hands shook as she took the body armor, its weight foreign. The vest felt more like a burden than protection. She fumbled with the straps, each click of the fasteners feeding her anxiety.

The reality of their situation crashed over her.

Matheo and Simmons' proficiency with the weapons underscored her alienation. She was just an engineer. One thrust into the soldier's world.

This makeshift war room was a far cry from her sterile lab. The arsenal before her was enough firepower to liberate East Berlin. It transformed her usual abstract concepts into physical instruments of violence.

"You can do this," Jessica said, putting her hand on Andrea's shoulder.

Andrea's gaze flicked nervously to the door. "Who's coming for us?"

"Doesn't matter who, just that they are," Jessica replied, chambering a round. "We're loose ends. So, we prepare for the worst case."

"How can I help?" Andrea asked, her hands still trembling.

Jessica gave her an approving nod. "For now, stay alert and be ready to follow instructions. It might happen fast."

It verified every fear. Gabrielle and John were gone. They were alone, a small band of misfits preparing for a last stand. And someone was coming.

The thought should have terrified her. But as she looked at these professionals and their preparations, she found odd comfort in the nearby table filled with loaded weapons.

They certainly wouldn't go down without a fight.

Chapter 46

CIA SAFEHOUSE

00:20

Flickering bulbs cast writhing shadows, their faint buzz a constant, grating backdrop. Stale cigarette smoke hung in the air, disturbing William's more refined sensibilities.

He should kill Olson. Here and now.

But Avery made an excellent point. The CIA operative had caught the troublesome Hyde. Durbin needed to build an army, and Olson could be his first recruit.

"Sit," Durbin said, gesturing to a nearby chair.

Olson hesitated, glancing at the two bodyguards. After a moment, John eased into the seat, with the men flanking him.

Durbin settled across from him with an air of relaxed authority. He studied the CIA officer, searching for any crack in the man's inscrutable front. John's gaze flicked about in a futile search for escape.

"Relax," Durbin said, slipping the gun into its holster. "You'd be dead if that was my intent."

He glanced at the two bodyguards. "Guys, give the man some space." The two men took a step back.

"I apologize for the muscle. Morozov sent them to monitor his investment." He leaned in. "He told me their names, but I honestly can't remember them."

John stared at him silently. He needed an alternative approach. And brute force wouldn't break this man. This demanded a subtler approach. Olson was on edge, but not reckless. The key was to appeal to his needs.

What did the man need?

The air conditioner's low hum punctuated the silence. Durbin relished these quiet moments; they often revealed more than words. Waiting provided glimpses into his adversary's mind.

There was interest in Olson's eyes. A slight shift forward in posture. An intellectual man craves debate. That was the path.

"John." Durbin leaned forward, elbows on his knees. "Do you see me as the villain here?"

A muscle twitched at his temple. "I'm not talking to you."

"That's your choice," Durbin said, tapping his pistol. "We can have a rational discussion between two intellectually gifted men, or I can put a slug between your eyes. Either way, I'll have a brandy in thirty minutes."

"What do you want from me?" John said at last.

"I want to talk. About you." He relaxed back in his chair. "You like to read, John?"

Olson stirred. That was a yes. "I suppose so."

"I knew it!" Durbin crossed his legs. "Personally, I love to read. Devoured books when I was a kid. Everything from dime-store novels to Verne's adventures. And as I grew, so did my tastes."

William scooted forward, adding excitement to his speech pattern. "You ever read Thucydides and his history of the Peloponnesian War?" He slapped his knee. "That really blew my mind when I was in college."

John retreated, shifting. "Is there a point to this?"

"Patience. I'm getting to the good stuff."

"Sorry. Go ahead."

"That's when I found game theory. Pardon the pun. Total game changer. The prisoner's dilemma, the Stability-Instability Paradox, Nash's equilibrium. Holy Jesus. Just... brilliant, counterintuitive concepts. Sharing control with the enemy creates a stable balance of power by allowing for controlled conflicts."

John smirked. "Is there an exam later, or are you just showing off?"

"Funny."

"It wasn't meant to make you laugh."

"Well, John. You're more right than you know. I lived and died by these theories. They were going to change the world." Durbin sighed. "And then I got to the reality of Washington. And you know what I realized about all those philosophies, all that Georgetown elitist doctrine?"

John's eyes lit up, and he leaned forward just a fraction. Durbin smiled on the inside. He was engaged now.

"Game theory, strategic balance, rational actors… it's all total bullshit."

John gave a short snicker. "First thing you said that made any sense."

Durbin beamed a smile. "We both know the theories don't work. The question is: do we keep pretending they do, or do we fix things?"

"I'm not sure the system is broken."

"Lie!" Durbin exclaimed.

Olson grimaced. "Fine. Yeah, it doesn't always work the way it should. But that doesn't explain what you're doing working with Morozov."

"Oh yes, him," Durbin said with a wave. "Not my first choice, trust me. Every deal I've cut with that psychopath and his superiors serves one purpose: keeping America safe. I'm trying to create a tomorrow where America is the world's dominant power. But this vision requires hard work and time."

Olson shook his head. "You're being a little overdramatic, don't you think?"

"Am I? Are you that blind to what's happening?" Durbin asked. "We're constantly on the brink of nuclear war. Locked in a deadly game of one-upmanship where everyone is a loser. I've got the launch codes memorized, John. Twenty-six characters that could end human civilization. I'm not the only one with them either."

"That's terrifying."

Durbin smacked the arm of his chair. "Exactly! How many Moscow kindergartens have to die before Brezhnev decides to glass New York?" He snapped his fingers. "One terrorist, one false radar reading, one drunk submarine captain. That's all it takes."

John leaned forward. "I won't gamble with humanity's fate."

"Neither would I. Gambling implies that luck is involved."

"Then why help the Russians? They're the enemy."

"Being a leader is about making the hard choices, John. It's a burden to be the monster, but it's a small price to pay if it means sparing the world from annihilation." Durbin looked directly into his eyes. "You want to hate me. But I love this country. I would die for it, just like you."

"That still doesn't explain it," John replied, shifting in his chair.

This was perfect. William had him totally engaged now.

"You know why the world hasn't ended yet, John? Fear. Pure, rational fear. The Soviets know we'll end Moscow if they push too hard. We know they'll return the favor. But what happens when one side gets desperate?" He leaned forward. "What happens if only one side has invisible aircraft?"

John scoffed. "Then we negotiate."

It was Durbin's turn to scoff. "Right. How could I forget? I'm sure the man who crushed Prague will listen to reason."

"There's no reason to be snarky about it."

Durbin patted John's arm with just the right amount of force. "I'm sorry. It's just that you haven't sat in those Cabinet meetings. I pore over every document that comes through that office. You haven't watched the President agonize over every ethical decision while Moscow builds bigger bombs."

John retreated slightly. "I happen to like Carter."

"I'm sure you do. But so do the Soviets. You know what they call him? *Slabak*—weakling. How long before they decide a Sunday school teacher won't stand up to their antics?"

John's eyes narrowed. "What are you suggesting?"

He asked the right question. Olson wasn't a mindless drone, but a man of reason. The walls were coming down, brick by stubborn brick.

"That you and I have the courage," Durbin continued, "to do what others can't. To bear the burden of being seen as the villain, if that's what it takes to save everyone else. You, of all people, understand this." His voice rose.

"I'm not evil; I'm a sentinel. Standing between America and oblivion. Just like you."

"There have to be other ways," John said at last. "We can't just accept this… this game of brinkmanship as the only option."

Durbin relaxed, taking a moment. He wouldn't rush this. How many times had he pondered the fate of the nation? Too many to count.

"Other ways? Hmm. Perhaps there are. I appreciate your optimism, John." He rubbed his chin. "Unfortunately, I've been proven wrong over and over again."

"By whom?"

"The masses." William picked up a newspaper and slapped it down.

John eyed the bold print: racial tensions, economic woes, political scandals.

"Look at the headlines," Durbin said, pointing. "Our nation is fracturing, torn apart by the divisions unleashed by Johnson and Nixon. And the media feasts on it, stoking manufactured fear and outrage. They've turned our lives into a circus in exchange for profit. These people are hopeless."

"That's a rather cynical view." Defiance burned in John's eyes. "The people may be divided, but they still have the power to demand change."

"Ahh, the idealism of youth. Tell me, how long do you think that fervor will last? They're a fickle mob."

Durbin noted the way Olson's fingers curled around the arm of the chair. He was beginning to understand.

With a flick, he tossed the newspaper aside. "My father died in Korea, fighting for his principles. He was revered. But within a decade, people wanted to sympathize with farmers in black pajamas more than with their own nation. They'll burn flags and cities just for the sake of hating something. I realized the important question is: do we let them destroy our country, or do we give them better enemies? "

"You want to know the secret to controlling 200 million Americans?"

John crossed his arms. "Sure."

"Give them someone to hate. Doesn't matter who. Russians. Arabs. Whoever's convenient. Watch how fast they'll hand over their freedoms for the promise of safety." He smiled coldly. "I've seen the data, John. Sixty percent of the country can't find Vietnam on a map. Now imagine giving that same group power. They can't handle it. An entire generation raised on television, consumerism, and the promise of endless government handouts. They'll vote for whoever promises to keep those checks coming."

"Hate it all you want. Someone must do the hard work."

John stood. A guard grabbed his shoulder and pushed him back down. The impact caused the chair to groan. Durbin motioned for restraint.

Olson eyed the enforcer, then turned his attention back to William. "You sound like you're describing the Morlocks."

Durbin leaped from his chair. "Exactly! See, I knew you were a reader. But Wells had it backwards—the Morlocks aren't the monsters. They keep civilization running while the Eloi remain fat, happy sheep watching television."

"You speak of ideals, but then undercut them. Morality isn't a liability; it's a necessity. It's what separates us from the animals." The words sounded as if Olson was trying to convince himself. "There are still good people who care."

"Not enough of them. And God knows I wish we could afford to be righteous," Durbin replied. "Morality is a luxury for people who don't have to live with the consequences. I do. And like it or not, the Russians feel threatened by our power. By our technological advantage. So we have to share—not everything, but some. Just enough to let their economic pyramid scheme collapse upon itself."

"That's the endgame here, John. I give them a poison pill that accelerates their demise. This particular end justifies the means."

"Tell me you understand."

John shook his head. "I don't."

One guard shoved a pistol against John's shoulder.

Durbin raised a hand. "No, no. Let the man speak. He's earned that right."

The guard backed up a step, giving John space.

"If what you say is true, why doesn't the President do it himself?"

Such naivety. The self-righteous, blinded by noble intentions, always fail to consider the malevolent forces that counter every necessary action. The President was the embodiment of everything wrong in America.

"Jimmy Carter." The name dripped from his lips like venom. "Is a good man, as you say. And that is precisely the problem. Good men have crusades. Carter's is human rights." Durbin stepped forward. "Meanwhile, the Soviets and Chinese expand unchecked, OPEC chokes our economy, and the Russians build bigger bombs. Our enemies see his reluctance to use force as a weakness."

This was Durbin's cross to bear. It was maddening knowing the inevitable consequences. "The nation doesn't need good men, it needs effective ones. Carter's moral compass spins uselessly while our ship crashes into the rocks."

"You've underestimated something," John said.

"Oh, which part?"

"The power of our institutions." Olson sat up a little taller. "They're filled with the same people you just dismissed. Some of them may surprise you, even if it takes time."

"Maybe I'm jaded, as you suggest." The CIA officer's devotion impressed him. "But who will have the guts to push the tea into the harbor or cry, 'Give me liberty or give me death,' when everyone else is glued to their TV sets?"

"I would," John said, rotating his hands back and forth across the arms of his chair.

Durbin walked back and sat down. This was it. He needed to stick this landing. Don't rush; just let him walk in slowly.

"That's why I need you, Officer Olson."

"Me?"

"Yes, you." Durbin stood, circling to the back of John's chair. He leaned down. "You've impressed me."

"I wasn't trying to impress anyone. Just doing my job. Lots of people in my position would do the same."

"You're wrong," Durbin said. "Do you know how many layers of security and misdirection I put in place? All the false leads? All you had to do was fail. And yet," he leaned in until their faces were side by side, "here you are."

Olson pulled against the armrest, the wood creaking. "Agent Vasquez was just as responsible as I was. But honestly, it was mostly Hyde. I hate to tell you, but she's on to you."

The fine line between intimidation and seduction begins with a minor concession. "Hyde was a curveball. That's why I had that idiot Vasquez assigned to the team. I was banking on his hatred of you and his disdain for Hyde to derail the entire operation."

"You sidestepped that landmine too, didn't you? Not only that, you went and stole the very data that everyone told me was untouchable."

Olson hated praise. This was better than Durbin could have hoped. John had no designs on a greater position, which meant he wouldn't develop into a rival.

"That's when I realized you've got a pragmatic streak. A willingness to bend the rules to win."

"I take no pride in that," John said after a moment.

"You beat her!" Durbin yelled. It made the two bodyguards flinch, taking a half step back. "Let's not forget, you also stole classified information," he continued, pointing at Olson. "Oh, I know you justified it as necessary. But the fact is, you crossed lines that most wouldn't dare approach."

Durbin's voice dropped. "I see a kindred spirit. You'll make the hard choices."

Olson didn't pull away. His breathing had quickened, his chest rising and falling in a noticeable rhythm.

"It's in your eyes. The fear that you're not enough. The knowledge that you could be special." Durbin extended his arms in a welcoming gesture. "I'm offering you exactly that," he said, leaning back. "Help me build a safer, stronger America. Architects of a new era."

He began pacing again. "No more half-measures, no more compromises. Just clear, decisive action," Durbin promised. "It's yours. All you have to do is say yes."

He fell silent. Olson had to make the next move. He scowled at the threadbare carpet. Ironic that the world's fate may be decided in this dump.

A torrent of emotions swept across the CIA officer's face. For a moment, it appeared his seductive logic had found its mark.

Something shifted. A hardness crept into John's eyes, a resolve. Durbin's satisfaction curdled. His instincts, honed over years, screamed that he was in danger.

But that was absurd. He was in control. As long as…

His attention darted to the guards. They had lowered their weapons, lulled into complacency by the lengthy debate. Amateurs. Too late to warn them.

Olson exploded into motion. He wrenched the arm off his chair cleanly, fingers gripped around the makeshift weapon. He surged forward, wielding violence.

The first guard crumbled under a swift strike to the temple. Before the second could react, Olson's palm shot out, connecting with the man's throat.

Hot air expelled from wordless lips.

In the same fluid motion, John swept the legs, sending him crashing to the floor. The wooden baton whistled. The sickening crack against the guard's forehead left no doubt in the ensuing silence.

John's stillness was remarkable. His gaze, blazing with cold fury, lifted slowly.

He had underestimated Olson.

William drew his pistol, trying to track his target. He fired twice, missing. John leaped and rolled forward, snagged a weapon from the fallen guard. He came up next to Durbin and struck the gun away.

The firearm rattled across the carpet and slid under the sofa. Durbin's mind reeled as he stared down the barrel of his own guard's weapon.

"William Durbin, you're under arrest for treason."

The tables had turned with breathtaking speed, and Durbin felt a trickle of genuine fear. It fell away immediately. He could work his way out of anything, including murder. It wouldn't be the first time.

"Damn. Avery taught you well. Shame."

In all his years of manipulating, John Olson was the first to surprise him.

Of course, Durbin would have to put him down.

Taking a calculated step back and to the side, Durbin guarded his eyeline. Olson followed as expected, now maneuvered into the correct angle. The noose was in place.

From the shadows emerged Sasha Morozov. Durbin was aware of the spy's reputation: a man driven by loyalty to the Soviet cause and a personal vendetta against Western operatives.

Before Olson could react, the spymaster pressed his own weapon against the back of John's head. The CIA officer stiffened.

"Drop the gun, Mr. Olson," Morozov growled, his Russian accent thick. "We wouldn't want any unfortunate accidents, now would we?"

Durbin savored the scene. "You should have taken my offer."

"You can't win this," John replied.

"It's not about winning or losing. It's about the outcome."

Durbin found there was a perverse humor in his fate being tied to the Soviet. He raised a hand as Morozov pressed his weapon harder against Olson's skull. One last point was required. He needed to share his truth.

"There are no heroes… only survivors," Durbin said. "And they write the history."

Morozov issued a final warning. "Drop it, Mr. Olson. Now."

Olson's options were gone, leaving him no choice but to relent.

Instead, the CIA officer smiled. This wasn't right. Olson was supposed to break.

"I made Nate a promise," Olson said. "'Give me liberty or give me death.' Patrick Henry was wrong, you know."

This wasn't a man defeated; he had made peace.

"It's not binary. I choose both."

Time seemed to slow as Durbin watched his finger tighten.

Click.

William flinched, bracing for the deafening report. But the gun remained silent.

Durbin's ragged breathing calmed. His eyes snapped open to find Olson looking equally shocked. Then came the laughter. Morozov's deep, rumbling chuckle was harsh and mocking.

"Ah, Mr. Olson. Did you think me that easy a target?" A sinister grin spread. "My Makarov pistols have modified safety. Only a select few know how it works."

Olson's shoulders slumped, the gun clattering to the floor as he sank to his knees. Anger replaced Durbin's relief. This principled fool had almost ruined everything.

The politician thrust the satchel containing the data reels towards Morozov. "Here. Take it. Everything you wanted." Reaching into his pocket, William pulled out a piece of paper. "These are the loose ends that need to be tied up. Courtesy of the FBI."

Morozov glanced at the list. "You sure?"

"My inside man has already replaced the records at CIA Headquarters. As far as anyone's concerned, this case never existed. After tonight, no one is left."

"And what of Avery?" Morozov asked. "He knows."

"Then make sure he gets an early retirement."

"My man is already in position," Morozov responded, tucking the paper into his jacket pocket. "What about the civilian woman?"

Durbin's eyes flicked to Olson, then back to Morozov. "No loose ends."

John lunged at Durbin, his hands outstretched like claws. With a swift, brutal motion, Morozov brought the butt of his gun down on John's head with a crack, sending the man crumpling to the floor.

Durbin didn't have sorrow for Olson, only in the wasted potential.

"You can kill him now. He served his purpose."

To his surprise, Morozov shook his head. "*Nyet*. I keep him alive. He may have additional intelligence we can extract, information that could prove useful. And later… he will make a fine prize to take back to Moscow. A trophy for the Motherland."

"You've considered all the angles, haven't you?"

"There is always something unexpected, Mr. Durbin. Always. You would be well to remember this."

Durbin inclined his head in acknowledgment of Morozov's ruthlessness, a quality that impressed and unnerved him. It was the key reason he had allied with this particular Soviet operative, despite the inherent risks.

"I will keep it in mind." He extended his hand, all business. "Speaking of our arrangement, I believe you have something for me?"

Morozov withdrew a folded page from his jacket, handing it over without ceremony. Durbin examined the list of 'approved' Soviet and Chinese spies operating in the United States. A treasure trove of intelligence, worth far more than money.

"List, as promised. A show of good faith."

The names were his ticket to the national spotlight. A phoenix rising from the ashes of Cold War paranoia. He could already see the headlines: "Durbin Thwarts Soviet Spy Ring."

Morozov tossed him a small burgundy velvet bag. Catching it, William felt the reassuring weight of African diamonds. The untraceable currency was perfect.

"Ten million—half of what we agreed upon. We must first verify the data you provided. Then the other half of the diamonds will come, along with another spy list, and support for your... political aspirations."

There were always conditions with the Soviets.

"Of course," he said, tucking both items away. "I understand completely. As you know, Senate campaigns can be so... expensive."

These Soviet fools thought they were buying a senator, a puppet to dance to their tune. Such hubris was expected. Soon they would be chess pieces in Durbin's international game.

The presidency would open in 1980, and with it, the ability to reshape the globe.

Durbin would seize the highest office in the land. Carter would either resign or meet with an unfortunate accident. The leadership vacuum would force the people to call for a national hero. Someone who had stood up to the Russians.

The only thing that mattered was POWER. Raw, uncompromising power. Everything else was just eloquent words to make small men feel better about being weak.

Everything was finally on track. He'd forge a world without weakness, unburdened by the shackles of morality. A society where the strong did what they must, and the weak endured what they had to.

Historians would write volumes about the golden age of President William Durbin.

Chapter 47

DOWNTOWN LA

00:42

Night enveloped Los Angeles. Neon signs flickered, gaudy reds and blues painting the underbelly of low-hanging smog. Inside his black town car, Lucas Avery sat in the plush back seat, processing the day's events.

He loosened his tie, the silk slipping through his fingers. With a flick, he popped open the top button of his shirt, relishing the relief. Dressing for fieldwork was becoming more troublesome by the year.

The driver weaved through the sparse traffic, jerking between lanes.

Avery watched the city roll by. The car's tinted windows offered a scant barrier to the outside world. He wondered how the administration, especially the director, would respond to the operation's unexpected outcome. It was clear there was something more to the backstory.

Nothing aligned. Not Hyde's capture. Not Olson's debrief. And especially not Durbin's sudden presence.

Avery had seen his share of unusual missions. He'd built his career wading through murky waters. Lucas had even bent some rules when the moment required it. Others remained unbreakable. Knowing the difference was the secret.

Hyde had been a forced gamble from the start, a wildcard in a game with too many unknowns. He didn't like being told who to include in an op. Her inclusion was the biggest puzzle of all, one he planned on addressing.

Olson was supposed to balance Hyde's unpredictability. The perfect choice, or so he'd thought. Despite a few concerning moments, the man had produced. It was over.

Yet… This didn't feel finished.

The car halted at a red light, the engine rumbling. Avery rubbed his temples, feeling the dull throb of an impending headache.

He reclined against the rich leather, but the tension in his muscles refused to relax. He should be able to unwind, but something in the back of his mind kept him on high alert.

A siren screamed in the distance, growing louder as a pair of police cars approached. Their flashing red and blue lights strobed across the car's interior, painting the upholstery.

The sirens crescendoed as the cruisers slowed. Then, with a burst of acceleration, they roared through the intersection. Avery's gaze followed the vehicles, catching the driver's face in the rearview mirror.

Avery had never seen him before. The man's eyes were locked on the receding police vehicles. There was fear in them. But why?

Intrigued, he looked closer. The driver's arm rotated deliberately. The man's head was unusually still, but the methodical twist of his wrist dislodged deep memories.

Years in the field, filled with close calls and hard-earned lessons, told Lucas there were few actions that specific. Avery's ears perked at the subtle sound of metal threads intertwining.

The driver was attaching a silencer. Who wanted him dead?

For a split second, Avery felt contempt. What kind of novice assembles his weapon in plain sight? He suppressed a bitter chuckle. A true pro would never be this careless.

Avery also knew he had precious seconds to act before it was too late.

Maybe he could make a run for it. He gauged the distance to the door and the likelihood of escape. He was too old, too slow. The shooter was now prepared. Any sudden movement would result in a bullet to the head.

He needed to buy time.

Lucas met the driver's gaze. "Time to the airport?"

The driver's eyes darted away, hands still hidden. "Soon, sir."

"Any problems?"

The driver's shoulders stiffened. "No, sir."

Avery's instincts screamed. He reached down towards his right ankle, where a backup pistol waited. Decades behind enemy lines had ingrained this habit. He wrapped his fingers around its grip, but was acutely aware of his disadvantaged position.

The light turned, casting an emerald glow throughout the car's cabin. But the vehicle remained stationary, idling. Lucas tried to keep his face a mask of calm indifference. His fingers curled tightly as his eyes remained locked on the threat.

"Hey, driver. Light's green." Avery hoped the man would take the bait.

The assassin turned. His earlier amateurish behavior was gone. Avery caught the gleam of the silenced pistol, now aimed squarely at his chest. Outwardly, he was calm, but inwardly, his muscles coiled with tension. His revolver was too heavy; his draw would never be quick enough to get off the first shot.

Time stretched as the world narrowed. He'd faced life-or-death situations before, but this… this felt different. Final. There would be no negotiation, no last-minute reprieve. Only death.

This was the price of operating in the shadows for too long. Avery's finger tightened on the trigger of his own weapon.

The muzzle flash flickered like distant lightning in the car's claustrophobic interior, illuminating the driver's face. The first muffled thud struck with brutal efficiency, driving into Avery's chest with bone-jarring force. A familiar pain exploded across his ribs, a searing heat that radiated outward.

A second impact, lower and to the side, sent shockwaves through his body. This agony was different. Sharper.

He recoiled against the leather, the once-comforting scent of the car's interior now tainted. For an instant, there was nothing but a high-pitched ringing in his ears.

A third shot shattered the deathly silence, the concussive force rattling Avery's teeth. The muzzle flash seared his vision, leaving spots on his retinas.

Warmth blossomed down his side, and Avery knew without looking that it was blood. His blood. The surprise of it was almost more powerful than the pain. His fingers lost their grip on the warm revolver. It clattered onto the floorboard.

His vision blurred, the world tilting sideways as darkness crept in. Avery lunged and grappled with the door handle, his blood-slicked fingertips trying to find purchase. He had to escape the confines of the car before it became his tomb. But the locked door offered no exit.

Fragments of Avery's life flashed before him. Faces of trusted allies and hidden enemies. He concentrated on the moment.

Why was he targeted? What had he missed? The answers remained frustratingly out of reach.

His fingers fumbled for his radio in a last-ditch effort. But it slipped from his grasp. The acrid smell of gunpowder mingled with the coppery tang of his blood. He eyed the smoking pistol on the floorboard.

He needed answers, but his vision dimmed.

Avery knew that a lifetime in espionage had finally caught up with him. Old Wild Bill himself had warned Lucas of this years ago.

Eventually, everyone's luck runs out.

Chapter 48

01:35

John's head throbbed as consciousness returned. Rough fabric scratched against his cheek. He blinked, squinting against the streetlight filtering through a car window. He took in his surroundings, finding himself lying in the backseat of an old sedan.

He tried to move his hands, but they were restrained. Handcuffs pressed into his skin, leaving raw, burning marks. Looped through the door handle, the restraints clinked as he strained, each movement intensifying the pain.

He shifted, wincing. Memories of the events leading up to this moment flooded back. An object had struck his head. But there was something else…

Andrea!

He needed to warn her.

A breeze wafted through the open window, carrying the unmistakable sounds of the city. He then caught a whiff of exhaust fumes and a hint of the ocean.

Voices drifted in from outside. Someone was speaking in Russian. He arched up, peering over the edge of the car door. Through the gap, he caught sight of a dozen men.

Morozov's voice carried. *"Eto mesto."*

John angled his head, straining to see more while being careful not to draw attention. He recognized the location immediately.

The warehouse district surrounded them, a maze of weathered brick and corrugated metal structures. They were just outside Hyde's headquarters, a nondescript building indistinguishable from its neighbors except for the fresh coat of gray paint on its loading dock doors.

He needed to warn his teammates of the impending danger.

John's mind drifted to Nate. The weight of that loss, still raw, threatened to overwhelm him. He'd sworn never to let another teammate down, yet here he was, helpless as history seemed poised to repeat itself.

Morozov pointed at one of his men. "Sergei, ensure they are inside. Eliminate everyone you find. If they are gone, extract the information from the prisoner by any means necessary."

"And if he gets… difficult?" Sergei asked, his thick accent carrying a hint of eagerness.

"Use your imagination. Have some fun. "

Sergei motioned towards the car holding John. "How much fun?"

Morozov chuckled. "Bring back most of him. Alive, if possible."

"I like the sound of that."

"Just remember," Morozov warned, "get information first. Don't let your enthusiasm ruin the mission this time."

The men shared a brief laugh. "It will be done."

Morozov turned to leave, then paused. "Oh, and Sergei? Once it's finished, rendezvous at the pier. I must provide an update personally."

Sasha entered a nearby idling car and drove away, leaving his men to their grim task.

John's pulse raced. Morozov's squad would hunt down and eliminate Hyde's team. If, by some miracle, they were already gone, then those same men would subject him to unimaginable torment for answers he didn't have.

Trapped, restrained, and outnumbered. Every conceivable factor worked against him.

John shifted in his seat, testing the strength of his bonds. The cuffs refused to yield even an inch. The frame was just as solid. Sweat trickled down his temple.

Through the open window, he could hear weapons being checked, the ominous clicks of ammunition being loaded. In a matter of minutes, the hit squad would breach the warehouse. Only chaos and destruction would follow.

The metal bit into his wrists, pain lancing through him. John's muscles tensed as he recalled a last-resort trick from his CIA training. A hidden pin in his shoe that could shim the handcuffs open. A long shot at best.

Twisting awkwardly in the cramped backseat, John bent his right leg up. With agonizing slowness, he maneuvered his foot towards his bound hands, the chain straining against the door. His fingers stretched, trembling with effort, until they brushed against the tip of his shoe. Just a little more…

Someone was approaching. John's muscles went slack as he resumed his prone position. Through slitted eyes, he watched a scruffy Russian guard climb into the driver's seat. The man's pungent body odor, a nauseating mix of stale sweat and cheap cologne, filled the small space.

A flare from a lighter illuminated the guard's harsh features as he took a slow drag from his cigarette. Thick, white smoke billowed through the car, searing John's nose with its putrid aroma. He fought the urge to cough, biting down hard on his cheek.

John watched as the guard settled into a rhythm. Puff on the cigarette. Check his watch. Glance at the prisoner.

From outside, he heard the distinct sound of rifles being charged as clips slid into their chambers. The muffled, accented voices drifted in through the open window. One voice bragged about how many Americans he'd kill by night's end. Another chimed in with a challenge, claiming that he'd win any such contest.

John bristled at their casual brutality. Every fiber of his being yearned to spring into action. But the guard's presence kept him trapped and immobile.

Each agonizing second ticked by as John's imagination conjured the horrors he alone could prevent. The guard's eyes darted between Olson's prone form and his watch. John's fingers trembled, yearning for the bobby pin, but the Soviet's vigilance kept him frozen in place.

Even if he could overpower the Russian and escape the car, the odds of reaching the warehouse alive were slim to none. The guard shifted, muttering under his breath, *"Da ladno, u menya net vsey nochi."*

John tensed. The men had entered the building. He was too late.

A single gunshot rang out.

More gunfire. Then there was an explosion. Rapid-fire automatic gunfire and shouted orders then followed. Something had interrupted the Russian's plans.

The guard jerked in surprise, his cigarette tumbling from his lips as he fumbled for his weapon. Eyes wide with panic, he secured the gun in his lap and whipped around to check on his prisoner.

He glimpsed worry on the man's face before another explosion erupted, snapping the guard's attention back to the mayhem outside.

There was an epic battle being fought outside, and John was pretending to sleep. He needed to escape immediately.

Chapter 49

Dr. Andrea Miles pressed her forehead against the window as she stared into the darkness. Streetlights blanketed the abandoned alleyways, doing little to ease her anxiety.

Fidgeting with the hem of her blouse, she turned. Each member of the team was packing equipment and checking weapons with frantic efficiency. The explosives made her queasy.

"How did I end up here?"

Andrea thought of her sterile research lab, where the greatest threat was a misplaced decimal point. Now she was in a world of espionage and danger. She'd joined this mission to protect her life's work and HAVE BLUE's data, but that was over.

This would be a desperate fight for survival.

Simmons hunched over his workstation, his fingers stuffing large wads of paper into pouches. He froze. His gaze locked on a flashing red light.

"We've got company!"

He switched on a closed-circuit television. The screen swirled to life, revealing a grainy black-and-white image of men approaching. Their military-style movements and machine guns left no doubt about their intentions.

"Oh, God," Andrea gasped.

These weren't FBI agents or police. They looked like mercenaries.

Simmons grabbed a cache of weapons from the loading table, his usual jovial demeanor now gone. As he distributed the arms, his hands lingered on each team member's shoulder.

Matheo snatched up a handful of explosives and placed each charge strategically around the room. He tossed a bundle to Jessica, who caught it with alarming casualness before stuffing it into her tactical vest.

Andrea froze, unsure what to do next. This wasn't equations or aerodynamics.

Jessica crossed the room in a few quick strides and grabbed Andrea by the arm. "Away from the windows."

"Who are those people? What do they want?"

"They want us dead, love." Jessica's grip tightened. "So stay close and do exactly as I say."

Andrea slumped against an interior wall. "There must be some misunderstanding."

Jessica fixed her with a hard look. "Listen to me. They're here to eliminate us all. No exceptions."

These men were here to kill them. To kill her. The reality of the situation crashed over her.

Matheo slipped past, tossing something into the stairwell before barricading the door. Simmons took up position behind a steel crate, weapon ready as he peered over its thick frame.

"Sixty seconds," Simmons called out as he watched the monitor. "They're moving fast."

She counted every second as it ticked by, each one longer than the one before. The anticipation was crushing.

A single gunshot shattered the silence with a sharp crack, making her jump. Before she could process it, Matheo triggered his remote. Flames erupted up the stairwell in a searing wave, illuminating the darkness with a violent burst of light. A surge of scorched air singed Andrea's eyebrows. The stench of burned chemicals and melted paint flooded the room.

The aftershock had barely faded when bullets riddled the door, splintering the sheet metal. Shards flew everywhere.

Andrea ducked, covering her head and trying to make herself as small as possible. Through squinted eyes, she watched Simmons step forward and return fire through a gaping hole in the entrance. Beside him, Matheo armed another charge, waiting for his chance.

Jessica appeared at Andrea's side, yanking open a large air duct. "Andrea," she called over the gunfire. "Get in!"

Andrea didn't move.

Jessica shoved her towards the opening. "Dr. Miles, get your arse in there!"

Andrea dropped to her hands and knees, backing into the small steel shaft. Once inside, Jessica stooped to face her.

"Take a left at the split. Crawl to the dead end with a ladder. Get to the basement and escape. Don't look back."

"I can't."

Jessica gripped her shoulders. "Listen to me. I've been watching." Rounds riddled the crate a few feet away, but Jess didn't flinch. "You are one badass engineer. You've got this."

She nodded as a fresh volley of bullets flew overhead. The terror threatened to overwhelm her as she stared into the vent.

She couldn't let fear win. She had to survive and see this through.

Andrea squared herself, committing the directions to memory. Left at the branch, dead end, ladder, basement. She repeated it.

Everything was going to be okay.

When she turned back, Jessica was drilling screws into the grate from the outside. Andrea's fingers interlaced with the metal, pushing against it.

The hatch refused to move.

The bitter truth hit her: they weren't coming.

"I'm not leaving without you!" Andrea screamed, unwilling to leave.

"Grenade!" Matheo's shouted.

Andrea flung herself down. Something heavy landed nearby, rolling. From the corner of her eye, she saw Jessica leap out of view just as it exploded. The concussive blast stole Andrea's breath as the pressure slammed her against the wall.

The world muffled, and the gunfire faded. There was only distant ringing.

"Jessica!" She clawed her way back to the duct entrance.

Fortner's face appeared on the other side, smudged with soot. "Go!" she insisted. "Get out of here!"

Jessica then charged ahead with her weapon raised, bullets spitting from the barrel in fiery arcs.

She was gone. No time for grief. Or goodbyes.

Tears stung Andrea's eyes as she turned. With trembling hands, she pulled herself forward. Behind her, the sounds of the firefight grew faint, then distant, as she crawled deeper into the void.

Andrea inched along. Rough steel dug into her palms and knees as the duct groaned under her weight. Darkness pressed in around her, thick and suffocating. Her elbows and hips scraped against the narrow walls as she trudged along.

Stale air filled her lungs, heavy with decades-old dust. She focused on her breath, trying to keep it steady.

Left at the branch, dead end, ladder, basement. The mantra repeated in her mind. Each distant explosion sent vibrations through the shaft, making the duct feel alive and malevolent.

After what felt like an eternity of crawling, Andrea reached a junction. She paused.

Think!

Left. You know what to do. Go left.

The tunnel seemed endless. Just when she thought she couldn't crawl another inch, her hands met solid metal. A dead end. Relief washed over her.

Andrea's fingers searched frantically for an opening in the door. No latch. No release. Fused by corrosion, it refused to budge. She pushed again, hoping for a different result. It still denied her. Years of neglect had locked it up. She was trapped.

No. Jessica would never forgive her if she quit.

Andrea had to think logically. Use the scientific method. If the first experiment failed, try something new. She thought immediately of Archimedes.

Leverage. She needed leverage.

With a grunt, Andrea turned herself around in the cramped space, bringing her feet up. Bracing herself against the sides of the duct, she drew her legs back and kicked at the grate with all her might.

The door wobbled, but held. Andrea struck again. And again. Each impact sent waves of pain through her lower body, but she didn't stop. She had to get out. For John. For the team. For herself.

With a final, desperate thrust, the hatch gave way with a groan. It fell into the vertical shaft, disappearing into the derelict hole.

Peering down, her eyes could just make out rungs fading to black.

Andrea scrambled onto the rickety ladder, its metal slick with condensation. Rust flakes coated her palms as she grabbed a handhold. She forced herself not to look down.

Move. Each second on this death trap was tempting fate. Falling was unacceptable.

She descended as fast as she dared; the darkness swallowing her.

Another explosion rocked the building, the shockwave slamming into her with the force of a dump truck. Her grip tore free, feet flailing in empty air. A scream escaped as she began to fall.

Andrea clawed at the ladder, desperate. Her left hand snagged a rung, jolting her body and slamming her against the railing. Pain shot through her shoulder, but she refused to let go. The thin metal strip was the only thing between her and the abyss.

A sickening crack came from the rung, followed by an ominous groan.

The bar, worn by age and strain, bowed under her weight. Andrea's mouth dropped in horror as she felt it deform. No, no, no! Her grip weakened as her fingers slipped. One by one, her digits peeled away.

With a primal cry, Andrea lunged upward.

Crack! The rung snapped.

For a heart-stopping moment, she floated. Then, her hand closed around hard metal, halting her plunge. The broken piece clattered, bouncing off the wall as it fell.

Andrea said a silent prayer and forced herself to move. She inched down the ladder until her feet touched solid ground. The smell of mildew permeated the basement corridor. In the distance, there was a faint glow.

An exit? Hope surged as she ran towards the light.

As she drew closer, Andrea realized it was a window set high on the wall. It was small, but it might just be big enough for her to squeeze through. She looked around for something to stand on, but the basement was empty except for a few broken crates.

Andrea backed up, then charged. With a desperate leap, her fingers caught the edge of the windowsill. She pulled herself up, every muscle straining, until she could brace her feet against the wall.

The window wouldn't move. It was painted shut. Andrea drew back her leg and kneed the glass twice. The pane shattered, shards exploding out.

Cool night air rushed in, washing across her sweat-streaked face. Andrea slid through the opening, wincing as broken fragments bit into her skin. She tumbled out onto rough gravel, gasping.

Andrea pushed herself to her feet, the warehouse towering behind her like a malevolent giant. She moved across the cracked asphalt, scanning for help.

She spotted a distant group of three cars. There was hope. Maybe someone could call the police. The team was running out of time.

She broke into a run, waving her arms.

"Hello! Please, somebody help me!"

Chapter 50

Andrea's cries for help floated through the car window. John wanted to sit up and call out to her, but he couldn't tip his state to the driver.

The scruffy Russian immediately noticed Andrea. He craned forward, peering through the windshield at the woman hobbling across the dark parking lot.

"*Eto slishkom prosto,*" he said, shaking his head.

Each plea twisted like a knife in John's gut. Every instinct urged him to move, but he remained motionless as the guard checked on him. Satisfied his prisoner was still out, the Russian grabbed his pistol and kicked open the car door.

His boots scraped on the asphalt. The pistol clanked against the frame as he moved forward and leaned over the hood. The gun remained behind his back as he waited for her to get closer.

"Over here!" He gave a wave, his attention solely on her.

John seized his chance. Curling up, he pulled his left leg toward himself and grasped the bobby pin from his shoe. His hands worked frantically, bending the metal. Sweat trickled into his eye as he focused on the evasion training techniques.

Andrea's footsteps were getting closer. The guard's fingers tapped the side of the pistol, as if counting down until he had the perfect shot.

John ripped the plastic tip off with his teeth and rammed the flat metal into the pawl, pushing back the locking mechanism. The ratchet released, and the cuff slipped open.

"Just a little closer," the Russian muttered.

The guard racked his pistol.

"Can you call the police?"

"Yes. But hurry. I heard gunfire," the Soviet said in perfect English.

He leaned forward and took aim, his finger tightening on the trigger.

"Hey!" John shouted.

The guard spun around, startled.

John launched himself at the man. Both men toppled over the hood and onto the pavement. The gun fired wildly in every direction. Olson ripped the gun from his hand and swung it down, connecting. The blow knocked the guard unconscious.

John staggered to his feet, the dangling handcuffs still attached to one wrist. The weapon slipped from his grasp and rattled to the ground. He was sure he looked like hell. He definitely felt like it.

He found Andrea as she limped close.

"John!" she called.

"Andrea!"

The air between them crackled with unspoken emotions. They moved toward each other as if pulled by an invisible force. Both limped forward at first, but picked up speed as they got closer. When they collided, it was in a tangle of limbs, John's arms wrapping around Andrea's waist as her hands cupped his face.

John drew her close, afraid to let go.

Their lips met in a passionate, unexpected kiss. John had experienced nothing like it. Soft. Yet fiercely genuine. He felt a rush of joy and warmth. For a brief instant, the world surrounding them vanished.

There was no mission. No danger. Just them.

A distant rumble grew.

BOOM!

A massive explosion shattered the tender reunion. Giant flames burst from the fourth-floor windows as the warehouse collapsed. The blast's force knocked them to the ground as debris launched outward.

John shielded Andrea with his body as chunks of concrete and glass deflected off his back. The air thickened with burning chemicals and oppressive heat. Once he looked, the warehouse was engulfed in an inferno, thick black smoke billowing high into the sky.

Andrea's screams pierced the roar of fire and crumbling walls. She struggled against John's hold, trying to crawl her way back towards the burning building.

"Jessica!" Anguish filled her voice as she tried to break free. "We have to help them!!"

"Andrea, we can't." He tightened his grip on her. "It's too late. They're gone."

Tears streamed down her face as she struggled. She gave one last surge and then collapsed into sobs. She looked back at the ruined building, raising her hand.

Before he could respond, injured Soviets began to stumble and limp from the building, their faces blackened with soot and blood. Some still clutched weapons despite their wounds.

They spotted John and Andrea. One shouted in Russian and took a shot.

A bullet whizzed past them, kicking up asphalt. John fished keys from the guard's pocket and yanked Andrea by the collar, pulling her around the hood.

"Get in the car! We don't have time!"

He shoved Andrea into the passenger seat before sliding behind the wheel. John jammed the key into the ignition. Bullets peppered the vehicle as the engine roared to life and he slammed the accelerator. The sedan lurched forward, tires squealing. The car's back end drifted in a lazy S pattern, the smell of burning rubber hanging as they sped away, leaving smoking skid marks.

His eyes darted between the road ahead and the rearview, watching for pursuit. Every sound made him flinch, expecting a roar of engines behind them.

POP!

The back windshield spider-webbed as a bullet sailed through. John checked Andrea, then himself. It missed both of them. He waited for another, but it didn't come.

In the side mirror, John watched the warehouse recede, flames licking at the night sky. The men stopped chasing, and the sputter of gunfire dropped off. They didn't give chase. The car keys were probably still on bodies inside the building.

The reality of what had just happened crashed over John, bringing a torrent of guilt with it. Jessica, Matheo, Simmons. They were gone. Only Andrea made it out alive.

Morozov's body count was adding up, and John wasn't sure the man could be stopped.

Firetrucks raced past them in the opposite direction, sirens wailing.

Andrea watched the flashing lights. "John, where are we going?"

"Somewhere safe."

"Is there anywhere safe left?"

John gripped the steering wheel tight. She was right. "We just need to survive another day."

Beside him, Andrea wept, her face pressed against the window. John's heart ached at the sight of her anguish. He longed to promise that everything would be alright.

Things would not be okay.

He reached over and gave her hand a gentle squeeze. They drove without speaking, leaving behind the destruction. He didn't know where to go. Only that their ordeal was far from over. He needed somewhere safe to plan.

Durbin would use his power to silence them. Morozov too. Hyde's team was gone. Vasquez was gone. For the moment, they were alive.

It was just the two of them now. It would have to be enough.

Chapter 51

SKUNK WORKS FACILITY

9 Hours Remaining

07:50

Exhaustion weighed on John as he and Andrea entered the Skunk Works facility. No one would expect them to come back here.

Their rumpled clothes and grime-streaked faces reflected the night's ordeal. Each step echoed in the unnaturally quiet hallways.

John grasped at fragments of their unraveled plan. The heist. The betrayal. The explosion. How had it all gone wrong? He peered at Andrea. Despite her haggard appearance, he realized she looked better than he did.

As they moved toward Andrea's office, John could tell something was off. Employees clutched cartons of belongings as they moved to the exit. Most averted their eyes.

They found Dr. Grant Wheeler hunched over Andrea's desk searching through stacks of paper. The sweet aroma of freshly brewed coffee wafted from his mug. Dr. Wheeler almost choked on the hot liquid as he registered their disheveled appearance.

"Good God," Grant exclaimed. "What happened to you?"

Andrea gave a faint smile. "You should see the other guy."

John chuckled, then grimaced, clutching his ribs. Everything hurt. At least Andrea could still make him laugh.

Grant looked them over once more. "Well, you both look like hell."

"That's exactly where we've been." She motioned to the people cleaning their desks. "What's going on here?"

Dr. Grant's face soured. "Listen, there's been an incident. The higher-ups are trying to keep it quiet, but everyone already knows."

Andrea sank into her chair, her shoulders slumping with exhaustion. "Knows what?"

"You haven't heard?" Grant leaned back, folding his arms across his chest. "There was a break-in last night. They're shutting down the project."

"Anything we can do?" John asked.

Grant replied with a weary shrug. "It's done. The President'll announce it tonight. A White House contact tipped me off."

"How long do we have?" She took in the grim faces of her colleagues. Everyone knew.

"A few hours," Grant said. He looked between them and added, "But it doesn't matter."

John rubbed the back of his neck. They had risked everything for the Stealth project, and now it lay in ruins. All their sacrifices, seemingly in vain. He noticed the glisten of fresh tears on Andrea's cheek.

John stood. "I need to call a friend. See if we can get some support."

He soon found an empty office with a phone. Removing a slick piece of vellum from the lining of his belt, he examined a list of emergency contacts. One of them was an old buddy who owed him favors.

The line rang twice before a man answered.

"Yeah?" a gruff voice said.

"It's Olson."

"John, what the hell?"

"My op's been compromised. I need backup, resources, anything."

There was a pause. "It's way worse than you think."

The man bombarded Olson with information, each detail worsening their situation. Visions of the cavalry coming evaporated, along with any hope for the Stealth Program's survival.

Durbin had been setting this trap from the beginning.

His friend sighed. "I'll see what I can do. Until then, lie low." The line went dead.

Olson hung up the phone and walked back to Andrea's desk.

She jumped up from her chair as he rounded the corner. "What did he say? Can they help?"

"My CIA credentials are gone. Erased. As if I never existed."

"That's impossible." Andrea's eyes widened with disbelief. "How could they do that?"

"It gets worse," John cut her off. "Avery's missing. And the FBI… they've branded us as Soviet spies."

Andrea recoiled. "What?" She slumped into her chair. "That's absurd! It's not true. That's ridiculous."

John put a hand on her shoulder. "Truth doesn't matter. In their eyes, we're guilty. And if they find us…"

"We'll be arrested for treason," Andrea finished.

"And we both know what happens next. We'd never make it to trial."

"Oh, God." The color drained from her face. "There has to be a way to clear our names."

"I won't let them get away with this. First, we stash you somewhere safe. Then I'll go after Durbin. I'll beat a confession out of him if I have to."

Grant cleared his throat. John had been so focused on their issues, he forgot the man was still there. "Dr. Wheeler, it'd be best if you kept your distance from us right now."

Grant's expression hardened. "I don't know what the hell you two have gotten yourselves into." His eyes focused on Andrea. "But whatever it is, I want to help."

John nodded. "I appreciate the sentiment, but my focus is on keeping Andrea alive." His mind moved to their next move. "It's not safe for her here." They had to stay one step ahead of Durbin. "Do you have a change of clothes here at work?"

Andrea pointed to a wall locker. "Yes."

"Good, clean up. Get changed, and collect some of these supplies. We need to be gone in less than an hour." John jotted down notes on a scratchpad.

Grant stood and approached John. "I have some fresh clothes you can borrow, and I can lend you my personal bath. It has a shower."

John shook his hand. "Thanks, Dr. Wheeler. I'll take you up on that." He turned back to Andrea. "Sixty minutes, Andrea. Then we're ghosts."

He followed Grant out the door. Within moments, he was stepping into the director's private bathroom.

John showered quickly, the scalding water carrying away grime and blood. But it couldn't purge the weight of lives lost. Breathing in the steam, he mentally cataloged potential escape routes and safe houses. They had to get out of the city.

Dressed in fresh clothes, he finished packing a go-bag, stuffing it with food and essentials. Andrea entered as he zipped up the duffle.

"Where's your bag?" John asked, frowning at her empty hands.

"I don't need one. John, we need to talk."

He slung the bag over his shoulder. "No time, Andrea. We've gotta get moving. I've still got friends who can help, but clearing your name will take time."

"John, forget about that." Her face hardened. "Follow me. This is urgent."

"Andrea, no detours. Every minute puts us at risk."

"Trust me." Her eyes locked onto his. "There's something you need to see."

John sighed, relenting. "Alright, lead on."

They found Dr. Wheeler in a briefing room, standing amid scattered papers and half-dismantled equipment. The scene was a mess. Frantic chalk diagrams riddled the far wall.

He smiled as John entered. "I trust you feel better?"

"Yes," John answered. "Make it quick, Doc. What do you want to show me?"

"I thought it was obvious." Grant adjusted his glasses, pointing at the chalkboard. "I solved your data tape problem."

John whirled around. "You told him?"

"Don't be mad. I had to."

John raised his hands in exasperation. "Now he's in danger too, Andrea. Durbin will kill everyone who knows about his involvement. You just made him part of this." He turned to the engineer. "I'm sorry, Grant. But the people involved in this are dying."

"That's why I insisted on being part of it. I know what I'm doing," Grant said, standing tall.

"Look, I appreciate whatever this is, but we don't have time. The Soviets are probably halfway to Moscow."

Andrea jumped in, "John! Hear him out. I think he can help."

"Alright, but make it quick."

Grant stepped forward. "At Skunk Works, we plan for any potential crisis. And this includes our data being compromised. As a precaution, all sensitive files are secured with double encryption."

"What does that mean?"

Grant allowed himself a satisfied smile. "Without the proper cipher, the data reels are useless."

"Can't they just decipher it? I mean, they have scientists who do that kind of thing."

"This isn't just any standard encryption," Grant replied. "We designed it with IBM for sensitive military intelligence. It's applied to all our TOP SECRET information, so… those stolen files require the proper key."

Andrea beamed. "See what I mean?"

"Ok. I believe you." John pulled out a chair, sitting. "Tell me how it works."

Dr. Wheeler leaned forward. "Think of it this way. The data on those tapes is like a letter written in a language only two people in the world can read."

He tapped the diagram he'd sketched. "The Soviets might as well be staring at hieroglyphics. Without the DES 64-bit block cipher, even the brightest minds at Bletchley Park couldn't crack it. They may have the source material, but they can't understand a word of it."

"So the tapes…"

"Nothing but glorified doorstops," Grant replied.

"How many keys are there?" John asked.

Grant held up two fingers. "Only two copies exist," he continued. "One is on the Cray-1 computers here."

"Those will be out of commission for months," Andrea said.

"Exactly," Grant confirmed.

"And the other?"

Grant paused. "The other key is at a secure offsite location. Its whereabouts are known only to a select few. Even as a director, I don't have access."

Andrea's shoulders sagged with relief. "So the Soviets are finished. The data they stole is useless."

"Not so fast. Don't underestimate Morozov," John replied. "He's resourceful, cunning, and now he has Durbin backing him. We can't assume the cipher will stay secure. They'll be looking for it."

"So, what do we do?" Andrea asked.

John considered the possibilities. "If we can pinpoint where the Soviets are hiding, we might intercept the encryption key or the original files. Either would work. We just need to act fast."

"Won't they have already fled the country?" Andrea asked.

John was confident in his assessment of Morozov's character. "He won't leave until his mission is complete. With Durbin and the resources of the Executive Office in his corner, we can't expect the cipher will remain safe for very long. The Ghost of Berlin never fails."

Grant smiled. "Then we don't have much time. I have city maps we could use."

"Perfect," Olson told him. "Morozov mentioned a pier outside the warehouse. We can start looking there."

A few minutes later, John and Andrea hunched over a map, tracing coastlines and harbor entrances. Dr. Wheeler hovered nearby, searching ship names from a registry with the city.

Andrea plotted several plausible spots. Each red dot represented a strong chance, yellow a moderate, and green dots were unlikely.

She circled a red dot. "This is a good start, but it's just guesswork at this point."

John's eyes darted from one location to another, trying to discern a pattern.

"Should we secure the encryption or the files?" Grant asked, lining out several of the cargo ship slots on the map.

"Both are crucial, but…" Olson trailed off.

He considered their situation. Limited resources and dwindling time. Durbin's involvement made their odds overwhelming.

Andrea voiced his unspoken doubt. "Can we handle this on our own?"

"I don't think so. We need help."

They needed Gabrielle. As much as he resented it, John knew Hyde's skills and unconventional thinking were the only way through this crisis. She had a knack for seeing solutions where others saw dead ends.

The irony of the situation wasn't lost on him. His actions had led to her capture. Now, when he needed her most, she was beyond reach.

Andrea placed a hand on his arm.

As he thought about what to say next, movement caught his eye. John looked up to see a Skunk Works guard standing in the doorway. The man's eyes were fixed on John and Andrea.

The guard's fingers rested on the grip of his weapon as he pointed at John. "Right there," he said.

Olson instinctively moved in front of Andrea, shielding her with his body, as he spotted a shadowy figure in the doorway.

John reached for his weapon, finding only empty air. What an idiot. He'd failed to take into consideration how vulnerable they'd become. The absence of an escape route left them trapped.

The overhead lights cast shadows across the guard's face. Grant stood frozen, his eyes darting back and forth, unsure of how to react. He took a cautious step backwards.

As the mystery figure entered, Olson's muscles coiled, ready to spring into action. Sweat prickled on his palms. He lacked a weapon, but he'd be damned if he'd go down without a fight.

He decided to tackle the armed guard first. Then he would go after the mystery guest. As he prepared to launch himself, John froze.

The figure stepped into the light, turning his world upside down.

Chapter 52

TEMPORARY EXECUTIVE FIELD OFFICE

8 Hours Remaining

Deputy Chief of Staff William Durbin savored his rare imported coffee in the White House temporary field office. His tall, imposing frame filled the leather chair as he shook off the weariness.

The decadent caffeine was a small indulgence he deserved. It had been a late night.

Zebra-like shadows danced along the walls as the morning sun slanted through venetian blinds. It was beautifully quiet. A lone secretary was on duty and he preferred it this way. Fewer eyes watching. His line of work demanded secrecy.

As he lifted the cup to his lips, a sharp rap on the door shattered the moment. His face darkened at the interruption. He had left explicit instructions not to be disturbed.

His secretary, Sarah, poked her head in. "I'm sorry, Mr. Durbin." Her eyes darted. "There's a call for you on the secure line. I know you said no disturbances, but the caller was quite insistent."

Durbin's grip tightened on the mug, but he hid his annoyance. He knew who was at the other end. They could report the murder of CIA Deputy Director Avery after his coffee cup was empty.

He remained seated. "I gave strict instructions."

"I know, sir." Sarah's shoulders hunched. "But he wouldn't take no for an answer."

He sighed, gesturing for her to patch through the call. "Fine."

The secretary nodded and retreated, closing the door behind her. He adjusted his posture, already preparing himself for whatever inconvenience awaited him.

The line crackled as he activated it. Durbin's irritation morphed into concern. The voice that greeted him was not the CIA, but someone both familiar and agitated.

"William," Morozov growled, skipping formalities. "What is this? We had a deal."

The lines around Durbin's steel-gray eyes deepened. "Sasha, we agreed. No contact."

"It is necessary," Morozov snapped. "The data you sent is defective. Scrambled and useless, like you. My engineer says there is encryption."

Durbin had not expected the reels to materialize in the hands of Officer Olson. It wasn't shocking that Skunk Works would encrypt their files. His original plan would have given him weeks to work out these issues.

The Soviets would just have to be patient.

"That's unfortunate. Calm yourself, Sasha. These things happen sometimes. It's not uncommon for sensitive programs to use encryption."

"Unacceptable!" he snapped. "You never mention this!"

"It's a minor setback, nothing more."

"This renders the entire operation pointless," Morozov said. "We need that data."

"I understand your frustration. This is merely temporary. I'll use my presidential code and contacts, and we'll have the decryption key within a couple of days. By Tuesday at the latest."

The silence was heavy. "Not good enough. I want it today. By 5 PM. Or the deal, and the treaty, are off."

Durbin curled his fist. The Soviet had no concept of discretion. This kind of short-notice move would raise suspicions. "Impossible. These things take time."

"No excuses!" Morozov snapped.

"You're overreacting."

"No, Mr. Durbin, I'm being realistic," Morozov added. "I will have my data today. If I don't, that would be very bad for you. Soviet secrets tend to 'leak' at inconvenient times."

"There's no need for that."

He knew Morozov well enough to appreciate his threat. Failure to deliver would have dire consequences, jeopardizing his path to the presidency. Until he held that power, he remained vulnerable.

"I'll get you what you want."

"See that you do." The line went dead.

Durbin gently placed the phone back in its cradle. The receiver settled with a soft thud, his fingers lingering. Motionless, he stood there in silence.

This was no time to be shaken. He was a master of control, a man who thrived in the shadows. And yet, Morozov had struck a nerve, opening doors Durbin normally kept sealed.

The space felt too small as a familiar pressure built in his chest. He strode across the room, pressing the door. The lock clicked as he turned the key, sealing himself away from prying eyes and ears.

His focus settled on the ornate fireplace. A brass fire poker rested against the brick, its length gleaming. He reached for the metal rod. Grasping it with both hands, he tested its weight, swinging it gently.

It felt good. Solid. Unyielding. The cool metal against his palm stirred a sensation deep within him, a memory long-buried but never truly forgotten.

Dr. Sheraton's face came into view. That condescending smile. Those patronizing eyes.

The childhood therapist, blinded by his ignorance, had seen only a troubled and violent teenager. He'd labeled young William as disturbed, oblivious to the raw potential packed within. Sheraton, fool that he was, had inadvertently given Durbin two invaluable gifts.

The first was the need for a mask. No one could ever see the true you.

William created a veneer of calm rationality to hide the rage inside. Mirroring others established rapport and made him instantly likeable. Mastering this had allowed him to excel in the cutthroat world of academia and politics. Channeled, his void became productive.

The second gift came through the doctor's sacrifice.

A wolf lurked in his soul, and it constantly demanded blood. It was always hungry, prowling the edges of his consciousness.

The psychiatrist's screams had taught him that these desires were only temporary. He could leash it and control its savage appetite. William needed to feed the beast only periodically to satiate its cravings. The wolf still clawed at its gilded cage, but it was now under his control.

Durbin's grip tightened on the poker, knuckles whitening. The weight of the rod in his hands bridged past and present, Dr. Sheraton's lessons merging with the frustrations of his current predicament. Long chained, the beast within yearned.

He closed his eyes, drawing in a slow breath. The air filled his lungs as reality sharpened into focus. The wolf stirred, hungry. It had been forever. He just had to give it a little.

His eyes snapped open. He hoisted the poker above his head, his 6'2" frame casting a long shadow. For a moment, he stood still.

The mask dropped.

With a snarl, he brought the rod crashing down onto the telephone.

Shards of plastic and circuitry flew across the desk. Durbin struck again and again, each blow accompanied by a grunt. The phone's casing splintered, revealing colorful wires. Fragments exploded like confetti. He reduced it to a twisted mass of broken components.

Durbin felt a weight lifting. The frustration and anger that had been building inside him dissipated. He continued his assault until nothing remained but a scattered pile of debris.

He tossed the poker, the metal clanking against the iron stand. A thin sheen of sweat glistened on his forehead. He shut his eyes, relishing the feeling. The wolf retreated, sated for now.

Durbin surveyed the destruction before composing himself. He straightened his tie and smoothed his disheveled dark hair. A single gray strand caught his eye. He plucked it out. Satisfied, he made his way to the door.

His mask was back in place.

Sarah stood near her desk, rigid. She had heard the commotion, but years of service had taught her when to remain silent.

"Everything okay, sir?"

William favored her with a reassuring smile. "Everything's fine," he said. "However, I seem to be having some trouble with my phone. Would you be so kind as to arrange for a replacement?"

Sarah's gaze lingered on the wreckage before snapping back to Durbin's unruffled presence. "Of course, sir. I'll take care of that ASAP."

"Excellent." He leaned in. "Oh, and one more thing. I need you to get a liaison with ARFCOS for me as soon as possible. It's rather urgent."

She nodded, retreating. "Yes, Mr. Durbin. Right away."

As Sarah busied herself with the tasks, Durbin watched her. A small part of him wondered if she would have to be dealt with once this was all over. She had, after all, been privy to more information than was strictly safe.

No, he decided. There were already too many bodies. Best to keep things simple. Sarah was efficient and discreet; there was no need to complicate matters.

Durbin retreated to his office, leaving the door open. He settled into his chair, feeling refreshed and focused. The path ahead was clear. He would secure the encryption key, satisfy Morozov's demands, and continue his meticulous march toward the presidency.

He swiped away the shards from his desk, a stray piece nicking his skin. A thin bead of crimson welled up.

The wolf growled, but he silenced it.

"Not yet."

He studied the blood's slow descent, transfixed. Gravity was inevitable. But so was he.

Chapter 53

US NAVAL STATION GUANTANAMO BAY

9 Hours Remaining

Sweat beaded on Vasquez's brow as he watched heat ripple off the tarmac. The sun, unforgiving and oppressive, bore down like an old adversary, reminiscent of Miami summers. With a deep breath, he drew in the thick, humid air, its salty warmth filling his lungs.

His family fled this country before Castro and his ilk took power. Now he was back, under vastly different circumstances.

Guantanamo Bay buzzed with activity. Soldiers traversed the ops area, their steps stirring small dust clouds from the parched earth. On the strip, a transport plane sat idle, its engines emitting a low, steady hum.

A military fighter jet taxied to a stop on the run-down airstrip nearby. Through a heat haze, Vasquez watched the marshaler's orange wands guide the aircraft. He was grateful for the armed escort, given the ongoing political tensions with Cuba. The last thing he needed was complications while transporting a high-profile detainee.

His gaze drifted to a group of MPs standing near a jeep, their uniforms sharp against the backdrop of scrub. A Marine Lieutenant, with short dark hair signaled everything was in place for the handover.

As Vasquez waited for the prisoner to disembark with Morris, a scraggly pig darted across the cracked taxiway, evading capture with an impressive burst of speed. It squealed with delight as it disappeared into the undergrowth.

The sight triggered a bittersweet recollection of his pet pig, Stuart, from when he was ten. Those days felt like another lifetime now, when simple joys were enough to fill his world. Despite his initial apprehension, Vasquez had bonded with that ridiculous animal when his uncle brought it over. The hog had brought an unexpected joy into their lives, his antics never failing to make them laugh.

Stuart was more than just livestock; he was a symbol of rebellion and freedom for two young boys living in a new country. Anyone could have a dog or a cat. The Vasquez brothers had a pig.

But Stuart had a secret: he wasn't really a pet.

Bruno's uncle had purchased Stuart with a different intent.

Noche Buena, the night before Christmas, approached with a harsh lesson in life's realities. Vasquez and his brother, determined to save Stuart from becoming part of the traditional feast, hid him. For five days, they'd kept the pig concealed, much to their father's growing anger and frustration.

Hiding Stuart? Pure defiance. A child's desperate grasp at control in a world dominated by adult decisions. Fairness be damned. Bruno wouldn't let expectations or tradition stop him from defending what he knew was right.

Vasquez remembered the pit in his stomach the moment his father found out about their clubhouse on the abandoned lot. He stormed off, intent on finding Stuart. The wait was excruciating; the worst of his life. Late that evening when his papa returned, it was without the animal.

To the day he died, Vasquez's dad never spoke about what happened. But Bruno had his suspicions. He believed that his father, faced with the reality of bringing Stuart home as the main course, couldn't do that to his boys. Instead, he told them that Stuart had escaped, leaving the details a mystery.

Bruno smiled as he stood on the sweltering runway. Part of him liked to imagine Stuart was still out there somewhere, roaming the streets of

Miami, free.

It was a comforting thought, even if he knew it was just a childish fantasy.

The memory of Stuart became legend within the Vasquez family. But his story served a greater purpose as a reminder of the complexity in life. Some things were meant for a higher calling, despite their humble beginnings. It was a touchstone that stayed with Vasquez throughout his career, reminding him that the right choice was often not the easy path.

Jet engines winding down brought Bruno back to the present. He looked at the small FBI jet and motioned to Morris. Time to get this done.

As Morris led the hooded prisoner off the airplane and down the stairs, Vasquez couldn't shake the feeling that something was off. His instincts rarely failed him. The problem was the silence since the transport vehicle. Not a word. More than that, the way she carried herself was different. Submissive.

He trusted nothing that was odd.

Vasquez scrutinized every detail as the prisoner shuffled. The black jumpsuit's fabric seemed baggier. He couldn't see Hyde's curves. Something else caught his attention. The blue forget-me-not pin Hyde always wore was gone. She would never part with it. He tried to recall when he'd last seen it.

"Boss," Morris said, "Congrats, sir. We did it." He turned to the hooded figure. "Ready for prison, Ms. Hyde?"

No reaction.

Morris cleared his throat. "Hyde? This is not the time for games."

Still no response.

Bruno's cheeks flushed. He knew it!

This entire scene was a lie.

Vasquez yanked the hood off the prisoner's head. "Hijo de puta!" The bag slipped from his fingers.

It was not Hyde.

Bruno stared into Clyde's wide, frightened eyes. The man who should have been driving the transport stood before him in Cuba, a poorly fitted wig sitting askew on his head.

"How?" His mind tried to piece together where everything had gone wrong.

It didn't matter. Vasquez seized the man by the collar. "Where is she?" he snarled, jerking the driver close.

Clyde's eyes were wide with fear, his body trembling. "I-I dunno, honest!" he stammered. "She just… she just told me to put this getup on, y'know? Said I couldn't say nothin', or the deal was off. I didn't have a choice, I swear!"

"What deal?" Vasquez demanded.

"It's Sonia. M-my wife." Clyde's voice cracked, tears forming. "Insurance company, they… they wouldn't lift a finger to help us. But Hyde, she…" He paused, blinking. "Somehow she got Sonia on the list. For a transplant. Probably in surgery right now." His shoulders sagged. "I'm sorry, sir. I'm so sorry, but… what was I supposed to do?"

Vasquez released him with a disgusted shove, sending the man stumbling back. A collective silence gripped the assembled personnel.

Bruno whirled around. "Check out his story."

"Yes, sir," the agent said before running off to find a telephone.

Morris stepped forward. "If Clyde is here," he began, "then who was operating the truck at the airport?"

"Morris," he bit back, "who do you think?"

Gabrielle had escaped right under their noses, driving away in an FBI-furnished vehicle while they celebrated.

The Marine officer approached. "Agent Vasquez. Orders, sir?"

"L-T! Get me the Air Operations Officer on the horn. I want these jets refueled pronto. I'm back in the sky in thirty minutes or it's your ass."

The lieutenant snapped a salute, his free hand already darting to his radio. Vasquez watched as the scene erupted into chaos, soldiers and agents scrambling to execute his directive.

Sweat slid down Bruno's back in waves. Hyde had somehow arranged this charade, pulling all the strings. His pride was bruised, but beneath the self-doubt, a fire smoldered. She didn't define him, nor would she win a game of wills.

Vasquez would find Hyde. Of that, he was certain.

Chapter 54

SKUNK WORKS FACILITY

8 Hours Remaining

09:15

Gabrielle Hyde stepped out of the shadows.

John blinked, unable to move. The scent of her signature perfume reached him, verifying it was not a trick.

She couldn't be here. She was in Vasquez's custody. He hauled her away in handcuffs only hours ago, bound for a maximum-security cell.

Yet, here she stood, completely unruffled. Gabrielle didn't even appear tired.

"Thank you for your assistance; that'll be all," Hyde said to the guard.

Andrea peeked over John's shoulder. There was a sharp gulp, then she let out a small gasp before pushing past. "Gabrielle!"

Andrea launched herself across the room. She threw her arms wide, enveloping Gabrielle in a fierce embrace. "I thought I'd never see you again," she confessed, her words lost against Hyde's shoulder.

Hyde returned the hug with equal fervor. "Oh, Andrea. You should know by now, I'm not that easy to get rid of."

Andrea let out a strange sound. Part sob, part joy. "But how? John said they arrested you."

"I left the party early," Hyde replied. "I just wish I could see Bruno's face when he gets to Cuba."

John remained rooted to the spot as unexpected emotions flooded through him. It was becoming maddeningly familiar.

As if sensing his thoughts, Hyde's gaze shifted. For a moment, everything seemed to stop. John saw in her a reflection of his own weariness.

John crossed the room, his steps slow and measured. Andrea stepped back, giving them space. He stopped in front of Gabrielle, the distance between them feeling like a canyon.

It was all his fault. The rooftop. The FBI. His failure to trust her. He owed her an explanation. But what could he possibly say?

"I know," she said softly. "Me too. We were both too damn stubborn." A rueful smile formed. "Can you forgive me?"

John swallowed the lump in his throat. All the pent-up pressure, the conflict, and the mistrust; it melted away.

Gabrielle stiffened, surprised by the vulnerability. But as John's arms wrapped around her, his hands splayed across her back, she leaned into it.

In the silence, John felt the old barriers collapse.

"Careful, Olson," she teased. "You're going to make me blush."

It was a rare thing to see Hyde let her guard down, even for a moment. He savored it, knowing it wouldn't last.

Questions flooded his mind. "How…" he began. "What happened with Bruno? As I recall, you were in FBI custody."

Hyde's smile broadened. "You didn't think a few FBI agents could keep me contained?" she said. "Especially not our old friend Agent Vasquez."

John folded his arms. "Alright then, enlighten us."

Hyde surveyed the room. Even Dr. Wheeler, who had been observing from the corner, leaned forward with a thoughtful expression.

"It all started with Vasquez bragging about shipping me off to Cuba during our briefing at the Oval Office," Hyde began.

John snapped his fingers. "That was oddly specific."

"They let you in the Oval Office?" Grant stroked his chin.

Andrea turned. "Dr. Wheeler, you have no idea. I'll fill you in later. By the way, this is Dr. Grant Wheeler"

"Charmed," Hyde said.

John waved his arms. "Introductions later. Continue your story."

"Right," she replied. "Bruno's threat. A private jet is the only way to get to Cuba without a security nightmare. The California FBI field office has only one approved location: Hollywood-Burbank. My sources informed me that Bruno requested a Tactical Vehicle and a driver for a high-threat prisoner transfer," Hyde continued.

John nodded, following her logic. "You were right."

Hyde shrugged. "I knew he'd find a reason to arrest me eventually, so I made preparations."

Andrea raised a finger. "Speaking of, how did the FBI know about the heist?"

John met Hyde's eyes. Would she tell Andrea? It was time to own up.

Olson sighed. "It was my fault…"

Hyde put a steadying hand on his forearm. "No. It was mine."

John's jaw fell. Why was Hyde protecting him?

"I did some things I'm not proud of." Hyde's gaze dropped to the floor. "The FBI found out, and it resulted in what happened." She cleared her throat. "I give Agent Vasquez a hard time, but he's an excellent detective. Underestimating him nearly cost us everything. I put all of you in danger."

John struggled with Hyde's admission. He'd never heard her acknowledge failure before. It was so unlike her. John felt he was seeing the real Gabrielle for the first time.

One glance at Andrea confirmed he wasn't alone. Her nose crinkled, eyes narrowing as she studied Hyde, then John. She could tell there was more lurking beneath the surface. But Andrea nodded and let the matter drop.

Hyde squared her shoulders. "So, because there was a high risk of capture, and since I knew when and how, it was only logical to put the right contingencies into play."

Andrea's eyes lit up. "Oh, I know! Operation Surrogate Starling!"

"Precisely."

Olson raised a hand, but Andrea interjected, "I'll fill you in later, John.

Let Gabrielle finish. This is fascinating."

John gestured for Hyde to continue.

"Swapping out the driver was child's play," she said casually. "I found an FBI operator named Clyde, who was in a desperate situation. A man who needed hope more than money. We switched places while Vasquez was waiting for the plane to refuel."

John knew Hyde was resourceful, but this level of manipulation was next level. "How did you know the plane would need fuel?" he asked.

A mischievous glint lit her features. "Simmons paid the FBO refueler fifty bucks to wait. Thus creating the window I needed."

As the pieces of Gabrielle's scheme fell into place, John shook his head. It was brilliant, audacious, and utterly Hyde. But something still didn't add up.

"Hold on," John said. "Vasquez would notice if he was escorting a different prisoner. How did you manage that?"

Hyde was clearly pleased that someone had picked up on this detail. "Ah, John," she said, "that's where things get interesting."

She moved in closer. "You see, Vasquez's ego isn't his biggest weakness. It's his history. We're all slaves to our patterns."

John considered his own tendencies and wondered how much Hyde leaned into those. He shook off the thought.

"Vasquez's psychological profile makes for a fascinating study. He tends to hood prisoners, a practice that has earned him reprimands in the past."

John's eyebrows shot up. "You read his psych eval? How did you even get access to that?"

"Details, details. The point is, I used it to my advantage."

"What do you mean?" John asked.

"I just needed to trigger Vasquez," Hyde continued. "Using specific verbal cues can guide someone down familiar paths. As we traded barbs, I slipped in markers like 'envision, see it, eyes opened, bagging the bad guy, and unveiled.' Then, I challenged his cultural background and authenticity. He had no choice."

Of course Hyde would know something like that. "So, you're saying it only took a few words."

"He already wanted to," Hyde continued. "I just gave him a nudge. By the time he was done fighting me, he'd forgotten to fight his own habits. "Vasquez saw what he expected, a hooded figure in handcuffs."

John understood all too well. "Perception is reality."

"Exactly," Hyde confirmed. "Clyde and I are similar enough in build that, with the right padding and posture, the switch wasn't immediately noticeable under the jumpsuit. Add in a wig, and presto."

Andrea leaned in. "What would have happened if the plane was ready when you showed?"

"Clyde would have waited for Bruno to exit and then driven off with me still in the back. Easy as pie."

John marveled at the meticulous planning. It was a masterclass in strategic thinking. This was Hyde at her best. "What about Clyde?" he asked. "Won't he be in serious trouble once Vasquez figures out what happened?"

"Clyde knew the risks." Hyde's expression softened. "And the rewards. His wife has a rare blood type and needed a new liver. The FBI's insurance wouldn't cover it, so I ensured she received the necessary care. Doctors performed her surgery early this morning. If my sources are correct, she'll recover well."

Dr. Wheeler slapped the table. "Unorthodox. Devious. Brilliant! You missed your calling as a scientist on our team."

"Sorry, Dr. Wheeler. I don't do nine to five."

Grant lifted his shoulders, as if expecting nothing less.

"Wait. How did you get away? Someone would have noticed," Andrea said.

"I commandeered the truck. I'll admit, it proved more challenging than expected."

John's eyes widened. "You've never driven a tactical vehicle?"

"It was my first time driving anything," Hyde admitted. "Not an easy vehicle to handle. Thank God the FBI includes manuals for everything. However, I might have hit a few curbs, maybe a fence."

John let out a whistle. "You never cease to amaze me."

"Then stop underestimating me."

John held up his hands in surrender. "I'm a believer."

Grant, who had been listening with a mixture of curiosity and amusement, cleared his throat. "As touching as this reunion is," he said, his voice carrying a weight of urgency, "I believe we have more pressing matters to discuss."

Hyde cocked her head. "Oh, do tell."

John's expression darkened. "While you were pulling your Houdini act, things went south on our end. Durbin took the tapes."

Hyde's eyes narrowed. "Why would you permit that? I warned you."

"I didn't intend to have that happen. He was working with Morozov. Who now has the stealth data."

"But he can't access it," Grant added. "Encrypted."

John looked at him and then back at Hyde. "We're trying to locate the Soviets' hideout before they leave the country. If so, they can be stopped. But we can't use law enforcement to help."

Hyde stroked her chin. "And why is that?"

"Um. John and I are wanted for treason," Andrea confessed.

"Oh, my. You've been busy," Hyde said with a laugh. "I suggest we finish what we started. I just need my team."

The room fell silent.

Andrea's face fell. "Gabrielle," she began, a tremor in her voice. "There's… there's something you need to be aware of."

Hyde placed a hand on her arm. "It's okay, dear. All is well."

"No, it's not." Andrea's eyes glistened. "Gabrielle, it's about your team…"

She took a shuddering breath. John knew she was finding the courage to deliver the devastating news about the explosion at the warehouse. He braced himself.

To her credit, Andrea was composed. "The Soviets sent a team to your headquarters to kill us. I escaped, but they didn't make it."

But before she could continue, a movement in the hallway caught her attention. John followed her gaze, eyes widening in disbelief.

Matheo trudged past, dragging equipment down the hallway.

"He's alive?" John and Andrea exclaimed in unison.

"They all are." Hyde stifled a grin. "Right as rain. I was trying to tell you."

Andrea's face transformed once again. Her eyes darted between Hyde and Matheo, as if she couldn't quite believe it.

"They escaped before the explosion," Hyde said.

Andrea blinked rapidly. "I'll process that in a minute. Second question: where did he get that equipment?"

John added, "And how did he gain access?"

Hyde took a conciliatory stance. "I know you're upset. And you have every right to be. What you experienced was real to a degree. A carefully orchestrated illusion."

Andrea wagged her finger. "I saw them die, Gabrielle. The warehouse exploded, and I thought… I thought they were gone."

John moved to her side. "We both did."

Hyde's shoulders slumped, a weary exhale escaping. "The explosion. The chaos. All of the show was necessary. The Soviets needed to believe. They saw what I wanted them to see." She paused. "But now, we hold the advantage. They think we're weak, broken. We're stronger than ever, ready to strike when they least expect it."

John listened as Hyde detailed the ruse. Matheo had rigged the warehouse with controlled explosions. The team had exited without harm through a pre-placed escape route. Meticulously staged, expertly executed.

Being kept in the dark, yet again, stung, but he was getting used to it at this point. The real problem was still Durbin.

Working with Morozov made him ten times more dangerous. But they both played by a certain set of rules, bound by reason and twisted logic. Hyde broke those norms in a way that infuriated everyone involved. It was their secret weapon.

Jessica entered the room, her presence a sudden interruption. She leaned over to Hyde, whispering something.

Jessica turned to Andrea, offering her a thumbs up. "Nice job with the vents, girl."

"The debriefing is ready," Hyde announced before turning to leave.

Andrea turned to John. "I assume we're going to follow her lead?"

"I'm in if you are."

A clearing of the throat caught both of them by surprise. They turned to see Dr. Wheeler still waiting in the back of the room.

"I'm not sure what I should do," he said.

"Come on, Grant." John motioned for him to join them. "We could always use another brilliant mind. Interested in saving the free world?"

"You know, why not?" He grabbed his bag. "It's certainly more interesting than packing my desk."

Grant charged out of the room, grabbing Andrea by the arm.

John lingered for a moment, staring at their maps and formulas on the chalkboard. The pieces were falling into place, but the real challenge lay ahead.

It was now them versus the entire US and Soviet federal governments.

Chapter 55

Hyde's team had taken over the cramped room. Now it smelled of coffee and gun oil.

Gabrielle hovered over a small table, absorbed in a map. Every inch of wall space disappeared beneath a medley of city schematics and blueprints. Dr. Wheeler took a seat in the corner, moving a stack of papers from his chair to the floor.

Jessica greeted Andrea with a warm embrace. Their reunion was brief but heartfelt. John hadn't realized how close they'd become, bonding through their shared ordeals. He was relieved to have Andrea acting herself again.

Jessica turned to John. "Thanks again for getting her out of there."

"Not a problem. That was one hell of an explosion."

Simmons gave a long, appreciative whistle. "Oh man, you should have seen it from my angle- it was wild!" He leaned against the wall, a lopsided grin spreading across his face.

"There was a garbage chute attached to the window, right? I'm talking proper industrial-grade stuff." Simmons flung his arms wide. "As soon as those flames came at me, I just jumped down it."

"You should have seen his face," Jessica added. "Thought he might need a cigarette and a cuddle after that stunt."

Simmons winked at Jessica. "You get me." His grin widened. "That fire chased me all the way down. Even melted some of the foam blocks in the dumpster. Think Disneyland, but better!"

A "theme park ride" combined with imminent danger wasn't John's idea of Saturday fun. "Sounds… exciting," was all he could muster.

Matheo rubbed his stubble. "Speak for yourself. I lost some of my favorite knives in that explosion."

John could listen to their stories for hours. But they simply didn't have the time.

"Okay, everyone, listen up." His tone sobered the room. "We're on a tight timeline here. The tapes are in the hands of the Soviets. My boss, Deputy Director Avery, is missing. And to make things more troubling, Andrea and I are now wanted as spies."

"Welcome to the family," Jessica said with a laugh.

"This is serious, Jess." John replied. "The President's Advisor, William Durbin, is the mole. And, worse, he's teamed up with Sasha Morozov. They have every resource available to both the United States and the Soviet Union. And it's all aimed squarely at stopping us."

Simmons exchanged a knowing look with Hyde. "Looks like you were right about that advisor fella, boss."

Olson took a step forward, pointing his finger accusingly. Hyde had known all along. "You…"

"Now, John, don't get all preachy. I didn't know for sure until you told me."

"How long have you suspected Durbin was the mole?"

"Since the White House." She sighed, examining her nails. "The man's a psychopath, but he's also a politician. Suspicion isn't validation. I just knew he was lying about something big. Maybe everything."

"And you didn't think to share that information? We could have…"

"What, John?" Hyde interrupted. "Stopped him? Exposed him? Right. You and Vasquez were in no mood to hear my thoughts." She shook her head. "No, I needed to force his hand. And with his proximity to the President, that wouldn't be easy. Flushing him out required calculated risks."

"Calculated risks?" John asked, his voice rising. "I almost died. Three times!"

Matheo, in his usual manner, interjected. "That made it very convincing."

John shot him a withering look, but the Frenchman shrugged, unfazed. But Matheo was right. And so was Hyde. Nobody would have listened.

Hyde held up her hand, silencing further argument. "What's done is done. We have a job to finish, and we should focus on that." She turned to John. "I know you have your reservations. But I need you to trust me, just this last time. Can you do that?"

John looked at Andrea. Her eyes told him everything he needed to know. These former adversaries were now his only hope.

"Yes." Hoping he wouldn't regret this moment, he then added, "But first, you need to hear something from Dr. Wheeler and Andrea. There is another angle to consider."

Grant stood up with a grunt and quickly brought the team up to speed on the encrypted tapes and the history of cryptography. To his surprise, Hyde seemed intrigued as Matheo struggled to stay awake.

"What are you saying?" Simmons asked.

Grant polished his glasses on the hem of his shirt. "The Soviets need that reader to access the data. There's only one remaining, hidden at a secure location in LA." He glanced at Andrea. "We have no idea where."

John moved to the table, looking at the map. "Knowing Morozov, he's using the Nuclear Treaty signing as leverage. So, that means he'll want the decryption device before 5 pm. If we could find that storage location, we could stop them."

"But we hit a dead end." Andrea shook her head.

"I'll find it," Hyde said.

Grant laughed. "Sure."

"She's not joking, Dr. Wheeler," Andrea responded.

Hyde rubbed her chin, eyes narrowing in thought. "The tough part is taking down both Durbin and Morozov simultaneously." She turned to Jessica. "Thoughts?"

Jessica pursed her lips, crossing her arms. "They know we'll be coming. Expecting some kind of trick."

Hyde waited.

"We lean into it. We go with a Kansas City shuffle," Jessica said.

Hyde nodded, a smile spreading. "My personal favorite." She looked at Andrea. "Dr. Miles, do you have another copy of those dummy files with the red rim?"

"I believe so."

"Good." Hyde studied the map. "Can you rig a secure encryption on those tapes?"

"I can handle it," Grant said, cracking a small smile. "Won't take long. Need to earn my keep anyway."

"Do it," Hyde commanded. "We need those decoy tapes ready, and the encryption airtight."

Olson raised a hand. "Hold up. You all deserve to understand something." His gaze swept the room. "What we're about to do… it's suicide mission territory. Far worse than anything we've faced before." He moved to the small board. "Durbin and Morozov have every advantage. Resources. Power. Hell, the entire government machine. They won't hesitate to crush us."

John grimaced. "I can't protect you. Not from them."

Hyde moved to his side. "You're right, John. The peril's real. But that's what makes this work." She grinned. "Durbin thinks he's won. He believes I'm in custody, my team is dead, and that you're on the run." Her voice rose to a crescendo. "As in all Greek tragedies, hubris shall be his downfall."

"Overconfident men make mistakes." Jessica added. "One tiny crisis is all it will take."

"And nobody sets a trap quite like our boss." Simmons rubbed his hands together.

Matheo released a grunt of agreement.

"I'm in," Grant said without hesitation. "This is shaping up to be the best Sunday at work, ever."

Andrea nodded. "We can do this."

John looked at the motley crew before him, ready to fight against hopeless odds. All for a country that labeled them as criminals. Olson built his CIA career by following rules and trusting the system.

That changed right now.

He took Andrea's hand. "You're right. We take them down, together."

"Excellent," Hyde said, clapping once.

"Now, we just need a plan," Andrea said.

Gabrielle turned, a mischievous grin on her face. "You heard Jessica, Kansas City shuffle."

"I have no idea what that means," John replied.

Gabrielle winked. "That's the beauty. No one knows the rules. What makes it so effective. Now, I require a cup of chamomile tea and ninety minutes to think."

"An hour and a half. That's all you need?" John asked.

Hyde glanced at her watch. "I would move faster, but you said no mistakes. And speaking of which, John, darling, try not to burn my tea. It's an unforgivable sin."

Olson sighed. Only Gabrielle could get away with this.

The odds were stacked against them, and time was running out.

Nevertheless, John felt there was finally hope.

Chapter 56

SKUNK WORKS FACILITY

6 Hours Remaining

11:05

John found Andrea in the Skunk Works kitchen preparing tea. The kettle whistled as steam billowed from its spout. The aroma of chamomile filled the air as she poured the hot water.

He approached, placing a hand on her shoulder. "Hey."

Andrea flinched, the cup teetering. "Oh, John." She set the mug down. "You startled me."

"Sorry. I didn't mean to sneak up on you."

Andrea chuckled. "It's alright. Just a bit on edge. Thinking too much. Occupational hazard." She wrapped her arms around herself. "I keep wondering about what's coming next. How crazy this is."

"You know. You don't have to do this. Going back into the field, I mean. If you want to sit this one out, no one would blame you."

Andrea fiddled with the metal tea infuser, her eyes filled with emotion. "This isn't just about me anymore." She looked towards the work areas. "When I started at Skunk Works, it was a dream come true. I was doing what I loved, pushing the boundaries of what was possible. But this..." she trailed off.

"It's about something more," John finished. "I get it."

"I thought all the challenges I faced in my life were meant to prepare me for working here. So I could become tough and resilient. I had it all figured out." She lowered her head, stirring the infuser. "But I was wrong."

She looked back at John. "This mission to stop the Soviets, it's about protecting something bigger than myself. I was meant to be part of it." Her jaw hardened. "I can't sit on the sidelines. My whole life's been leading up to this."

"And I'm damn sure not going to walk away just because I'm scared."

Faced with unimaginable danger, she was choosing to stand her ground, to fight for what she believed in. It was courage Olson rarely saw, even in the CIA.

"Me neither," he said, leaning closer.

A faint blush colored her cheeks. "I'm just following my heart."

Andrea's chin tilted up.

John could feel her breath. "Yeah," he said, "you gotta follow your heart."

She moved closer, millimeters away. "Even if it doesn't make sense?"

"Especially then."

John's thumb traced the curve of her jaw. Andrea's eyes fluttered closed.

Before either of them could second-guess the moment, John leaned in, capturing her lips in a gentle kiss that turned more passionate. Andrea melted into him as she returned the embrace with equal fervor.

A loud throat clearing shattered the spell, causing them to spring apart like startled rabbits. John whirled around to see Simmons leaning against the doorframe, a knowing smirk in place.

Behind him, Jessica stood with her arm outstretched. Simmons slapped a crisp hundred-dollar bill in her palm.

"That's only half." Her tone was smug.

Simmons fished a matching note from his pocket. "Damn it, Olson." Douglas shook his head. "Couldn't you have waited another day? I was so close."

"Mama needs new shoes."

John felt his face flush with embarrassment. He opened his mouth to retort, but stopped. Andrea's cheeks still burned red. "We'll talk later," he murmured.

Simmons jerked his thumb over his shoulder. "Boss has the plan ready. Oh, and… she wants her tea."

As if on cue, Matheo whisked by the kitchen, pushing a cart laden with an assortment of gear.

Andrea's eyes widened. "Is that…" She darted after Matheo, following him down the corridor. "Matheo, that's classified equipment!"

Simmons chuckled as he trailed behind.

John moved to follow, but Jessica's knowing gaze stopped him.

"Oh, shut up." John held up a hand. "You were right, okay? Happy now?"

Jessica tucked the cash into her bra. "Yes, John," she said, "yes, I am."

He followed her down the hallway, trying not to think about the tender moment with Andrea. As they approached a doorway, he stopped. He knew he needed to compartmentalize. There would be time to sort out his feelings later. Right now, the task demanded his full focus.

Exhaling, he squared his shoulders and entered. The room felt uncomfortably warm from all the bodies cramped inside. A complex web of information sprawled across the walls and on every horizontal surface. Red string crisscrossed the wall haphazardly, connecting notes attached with pins and tape.

A whiteboard on the far wall hosted an intricate plan in multiple colors, including arrows, exclamation points, and underlined steps that traveled from top to bottom. Hyde had a marker clutched in her fist.

She gestured to the board. "This marker board," she said, "is brilliant. So much more efficient than chalk. Douglas," she called over her shoulder, "be a dear and procure two of these for me, would you?"

Simmons snapped a crisp salute. "Roger that, boss."

She turned, noting everyone's attention. "It appears we have a quorum. So listen up, I don't have time to repeat myself." Hyde crossed her arms. "Let's not forget the gravity of our situation. What we're dealing with here is perhaps one of the most significant military secrets ever developed. Its implications and applications are endless."

Olson felt reassured to see that Hyde was treating the matter seriously.

"Normally, we'd steal this for ourselves," Gabrielle said.

John glared at her.

"But given recent events, we're focusing on the unusual position of protecting the nation and its secrets."

Jessica jabbed a sharp elbow into John's ribs. "We could do both, you know. Have our cake and eat it too." John shot her a withering look, and she withdrew with a pout. "Bloody hell, you government boys are duller than dishwater."

"Jess, dear. Behave and listen up." Hyde said with a sharp tone.

Jessica held up her pen. "Yes, ma'am."

Hyde leaned on a long wooden pointer. "Time is not our friend. In six hours, the world as we know it could change forever."

"No pressure," Simmons quipped.

"We have one shot at this. A single chance to outsmart every agency, spy, and operative gunning for us. More than I care to count, honestly," Hyde added. "Failure isn't an option. Pay attention as if your life depends on it. Because it does."

She pivoted to face the elaborate script flowing across the board. John admired her penmanship, a blend of calligraphy and cursive that gave the plan a scholarly air.

"It's quite simple. We start here," she pointed to the top, "and if we don't end up dead, we finish here." Her stick landed at the bottom.

Hyde flew through the meticulous steps in a matter of seconds.

She whirled around. "Questions?"

John and Grant looked at each other. Dr. Wheeler shrugged. "I have two doctorates, and I have no idea what she just said."

Andrea squinted at the board, trying to extrapolate the arrows and cryptic notations. "I'm sorry, but I'm still lost. How are we supposed to do any of that?"

John squeezed her hand. "One step at a time."

Hyde inclined her head. "Officer Olson is right. I let my excitement get the better of me. I'll break it down into more manageable pieces. Let's start at the beginning."

Turning back to the board, her finger traced a path. "Our first critical objective is to intercept the courier."

"Wait," John interjected. "Why not find the encryption key directly? Go straight to the source."

Grant raised a finger. "They use multiple sites for storage. The location changes based on the encryption type. Gabrielle's right. The courier is the only one who knows where to go. That courier should be our top priority."

"Precisely," Hyde confirmed. "But there's a catch. No one knows his identity. It's a precaution to prevent compromise."

Andrea rubbed her chin. "Why not just stake out Durbin?"

"Or just take him out," Simmons said.

John turned. "As much as I would like it, we can't kill him. Not till the tapes are secure and our names are cleared. And as for following him, he may not meet the courier at all. He could send it directly to Washington, Morozov, or somewhere in LA. Any of those scenarios ends in a firefight, no doubt."

"I want to avoid gunplay until the timing is right," Hyde replied. "We must control that."

"Then how are we supposed to find the decryption?" Andrea asked.

Hyde tipped her chin. "Ah, Mr. Durbin is asking the same question. He'll discover that he needs to use an official service. And the answer already presented itself to me last week."

"The binders on the President's desk," he said. As usual, there had been method to her madness. "I thought you were just messing around."

"Everything has a purpose, John." Hyde tapped the marker against her board. "Among other tantalizing documents, I spotted an ARFCOS stamp on every sensitive file from the West Coast."

"ARFCOS?" Andrea questioned.

"The Armed Forces Courier Service," Hyde explained. "Renowned for its secure and discreet transfer of classified information. They are also under contract with the administration."

"So Durbin has to use them," John finished.

Hyde gestured to a regional map pinned to the wall. "The nearest

ARFCOS office is in San Francisco. Given the treaty deadline, Durbin will need an expedited transfer."

"How does that help?" Andrea asked.

"ARFCOS uses circuitous routes. Boats, trains, multiple vehicle changes. Tracking them is a nightmare." Hyde tapped the map. "But a fast-track request forces them to use air travel."

She traced a yellow line from San Francisco to Los Angeles. "Considering he made the request in the last three hours and will need this finished before the treaty tonight, only one flight fits our window. It arrives at LAX in two hours."

"That's great news, boss!" Simmons exclaimed. "We know where and when. I'll get the gear set for a nab and grab."

"It's not that easy," Hyde cautioned. "We still have no idea who he is. No name, age, or description to go on."

Andrea leaned closer to John. "This seems…"

"Impossible? Don't let Hyde hear you use that term."

"I was going to say 'insane,'" she replied with a nervous chuckle.

Grant rubbed his temples in frustration. "So, we're back at square one?"

"Don't be discouraged," Hyde chided. "He'll identify himself if we're observant. I have a plan to spot him using tested methods. Remember, subtlety is key. Success requires everyone being ready."

Over the next twenty minutes, Hyde laid out her intricate scheme. The web of arrows and notes became a clear roadmap.

With each step, John's pen flew across the page. He glanced at Andrea. She jotted details in neat handwriting, her nose crinkled in concentration. Their roles at the center of this op would demand not just skill, but courage.

Hyde's explanations were thorough and precise. Anticipating questions before anyone could ask.

"My God," Dr. Wheeler muttered, "that's either brilliant or utterly mad."

"Questions?" Gabrielle asked as she capped her marker.

Matheo, typically ready with a biting remark, grunted his assent. "*C'est fou.*"

"As intended," Hyde said. "Dr. Miles, did you bring the data reels?"

Andrea pulled out a set of red-tipped reels along with a small, unfamiliar device. "Right here," she confirmed, holding them up for everyone. "Dr. Wheeler can explain how to use these."

Grant took both items and placed them on the table in front of Hyde.

"This," he said, indicating the mechanism, "is the decryption unit. It's the key to unscrambling the information on these reels. These connections here," he pointed to a row of pins, "interface with the reader, giving you a clean output."

Andrea noted the distinctive red tips on the reel as Grant hooked them up. "As you can see, these look identical to the ones we used before. To the untrained eye, everything will appear legitimate."

"Like on the Cray-1 computer?" John asked.

"Exactly."

Grant inserted the reels into the device, demonstrating how it operated step by step. "Anyone who tries to use this corrupted data is doomed to fail." He peered over his glasses. "Dr. Miles, that is an ingenious misdirect, I must admit."

After running the decryption sequence herself, Hyde nodded, confident she could do it again. "Mr. Simmons, were you successful?"

Simmons reached for a gleaming silver briefcase on a nearby shelf. "I've got just the thing," he said, arranging the reels and decryption device inside. "To your specifications, and it all fits perfectly."

Hyde inspected the case, running her fingers along the edges. "Perfect," she declared, snapping it shut. "Well done, Douglas." She checked her watch. "We move in five minutes. Get ready."

The room erupted as everyone gathered their equipment. Andrea fumbled with her comm unit, trying to secure it to her ear. Jessica stepped in, adjusting the earpiece for her.

"Deep breaths, doc," Jessica said, "we've got your back."

John marveled at how far they'd come. Just days ago, these people were strangers. Now they moved in sync, anticipating each other's needs without speaking. Even Dr. Wheeler seemed to have found his place, conferring with Matheo about signals and frequencies.

Hyde's distant expression as she traced the plan's outline caught John's attention. Her uneasy posture compelled him to approach. For a while, they stood in silence.

"It's a good plan," she said. There was a hesitant undertone in her voice. "But something's missing. I can taste it."

"I know," John replied. "I feel it too."

John's finger traced the 'Run for your lives' section. A simple ruse wouldn't sway Durbin. They needed something more potent. True danger.

"This. It has to be stronger."

"Mr. Simmons has it covered," she assured him.

"That won't cut it." John shook his head, unconvinced. "You know what's necessary. It has to be a real external threat. Something he knows, and fears." He tapped his lips with his finger.

"We need one more player. Someone Durbin would never expect."

"No," Hyde replied.

She knew what he was suggesting, and her response was unequivocal.

He stepped closer. "Look, Gabrielle, we've both come a long way from where we started." She opened her mouth to argue, but John pressed on. "Two weeks ago, I was in Somalia. I didn't know if I'd ever escape or make any difference at all."

"And you," he added, "were stuck in that black site painting away your frustration and boredom in watercolor."

Hyde remained silent.

"Look how far we've come. We've both changed. And it's time we trust each other."

She averted her gaze. Fingers drummed against her arm.

"I can make it work," he assured her.

"Fine."

"There's just one more little thing," John added.

"What do you need?"

"Something you won't like."

Hyde swiveled around. "Well, spit it out."

"A symbol of trust." She followed his gaze.

Her head snapped up, eyes narrowing. "Absolutely not."

"It's necessary."

Hyde's body tensed as if preparing for a fight. He waited, watching as she paced the small space between the whiteboard and the table. She took measured steps, buying time while she weighed her options.

Hyde stopped, her back to John. He could see the subtle rise and fall of her shoulders. When she turned, her expression had shifted. The usual mask of confidence was gone.

Gabrielle nodded, a small, almost imperceptible gesture.

"Alright," she whispered. "I trust you understand."

Hyde wasn't just trusting him with the mission; she was dismantling years of carefully constructed walls.

"I do."

She pressed the cool metal into his palm, her fingers lingering for a fraction longer than necessary. He saw the vulnerability.

Gabrielle departed without another word, leaving John alone. He didn't need verbal confirmation. Actions spoke louder than words.

Checking his watch, he realized he was already running late for step one.

As he exited the facility, Olson glimpsed a television displaying the news. The screen showed live footage of preparations for the treaty signing at the White House. Dignitaries and officials milled about behind the reporter.

The world teetered on a knife's edge, and they were the last line of defense. This team would either pull it back from the brink or fail spectacularly.

The fate of millions depended on what they did next.

Chapter 57

LOS ANGELES INTERNATIONAL AIRPORT

3 Hours Remaining

13:58

John and Gabrielle stepped into LAX. A horde of faces blurred past as luggage clattered and the PA crackled overhead. Businessmen, harried families, and darting staff created a human obstacle course.

As they arrived at the terminal, Hyde gathered them close.

"This is it. Our only chance to intercept the courier before he disappears into the wind. As discussed, he'll be a single male, under 35, college-educated, and ex-military. Look for someone in business attire, traveling light with little to no luggage. No kids, no wife."

John glanced around at the endless faces. This op needed a larger team, but that was out of the question. He would have to rely on what they had.

"And remember," Gabrielle added, "he's on the clock. No booze, no long lunches, and definitely no chasing skirts."

"Got it." John adjusted the earpiece wire. "Alright, everyone remain covert and alert. We're on Channel 5. Simmons is at ground transportation as our wrangler. He's our last line of defense should you need backup."

"Stay sharp," Hyde added, "and trust your instincts."

The team split up, each moving to their designated position.

Andrea headed for the coffee shop near Gate 14, while Matheo drifted toward a shoeshine vendor fifty feet away. Jessica melted into the crowd, disappearing within seconds. John positioned himself to have a clear view of the arrivals.

Standing beside him, Hyde watched the waves of people. "It's a lot to take in, isn't it?"

John felt overwhelmed. "How are we supposed to filter through all this?"

"There is a way," she said. "In fact, it's time you learned a recall technique my father once taught me."

John grimaced. "Right now?"

"Yes, now," Gabrielle insisted. "We have a few minutes before the flight arrives, and you've earned the right."

"I'm listening."

Hyde's voice softened. "This is an art my family has practiced for generations. A way to access your deepest memories."

"Hypnosis?" John frowned.

Hyde laughed. "Oh no, you're way too pragmatic for that. But this can open you up to what's already there. Even details from years ago." She positioned him squarely in front of her.

"Sounds tricky."

"It is," she acknowledged, "but valuable. Eventually, you'll be able to do this on your own." A sly smile crossed her lips. "But first, I need to open your blocks. Peyote would be ideal."

John cringed.

"But I'm fresh out. We'll just have to do this the hard way." Hyde laid her palm over his face. "Close your eyes. Imagine yourself somewhere calm. Somewhere you feel safe. Let yourself be open."

Her hand slid to his shoulder, her touch almost reverential. She leaned in, her breath warm against his ear as she let out a sharp, percussive snap. John flinched, but Hyde's grip tightened, holding him in place.

"Trust me. And don't move."

John forced himself to be still as Hyde's fingers trailed along his neck, tracing delicate patterns. Her touch was unsettling as the patterns left a tingling sensation. He suddenly felt vulnerable. Maybe that was the point.

She pressed hard against his cheek, then snapped again, pulling him deeper. He felt a strange lightness in his shoulder, his eyes dilating. She tugged at his earlobe, then cradled his head, her palm flat against his skull as she tapped out a measured rhythm.

"This was handed down and guarded by my ancestors. The Nazis feared it because they couldn't control the Sinti people," she whispered. "Some think it's mysticism. That's a lie. Our internal connections are as real as the sun and moon. This sanctuary is meant only for those who are pure. I'm trusting you with my family's gift."

John felt strange, as if floating. "I don't deserve that."

Her hands poked and prodded further. "That's my decision." She squeezed. "I'm reestablishing the pathways to your inner self. Letting you tap into what your mind already knows. Things buried deep."

Hyde moved in close, her words faint. "Let go," she said. She pressed her thumbs against his eyes, muttering, *"Khud ko paane ke lie khud ko chhod do."*

John's pulse dropped, the room fading as if he were sinking into a dream.

"Let's begin," Hyde's voice sounded distant. "Envision an empty place. Clear your mind of everything. Forget me, the courier, Durbin, Andrea."

The surrounding noise was gone, replaced by the sound of his heartbeat. John pictured himself standing in Grand Central Station. Alone, he stared at the towering columns and marble floors.

"Transport yourself to Somalia as an external observer. Watch without judgment. Feel nothing."

John stood on a sweeping desert, dunes rising around him.

"See only your surroundings. Go to the courtyard." Hyde's voice seemed to float in.

John was now in the empty street market. "I'm there. I'm alone."

"Good. Envision Morozov's arrival. Nothing else."

The black sedan's door opened. A single foot stomped out, dust swirling around the shoe. Sweat beaded on John's forehead as the memory crystallized. His fingers twitched.

Hyde's voice came in from beyond. "He can't hurt you. What color is his belt?"

His fists clenched. Morozov looked directly at him with an icy stare. "Don't lose control."

People started to appear. Vendors yelled once more. Morozov laughed. Nate's lifeless body lay on the ground, blood spreading out. Olson's eyes snapped open.

"I can't do it." John hung his head.

"No one expects you to master this right away. It takes time." She put a hand on his shoulder. "I could tell you were close. You must first lose yourself. Trust yourself. Then you can master yourself."

John knew she was right. He had to learn control. "Okay," he said, shaking the tension from his arms. "Let's go again."

"Plane's here," Matheo's accented voice reported over the radio. "Passengers any moment."

Gabrielle tapped John's shoulder. "We'll continue later. Focus on the task now." She lifted her radio. "First-class passengers are our priority. Look for our courier among the first group."

The Pacific Southwest Airlines gate slammed open with a metallic clang. John's training kicked into high gear as he analyzed each disembarking traveler, his eyes darting from subject to subject.

A procession of men in dark suits emerged, each one with a briefcase and bearing an uncanny resemblance to the last. Years in the field had taught Olson to focus on subtle nuances. The slight hesitation in a step, a discolored article of clothing, the length and style of their haircut.

He dismissed three older men; their graying hair and slower gaits ruled them out as potential couriers. That left four more targets.

John doled out assignments. "Andrea, take the businessman with the red tie. Matheo, watch the guy with the leather briefcase. Jessica, focus on the one in the navy suit. I've got the last one. Report anything suspicious."

"Copy that," Andrea responded.

"*Mallette en cuir* in sight."

"Dapper Dan acquired," Jessica chimed in.

Olson's gaze settled on his traveler, a younger gentleman wearing a tilted gray hat. He was the last man to exit before a frazzled family burst through the gate, corralling two shrieking four-year-old twins. The mother held one girl around the waist, the child's toes dragging along the floor.

John focused on his target. The man's pace was brisk but controlled. "I'm on Hat Man," he informed the others. "Hyde, stay put. Maintain overwatch."

Olson fell into step twenty feet behind his target. John grabbed a discarded newspaper, the pages providing cover as he maintained visual contact. The target's movements were purposeful. Ex-military. John kept a casual demeanor to avoid drawing attention.

The suspect wove through the traffic, his pace picking up. John matched his stride, keeping a discreet distance while never letting the mark out of sight.

The Hat Man paused at an intersection, checking his watch. John ducked behind a pillar, suddenly interested in his paper. Years of fieldwork gave him a sixth sense of when to disappear.

Through his earpiece, Andrea's voice crackled. "My guy just met his wife and kids. Not our courier."

"Copy that," John replied. "Fall back and regroup."

The man in the hat pivoted, changing direction. John adjusted his trajectory. He jinked, checking his watch before looking around. Olson kept moving, trying to act natural.

The man sighed, then barged into an airport bar, settling at the counter.

"Target four is down."

Matheo's voice filled his ear. "Mine as well. Too young, fresh out of college."

"Jessica here. My target's complete codswallop."

Their options evaporated, John replayed every detail. What had he overlooked?

"All units negative on courier identification," John reported. "Andrea, Matheo, Jessica, converge on baggage claim. Simmons, standby at your position. Hyde, rendezvous with me at Gate 23. Confirm."

Everyone checked in as John raced back through the terminal. The gate numbers blurred as he sprinted to reach Hyde.

Catching his breath, John reported, "None of the passengers matched the profile. Too old, with families, or breaking protocol."

Hyde's expression remained neutral. "He had to be on this flight. We must have overlooked something."

John let out a heavy sigh. "What are our options?"

"We have to take another look. We have to watch the deplaning process and find the error." She paused, her eyes locking onto John's. "And you're going to do it."

He grimaced. "Too many distractions." The words were an excuse. The problem wasn't the commotion.

"I'll guide you. It's about time you trusted yourself."

"Breathe," she whispered. "Let go." Hyde's fingers tightened. "The noise, the chaos, your anger, your fears, your pain." She leaned in. "Do you remember the trigger words?"

"Khud ko paane ke lie khud ko chhod do," John recited, shocked the words came so easily. Everything seemed to recede.

"Excellent work." Hyde's tone took on a dreamlike quality. "We are in your memory now. Picture yourself standing in the middle of the airport terminal."

John visualized the scene, the bustling movements slowed to a frozen spectacle. Travelers stood motionless, their expressions a snapshot of everyday life.

"Are you there?"

"Yes," John replied, his voice detached.

"Good. Now imagine I'm there with you." She joined him in his mind. "Let's walk through the terminal and find our man."

They navigated the mental construct with calm deliberation, approaching the gate. The jet bridge extended into the unknown, the crowd standing as statues.

"Ignore people who don't matter. Let them fade away."

John focused on the faces of the disembarking passengers. The elderly couple with their matching luggage dissolved into mist. He erased each person from his field of view, one by one.

"The men we followed. They're not important anymore. Remove them."

John released his hold on the four suspects, watching as they melted away.

"What do you see?" Hyde asked.

John focused on the figure crouched near the door. The family with the screaming twins approached, bumping against the kneeling man before rushing past.

"There's someone," John said. "On the jet bridge. Tying his shoe."

"Go to him."

John closed the distance, details emerging. A battered brown briefcase rested at the man's side, its edges worn.

"Describe him."

John studied the man, taking in every aspect. "About six foot, twenty-eight to thirty years old. Wearing a charcoal jacket with navy pants. Black tie with a silver pin. Some kind of animal on it. Short black hair, polished shoes. Except the right one has a fresh smudge where the little girl stepped on it."

The words flowed. He pulled each detail from his memory with startling clarity.

Hyde snapped twice in his left ear. "Come back."

John's eyes popped open, the bustling airport rushing into focus. He blinked, disoriented. Hyde was holding the transmitting radio inches from his mouth.

"You have the description. Find him," she added to the radio transmission.

Jessica was the first to respond. "Got eyes on the subject near baggage claim," she announced. "Engaging now. Going open mike."

Without hesitation, John and Hyde took off running towards the ground transportation area. His dress shoes squeaked against the polished floor. Beside him, Hyde moved with her usual grace, slipping between people.

As John reached the stairwell, he skidded to a halt. Hyde caught her breath as he scanned the crowd below, soon finding Fortner in the crowd.

Jessica pulled her hair back in a fluid motion as she was passing an information counter. She grabbed a clipboard and pen while a distracted agent looked the other way.

"There!" John pointed out the courier to Hyde as they listened to Jessica on the open channel.

Jessica sashayed into the courier's path, forcing him to react. The man halted to avoid a collision, his expression a mix of curiosity and annoyance.

"Excuse me, sir?" Jessica's voice dripped with charm. "I'm collecting signatures to ban the use of firearms. Could you sign my petition?"

"Boy, did you pick the wrong guy," he said with a laugh. "Prior Army, 101st Airborne. So, no, I won't be signing that."

He moved to step around her, but Jessica wasn't finished. She lightly touched his chest, her eyes locking with his. "That's okay, sugar."

Her fingers traced small circles on his jacket. "I don't care about that stupid petition. But I do love a handsome man who wore the uniform. So brave. Why don't we grab a drink so you can tell me about your time in the 101st?"

The courier politely declined her offer and maneuvered around the temptress, eager to escape her advances. The man's commitment to his job marked him as a professional.

As the courier walked away, John noticed Jessica holding up a wallet and an ID card, a triumphant grin on her face. She had pulled the same trick on him at the warehouse. It worked then, and it worked now.

"She's way too good at that," John told Hyde.

"Our courier's name is Karl Robertson," Jessica reported, "and he's headed to the driver's area."

John's grip tightened on the transmitter. "All teams, converge on Robertson. We need to intercept and distract him until Simmons is ready."

"I'm here with the drivers." Simmons' voice was tense. "Robertson's arrived. Visual contact established, but swap is compromised. Cannot proceed with a switch with the mark on site."

John's stomach dropped. He glanced at the distance between himself and Simmons, realizing there was no way he could reach him in time. Their plan to trap the courier by replacing his driver with Simmons was falling apart.

"Copy that," John responded. "Hold position. Hyde and I are inbound from the upper level. Andrea, Matheo, get there ASAP!"

John bolted, zigzagging through travelers and vaulting over obstacles. Hyde was close behind.

Robertson scanned the waiting drivers holding name cards. John's lungs burned as he pushed himself to bridge the impossible distance.

Simmons' voice crackled, panic bleeding through. "He's coming straight at me. I need help now, or this is over!"

John yanked the radio from his belt. "Someone do something!" As he finished speaking, he clipped a woman, who let out a shriek as she nearly fell over. The noise carried through the terminal.

Robertson stopped in his tracks, pivoting toward the sound.

Chapter 58

After the collision, John fell to the floor and slid several feet on the polished tile. Robertson craned his neck, trying to see the commotion. The second Olson stood, the courier would spot him.

Simmons remained frozen, panic in his eyes. Both of them were stuck.

Out of nowhere, Matheo lunged forward. The compact Frenchman collided with Robertson, the impact sending both men sprawling to the ground as luggage and personal items flew everywhere.

Matheo sprang up, leaning over Robertson. His voice rose above the startled crowd, his French accent thick with indignation. "Watch it, Dirty American!"

Robertson scrambled to his feet, swiping at his jacket. "Hey, what's your problem, buddy?" he barked back.

Seizing the distraction, John dashed towards the line of drivers. He gave Simmons a subtle nod, signaling him to proceed. Simmons instantly moved to the driver holding a sign that read: "ROBERTSON."

John strategically placed himself to block the real courier's view of the exchange.

"I'm Karl Robertson," Simmons said to the driver.

"This way, sir," the driver replied, still distracted by the commotion.

Simmons slipped the keys to John, who quickly pocketed them before adjusting his suit, flipping up his collar to blend in.

Matheo and Robertson hurled insults at each other, drawing more attention to their confrontation. Matheo, playing his part to perfection, seized Karl's briefcase, his voice rising in a torrent of rapid-fire French curses. Robertson's face reddened with anger, grasping the intent.

"Give that back!" Robertson demanded, lunging as Matheo held the briefcase aloft.

John noticed a crucial flaw: he was the only driver without a sign. Thinking fast, he turned to a friendly-looking older gentleman standing nearby.

"Hey, can I borrow a piece of paper? It's my first day." John offered a sheepish grin.

The driver chuckled and reached into his bag, producing a sheet and a pen. He handed them to John with a knowing wink. "You've gotta plan better, kid. Here you go. Good luck."

John accepted the items. "Thanks."

Robertson wrenched his briefcase from Matheo and stormed towards the chauffeurs, his face contorted with rage.

John ducked out of line, scribbling Robertson's name in bold letters. Keeping his head down, he rejoined the other drivers, the ink still glistening on the impromptu sign.

Robertson's eyes locked on the paper in John's hand as he scrutinized the unprofessional signage. "I'm Karl Robertson."

John nodded, forcing himself to maintain his composure despite the discomfort of his sweat-soaked shirt.

"This way, sir."

Robertson eyed him critically. "You alright? You look a bit off."

Olson hastily wiped his forehead. He kept his gaze downcast, avoiding eye contact. "I'm new, sir. Sorry," he apologized. "The airport's just so confusing. I was late. Sprinted all the way from parking."

"Yep. That's it," Robertson said, his stance easing. "I saw you running. Knocked that lady over. That was quite the mad dash. Let's try to stay on time from this point forward."

Olson jumped forward, adopting a posture of eagerness. "Don't you worry, sir. I'm a great driver." Gesturing towards the briefcase, he asked, "Want me to take your bag?"

Robertson's grip on the case tightened. "No," he replied, shielding it with his body. "Just get me to the car."

John strode toward the exit, courier in tow. They emerged from the air-conditioned terminal, the fall afternoon sending a shiver down Olson's sweat-drenched neck. The distant roar of jet engines mixed with the rumble of idling cars and honking taxis.

"This way, sir. Your car's just up ahead," John announced, heading towards the parking structure.

As they approached the town car, John felt a momentary surge of relief. The vehicle was exactly as Simmons had described it through the radio. He opened the door for Robertson, standing aside as the courier slipped inside.

"Nice ride." Robertson ran his hand over the leather seats.

John eased behind the wheel, gripping it to steady his nerves. He reached up and slid the partition open.

"Where to, sir?"

Robertson's earlier suspicion melted as he admired the luxury interior. "3355 Sycamore. Off Sepulveda in Culver City."

"Yes, sir. Right away," he acknowledged, starting the engine and easing out of the parking space.

As they neared the exit, John spotted Jessica and Hyde standing casually at the curb, appearing as though they were waiting for a taxi. Slowing the vehicle, he pulled over next to the women.

Robertson leaned forward. "Why are we stopping?"

John eased the car to a smooth stop, offering a calm smile. "It'll just be a second, sir."

"I don't have time for this. I'm on a schedule."

Robertson's hand disappeared into his jacket. John knew the man was likely packing. His hand came back out empty. Karl flung open his jacket, revealing an empty holster.

The rear door opened, and Jessica slid into the backseat next to the courier. She held Robertson's missing gun in her hand, pointing it directly at the man.

John flashed back to when she had pickpocketed his badge on the day they met. He had to admit, it was more entertaining to see it happen to someone else.

Jessica twirled the weapon. "Looking for this?"

Robertson's eyes went wide. "How did you…?" He sputtered. "Wait, I know you. From the airport, with the petition." His shoulders deflated. "I thought you hated guns."

Jessica gave a disarming smile. "What would give you that opinion? Yours, for instance, is very nice."

From the opposite side, Hyde slipped into the back, her presence commanding attention. Robertson's head whipped around, his concentration now split between the two women.

"Hello, Karl." Hyde raised the tranquilizer pistol and fired, the dart striking Robertson in the bicep. He looked at her incredulously as he reached over to remove the projectile.

"You shot me." Karl's words slurred.

John bit his lower lip as the courier slumped forward. Karl had just been doing his job. The way they'd manipulated and incapacitated the man felt too close to home. That had been him in Toronto.

As he drove, John couldn't help but wonder how many more lines he'd have to cross before this was all over. National security often demanded more than anyone realized.

"Where to?" John asked as he merged into traffic.

Jessica turned to Hyde with a mischievous grin. "The usual?"

Hyde let out a short laugh. "Oh, I love the usual."

John changed lanes. "Which direction?"

"South, Officer Olson."

John watched the airport disappear behind them. They'd stumbled through part one of the plan despite the setbacks. He considered the next stage, a scowl forming. A one-man operation. No Hyde. No backup.

This time, he'd be at the center of the chaos.

Chapter 59

BURBANK REGIONAL AIRPORT

2 Hours Remaining

15:10

Bruno Vasquez stepped off the FBI jet at Burbank Regional Airport. Heavy ocean air clung to him, mingling with the smell of fuel. His mood matched the ominous clouds gathering over the distant Pacific.

He rolled his shoulders with a wince, trying to work out the kinks that had settled into his muscles. The flight to Cuba had been grueling, but the return felt interminable.

Bruno shielded his eyes against the afternoon sun. Long shadows stretched across the tarmac.

An FBI field agent approached from a waiting car. "Agent Vasquez," he called out. "Word from the Director. You're to refuel and head directly to D.C. You're briefing him personally. He wants to know what happened last night."

Vasquez's exhaustion was forgotten as Agent Morris joined him. "Didn't the CIA debrief him?" Bart demanded.

"No, sir. The White House has appointed you both to a task force to hunt down the threat."

"We know about Hyde," Morris responded.

"New orders, sir. John Olson's now the priority target."

"That's ridiculous. Officer Olson's with Deputy Director Avery," Vasquez responded.

"Director Avery's missing." The agent's expression soured. "Olson and Dr. Miles from Skunk Works are Soviet spies, deeply embedded. We have everyone searching for them."

"Thank you. I got this. Dismissed," Vasquez said.

A cold shock of disbelief surged through him as the agent scurried off. John, a traitor? It didn't add up.

Bruno recalled the restaurant where he'd shown John the pictures of Hyde. Olson's devastated reaction and his dogged determination bordered on obsession—something Vasquez understood. Olson was no turncoat.

Someone was lying.

Morris eyed the surrounding agents. "Boss, you buying any of this BS? "This stinks."

Bart let out a low hum. "Someone's yanking our chain."

As Vasquez grappled with his thoughts, a familiar figure approached. The maintenance man was still sporting his Lakers cap and grease-stained overalls. Vasquez's fists flexed. He was in no mood to deal with this guy again.

The man carried a stuffed envelope. "One of you guys Bruno Vasquez?"

Vasquez jerked his chin. "Yeah, that's me."

"This is for you." The worker held out the envelope. "Some lady paid me a hundred bucks to deliver this. Said it was important."

Morris took the parcel, turning it over in his hands. The plain brown paper crinkled. Someone had written 'Vasquez' on the front in what looked like calligraphy.

"What is it?" Morris asked.

The man in the Lakers cap shrugged. "Dunno. Not my business. Good day." He turned and ambled away.

Vasquez sighed as Morris flipped over the envelope in his hands, holding it up to the light for inspection like a bomb tech.

"There's something inside, boss."

"I'm not in the mood," Vasquez growled at Morris, waving him off. "You can open it on the flight to D.C."

Morris clutched the envelope. "What about Olson and Miles? If they're spies..."

"One thing at a time." Vasquez silenced him with a hand. "We brief the Director first, then we'll deal with them."

But doubt lingered. He'd worked with John for years. It seemed absurd. And Dr. Miles? She was a scientist, not an operative.

"Morris. You're right. Something doesn't add up." He looked around to make sure no one was listening. "Look into Avery's last known position. Did he leave LA? And see if you can verify these orders. I want to know who's calling the shots. Trust nobody, question everything."

"Yes, sir."

As the refueling concluded twenty minutes later, Morris returned at a sprint. "Boss," Morris said, still huffing. "Orders confirmed. We're to head straight back to D.C. Also, affirmed the news about Officer Olson. The Director's aide wanted to know why we weren't already airborne. I told them we would be any minute."

Bruno scrubbed a hand over his stubble. The whine of a starting engine filled the air. The accusation against Olson still made his skin crawl.

"Time to go," Vasquez said.

The second motor hummed to life as Vasquez settled into his seat. He glanced over at Morris, who twirled the mysterious package in his hands.

"Go on, then," Bruno told him.

Morris tore open the envelope. His eyes widened, and he looked up at Vasquez with disbelief as he thrust out the folded note.

"Sir, you need to see this. It's from Olson."

Vasquez hesitated, not wanting to complicate the situation further. But the look on Morris's face told him it was important.

He scanned the words, trying to understand what he was reading. He blinked, then reviewed it again, more slowly.

It started simply: "*Dear Bruno, You taught me that trust begins where secrets end.*"

Each word seemed more unbelievable than the last. It was nonsense.

Yet, it explained everything.

"I don't know, sir," Morris said, shaking his head. "This another one of Hyde's tricks?"

Vasquez looked back at the page. It defied logic, yet felt right. The message and ensuing instructions were crystal clear. One could also consider it treason.

"No. I believe every word."

Morris held out a small object wrapped in tissue paper. It had been hidden beneath the note. "Boss. There was this too."

Bruno peeled away the delicate wrapping. The object tumbled into his palm, intricate and fragile. He recognized it immediately.

Vasquez stood suddenly, banging his head on the low ceiling. This wasn't some intricate ruse. His hand grew heavy as he eyed the jet's door.

The pilot's voice crackled over the intercom, announcing they were taxiing. Vasquez moved to the window. The vast expanse of the Pacific Ocean stretched before him, its waters shimmering in the afternoon sun. Then, his eyes surveyed the distant horizon where Washington D.C. awaited.

"What do you think, Bart?"

Morris straightened. "Whatever we do, sir, I'm here for you. You know that."

"Not what I'm asking."

Bart looked at the letter. "It's legit. I'm in if you are."

"Damn." The paper crumpled in Vasquez's grip. With a sigh, he sank into his chair as the aircraft jerked forward.

They were at a crossroads. If the accusation was true, he was playing the fool. If it was a lie, acting on it would be equally foolish. Either way, the decision he made now could alter the fate of the nation.

"Bart, what does loyalty mean to you?"

Morris considered. "Following orders, I guess."

"What if those orders are wrong?" Vasquez's eyes remained fixed on the horizon.

"Then..." Morris hesitated. "I suppose. Wow. That's tough. I guess true loyalty is to your conscience. Aren't you the one who told me you'll know the right thing to do…"

"Because it's hard," Bruno finished.

Vasquez smirked. Here he was, a seasoned FBI agent, and once again he contemplated trying to save someone from a fate that seemed all but inevitable. He'd felt the consequences of following his heart before. But he never regretted that choice.

After all these years, after all the cases, and all the criminals, Bruno still felt like a lost child trying to do the right thing.

It all came back to saving Stuart the Pig on Christmas Eve.

Chapter 60

THE BAD MONKEY

2 Hours Remaining

15:12

John emerged from the bathroom at The Bad Monkey Gentleman's Club. His skin crawled as he tugged at the collar of Robertson's suit. While the fit wasn't bad, the fabric felt off. The real problem was that he was wearing another man's life.

The air reeked of stale beer and cheap perfume, with an undercurrent of regret. John grimaced, vowing never to return.

As he made his way back to the front door, John found Robertson sprawled across the leather seat of a booth. His limbs dangled while two scantily clad dancers flanked him. At the edge of the table, Jessica slipped a thick wad of cash to a burly man with a shaved head, his neck bulging above a black t-shirt.

"Make sure he's comfortable and confused," Jessica said over the blaring music.

John approached. "A strip club? Really?"

"Think about it. If you woke up in a place called 'The Bad Monkey,' how quickly would you report that to your superiors?"

John rubbed his chin. "Good point." It was definitely an effective deterrent for someone in Robertson's line of work.

"Here." Jessica handed over a small bundle. "Your new credentials. Not perfect, but they'll do."

He examined them, noting the quality of his picture. "These are good."

"It was a rush job, but I'll let Matheo know you complimented his work." She turned toward the exit.

"Hey, we don't need to do anything rash, Jess," he said, chasing after her.

John cast one last glance at Robertson, now just another lost soul. He felt bad for abandoning the man, but there was no time for second-guessing.

As he stepped outside, Olson spotted Hyde at a nearby payphone. Her body language was animated despite the constricted space. Curiosity drove him closer as he hoped to overhear the conversation.

"He'll be there shortly," Hyde whispered into the receiver. "Yes, I can do that." She paused. "Double my usual fee is agreeable… Yes. One hour."

Hyde hung up the phone and exited the booth as John stepped forward. Gabrielle's eyes raked over him as she assessed the fit of Robertson's suit. Her lips pressed into a thin line.

John spread his arms. "How do I look?"

"It will work."

John's curiosity got the better of him. "Who was that?"

Hyde's expression remained flat. She dismissed his question. "Some things are best left unsaid. But, rest assured, all part of the plan."

Before John could press the issue, the town car pulled up to the curb, its engine purring. To his surprise, Andrea sat behind the wheel, her face scrunched in concentration as the vehicle came to a sudden stop.

"Sorry!" she called from the driver's seat.

John and Hyde climbed into the backseat. Jessica popped in the other door, squeezing John into the middle. He frowned, remembering Robertson being in a similar position.

"So, what's next?" John asked as Andrea pulled away.

Hyde tapped his knee. "Are you prepared to become Karl Robertson?"

"As ready as I'll ever be." John shifted, then cleared his throat. "About this insurance policy you mentioned…"

Andrea glanced over her shoulder. "Maybe we should destroy the decryption key as soon as we get it. It's safer, and we'd eliminate the risk entirely."

"If we do that, the Soviets will just come back stronger," Hyde countered. "Worse, Durbin will know we're onto him, limiting our options. We need leverage, not destruction."

"Alright," John conceded. "We move forward. Tell me about how we safeguard this thing."

Hyde produced a slim envelope and a keychain from her purse.

"Your insurance package," she said, pressing them into John's palm. "Courtesy of Matheo and Simmons."

John's brows shot up. "What exactly am I holding here?"

"Let's just say it's enough to make a very loud statement if required," Hyde replied.

John pressed the envelope with his thumb. It gave a little, like Silly Putty. He caught a faint, almond-like odor.

"You can't be serious," he sighed. "Your insurance policy is plastique?"

"Wait a second," Andrea interjected. "You're asking John to carry a bomb into a secure facility? That's insane."

"It's necessary." Hyde met her gaze in the rearview mirror. "You wanted certainty. This is it." She nodded at the envelope. "Slip it into the case once you have the decryption device. It's the only way to ensure the key doesn't disappear."

"And the keychain?" John asked, holding up the small metal trinket.

"A proximity sensor. Think of it as a very aggressive leash," Jessica said. "If it gets more than a hundred meters from the envelope, it'll give a warning tone. You'll have, um, about five seconds before..." She mimed an explosion with her hands.

John's mouth went dry.

Jessica patted his knee. "So, don't get separated."

"I'm not thrilled about this," John muttered.

"Don't worry, love. I carry explosives all the time." She took the package and clicked the corner twice. A soft beep emanated. "There," she said, handing it back. "Armed and ready."

John accepted the envelope with care and slipped it into his jacket pocket. He clipped the keychain to his belt loop with a metallic click. The responsibility of carrying such a dangerous device was unpleasant, but necessary.

"Gabrielle. You're sure about this plan?"

Hyde met his gaze. "John, you're the only one who can pass for the ARFCOS courier. There will be multiple layers of security. You must work through all of them alone."

"Not helping."

Jessica placed a hand on his arm. "John, you belong there. Relax; this is your job."

John repeated the words, "I belong," trying to convince himself.

He closed his eyes, picturing himself as Karl Robertson, the confident ARFCOS courier he remembered from the airport pickup line.

"Any problem is not your fault. Condemn the person asking," Hyde added. "To you, this is like any other assignment."

Just another day at the office, he told himself. But the explosives in his pocket made that illusion difficult to maintain.

"You play roles all the time in the CIA," Hyde told him. "This is no different."

"Yes, it is. This op is against Americans. And I'm not exactly working for the government anymore."

Hyde's expression softened. "You're still serving your country, John," she assured. "Maybe more now than ever before. You're doing what needs to be done to protect the nation from those who would betray it."

Could he justify his actions as patriotism? The line between right and wrong had blurred beyond recognition. He knew they were on the side of justice, but that didn't make it easier.

"You've got this, John," Andrea said from the front seat. "I believe in you."

John drew strength from their words, feeling a renewed purpose. After all, in many ways, he was doing what he'd always done.

"How much farther?"

"About another half mile," Andrea replied.

Hyde pointed at a stretch of pavement. "Let us off here, my dear."

Andrea guided the town car to a stop along the curb. Behind them, Simmons pulled up in his van. The car door opened with a soft click, and Jessica slid out.

She leaned back through the open window. "Remember this above all else. People are more likely to comply with abrasive authority figures."

John nodded, appreciating the behavioral psychology behind her words, even if it was counter to his personality.

"If in doubt, be a jerk. It's science," she advised with a wink.

Leave it to Jessica to find humorous advice in the worst of situations. But her unorthodox counsel had saved him more times than he cared to admit.

Hyde folded her hands. "The rest is going to be rough for both of you." Her tone was serious. "There will be unexpected turns. No matter what happens, don't break role. Your lives depend on it."

John started to speak, but Hyde cut him off. "Never."

"I understand."

"Me too," Andrea echoed.

"I hope so." Hyde opened her door and slid out gracefully. "And don't blow yourselves up either," she added before shutting it.

John watched as Gabrielle jumped into the passenger seat of Simmons' waiting van. He turned his attention back to Andrea.

"You ready?" he asked, trying to sound confident.

Andrea shook her head. "No."

John laughed. The absurdity of their situation hit him all at once. Here they were, a CIA officer and an aerospace engineer, about to infiltrate a secure government facility with a bomb in his pocket. It was like the setup of a bad joke.

"Me either," he confessed, "but we do it together."

"Agreed. Unless you set off that explosive, then feel free to do that alone."

Andrea put the car into gear and pulled back into traffic. The drive seemed both too long and too short. As they neared their destination, the bustling city gave way to a more industrial landscape.

An inconspicuous entrance came into view, marked only by tall fencing topped with barbed wire that glinted under the afternoon sun. This was their target.

Andrea eased off the accelerator as they approached the first security checkpoint. The car rolled to a stop in front of a squat, gray booth that seemed to absorb the harsh sunlight. Two armed men waited inside, eyes hidden behind mirrored sunglasses.

John took a deep breath, mentally preparing himself. Adrenaline made his fingertips tingle. Sweat formed at his hairline.

He patted the stolen credentials in his pocket, right next to the envelope. Five seconds, he repeated to himself.

"Just another day," Andrea said.

John straightened his tie and adjusted his posture, adopting the confident demeanor of a seasoned courier. Drawing a deep breath, he rolled down the window and fixed the man with a look of mild impatience.

"Identification?" The guard's gruff voice matched his stern expression.

John reached into his pocket, his movements deliberately casual. Careful not to disturb the explosives, he produced the forged credentials and passed them over with a bored scowl.

The guard scrutinized the ID, his head darting between the photo and John's face. Olson remained calm, fighting the urge to fidget. After what felt like an eternity, he handed the identification back.

"Purpose of visit?"

"Classified," John replied, as if the question were an insult. "Courier Robertson. I'm here on ARFCOS business. You should've been notified and ready, so I could already be on my way. I'm on a tight schedule."

The guard frowned. "One moment, please," he said, stepping back to his booth.

As they waited, John sensed Andrea's tension. He wanted to reach out and reassure her, but he knew they had to maintain their roles. Instead, he drummed his fingers on his leg, projecting annoyance.

The guard returned. "You're clear to proceed," he said, handing John a visitor's badge. "Display this at all times. Follow the signs to Building Two.

You'll need to check in at the main security desk there."

John grunted, clipping it to his lapel. "About time," he muttered, loud enough to be heard.

As Andrea drove through the open gate, John allowed himself a small sigh of relief. They had cleared the first hurdle, but now it was time for the serious challenge. The car's tires hummed on the smooth pavement inside the compound as maintenance teams worked cutting hedges.

"Nice work," Andrea said, her eyes fixed on the road. "You had me convinced you were a real jerk."

"Who says I was acting?"

The car entered the ground floor of a nearby parking garage. The engine faded into silence as Andrea cut the power.

He sighed. "Time to commit some treason."

Chapter 61

TEMPORARY EXECUTIVE FIELD OFFICE

90 Minutes Remaining

15:30

William Durbin sat at his station, scanning the intelligence reports on his mahogany desk for hidden patterns. The recent race riot between Puerto Ricans and the Chicago PD in Humboldt Park drew him in. Tension and disorder were power, creating the perfect environment for his particular breed of politics.

He snuck a peek at his Rolex, scowling. The ARFCOS courier was overdue. Each passing minute assailed his patience, as did the mounting pressure from his Soviet partners. Their demands were becoming as volatile as Chicago. He needed that encryption key to placate them.

Raised voices pierced the office's peaceful atmosphere, shattering his concentration. William rose from his chair and smoothed his suit jacket. He strode into the lobby, where his secretary was attempting to stop Sasha Morozov.

This confirmed his worries. He'd cut ties with the Russian soon enough, but for now, he would have to endure.

"Sarah." Durbin held up a placating hand. "It's okay. Sasha, please come in."

She hesitated, then moved aside. He waved Morozov in, his mind already racing to regain the advantage. His secretary followed behind, waiting at the door to take notes.

Durbin couldn't shake the feeling that Sasha was becoming unhinged. He felt a surge of irritation at Morozov's brutish approach. Durbin prided himself on finesse, a quality most Soviet operatives lacked.

He knew he had to assert control, but Sarah hovering about would complicate matters. "I can see you are concerned about the treaty this evening," Durbin said. "We have diplomatic channels for this kind of engagement."

Morozov regarded him with a bitter smile. "Of course, William. I apologize for my ignorance of international etiquette."

Durbin sensed the apology was a setup. Morozov's gaze shifted to Sarah by the door. "Sarah? It is Sarah?"

"Yes," she replied.

"Would you mind joining us for a moment?" Morozov asked, his voice pleasant.

"That won't be necessary," Durbin objected.

Morozov smiled. "It's okay," he insisted.

She hesitated, then stepped into the office. Her hands fidgeted as she tried to maintain professionalism.

"My deepest apologies for the disruption," Morozov said, his tone mocking.

The secretary nodded, her eyes darting. "I understand, sir. No trouble at all." She took an instinctive half-step backward.

Durbin cursed internally. He could diffuse this, send her away, but she knew too much. Morozov's stance told him it was already too late. The metallic click of a safety unlatching confirmed his suspicion.

Morozov drew his gun. Sarah's mouth opened, a scream forming.

Two thunderous cracks split the air. The secretary's frame jerked violently, then crumpled to the ground.

Durbin observed with calculated indifference, aware Morozov was probing for weakness. He watched as the life drained from Sarah's irrelevant eyes, her body twitching. Blood pooled beneath her, spreading outward like a blooming crimson flower.

It would be a pain to replace that carpet.

A twisted regret welled up. Not for her lost life. But for the lost opportunity to dispose of her on his own terms. He would never get to savor the control as she begged for her life. The wolf inside stirred, hungry for what Morozov had stolen.

"Consider that your last warning."

"Was that necessary?" Durbin modulated his voice to convey annoyance.

Morozov shrugged, tucking the pistol into his waistband. "You're too soft. You need reminders now and then."

"I understand clearly. But actions like this jeopardize all we've worked for. Be patient."

Morozov's lip curled as he plucked a handkerchief from Durbin's breast pocket. He wiped the mist of blood from his hands with the silk fabric. He crumpled the stained cloth and tossed it onto the body.

"Everything is not fine, William," Sasha said. "That CIA Agent, Olson. He escaped and is now attempting to recover the decryption device."

John got away? Impossible. He'd accounted for every detail, every possibility. All threats were supposed to be neutralized. This was devastating news.

Years of political maneuvering had honed Durbin's mask. He maintained a neutral expression, concealing his concern from Morozov. Effortlessly, he formed a new strategy.

Olson's escape was an opportunity. He would use this crisis to prove his worth, and when the time was appropriate, rid himself of Morozov. For now, though, he needed to play the concerned partner.

"Sasha," he started, injecting just the right amount of worry. "This is troubling news. Olson is a threat to both of us." He placed a hand on Morozov's shoulder. "Let me handle this. As soon as I get word from the courier, Olson will be dealt with appropriately. Until then, we're still on track."

"That," Sasha growled, shrugging off the politician's touch, "is not what I hear." His eyes narrowed as he stepped closer. "Your operations need more attention. Your courier? Out of commission."

William raised a hand. "I promise, whatever…"

"Enough!" Morozov cut him off. "I'm finished with your promises."

"I assure you…"

"*Nyet!*" Sasha barked. "I want the encryption device and Olson, alive. One hour. Meet me at the pier, or we're done. And so are you."

Morozov's expression remained inscrutable. "And don't send one of your lackeys. Bring both yourself."

"Sasha, that is hardly enough…"

"One hour."

Durbin knew how to pivot. "I'll handle it. You'll get what you want."

Morozov nodded. Without another word, he strode out of the office, leaving the politician alone with the body of his secretary still sprawled on the floor.

As the door closed, Durbin's hands clenched into fists, knuckles white with the strain of containing his rage. For a moment, he considered giving in, to release that fury, imagining the satisfaction of destroying something precious.

No. He needed clarity.

Durbin considered the possibilities, working them through one after another. He certainly couldn't trust Morozov. He'd have to play along with the Soviet's demands, for now.

William reached for the phone, dialing a familiar number. "Bring the car around," he ordered. "We leave in two minutes."

As he hung up, Durbin eyed Sarah's lifeless body. Just another problem to solve. He'd deal with her later.

For now, the board had shifted. He would seize it, mold it to his will.

Durbin was the one in control. No one could stop him.

Chapter 62

SECURE STORAGE FACILITY

60 Minutes Remaining

16:00

John approached Building Two's secure entrance with Karl Robertson's stolen ID burning a hole in his pocket. This time, it was just him against the world.

His visitor badge stood out against the dark fabric of his suit, declaring his right to be there. Two gruff security guards flanked the door, their faces pinched as they assessed him. John flipped out his credentials, tapping his foot.

He glared as if the delay offended him. "I don't have all day. You gonna do your job or what?"

The officers, suitably intimidated by his brusque manner, stepped aside and opened the heavy door. John brushed past them without a second glance, his posture radiating authority.

The sterile lobby greeted John with its white walls and polished floors, fluorescent lights humming a monotonous tune overhead. Feigning disinterest, he scanned the room.

Hyde's voice crackled in his earpiece. "Remember, you're in control here."

His eyes landed on a mousy receptionist sitting behind a desk, her attention absorbed in an animated phone conversation. She barely glanced up as John approached, absent-mindedly twisting the cord around her fingers.

Karl Robertson, ARFCOS courier, wouldn't tolerate such nonsense. John pressed the cradle button on her phone with deliberate force, cutting off her conversation mid-sentence.

Her head snapped up. "Excuse me! That was an important call!"

John leaned in. "Not as important as I am. I've been standing here for ages while you gossip. Guess your job doesn't matter much to you."

The receptionist's cheeks bloomed with color, her fingers fumbling to replace the handset. "I-I'm sorry, sir. How can I help you?"

John planted his hands on the desk. "Robertson," he said curtly. "Here for a pickup. I hope your social life is more important than national security."

Under John's withering gaze, the receptionist's shoulders hunched. She looked down, straightening paperwork. "Of course not, Mr. Robertson. Let me just notify the manager that you're here."

She scurried away from the desk, tripping over her own feet. Olson watched the woman vanish through a door, a small part of him feeling guilty.

In his ear, Jessica's voice chimed in. "I told you. Jerk works."

John fought the urge to grin. There was a certain thrill in playing the role of the demanding courier.

The receptionist returned moments later, followed by a heavyset, balding man in a crisp suit. The manager waddled forward, arm outstretched. In his other oversized fist was a silver briefcase.

The decryption device.

"Mr. Robertson, I apologize for the delay." His rich baritone oozed feigned politeness.

John ignored the offered hand. "I thought couriers were always expected," he said coldly. "Or has protocol changed since my last visit?"

The smile faltered. The fat manager struggled to maintain composure. "No, of course not. We're constantly prepared for ARFCOS. If you'll just follow me, we'll get your paperwork processed and have you on your way."

The supervisor gestured towards a door marked 'Authorized Personnel Only.'

John fixated on the case, aware the decryption device was inside. Time was of the essence. With his brusque demeanor intact, he reached out and snatched the briefcase from the manager's grasp.

"I'll take that." He turned to leave.

He had taken only three steps when a protest stopped him short. "Mr. Robertson, wait! The paperwork, I can't just let you depart without..." panic seeped into the man's deep voice.

The security guards tensed, their hands resting near their weapons. John couldn't allow this to fall apart now. This was about authority and confidence.

"Listen," he snapped. "I'm already behind schedule. Do you have any idea how much trouble you've caused me with your incompetence? I don't have time for this bureaucratic nonsense."

The manager's complexion took on the hue of antique porcelain. "Mr. Robertson, the paperwork... I-I can't break protocol. It's mandatory for all pickups."

Hyde chirped in his ear. "Take charge."

Olson pivoted and advanced on the manager in two swift strides. The man's Adam's apple bobbed, his eyes wide as John towered over him.

"Let me make something very clear," John declared. "I work directly for the President. Have you not read the latest ARFCOS memo on pickup protocol put out by DC HQ on the first of September?"

The manager's eyes darted. A sheen of sweat formed on his forehead. "I, uh... of course," he lied.

John pressed his advantage. "Then you know that the field office will telex you the signatures within the hour. We're modernizing at ARFCOS. The Director is cutting anything, and everyone..." he let the word hang for a second, "that doesn't follow the new procedures."

He could see doubt taking hold. The fear of being pegged as a problem could cost the supervisor his job.

"I might take a moment to review your regulations if I were you," Olson added in a tone dripping with condescension. "It seems you're not as up to date as you should be."

"Yes, sir. That's… that's a good idea. I'll do that right away. You tell the Director we embrace efficiency around here. Do more with less, I always say."

"Glad to hear it." John spun, the decryption device in hand as he strode forward. The security officers stepped aside, their expressions dour as they jumped to open the doors.

Just as he reached the exit, the receptionist's voice called. "Mr. Robertson!"

Olson fought the urge to sprint. He turned, half-expecting to see guards rushing at him. Instead, he found only a cheerful smile. "Have a nice day!"

"I will."

Sunlight streaked in as the guards popped to attention. As the heavy door swung shut behind him with a muffled thud, Olson let out a shaky breath. He had done it. The decryption device was in his hands, and he had bluffed his way through the pickup.

He maintained a brisk but measured pace down the sidewalk, never looking back. Every second on the grounds increased their risk of discovery. But first, he needed to prepare.

Seeking a secluded spot, he quickly found a large ornamental plant nestled against the building. Its dark green leaves offered just enough cover. The scent of damp soil intertwined with fresh asphalt from the nearby drive.

John ducked behind the shrubbery, setting the briefcase down. With still-shaking hands, he popped the latches. Inside, molded foam padding cradled the decryption device. He pulled the envelope of explosives from his jacket pocket, aware that it could level half the building.

Peeling back the lining, John tucked the bomb into place. The soft package fit snugly, barely noticeable unless someone knew what to look for. He ran his fingers along the edge, making sure it was secure.

Satisfied, he closed the case with a decisive snap, the latches engaging. He stood up, brushing off his knees and straightening his tie. To anyone watching, it looked like nothing more than a courier adjusting his suit.

Prize in hand, John jogged towards the car where Andrea waited. They had the decryption device. For the next phase, they just needed Durbin to take the bait.

Hyde's voice crackled over the radio. "Perfectly executed, John."

"A natural jerk. That manager didn't stand a chance," Jessica chimed in.

"Thanks," he murmured. "Couldn't have done it without you."

Rounding the corner, John spotted the town car. "Approaching the vehicle now. Five minutes to rendezvous."

"This is where it gets tricky. Be ready," Hyde replied.

John slid into the back seat, clutching the briefcase. Too late, he realized something was wrong. A strange man sat behind the wheel.

William Durbin held Andrea hostage, his haughty face gleaming with triumph as he pressed a weapon against her temple. Andrea's eyes were wide with fear. John tried to comprehend how Durbin had found them so quickly.

He had to warn Hyde.

"Quiet," William mouthed, pressing a finger to his lips with exaggerated slowness. The click of the gun's safety disengaging punctuated his order.

Durbin's free hand moved to John's holster, relieving him of his weapon. He then plucked the radio and earpiece from John, his fingers finding the power switch. He silenced it with a soft click.

"There, we're alone again." He looked at the case in John's grip. "Put it down."

John briefly entertained shoving it right in Durbin's perfect teeth. The risk was too high. The gun would fire. Instead, he placed it on the floorboard. The driver started the car and drove through the exit.

"You've turned out to be quite the thorn in my side, Mr. Olson." Durbin pressed the pistol harder into Andrea's ear, making her squirm. "I should make you pay for that."

John opened his mouth to object, but Durbin cut him off. "But that will have to wait. Stay silent, Officer Olson, or she gets extra holes." He dug the muzzle even deeper into Andrea's temple. "This ride shall be conducted without commentary. I think we've both said quite enough already."

Durbin rolled down the window and tossed the radio out. It bounced once on the pavement before disappearing from view.

The politician tapped the driver on the shoulder. "Lose any tails and head for the pier. Our friends here are late for their trip overseas."

The man nodded, weaving the large car with finesse around the bollards at the exit. This man was no amateur.

As the car wove through traffic, John searched for any sign of Hyde. He soon spotted Simmons' van a few cars behind them, trailing at a discreet distance. Perfect. They just needed to maintain visual contact.

Olson stared at the case, considering the explosives within and the keychain clipped to his waist. He could leap from the car, leaving Durbin to face the force of the blast.

It was futile. There was no way to get Andrea out safely. Despite what she may say, he wouldn't make that kind of sacrifice.

As if sensing John's thoughts, Durbin tsked. "No heroics." His finger tightened against the trigger. He motioned back at the van. "Lose them."

The driver took a hard turn, tires screeching against the pavement. The car lurched as they narrowly avoided colliding with a parked truck. After another unexpected swerve, John watched helplessly as a passing vehicle cut Simmons' van off, veering to avoid the collision.

The driver executed a series of quick maneuvers, winding through back alleys. The van behind them soon disappeared from sight.

The strategy Olson had envisioned was now gone. His and Andrea's only hope was that Hyde would know how to find them. Every new variation to the plan increased the likelihood of disaster.

Durbin settled back, a smug smile plastered on his face. He seemed to revel in his need for control. This was his only vulnerability.

And as the car sped towards the pier, John knew for certain that this ordeal was about to come to an end. William Durbin was taking him directly to Morozov.

Chapter 63

PIER 53

18 Minutes Remaining

16:42

Durbin marched John and Andrea into the damp, cavernous warehouse. He kept one hand on Andrea's shoulder, the other pressed the gun's muzzle into the back of her head. The driver kept his weapon trained on Olson.

The abandoned shipping area stretched upwards, its cathedral-like ceilings built for towering cranes. Weathered concrete columns stretched to the iron structure overhead. Oppressively cold, the air hung heavy with saltwater and rust. Waves lapped against the edge of the building, punctuated by the distant cry of seagulls.

A makeshift meeting area of metal chairs and battered tables stood incongruously in the center, near a small, dark-windowed office.

John spotted a sleek cigarette boat docked only fifty yards away. A man waited in the vessel, his hand resting on the throttle. Morozov's escape route.

Durbin drove them forward. John fought to keep his face a mask of controlled defiance despite the fear coursing through him. He carried the case in his left hand, the hidden explosive within never far from his thoughts.

William set his black briefcase on the concrete and snatched the silver decryption device from John's grasp. He shoved John forward, a celebratory sneer on his face as he presented his captives to Morozov.

"I deliver what I promise, and more." Durbin set the case at Morozov's feet. "The decryption device and…" he grabbed a handful of Andrea's hair, forcing her to rise to her toes as he continued, "one of their engineers. Just in case your scientists run into a dead end."

The Spymaster gave a stiff smile. "So you have." Morozov's attention shifted to John. "Ahh, the troublesome CIA man."

He took a step closer. "Mr. Durbin assured me that Africa was a secure location and there would be no interference. I lost good men there." His breath was hot and foul, reeking of unfiltered cigarettes. "Unfortunate."

John thrust forward, cutting the distance. "So did I."

"I should have killed you along with that boy you abandoned."

John clenched his fists in anger, but then forced it down. He refused to give Morozov the satisfaction. "His name was Nate Balik," John growled. "He was more man than you'll ever be."

Without warning, Morozov punched John in the stomach, driving the air from his lungs. His two goons grabbed Olson's arms, and Sasha hit him again. The Soviet leaned in, tapping John's cheek. His gaze flicked to Andrea.

"Maybe after I make your friend scream, you will be nicer to me."

With a roar, John lunged, almost striking the stunned Morozov. "Don't you touch her!" The guards yanked him back just in time.

"You have spirit. A worthy man."

John wanted to wrap his hands around the Soviet's throat. But it was useless. The guards held him fast, their fists digging into his arms. John could only glare with impotent rage.

Seizing the moment, Andrea sprang forward, catching the Soviet by surprise. Her small fist connected with his cheek. The driver recovered and pulled her back, legs flailing in the air. Morozov wiped a bead of blood from his lip, licking it with his tongue.

"Let him go and see what happens, you cowards!" she screamed.

The Soviet chuckled as he turned to Durbin. "You've brought me quite the pair, William. This should be entertaining."

Durbin looked to the exit. "Sasha, do we have a deal? I have other places to be."

Morozov fixed the politician with an icy stare. "First, I check the data."

"I've given you everything. The intel, the access, the tapes. Even human assets. Time to hold up your end."

Morozov signaled to one of his men, who entered the office. John strained against his captors, craning his neck for a better view. What or who was in that office?

The man returned, handing Morozov a black bag. After a wary look, the Soviet handed him the package. Durbin hefted the bag once before opening his briefcase. He withdrew a second bag, this one was burgundy in color. He poured the contents of the black bag into the other, cinching it shut.

He tucked both into the briefcase and closed the metal clasps shut. He finished his ritual with a quick spin of the combination lock. The presidential advisor stood, ready to exit.

"Good day, sir."

"Not yet. You stay."

Durbin froze mid-step. "Why?"

"No offense, friend," he said, resting a hand on his handgun. "You are a politician. Your assurance means nothing to me."

Morozov motioned to his men. "Bring her out."

One man banged twice on the office door, and a familiar figure emerged. Gabrielle Hyde carried a large black bag, its contents a mystery. Her face remained impassive as she surveyed the scene.

"What are you doing?" Olson demanded. "You're our backup. What the hell is this?"

Hyde remained still. A slow smile stretched across her face.

Morozov leaned in to Hyde. "I treasure this. That moment right there…" he held his hands up to frame John's face. "That look when they realize all hope is gone." He laughed. "She's not here for you, American. She's here for me. You were deceived."

With a roar, Olson lunged forward. His muscles strained as he fought to break free from his captors. "Hyde!" he shouted. "What the hell are you doing?"

Durbin's reaction was no less dramatic. He yanked out his pistol, pointing it at Gabrielle. "You're supposed to be in prison!"

Hyde, for her part, looked utterly nonchalant. She shrugged, almost bored. "Obviously, that was temporary."

William's face twisted. He swung his weapon at Morozov, eyes wild, finger on the trigger. Sasha's men trained their guns on him.

"Whatever she told you, she's lying!" Durbin screamed.

Morozov stepped forward, pushing the muzzle down. "William, put that away."

"No!" Durbin reddened with fury, raising the weapon again. "You don't understand. She's deceiving you! She and Olson are partners!"

Gabrielle and Sasha exchanged a look, then burst out laughing. The sound was harsh and mocking. Hyde placed her large case on the floor, and then stood next to Morozov, resting a hand casually on his shoulder. She gave a dazzling smile.

"And who do you think arranged that?" Morozov asked. "You are not, as they say, the only fish in the sea."

Durbin's mouth fell open in stunned disbelief. The questions were obvious. Had Hyde been working with Morozov all along? Had everything been just an elaborate ruse?

John struggled with renewed vigor. It was crucial that he do everything he could to get to Hyde. He would demand the truth.

"Look for yourself," Sasha taunted, gripping John's cheeks with a squeeze. "Does he seem happy to see her?"

John jerked to free himself. "You lied to me!"

Morozov gave a lazy flick of his fingers to the men. "Shut him up."

A guard's rough fist met John's chin, snapping his head sideways. Pain coursed through his jaw and cheekbone as he staggered back.

"You can't trust her," Durbin argued, gesturing wildly.

Morozov scoffed. "No one should ever believe Gabrielle Hyde. She's been my best pupil since childhood."

John's eyes darted between Hyde and Morozov, searching for any trace of the woman he knew. Nothing remained. Only the monster forged by trauma and honed by cruelty.

Morozov pointed at Durbin. "I'll tell you what's real. Until then, be quiet like the puppet you are."

Andrea broke free of the driver's grip. "How could you? You were my friend!" she cried, lunging with a vicious swing.

Hyde caught her hand mid-swing, pressing the arm back with surprising strength until Andrea relented. Gabrielle showed no reaction as the driver restrained Andrea. Durbin watched the scene, still unconvinced.

Hyde stepped to the table. "Are we doing this or not? I get paid either way."

The guard next to the office disappeared for a second and then returned with John's satchel tucked under his arm. He passed the bag of tapes to Gabrielle.

"And the decoding device?" Hyde asked.

Durbin picked up the silver case and handed it to Hyde with reluctance. John watched as she assembled the decryption machine. First connecting the magnetic reels to the arms, then turning it on. The instrument hummed to life, needles dancing across the analog gauges.

The indicators jiggled, then synced up in a steady rhythm. Hyde turned and gave an affirmative nod. "Data's verified and decrypted. You have what you wanted."

Her fingers lingered on the device for a fraction too long before pulling away. The Soviets now had everything they wanted. They no longer needed him. Or Andrea.

Sasha handed a thick envelope to Hyde. "Thank you for your services."

"*Merci*," she replied, tucking the cash into her jacket.

She swiftly disassembled the kit, packing both the reel and original disks into the silver case. She deposited it on the concrete next to her black bag.

This was it. They were out of time.

"Hyde, was this your plan all along? To betray everything and everyone?"

John spat. "They'll hang you for this! Traitor!"

Her face froze, the insult having its intended effect. Hyde's hand darted to her jacket, emerging with a sleek pistol.

"Gabrielle, allow me, my dear." Morozov's tone was almost fatherly. "You need not bother. I was going to kill him, anyway."

Ignoring him, Hyde stepped forward and pressed the steel to John's temple. "I handle my business. As always."

John stared down the barrel, knowing he should be afraid. He searched Hyde's face for regret. All he found was her mask. The facility was now a tomb; the shadows ready to close in with the ruthless embrace of death.

Durbin stepped forward. His hand shook as he waved his pistol around, unsure of where to aim. "Sasha, please… They're in this together!" he pleaded. "Can't you see it's all a sham?"

He pointed the pistol at Hyde. "Her gun isn't even loaded!"

Without a word, Gabrielle shifted her aimpoint downward, the muzzle of her pistol now pointing at Durbin's black briefcase. Her fingertip squeezed the trigger decisively.

CRACK!

The gunshot shattered the air with a deafening bang. A bright flash illuminated Hyde's impassive face as the bullet hit home, tearing through the leather and latching mechanism. The briefcase's handle and lock exploded into fragments, shards of hot metal and torn fabric spraying outward. Smoke curled from both the weapon's barrel and the newly formed hole in the ruined case. Durbin staggered back, shock plastered on his face.

John struggled against his captors. Morozov was right. You couldn't trust Gabrielle Hyde. He'd been so sure about her, but now, facing the barrel of her smoking gun, it felt different.

"Your father would be ashamed. The Nazis did him a favor," he said bitterly.

She hadn't expected the response. Morozov watched as Hyde's pistol faltered for a moment. Then, as if it had never happened, she pointed the weapon at John's face.

"Don't you ever presume. Tata is dead," Gabrielle responded. "And you shall join him. I warned you this was coming."

"You can't hurt me anymore than you already have."

Her lips curled down. "No?"

Hyde shifted her aim, the gun now pointing at Andrea. A muscle in her jaw twitched. Time seemed to slow as she squeezed the trigger.

BAM!

The gunshot cracked thunderously, the muzzle flash blinding. Andrea's body jerked violently, spinning as the projectile struck just below her left collarbone. A scream of anguish tore from her throat as the impact hurled her backward, arms flailing. John watched in horror as she twisted, her legs buckling, before crashing face-first onto the concrete floor.

"No!" John's cry echoed.

His world narrowed to a single point. Andrea's body lay crumpled like a discarded rag doll. With a surge of adrenaline-fueled strength, he wrenched free and raced to her collapsed form.

He fell to his knees, trembling uncontrollably as he hovered over her. Panic gripped him as he desperately searched for the wound. He found the spot, and his head dropped. It confirmed what he knew to be true.

There was a dreadful silence.

His hands wobbled as they came away slick with warm, red liquid oozing down his fingers. John's eyes snapped up. "You're a monster."

Hyde took a step forward, whipping her pistol toward John's chest. The motion seemed devoid of remorse. All the warmth, the breaks in her armor, all of it was gone. There was nothing but the monster Morozov created.

Hyde's finger tightened on the trigger. "I am what the world made me."

Was this how it ended?

John raised his chin in defiance.

He thought of Nate, of Andrea, of all the people who had suffered in this twisted game. He refused to close his eyes. Durbin and Morozov would not get the satisfaction.

His death was the last move in Hyde's elaborate scheme.

The pistol barked again, the sound deafening. John saw the flash and felt the impact simultaneously. It was a sledgehammer blow to the center of his chest. The force lifted him, sending him reeling backward.

Pain exploded through him as his back hit the ground, the rough concrete scraping against his skin. His vision swam, the dim lights above blurring into hazy streaks. John struggled for breath, feeling like shards of glass splintered in his lungs.

Olson's hand moved of its own accord to his chest. Pulling it away, he saw red spreading across his shirt, the fabric becoming saturated.

Through the haze, John watched as Morozov seized Durbin, the politician's face contorted in disbelief. The Soviet's grip tightened.

"I love this woman!" he bellowed.

Hyde stood motionless, her eyes fixed on John's fallen form, her expression unreadable. She stowed the weapon in her jacket.

John studied Durbin's frozen shape. He had held on to the faint hope of finding some shred of humanity, some remorse. But the politician's gaze was hollow. Their lives meant nothing. Ambition was the only thing he valued.

Hyde was right. The man was a psychopath.

Olson's eyelids fluttered, the darkness creeping in at the edges.

He clung to the one thought that brought him joy. The unflappable William Durbin was, at last, caught off guard.

John's body went limp.

Chapter 64

10 Minutes Remaining

16:50

Vasquez stood before the assembled FBI task force, his face filled with apprehension. The salty sea breeze tugged at his suit jacket, the briny scent mingling with the faint aroma of exhaust from a dozen idling vehicles lining the street.

His men, clad in riot gear, stood rigid. Vasquez felt their eyes boring into him. Wondering.

The pier stretched out before him. Five minutes had elapsed since the targets had entered the warehouse. Now they waited.

The tactical team stood ready for his command. Bruno's fingers traced the worn creases of the note in his pocket, its rough texture somehow soothing.

Agent Morris approached and reported, "Sir, all units are in position."

Vasquez's eyes remained fixed on the warehouse. "Tell them to stand by."

Bruno thought about the message in his pocket. He had read it countless times in the last two hours. The words still had him speculating. Was he being played? Or was he finally seeing the real world?

His rational mind waged war against his intuition.

The letter warned of danger lurking within the White House. The note told of a truth that could shake the very foundations of their nation. John insisted that William Durbin was using their history, their previous animosity, as a weapon. To counter this, Olson was asking for his trust. Durbin was behind everything. To choose a field agent's word over the FBI Director and the entire national intelligence apparatus.

That was a tall order. He should be halfway to DC.

Then again, he never really liked the FBI Director. Too political. Always swaying with the wind.

He looked at the item in his hand. Bruno turned over the small blue forget-me-not pin, its petals cool against his skin. Hyde's signature accessory was now a symbol of good faith.

Hyde embodied everything Bruno despised. Capricious. Eccentric. Unbound by the rules. But at least she was true to her word. And the brooch mattered to her. He knew that with absolute certainty.

Then there was Olson. The CIA cowboy. Just like Hyde in so many ways. But he couldn't help but respect the man's dedication. He never seemed to get caught up in petty rivalries like so many others.

Vasquez considered the allegation one last time.

The White House was supposed to be an American symbol of freedom. But if John's accusation was true, there was a cancer eating away at the heart of the country.

Normally, he'd ignore such wild claims. But this had far exceeded his tolerance for normality.

The final straw was the warrant for Olson's arrest as a Soviet spy. Vasquez had seen the man in action. The idea of John as a traitor was laughable. A blatant cover-up.

It was made all the worse that the order came directly from headquarters. It supported John's letter to a T.

Vasquez faced a choice.

He could follow orders, trust in the chain of command, and arrest Olson. That path offered simplicity, promising to keep him in good standing with his superiors.

His radio chattered with an unheard statement. Morris shifted. "Sir, the men are getting restless. What are your orders?"

Vasquez noted the confusion in their postures. His forces were likely wondering why they weren't already storming the depot.

"Hold position," Vasquez replied.

Morris hesitated before nodding. "Understood, sir. I'll pass the word."

By now, his absence from the flight to DC would be noticed. Superiors would demand to know his whereabouts, phones ringing unanswered across offices and homes. They would soon find him. Each passing minute dug him deeper into a hole.

There was only one way out. They had to follow it through, come hell or high water. He had to follow the hard path.

Vasquez thought of his father. He was a stern man with a steel backbone and unyielding beliefs. His father's eyes had a mysterious way of conveying affection and discipline simultaneously.

"Be brave, Mijo. Always follow your heart," he would say. "It's acceptable to be afraid, but it's never okay to be a coward. You have to walk the hard path."

True strength was the willingness to stand up for what you believed in, even when the odds were against you. Especially if there were consequences. Bruno's brother had proven himself. Now it was his turn.

He checked his watch again. "Olson, I swear to god…"

The crack of a gunshot split the air. Vasquez flinched as he strained to hear. A second shot followed a moment later, equally jarring, confirming it was no accident.

Bruno's body tensed, ready for action. He waited, breath held. The letter promised a third discharge. That was when he should pounce.

When it came, the sound seemed to pierce right through him. His hand moved up, forming a fist. His FBI team crouched, but held fast. Before they could move, he had to wait twenty seconds.

He mouthed the words, counting in his head. One… two… three… He wondered what was unfolding inside. Eleven…twelve…

Time to see if his gamble would pay out. He had chosen his path, consequences be damned. Vasquez knew his brother would have done the same. Even his father would crack a rare smile.

…eighteen… nineteen… twenty.

Bruno nodded to Morris, raising the megaphone. "This is the FBI." His voice resounded across the pier. "Lay down your weapons and come out with your hands in the air. The building is surrounded."

No response.

Vasquez took the lead, charging forward in an all-out sprint. His team's boots rumbled against weathered timbers as they approached the soaring structure, its corrugated walls rippling in the waning afternoon light.

Rusted metal groaned underfoot as they transitioned to aged concrete, cracks spider-webbing beneath their feet. As they neared a towering steel door, a man in riot gear stepped forward with a shaped charge in hand.

The agent worked quickly, his ungloved fingers deftly attaching the explosive. The sharp click of the detonator cover told Bruno it was time. He tapped the man's arm and then ducked, bracing himself.

The detonation released an ear-splitting boom that radiated shockwaves, the force of the explosion ripping the door from its hinges. Searing heat blasted outward. A billowing white cloud enveloped him and obscured their view as twisted shards of metal rained down.

Vasquez tapped his men on the shoulder, a silent command to move. They dove into the breach, weapons drawn. They immediately encountered resistance.

Two more agents entered. More shots fired.

Bruno paused at the threshold, offering a prayer. This was the defining moment of his life.

He raised his weapon, made the sign of the cross, and charged inside.

Chapter 65

PIER 53

9 Minutes Remaining

16:51

John remained motionless on the concrete, struggling to keep up the appearance of death. He finally heard the unmistakable sound of a bullhorn. Thank God, it was about time.

Vasquez's commanding voice boomed. "This is the FBI. Lay down your weapons and come out with your hands in the air. The building is surrounded."

John forced himself to stay still. He had an overwhelming urge to spit out the foul chicken blood that filled his mouth. Why he had agreed to this detail was beyond him.

His chest ached from the impact of Hyde's rubber bullet. Non-lethal or not, it hurt like hell. But Morozov and Durbin needed to believe they were standing over dead bodies. John just had to maintain the fantasy for a few more minutes.

Morozov's men and the politician scrambled, spooked by the FBI's sudden arrival. Their earlier bravado had evaporated. With an existential threat at hand, the tables had turned. Not to mention their attention.

Hyde moved swiftly. With the press of a button on the top of her large black suitcase, a false bottom released. A silver case emerged as she lifted it.

In a single motion, she placed the black bag over the other case containing the real data, concealing it from view.

The swap was complete.

At John's side, Andrea stirred. The sounds of the scrambling men drowned out her soft groans.

The wild accusations. The staged shooting. Even fake blood. Every element was part of a dangerous gambit to catch everyone off guard.

Durbin suspected a con and believed in people's self-centered nature. Hyde simply played into his expectations. His attempt to control every variable was his undoing. His greatest strength was his biggest weakness.

Just as Jessica suggested: The Kansas City Shuffle.

The panic among Morozov's men was unmistakable now, their earlier discipline giving way to a frantic scramble. This was exactly the reaction Hyde had predicted. Sasha tossed his weapon aside, moving towards the waiting boat.

"Grab the case and get to the boat!" Morozov shouted. He tapped another lackey on the shoulder. "Cover our escape."

One man grabbed the silver case beside Hyde's bag. The other took up a defensive position, ready to lay down covering fire.

Durbin, meanwhile, remained frozen in place, his head swiveling between the boat and the door like a spectator at a tennis match. He was stuck in a ruthless loop of indecision.

John could almost see the wheels turning as Durbin weighed the dwindling options. Flee with Morozov? Or take his chances with the FBI? The man had fallen into his own trap.

Theory was great, but Durbin was now experiencing an authentic version of 'The Prisoner's Dilemma.' Everybody has a plan until the shooting starts.

The pier door burst inward in a shower of metal, sending a shockwave through the air. John felt the vibration in his bones as debris rained down around him and agents poured in.

"FBI!" one shouted.

"Don't move!" the man behind him added.

Morozov's guard reacted first, opening fire. The first two men took the brunt of it, their bodies hitting the ground in quick succession.

Through the smoke, another agent leaped through the doorway to avoid the gunfire. The man executed a perfect forward roll, landing in a crouch. The Soviet fired again and missed.

Two swift shots rang out from the FBI agent's gun, and the Soviet gunman twisted sideways, his weapon clattering to the ground.

Durbin spun towards the entrance, his gun still clutched in his hand. His eyes were wild with panic.

Special Agent Bruno Vasquez burst into the warehouse. He swept the room with the practiced eye of a veteran, zeroing in on Durbin.

The two men faced each other.

"Freeze!" Vasquez yelled.

William's mouth opened, perhaps to plead or threaten. His pistol inadvertently rose toward the agent. Before he could utter a word, fire erupted from Vasquez's service pistol.

Durbin's body jerked, a look of shock frozen on his face. His gun fell from limp fingers as his frame buckled to the ground. A dark stain spread across his chest, the blood seeping through his crisp white shirt.

He took two ragged breaths and then stopped. His eyes stared blankly at the ceiling, unseeing.

The room faded into an eerie silence, broken only by John's sudden gasp as he sat up. He spat out the disgusting mixture, the fake gore splattering across the concrete.

The movement sent pain through his chest, far more intense than he had expected. Despite the protective vest hidden beneath his shirt, the non-lethal round had left its mark.

Beside him, Andrea coughed and sputtered. She wiped at her face with her sleeve, smearing red saliva across her cheek. Her expression was a mix of relief and disgust as she propped herself up on one elbow.

"I'll never be able to eat chicken again," she said with a grimace.

Hyde leaned casually against the office wall, her hands raised in surrender. She looked almost bored, as if the firefight were a mere inconvenience. She nodded toward the dock area.

Morozov was making a break for it. The Soviet operative vaulted into the back of the cigarette boat with surprising agility for someone his age. He screamed an order. The pilot revved the engine as the bodyguard with the silver case leaped aboard.

With a deep baritone rumble, the boat's motor roared to life. The driver slammed the throttle to full power, sending up a high plume of water as the vessel accelerated.

John struggled to his feet as Vasquez sprinted by him, barely acknowledging Olson's condition.

The FBI agent's focus was on the fleeing boat. Without hesitation, Vasquez aimed his pistol at Morozov and his men. Sharp cracks of gunfire rang out as bullets skipped across the water. Bruno fired his entire clip, running full tilt to the edge of the dock.

John jumped up and raced after Vasquez, his shoes pounding the pitted concrete and sending up splashes from puddles. He had to stop Bruno before it was too late.

"Bruno! Stop!"

Vasquez didn't listen as he inserted a new clip. Instead, he rolled his shoulder, settling into a shooting stance. Two quick gulps of air and then Bruno held his breath, giving him the most stable platform. He had Morozov, dead-to-rights.

Lunging, John tackled Vasquez just as the gunfire erupted. The bullet whipped through the air, missing the Spymaster by inches. Instead of a strike, it smacked into the boat's bow with a metallic ping before ricocheting off.

John hit the ground alongside Vasquez. They tumbled in a tangle of limbs, the impact sending fresh pain through John's torso.

Vasquez sprang up to take another shot.

Ignoring common sense, John positioned himself between the FBI agent and the escaping Soviets.

"Move it!" Vasquez ordered.

"Can't do it, Bruno."

Vasquez tried to duck and weave, desperate to get a clear view. But John matched his movements, persistently blocking his line of fire.

Frustration twisted Vasquez's features. The man wanted retribution for his murdered men. "He's getting away!" he bellowed. "I said move, John!"

"I want him dead, too!"

He understood the fury. Morozov deserved death a thousand times over. The man had killed Nate in cold blood. But this wasn't about revenge anymore. The world was at stake. The Stealth data had to stay out of Soviet hands.

Ironically, only Morozov could deliver the fake tapes convincingly.

"Move!" Vasquez demanded.

"Bruno, you don't understand." John had to protect the Russian spy, no matter how much it tore him apart inside. He put his hand on the pistol, pushing it down gently. "Morozov has to live for this to work."

Vasquez hesitated, considering John's plea. The boat's engine roared, then faded as it passed behind a cargo ship.

Anger gathered on Vasquez's face. With agonizing slowness, the FBI agent withdrew his gun. "What the hell, Olson? I'd swear you were on his side."

"I'm not. There is more to this. It's as Hyde says," he began, feeling the pain in his chest surface again. "Sometimes you have to stare at the monster."

Vasquez stared at John in confusion. He holstered his weapon with an aggravated sigh and rubbed his temples. "I don't get you CIA boys."

Footsteps announced Hyde's arrival. "John, I never said such rubbish."

Olson cast a glance towards where Morozov's boat had vanished. "Sorry," he sighed. "What I meant was… sometimes monsters can be useful."

Hyde clapped him on the back, the impact making John wince. "That, I did say."

"I don't get it. Don't want to." Vasquez pointed at Hyde. "Don't go anywhere. We're not done. But right now, I gotta take charge of the scene," he said as he walked away.

Andrea limped towards them, her face pale and eyes wide. She looked shaken, but otherwise unharmed.

"You okay?" John asked.

"I think so," she replied. "How about you?"

John turned and stared out at the choppy water. The boat had long since disappeared from view, but the sense of failure lingered. The distant wail of sirens and the rustle of FBI agents faded into the background as he thought of Nate.

"I know what he meant to you," she whispered, placing a consoling hand on his arm.

John swallowed hard. Letting Morozov escape was a betrayal of his vow, even if it had been necessary. Yet, somehow, he knew Nate would approve.

"Someday, he will get what's coming," Hyde said with a quiet intensity. "Trust me."

There was a conviction in her words that offered a strange comfort, and John couldn't shake the feeling that it was more a promise than reassurance.

He wanted to believe her, but he knew all too well the unpredictable nature of their world. The line between right and wrong was now blurred beyond recognition. There was no black and white left.

Andrea winced as her fingers pressed against the spot where the bullet had struck. "This hurts like hell."

"You had me going for a minute there," John admitted, turning to face Hyde. "I thought maybe you'd actually turned on us."

"Same here," Andrea agreed. "I was completely fooled."

Hyde's earlier hardness was now gone. She shrugged, a small smile forming. "The truth is always complicated," she said cryptically. "Morozov was a client, yes, but no longer my master. He has one rule: no one's to be trusted. He should've known better."

Her eyes landed on John and Andrea. "I simply picked a superior investment."

She would say nothing more, but it was the highest of compliments. In her line of work, betrayal was common currency. But Olson had earned her trust, and that was a rare commodity. One he now cherished.

Hyde looked out at the water. "In the end, I think we all got what we needed. Morozov secured his data, Durbin received his comeuppance, and we got our lives back."

John cringed. "I think you cracked my rib."

Hyde was unapologetic. "I owed you for Toronto. You ruined my bikini season on the Riviera." She arched an eyebrow. "At least I used a rubber bullet."

"What about the live round?" John asked. "Are you insane?"

"The look on your face sold the entire thing. Besides, the first bullet in the chamber is always real. Didn't they teach you anything in spy school?"

"I never went to evil spy school like you," John retorted.

Andrea, still attempting to wipe fake blood from her mouth, chimed in, "Durbin could have known."

John shook his head. "I think he attended Harvard."

Andrea's response was quick and dry. "Same difference."

Her smile was all he needed. He chuckled, wincing as he tried not to breathe. The moment of levity ebbed as quickly as it had come. John and Andrea looked back at the waves, now fading. FBI agents moved around them, securing the surrounding scene and collecting evidence.

They wouldn't find much; the real action was over.

Andrea stepped closer. "Do you think Morozov bought it?"

"I believe so. Everything depends on it."

Chapter 66

PIER 53

4 Minutes Remaining

16:56

Spray crashed over the bow as the cigarette boat surged forward, leaving the pier behind in a frothy wake. The vessel knifed through the water, waves pummeling the hull. Sasha Morozov leaned into the wind, his scarred hand gripping the rail.

There was freedom in the sea's embrace, its salty mist caressing his ruined face. He savored the sensation, the raw power surging beneath him. The primal force made him feel alive despite the danger.

The silver case jostled against his feet. He delivered on his end of the bargain. It was the culmination of months of planning and manipulation. Inside lay the data tapes holding the secrets of American stealth technology. With these, the balance of power shifted, and the Soviet leadership would be ecstatic.

He couldn't care less about what they thought or shifts in power dynamics. All of this death and destruction was for his *vnuchka*.

"*Obnovleniye statusa?*" Morozov shouted.

"We're clear, Commander," the pilot replied, his eyes fixed on the horizon.

A sudden ping came from the hull. Morozov ducked, his body reacting before his mind registered the threat. He glanced back, squinting against

432

the sun.

Chaos ensued on the pier, with swarming bodies and flashing lights. Morozov made out a scuffle, someone restraining the FBI agent. But the details vanished as the boat swung around a container ship.

He settled down into a seat, his attention never leaving the precious cargo at his feet. He ran a hand over the outside, the cool metal smooth against his fingertips.

Sasha hoisted the silver case onto his lap. With a click, the latches released. He lifted the lid, eyes drawn to the contents. There, nestled within, lay the decryption device and tapes.

Morozov dragged his thumb along the edge of one of the red-rimmed reels, noting every dent. He marveled at how something so small could hold such immense power. It was all there, just as promised. This prize would satisfy the demanded ransom.

He raised a modified walkie-talkie and depressed the button. The familiar Slavic rolled off his tongue. *"Imamo stealth podatke."* We have the data.

Now came the reckoning.

As he waited for confirmation, his mind drifted, carried back to a time that seemed beyond reach. Once, the world had believed him dead, consumed by the flames of a car bomb. And in that death, he had found a measure of peace.

It was a concept so foreign to him it scarcely felt possible.

His enemies not only exaggerated his demise but celebrated it, unwittingly easing his escape into obscurity.

For two precious years, he lived simply, tending his small farm, coaxing life from the earth instead of snuffing it out. The feel of dirt between his fingers, the satisfaction of watching crops grow. It connected him to a long-forgotten natural world of quiet fields and mottled sunlight. In his mind, he could almost smell the rich, freshly tilled soil.

A gull's cry pierced the air. Morozov's eyes focused, scanning the horizon for pursuit. Nothing. He relaxed, settling back into his chair to think about what really mattered.

Galina. His tiny, perfect granddaughter.

That car bomb, while granting him freedom, had exacted a terrible price: the lives of his son and daughter-in-law. Wracked with guilt, Sasha knew he had been the intended target. Yet, by some cruel twist, both he and the newborn Galina had escaped harm.

Cradling the innocent baby, Morozov felt duty take hold. He was all she had. Political games lost their luster; his new mission was to protect her. It proved to be just what he needed. A balm for his weary, bloodstained soul.

Galina became his saving grace, her laughter and curious eyes promising a future untainted by his past. Each morning, her smile renewed his purpose. As *Dedushka*, he swore to provide the normal, happy life she deserved.

For the first time in his miserable existence, he was free. But like most dreams in the Soviet Union, it was ripped away.

They came in the night, taking Galina right from under him. They should have killed him, but that was not their intent. That was too straightforward. The next day brought a chilling ultimatum: trade the stealth data tapes for Galina's life. A Faustian deal he had no choice but to accept. He donned the dark mantle again, becoming once more the monster the world knew as 'Chort'—The Demon.

He'd rip the world apart just for one more moment with his sweet girl. The mission was complete, but his heart was hollow.

Morozov's eyes narrowed as the radio crackled, his handler's static-laced voice piercing the engine's roar. "Excellent work, Ghost. The treaty is off. Moscow has the advantage."

The Soviets, armed with stealth tech, had walked away from the table. They believed they were finally standing up to the imperialists. He knew it was all pointless. The geopolitical chess game was no longer his concern. He did his part.

Now to focus on his true goal: Galina. He could not let her down.

The man who held her captive had made two demands. First, Morozov would steal the stealth data for the USSR. This task he'd accomplished.

But the second condition was more puzzling, and infinitely more perilous. Gabrielle Hyde was to play a central role in the operation. That had taken time to orchestrate.

Hyde's involvement baffled Morozov, a twist he struggled to decipher. Was it fate or a strategic move by forces he had yet to understand? Gabrielle's resourcefulness had proven invaluable, weaving her way through with a deftness only she possessed. Morozov understood that with Hyde, every smile concealed a dagger.

Even he could never fully trust her. The thought made him squirm, a brief flicker of unease crossing his scarred face. Morozov's grip tightened on the disk as he inspected it again, searching for any sign of tampering. All seemed in order.

With a soft click, Morozov closed the case. He had held up his end. Now it was their turn to do the same. He would deliver the intel, and then he would find Galina.

As the shoreline approached, Morozov braced himself. A new war was brewing, with him at its epicenter. The simple life was gone, and there would be no third act. When death came this time, it would be final. But if it meant saving Galina, he would do so without hesitation.

Like a snake, Sasha had shed his skin many times. He would do it again and again, until he had what he wanted. The blood he had spilled was pale compared to what was coming. Cracking his knuckles, he thought of those who deemed him a relic. Their first mistake was leaving him alive.

Their biggest folly was threatening the one thing he cherished more than life. This mystery man would pay an unbearable cost. He should have known the devil doesn't bargain.

Morozov had to play their game for now. He raised the walkie-talkie to signal the delivery. *"Kudryavka."*

"Approved."

"Maintain radio silence until visual confirmation," he ordered.

"Dlya natsii, Prizrak." The channel fell silent.

Sasha would be patient, bide his time. Then, when they least expected it, he would have his vengeance.

Never make a deal with the damned.

Chapter 67

PIER 53

17:24

A breeze tousled Agent Vasquez's hair as he approached John and Hyde with the letter in hand. The sheet was no longer crisp, but worn from constant folding.

Vasquez held it up. "It's time we talked about this."

"Glad you got my message."

"Almost didn't. Director wanted me in DC for a debrief."

"Why'd you stay?" John asked.

"You made a convincing case." Vasquez held out the blue forget-me-not pin, his eyes softening as he returned it to Hyde.

"Thank you." Hyde's face brightened as she fastened it to her lapel.

"I know some things are valuable beyond measure," Vasquez added. He glanced around. "And I sure as hell wasn't going to miss taking down that smug sonofabitch Durbin."

"Hell of a thing," John said.

"Yeah." Vasquez's expression hardened, his eyes sharpening. "Now, are you doing this, or am I?"

John nodded. "I'll do it."

Vasquez unclipped a set of handcuffs and tossed them to John. The metal was heavier than he remembered. He had used restraints many times in his career, but this was different.

He prepared himself. The line between criminal and hero had blurred beyond recognition. He was about to arrest someone who had just saved countless lives.

Hyde raised her chin defiantly, but he saw the vulnerability. She held out her wrists, ready to play her part.

"Gabrielle…"

"It's okay," she whispered. "I'm glad it's you." She offered a bittersweet smile. "I told you never to break role."

This was just one more mask, another performance in the grand theater of espionage. But knowing that didn't make it any easier. When did the lies they lived become truth?

The cuffs clicked into place around her wrists.

"Gabrielle Hyde, you're under arrest."

Hyde turned to Vasquez. "Thank you for your help, Special Agent Vasquez." Her tone was sincere. "You should be proud. You're one hell of an agent."

Bruno seemed taken aback. "Gotta say, I imagined this going down differently."

"It's okay if you need a hug," she teased.

Vasquez grimaced. "No, thanks."

It felt strange for Olson to see her restrained, even if it was all part of their plan. Bruno hesitated for a second before accepting the transfer of custody.

He nodded to John. "You kept your promise. I'll do what I can for her."

The words hit harder than expected. John respected Vasquez, even when they were at odds. "What do you have in mind?"

Vasquez gestured with his free hand toward the door. "That depends on your boss."

He and Andrea exchanged a confused glance before turning. In the rubble-filled entryway, Deputy Director Lucas Avery ducked through.

"My God," Andrea whispered.

The man was alive. Metal and debris crunched beneath his feet as he approached. He had a noticeable limp and wore a sling on his left arm. His once neatly trimmed hair was disheveled, and a layer of dust coated his suit.

"Sir, how on Earth…" John stammered.

"Our Russian friends need to work on their marksmanship." Avery's hand instinctively moved to his ribs. "Their man was using low-velocity .22s. Body armor caught the first shot. Second one made it through…" He gestured to his bandage. "To put it mildly, I won't be doing wind sprints for a while."

Andrea eyed his sling. "What happened to the other guy?"

"Met the business end of my snub-nose .38. Our would-be assassin will not be troubling anyone else."

"Sir, we were told you were dead." John swallowed. "Where have you been?"

"Response team found me unconscious. Exfiled me to a CIA stash hospital under a false name." Avery's expression darkened. "Finally woke up a few hours ago. Ever since, been arguing with doctors who seemed to think a national crisis was less important than my blood pressure." He locked eyes with John. "Vasquez's team filled me in on everything."

John glanced over at Andrea, expecting to see relief. Instead, she was pensive. She wanted to know about her program, but couldn't ask. That part was up to him.

"Sir, I hate to ask. But…" John cleared his throat. "The SALT Treaty? Did the Soviets follow through?"

Avery's face clouded. "I just spoke directly with President Carter, and he's been thoroughly debriefed on the situation. I'll give it to you straight." He rubbed his shoulder. "The Soviet coalition walked away from the White House a few minutes ago. No doubt tied to their perceived success here in Los Angeles. They think they have the advantage."

"So, no, they won't be signing. At least, not today."

John heard the air leave Andrea's lungs, her body deflating. Her face paled. Despite all their efforts and risks, the Soviets still derailed the nuclear talks.

Avery held up a finger, gaining her attention. "Don't let that worry you.

Soviet diplomats do this sort of thing all the time. When they realize they can't figure out the data, they'll be back."

Usual political maneuvering. The Russians were posturing, trying to gain the upper hand. But once they poured all their resources into a defunct idea, their position would be weaker than ever.

Durbin may have been misguided, but he was right too. Diplomacy was often a game of endurance.

"And the Stealth Project?" John asked. "What about it?"

Avery's mouth clamped. "President was mad as hell. I swear I heard him curse." He paused. "Demanded we shut everything down, pronto. Including the Stealth Program."

Andrea's face crumpled, a tremor running through her body as she fought to maintain composure. Her fingers balled into fists. A spark of determination filled her eyes as she swallowed back the tears.

She looked at Avery, defiant. "We did our best, sir."

John reached for her hand, feeling the trembling in her fingers. "You were extraordinary."

Avery nodded with respect. "I agree entirely."

His tone turned conspiratorial. "Which is why I had a little heart-to-heart with the President. Let's just say… promises from the CIA and FBI to keep certain advisor activities under wraps led to some… reassessment." He smiled. "You know, after that, he was more than willing to consider alternatives."

Andrea's eyes went wide. Her fingers gripped her sleeve as if bracing for the worst. Even Hyde, still in handcuffs, leaned forward, her interest piqued.

"First," Avery began, "your research program is reinstated. Effective immediately. You will also receive an expanded budget."

He turned to Andrea, his smile widening. "Go get 'em, Dr. Miles."

For a moment, she stood frozen, the words not quite registering. Relief finally came as Andrea threw her arms around Avery, giving him a hug. Lucas winced, and she immediately let go.

"Sorry! I'm just so happy we did it," Andrea said as she wiped the tears from her eyes.

John looked at Hyde. The thief's expression was almost tranquil. "What about Gabrielle? Will the President honor her immunity?" he asked.

"That's a little more difficult. Miss Hyde has walked a fine line between friend and foe throughout this ordeal."

John sighed, knowing it was true from an outsider perspective.

"However," he continued, "President Carter left that decision up to the FBI Agent in charge. He figured the men on the ground would know best what to do."

All eyes turned to Vasquez. His jaw clenched and unclenched as he stared at Hyde. He stood silent for ten long seconds, a statue of contemplation.

"Fine," he relented. "I'll honor the amnesty deal."

John hadn't realized how much he'd been hoping for this outcome. "I knew you would come around."

Deputy Director Avery's face broke into a pleased smile. "That was what I hoped would happen," he said, producing a folded document. "Your signed immunity deal, approved by the President himself."

Hyde took the paper with both hands. For a long time, she stared at it, her eyes tracing each official seal and signature. John was transfixed by the subtle play of emotions across her face.

Her fingers tightened on the document, crinkling its edges. She exhaled slowly, her body relaxing. For the first time since he'd known her, Hyde seemed at a loss for words. John saw moisture in her eyes, which she quickly blinked away.

Gabrielle cleared her throat. "Thank you, Director Avery. This… means more than you know." She nodded respectfully to Vasquez. "Bruno."

"That's Agent Vasquez to you," he grumbled, as if he already regretted it. "And don't think this makes up for Cuba. I had to fire a very skilled driver because of that mess. But I hear his wife's recovering."

"Glad to hear it. I knew you were a big softy."

"You're still a pain in my ass."

John strode over to Hyde, unlatching the restraints that bound her wrists. No longer able to bear the sight of the handcuffs, he hurled them toward the nearby ocean. They arced high, a brief silver flash against the sky, before plunging into the churning waves with a distant plop.

Bruno's eyes followed their path with a look of shock. "What the hell, John?"

"Just felt like the right thing to do."

"Those were my favorite cuffs." Bruno glanced back at the water.

Olson gave him an apologetic grin. "I'll get you a new pair. A better set."

Andrea stepped forward, her hand resting on John's arm. "You two boys can work that out later," she said. "We have more pressing matters to attend to."

Two FBI technicians waved for Vasquez's attention.

"A new pair, Olson. None of that cheap CIA crap either." Bruno pointed at John before walking off to address his team.

"You got it."

As John turned back, he found Andrea searching the area frantically. She looked right, then left. She stepped around him, a quizzical look on her face.

"Where did you put the decryption case and data reels?" she asked.

The question hit him like a bucket of ice water. He turned to where the black bag should have been, only to find empty space and a wave of FBI agents. Panic set in as he desperately searched the area, his eyes darting from one corner to another.

"Vasquez!" John shouted. "The briefcase with the stealth data. Where is it?"

"Technicians already secured it," he responded. "Standard procedure for evidence. Don't worry, you'll get it back."

John remembered the explosives hidden in the lining. Bruno didn't know about it, and the proximity sensor was still on him. If the FBI moved the case out of range…

The transmitter clipped to his belt beeped, then turned to a solid tone.

John's eyes widened in horror. It was too late to stop what was about to happen. "Get down!"

Acting on instinct, John lunged towards Andrea, wrapping his arms around her and dropping to the ground. He shielded her with his body.

A second later, the world erupted. The explosion tore through the air with a thunderous crack, followed by a deep, reverberating boom. Concrete rippled as the pier bucked beneath them. Shards of glass and metal rained down, tinkling as they landed on the warehouse roof.

The case had detonated outside. Thank God.

John checked Andrea for any signs of injury. "Are you okay?"

"Yeah," she managed. "What just happened?"

"We forgot about the insurance policy." Olson pushed himself up onto an elbow. "We blew up the data."

Chapter 68

John and Andrea raced outside, plunging through the mangled door into the sunlight. The smell of smoke hit him immediately. A smoldering vehicle carcass hung precariously on the edge of the pier, threatening to fall at any moment.

Vasquez, Avery, and Hyde emerged from the building close behind. FBI agents darted about the gangway in a flurry of activity, trying to secure the scene. Agent Morris jogged over, his face smudged with soot.

"There was an explosion in one of the trucks," he shouted. "Thankfully, nobody was injured. Just scrapes and bruises."

A plume of black smoke rose from the remains as ash drifted on the breeze.

"What about the driver?" Vasquez asked.

"We got lucky, boss. No one was in it."

Avery scowled. "Bruno, what the hell happened to our crime scene?"

Vasquez stared at Morris and then back at Avery. "Sir. I have… um."

"Sir, it wasn't him," Olson said. "It was me. The case was booby-trapped." All eyes turned his way. "To ensure the Soviets didn't escape with the original data, there was a proximity charge in the bag. Agent Vasquez didn't know about it. It got out of range and exploded."

"Jesus H. Christ. I appreciate having a backup plan. But what the hell made you decide to put…" Avery surveyed the destruction, "a couple sticks of dynamite in there?"

Gabrielle let out a whistle. Avery glanced at Hyde. "Nevermind, I know how."

John cursed himself for neglecting such a crucial detail. "In all the commotion, I forgot about it. Honest to God."

Morris added, "Sir, just to be clear, the blast only took out the truck. No civilian property damage. Nobody seriously hurt." He popped a thumb at the wreckage. "Could've been worse."

Vasquez wearily shook his head. He opened his mouth, but a loud crash from inside the warehouse drew his attention.

"What now? Morris, you're with me," he barked, already moving. He skidded to a stop and fixed Gabrielle with a glare. "You," he said, pointing, "no more trouble."

Hyde raised her palms. "Intention is a promise that's never kept. So I make no such pledge." She added, "However, I shall do my best to stay off your radar."

"Whatever. Just be good, okay?" Vasquez grabbed Morris and disappeared into the industrial building.

Hyde checked her watch with a pensive look. She studied the horizon and the encroaching dusk. The wistful expression on her face was a clear sign she was already planning her next move.

"My dear, I'm afraid it's getting late. I should go," Gabrielle said to Andrea.

"Next time, I get to shoot you with rubber bullets," Andrea teased, her words muffled against Hyde's shoulder as they hugged.

Gabrielle's laugh was rich. "Careful what you wish for, darling." She stepped back, her gaze settling on Olson. "John, do look after our favorite doctor. I've got quite the ideas in mind for you two."

"Yes, ma'am."

Despite their complicated history, a deep sadness washed over John at the prospect of her leaving. She had proven herself to be an invaluable ally, and even more surprisingly, an unlikely friend.

"So, what's next for the great Gabrielle Hyde?"

"I'll think of something," she replied cryptically. "Now, you two behave." Andrea blushed. "You too."

"You know me better than that. Now, I truly must be going. Places to be and such."

Hyde turned and walked toward the pier entrance. John wished she would stay. There was still so much he wanted to understand. He raised his hand, trying to figure out what to say.

Before he could speak, Gabrielle Hyde rounded the corner and vanished.

Her absence created an immediate void. It was hard to believe she was gone. She was a force of nature, like a hurricane that swept across the land. In her wake, she left a swath of destruction and, ironically, new opportunities.

"You know," he said to Andrea, "we never took back that cash Morozov gave to Hyde during the sting. It was a lot of money."

"Let it go, John. After all, she needs something to get started. Consider it a severance package."

He couldn't argue. Hyde had risked her life, put everything on the line to help them. And in the end, she had sided with them over Morozov. She deserved a fresh start.

Olson watched the last of the smoke snuff out from the charred vehicle. "How will you finish without the data? I destroyed your only copy."

"We'll be fine," she assured him. "The project's past development phase. We're in operational testing. We'll move forward while the computers are repaired, and once that happens, we can make new ones." She squeezed his arm. "Within a few months, no one'll even know the difference."

She was right, of course. The Stealth program was bigger than a single set of data tapes. They had the knowledge, the expertise, and the determination to see it through.

The struggles, the pain, the sacrifices. They had all been worth it. They had accomplished something extraordinary. "I will," he said. "I'll always remember."

Andrea laughed, leaning in. "I'll hold you to that."

Unable to resist any longer, John pulled her close. He leaned down, capturing Andrea's lips in a tender kiss. The world around them diminished in a familiar way, but approaching footsteps broke the spell.

They pulled apart. An FBI agent, who seemed determined not to intrude, gave them an apologetic cough.

"I guess we'll have to find a more private spot," he joked, earning a playful swat from Andrea.

Her cheeks flushed from the tender moment. In her presence, he felt calm and clarity, as if he had found the place where he belonged. If he wanted to hold on to this, he would have to make a choice. A hard choice.

John looked around, spotting Avery nearby. "Come with me," he told Andrea.

The two walked over to the Deputy Director, John taking the lead.

"Sir, a moment of your time?"

"Of course." Avery dismissed the FBI agent he was speaking with and directed his attention to John. "Impressive work, Olson. Unorthodox. But you got it done. That's what matters to me."

"Thank you, sir."

"Take a couple of days to heal up. Then I need you back in D.C." Avery clapped Olson on his shoulder with his good arm. "I've got big plans for you."

John took a deep breath. "You know, sir," he began. "I finally hit that 100% closure rate. No one's ever done that before."

"Quite an accomplishment."

John reached into his pocket and withdrew his badge. His fingers brushed over the worn leather, then held it out. "Consider this my resignation, effective immediately."

Lucas made no move to take it.

"I'm going to explore new opportunities." John looked at Andrea. "It's time for a change."

Avery's voice lowered. "Are you certain? Your future here is bright."

"I'm writing a different chapter, sir."

Avery took the shield. "The Agency's losing one hell of an officer, Olson."

John nodded, a lump forming in his throat. "Thank you for everything."

"If you ever need a client, the CIA's always here." Avery pocketed the credentials. "Off the books, naturally."

"Naturally."

A fresh string of expletives from Vasquez could be heard from inside. Avery sighed and started walking gingerly toward the building. He turned back. "Dr. Miles," he called. "Since Officer Olson will not be filing a final report, I was wondering if you could fill in a couple of blanks for me?"

"Go ahead." John gave her a reassuring nod. "I'll catch up."

"Coming!" she called. She grabbed John's collar and pulled him down, giving him a kiss. "We have more to discuss, so don't you go anywhere."

"Yes, ma'am."

Andrea jogged over to the Deputy and they disappeared into the warehouse, leaving John alone on the pier.

Silence settled around him as he surveyed the destruction.

A nagging thought nipped at him. He couldn't shake the feeling that something was off. Hyde had taught him, inadvertently perhaps, to question everything.

He approached the charred truck.

Heat from the dying flames radiated onto his skin as he drew close. Debris crunched beneath his feet. There was a somewhat sweet chemical odor, almost like burned plastic.

How did the decryption device end up in the back of this truck?

More importantly, how was it that no one was hurt? The odds of such an outcome seemed too good to be true.

John paced the area, struggling to piece together the sequence of events. The proximity sensor went off while he was standing still. The vehicle had to be moving.

But where was the driver? And why wasn't he hurt?

Something caught his eye. A small, inconspicuous object, half-buried in the soaked rubble. John bent down, fishing it out. As he lifted it, the scent of tobacco hit his nostrils.

He turned the filter, examining the crisp lettering on the side. It wasn't just any generic cigarette butt. Ducados. The same rare Spanish brand Simmons favored.

Was Douglas responsible for the burning car?

Now that he considered it, Hyde's crew was absent during the showdown with Morozov and Durbin. Where were they? This cigarette was proof they were here. How could he have missed them?

John let the trash fall from his hand and took a deliberate breath. The memories were buried deep within the recesses of his brain. But unearthing them would require complete focus.

He closed his eyes, recalling the technique Hyde taught him at LAX. It was time to put it to the test.

His breathing settled into a measured rhythm. Somehow, he remembered the words Hyde had used. *"Khud ko paane ke lie khud ko chhod do."*

His pulse steadied. The cries of gulls faded, replaced by an ethereal silence. It felt like descending into a dream. He pushed away external influences, layer by layer, until he was alone. John surrendered to the stillness.

He was back at the warehouse. FBI agents swarmed like ants, weapons drawn. On one side, he saw himself and Andrea conversing with Hyde and Vasquez. They were irrelevant, and he pushed them from his vision.

He focused on the black case sitting isolated on the concrete floor. Someone would come for it.

Most of the men ran in zigzag patterns, stomping their feet. But one agent differed from the rest. This individual had grace. Unlike everyone else, this person moved with an unhurried stride, face obscured by a hat pulled down low.

He fixated on the anomaly, tracking the agent as they crossed the room unnoticed. This one didn't care about threats. A slender, feminine hand shot out from beneath the bulky FBI blue jacket. She picked up the case and pivoted.

As she turned, a yellow ponytail popped out from beyond the collar. The sight lasted only a second. But it gave him everything he needed. A woman. Early to mid-thirties. Tall and slender, with long blonde hair.

Opening his eyes, John returned to reality with a jolt.

He jogged the length of the pier, searching for the mysterious operative. But there was no trace of the woman he'd seen. The agent had vanished.

John noticed Vasquez stalking through the door and ran to him. "Hey,

Vasquez!" he called. "I need to know. Any female techs on your team?"

"No," he replied, shaking his head. "Why do you ask?"

John couldn't reveal too much, not without raising suspicion. "Just curious," he said. "I thought I saw someone, but I must have been mistaken."

"Jesus, John. Either get over here and help or stop asking me stupid questions." Vasquez didn't press the issue further, instead turning his attention to the arriving fire department.

Bruno's response confirmed it. The FBI agent was Jessica. Then there was Simmons. Of course.

All the pieces fell into place. He'd been played. Again.

"Son of a bitch."

But this was significantly more than a con; it was a symphony of misdirection.

Hyde had applied the Kansas City Shuffle to him as well as Durbin. It was so obvious. The precision. The timing. Every piece executed with audacity.

In the aftermath of the FBI raid, Jessica seamlessly integrated herself amongst the technicians. Once in, she simply secured the real data tapes during the confusion. No one noticed as she made her way to the designated rendezvous point outside.

There, she and Simmons must have removed the explosives and put them in a waiting truck. Once the path was clear, Simmons and Matheo had put it in neutral and pushed the vehicle into a roll. The explosion covered their tracks.

It bore all the hallmarks of Hyde's unique brand of brilliance and recklessness.

Then Gabrielle simply walked away from the scene. In one hand, she held immunity; in the other, deniability.

She had not only secured the stealth data for herself, but ensured nobody would ever come looking. Who would? The explosion destroyed it. Everyone witnessed it.

She had the money, the immunity, the tapes, the decryption device, and an airtight cover story. All courtesy of the U.S. government.

John marveled. He couldn't deny there was something unsettling about the ease with which she had outmaneuvered them all.

It was by all accounts, the perfect con.

Gabrielle would scold him for such a thought. There was always a catch. He laughed. This was the major difference from when they first met in Toronto: she had taught him how to play her game. But more importantly, she had given him the proper mindset.

Nothing is perfect.

Chapter 69

CORPORATE LIMOUSINE

3 Days Later

Sonny "Duke" Ellington reclined in the leather seat of his limousine, the tinted windows obscuring him from the outside. The vehicle's polished wood accents and plush carpeting provided a cocoon of comfort and privacy.

Duke's posture remained rigid, as if still bearing the weight of military command. Faint lines etched by years of stress surrounded his keen eyes. On his knees rested large hands, still stiff from the frostbite he had suffered during the war.

The executive wore a three-piece suit, a rich navy with a subtle windowpane check that draped impeccably. The crisp white shirt stood in sharp contrast to his silk tie. His lapel was adorned with a pewter P-51 Mustang pin. Every element of his ensemble spoke of a man who demanded perfection.

Duke unconsciously massaged his damaged fingers with his thumb, a habit he had long given up trying to break. He felt the sleek silver case resting next to his leg, knowing what it contained.

Ellington flipped through the classified documents in his lap, each word and diagram representing a quantum leap in aerospace technology. It was a glimpse into a future he had never imagined possible during his days as a World War II ace.

The design aesthetic was revolutionary. With this data, Duke's company could secure a stranglehold on lucrative government contracts, leaving competitors in the dust. It was a high-stakes game where even a minor advantage was the difference between success and bankruptcy.

Across from him, Gabrielle Hyde reclined with an ease that bordered on arrogance. Even in the soft light, her features were a study in contrasts.

Duke had first heard of this woman only two days earlier. But in his inquiries, he had learned enough to know she was as dangerous as she was clever. Hyde made him uneasy, and that was no minor feat.

The risk added to her allure. It was the reason he'd flown on a moment's notice to Los Angeles. The threat of a competitor getting their hands on this gold mine was more than sufficient to pry Ellington from his Vermont estate.

"Appears to be in order." Duke closed the case with a decisive snap.

Gabrielle leaned forward. "It's all there, Mr. Ellington. Exactly as promised."

There was something disconcerting about her confidence. The risks were immense, but so were the rewards. "Anyone suspect the data is missing?" Duke asked.

Hyde gave a cryptic smile. "As far as the world is concerned, this information is smoke and ashes. No one's coming for it."

"You're sure?"

"I've tied up every loose end, Mr. Ellington." She examined her nails. "It's what separates the amateurs from the professionals."

"I just don't need government trouble."

"My dear Duke, there is one simple rule to success in my world." She leaned forward, her presence suddenly more intense. "The best heist is the one no one ever knows happened."

In Duke's experience, even the tightest security could be broken. No plan was perfect. But that was Hyde's dilemma, not his.

"Just so long as this data stays in American hands." She tapped the silver case with the tip of her shoe. "That's non-negotiable."

The caveat struck him as oddly patriotic, a sentiment he didn't expect from someone in her line of work. But he appreciated it nonetheless; it aligned perfectly with his vision of American superiority. The U.S. had the best pilots in the world. He would build them an invincible aircraft to match their spirit.

A new era of global dominance. More government contracts were on the horizon; he felt it in his bones. And with this head start, they could outmaneuver and outclass anything the Soviets produced.

"During the war, I lost good men. They died for this nation. This technology… it'll stay out of the hands of our enemies. It's about protecting our nation."

Hyde raised an eyebrow. "How noble. And I'm sure the billions in potential revenue are just a fortunate coincidence?"

Ellington's jaw tightened. "You wouldn't understand…"

"Oh, I understand." Hyde's smooth interruption cut him off. "Are we in accord?"

"Yes."

He reached into his jacket pocket and withdrew a crisp envelope containing a single cashier's check. "As agreed," he said, handing it over.

Gabrielle accepted the note with a nod. She tucked it away unopened, a display of trust that unsettled him. Perhaps it was calculated indifference. Either way, it characterized their transaction.

"If you don't mind my asking, what are you going to do with forty million dollars?"

Hyde offered no answer. Instead, she gave him a curt nod, acknowledging both his inquiry and its irrelevance. "I think that concludes our business."

Duke chuckled. In truth, her plans were probably best left unspoken.

Gabrielle glanced at her antique gold timepiece with satisfaction. She cracked the door, letting a sliver of the Los Angeles afternoon light spill through. Through the gap, Duke caught glimpses of sun-bleached palm trees lining the boulevard, their fronds swaying.

"A pleasure, Mr. Ellington," Hyde said, sliding gracefully out. And with that, the door closed.

"Drive," he instructed his chauffeur.

Duke sank into his seat, his hand resting on the case in his lap. He didn't bother to look outside. Hyde was gone. The data was now his.

Ellington knew that war was ugly business. In youth, it had seemed straightforward. There was good and there was evil. But survivors soon learned that things were not always so clear-cut. Good people did bad things. Bad people did good things.

Which one was Gabrielle Hyde?

Ellington decided she was beyond simple categorization. Part angel, part demon. She was a mystery that no man was meant to fully understand.

Chapter 70

LOS ANGELES

John leaned against a sun-soaked wall on an unremarkable Los Angeles street. His discarded tie waited in the car, a relic of another life. Nate's gold aviator sunglasses dangled from his shirt collar as sweat trickled down his neck in the warm afternoon air.

He was free. The CIA no longer dictated his actions.

The first day after the episode at the pier had been a whirlwind, with dead ends wearing on him. But Andrea had taught him the power of thinking about problems from a new angle.

He didn't need to find Hyde. He'd never be able to do that.

John shifted his focus from chasing Hyde to tracking potential clients. After all, she had something to sell.

He pursued leads on aerospace executives, scouring financial records and following whispers of secret meetings. The breakthrough came when Vasquez flagged a suspicious private flight from Vermont.

Sonny "Duke" Ellington was an aviation executive with just enough discretion and money to be a good fit. Olson had tracked the careless businessman to this very spot, his stretch limousine hardly discreet.

The black limo idled across the street, its obsidian exterior easy to follow. The low purr of its engine was barely audible as the door cracked open. Olson pushed off the wall, the rough stucco scraping his shoulder blades.

Time for answers.

Hyde stepped out, sporting her usual grace as she tried to put distance between herself and the car. John soon maneuvered behind her retreating form.

"You're not an easy woman to track down," John said, keeping his tone casual.

Hyde pivoted. "And here I thought I was being discreet." Her eyes narrowed. "I suppose you're here to arrest me."

"Those were my orders."

Hyde scanned her surroundings. "Where's your backup?"

"Everywhere. Watching from above." John nodded towards the windows. "Now, are you going to make this difficult?"

"Go ahead." She held out her wrists.

He could no longer contain his smile. "Put your hands down; it's unseemly. Plus, I already arrested you. Remember?"

Gabrielle lowered her arms, the tension leaving her shoulders. "What about the CIA and your orders?"

"I quit."

Surprise crossed Hyde's face. John felt a rush. It was a rare occurrence to get one up on Gabrielle, and he intended to enjoy it.

"You quit?"

"Walked away."

"You?" Hyde shook her head. "I didn't think it possible to pry you from the CIA."

Olson waggled his finger. "Turns out, just improbable."

"You stole my second favorite line."

"Learned from the best."

As they stood there on the sidewalk, John marveled at the absence of the responsibility that had burdened him for so long. The agency had been the very foundation of his identity, dictating every decision.

Without the badge, he felt free. For the first time in years, he had no orders to follow. Only his personal code.

"So, if you're not here to apprehend me, why are you here?"

He considered the question. Why was he here? "I needed to confirm," he said, "that I could match your game."

Hyde's expression remained neutral.

"Brilliant, really. Jessica as the FBI tech, Simmons and Matheo on the pier. Everyone fooled into thinking the data was destroyed."

"Hypothetically speaking, of course."

"Of course." John nodded. "I just have one question."

"Just one?"

"Did you intend for me to figure out what you did, or did you finally make a mistake?"

"You know," Hyde cocked her head. "Never thought I'd see the day CIA golden boy Olson let a criminal walk away."

John chuckled. "Is that what I'm doing?"

"Maybe you miss your partner."

"That I did," he replied. She certainly had charm. "What's next?"

Gabrielle looked to the horizon. "I have some unfinished business in Virginia. A gate agent in need of help with a problem. Perhaps I can use my talents to do some good for once."

John stepped forward, extending his hand. Hyde looked down at his upturned palm. After a second's hesitation, she reached out and accepted his gesture.

"There's a lot of good to be done in this world. Good luck."

"Indeed." Hyde turned to leave, but then hesitated. She stared as if committing him to memory. "John?"

"Yeah?"

"What will *you* do next?"

He had thought little beyond tracking Hyde. Now that he had accomplished that, the future stretched out, vast and uncertain.

"I don't know," he admitted. "Maybe I'll try consulting." It felt different, yet appealing.

"Consulting," she repeated, laughing. "Interesting choice."

Her head tilted to the side as if making a split-second decision. She reached into her pocket and pulled out a burgundy bag no larger than her palm. Without warning, she tossed it to John.

"Maybe you can put that to good use. I found it among Durbin's things in a discarded briefcase near the pier."

The pouch looked familiar, and it took him a moment to place it. This was the same one Morozov had given Durbin during their meeting.

"What is it?"

"A retainer," she said, her voice laced with amusement. "After all, consultants get paid."

Unable to contain his curiosity, John opened the bag and peered inside. He felt a sudden tightness as the diamonds caught the sunlight, exploding into a kaleidoscope of colors.

The jewels represented millions of dollars, the price of Durbin's betrayal. It was a life-changing amount of money, all contained in a single pouch. He cinched it closed, fearing he might spill the contents.

Why would Hyde give him this? No one knew this existed. She could have walked away, and nobody would have ever known.

John's head popped up, a thousand questions swirling. His eyes darted across the empty street, finding only the rumble of traffic and hasty commuters.

Hyde was gone.

He spun around to search the passing faces, but found no trace of Gabrielle. She had vanished, as if she had melted into the very fabric of the city.

John should have known better than to take his eyes off her, even for a moment. His muscles tensed, ready for pursuit. But he caught himself. That wasn't his mission anymore.

With a sigh, he slipped the bag into his pocket.

John found himself adrift in a crowd of hurried pedestrians, each one brushing past him. The diamonds were the only proof that any of this had really transpired.

Yet, as the thrill of catching Hyde faded, his thoughts drifted to more personal matters. He checked his watch, a habit ingrained from years of covert operations. But this time, the gesture brought a surge of delight.

He had a proper date with Dr. Andrea Miles, and he had no intention of being late. Dinner and a movie. He would finally experience the simple pleasures of life.

Andrea had promised to let him pick the film if she got to choose the restaurant. John considered his options, knowing he needed to make a smart, modest choice. No political intrigue, explosions, or impossible missions against the government.

Simmons had been raving about a character-driven western set in space that had been popular since May. John figured it was winding down its run by now. Knowing Douglas, it was likely a hidden gem. Small and forgettable. Perfect for a quiet evening out.

John gave a hopeful smile as he gazed up at the sky. He retrieved the gold sunglasses from his collar and pushed them up to the bridge of his nose. Nate would have approved.

The world took on an amber hue. The cityscape brightened with possibility while his past receded.

It wasn't the glasses that had changed. It was him.

A fresh beginning. No more orders from on high, no compromising choices for the sake of someone's career. From now on, he made the decisions. Except for the restaurant, that was all Andrea.

Stepping off the curb, Olson felt excitement. He was just an ordinary man with a date to keep.

Propelled by the light, John enjoyed the sounds of life, knowing happiness came from within.

Thank you for reading Stealing Stealth.

If you enjoyed the journey, you can give this book no greater gift than leaving a brief, honest review on the site where you purchased it.

Reviews are the lifeblood of independent authors and help new readers discover this story. Your voice makes all the difference.

REVIEW LINK: https://mybook.to/reviewSS

If you enjoyed the high-stakes world of *Stealing Stealth*, prepare for something darker.

Coming April 13, 2026

Zoe Nichols came to Alaska to bury her past. It didn't work.

A damaged Marine Major haunted by survivor's guilt, Zoe is drowning in whiskey at a dead-end government job with the Bureau of Land Management. In the middle of nowhere, she's not looking for a fight. She's looking for oblivion.

But when a rigged land lottery sparks a war between a legacy homesteading family and a ruthless natural gas executive, Zoe is dragged into a conflict she wants no part of. Sebastian Fisher has built an empire by stepping on the throats of his enemies, and the Masons are the last obstacle on his path to a global energy monopoly.

Left for dead in a frozen river, betrayed by the only person she thought she could trust, Zoe must become something more dangerous than a soldier. She must become a reckoning. Allied with Guwaii Stonefoot, a Haida survivor haunted by his own lost tribe, she will learn a hard truth: in the Alaskan wilderness, you don't outrun your past. You turn and face it with a gun in your hand.

Some wounds don't heal. They just stop bleeding.

In the far north, justice isn't found. It's taken.

ORDER YOUR COPY: https://mybook.to/arcticfire

About the Author

Brian L. Reece is a retired Air Force Colonel with twenty-six years in special operations and strategic command, decorated with 2 Legions of Merit, a Bronze Star, and 9 Air Medals. His career included classified operations, intelligence work, and strategic planning that informs the authenticity of his fiction.

During his career, he flew MH-53, UH-1, and Mi-17 helicopters with over 350 hours of combat time.

Brian holds master's degrees in business, history, and strategy. At Air War College, he won the Nowak Award and graduated with highest distinction. As an adjunct professor at the US Army Command & General Staff College, he taught international engagement and interagency affairs, providing unique insight into governmental complexities.

His creative background includes work as a SAG actor, semi-finalist in the PAGE International Screenwriting Awards, and experience as a film industry technical advisor. This combination of cinematic storytelling knowledge and firsthand military expertise uniquely positions him to craft technically accurate yet cinematic stories.

He is currently the president of a consulting firm that specializes in education and military instruction. He lives in Texas with his wife and three children. This is his debut novel.

You can connect with me on:
- https://www.brianreeceauthor.com
- https://x.com/BrianLReece
- https://www.facebook.com/profile.php?id=61580374395565

Subscribe to my newsletter:
- https://www.brianreeceauthor.com/contact

9 781969 584022